*Shadows and Strongholds*

# ELIZABETH CHADWICK

sourcebooks
landmark

Published by Sourcebooks Landmark, an imprint of Sourcebooks, Inc.
P.O. Box 4410, Naperville, Illinois 60567-4410
(630) 961-3900
Fax: (630) 961-2168
www.sourcebooks.com

First published in Great Britain in 2004 by Time Warner Books. Most recently published in New York in 2005 by St. Martin's Press.

Library of Congress Cataloging-in-Publication Data

Chadwick, Elizabeth.
  Shadows and Strongholds / Elizabeth Chadwick.
    pages cm
  (pbk. : alk. paper) 1. Knights and knighthood--Fiction. 2. Great Britain-
-History--Stephen, 1135-1154--Fiction. 3. Shrewsbury (England)--Fiction.
4. Historical fiction. I. Title.
  PR6053.H245S47 2013
  823'.914--dc23
                        2012045155

Printed and bound in the United States.
VP 10 9 8 7 6 5 4 3 2 1

Also by Elizabeth Chadwick

# Boy and Girl

# 1

## St. Peter's Fair, Shrewsbury, August 1148

O N THE DAY THAT BRUNIN FITZWARIN ENCOUNTERED THE MEN
who were to change and shape his life, he was ten years old
and wandering the booths of St. Peter's Fair unchaperoned.

Mark, his father's serjeant, who should have been keeping
an eye on him, had allowed his attention to be diverted by a
brimming pitcher and an alewife's buxom daughter at one of the
refreshment stalls. Growing bored with the adult dalliance, Brunin
had meandered off to explore the booths on his own. He was a
lanky child with an olive complexion and eyes of so deep a brown
that they were almost black, hence his nickname, his true appellation being Fulke, the same as his father. His five brothers were
fair like their parents. Brunin, it was said by the charitable, was
a throwback to his grandsire, a Lorraine mercenary of doubtful
origins. Those less generous muttered that he was a changeling
child, a cuckoo laid in the nest by the faery folk of the Welsh hills.

He passed a cookstall where soft oatcakes were being smartly
turned on a griddle and sold to passersby. A woman had bought
several and was dividing them among her swarming offspring.
She reprimanded one child with exasperation, but a moment later
ruffled his hair. Catching Brunin's wistful gaze, she smiled, tore a
side from a remaining oatcake, and offered it to him as if coaxing
a wild thing. Brunin shook his head and moved quickly away. It
was not the oatcake that had caused his yearning look.

"Jugs and pitchers!" a trader shouted in his ear. "Pottles and pots! Finest wares of Stamford and Nottingham!" The man waved aloft a green-glazed jug with the design of a grinning face carved in the spout. A pugnacious housewife was haggling vigorously with his assistant over the price of a cooking jar.

For three days every summer, traders came to Shrewsbury and arrayed their wares in the shadow of the great Benedictine abbey of Saints Peter and Paul. Even the unrest of the civil war between the supporters of King Stephen and the Empress Matilda could not dampen people's enthusiasm for bargains and rarities. Brunin's father said that, if anything, the unrest made the fair even more popular because men could meet allies and discuss common ground while seen to be engaged in legitimate pursuits.

That's where his father was now, talking to old friends, and that was why Brunin had been put in Mark's charge. They were supposed to meet FitzWarin at the horse market when the abbey bell rang the hour of sext. Brunin was to have a new pony since he was rapidly outgrowing the small Welsh bay that had served him since he was six years old. Spider legs his grandmother had called him last week, as if his sudden growth spurt was a sin.

The language of trade assaulted his ears from all quarters. The Latin and French of wealthier stall-holders were familiar to him. Here and there, a Welsh voice soared above a babbling undercurrent of English. Brunin spoke a smattering of the two latter tongues—but never in his grandmother's hearing unless he deliberately wanted to annoy her.

The cloth stalls were heaving with women who eyed and fingered, discussed, longed for, and occasionally bought. Brunin's mother had a silk dress of the same shimmering red-gold as one of the bolts draped over a booth counter. He had seen it in her clothing coffer, but she rarely wore it. She had told him once with blank eyes that it was her wedding gown.

Brunin paused at a trader's cart to fondle a litter of brindle hound pups. The trader also had a pair of tiny dogs with long, silky fur and colorful ribbons tied around their necks. The sound of their yapping hurt Brunin's ears. He tried to imagine his father entertaining such lap rats in his household and grinned at the image. FitzWarin was strictly a hound man, the larger the better.

Ambling toward the horse market, Brunin wondered if he could steer his father's eye in the direction of a pied or jet-black pony this time—something that would stand out from common chestnut and brown. Of course, unusual colors cost more and if the price was not reasonable, his father would refuse to buy.

To reach the horse fair, Brunin had to cut down the thorough-fare where the weapon smiths had set out their stalls. The sight of the shining sword blades, the axes, daggers, hauberks, helms, and sundry accoutrements of the warrior's craft seized both his sight and his imagination. Here was a knife in a tooled leather sheath just like the one Mark wore at his hip, here a sword with a grip of red braid and an inscription scrolled in Latin down the blade. Brunin's mouth watered. Sometimes he would draw his father's sword from its scabbard and pretend that he was the great warrior Roland, defending the pass at Roncesvalles against the Infidel. His grandmother had caught him once and thrashed him for leaving sticky fingerprints on the polished iron. He had been more cir-cumspect since—and, mindful of her words, he always cleaned the sword on his tunic before putting it away.

A nobleman and his entourage arrived at the booth where Brunin was eyeing up the weaponry and began inspecting the swords. Brunin watched the lord heft the blade that the craftsman handed to him.

"Good balance," the lord nodded. "Grip's a little short. I don't want to lose my finger ends in battle." He swiped the sword through the air, testing the feel, following through with a deft backswing before handing the weapon around for an opinion.

"That can be changed if you like the blade, my lord," said the trader. "Or there's this one." He presented another sword, this one scabbarded in tactile, rose-colored leather.

Captivated, Brunin moved closer and was immediately pushed aside by a fair-haired squire attending the noble. "Out of the way, brat," he sneered. "Get back to your nursemaid."

Brunin flushed. The youth was wearing a tunic of blood-red wool and had a knife at his belt not much smaller than Mark's. One hand hovered close to the hilt as if he were thinking of drawing it. Eyeing the implied threat, Brunin began to feel queasy.

"He's lost his tongue," grinned a younger, stocky youth in blue. "Unless he's Welsh and doesn't understand us. He looks Welsh, doesn't he?"

Brunin lifted his chin. Every muscle was stiff with the effort of holding his ground. "I'm not W-Welsh," he said.

The lord ceased examining his second sword and glanced around. "Ernalt, Gerald, leave the boy alone. Let him look if he desires." His tone was tolerant. "What's your name, boy?"

Brunin delved for his manners. "Fulke, sir," he said, using his formal birth name. "Fulke F-FitzWarin…"

The humor faded from the man's eyes. "Of Whittington?"

"Yes, sir."

"And what might you be doing strolling the booths on your own?"

"Waiting for my father," Brunin answered.

The noble raised his head and gazed around as if expecting to see Brunin's father among the crowd. "Then perhaps you would do better not to wait in my vicinity," he said. His voice had lost its warmth. "If your sire is as careless with his lands as he is with his son, he may well end up losing both." Turning his back on Brunin with a deliberate air of dismissal, he handed the sword to the craftsman and set about discussing terms.

Brunin was bewildered. He did not understand the sudden change, but knew enough to realize that his presence was unwelcome and that it must have something to do with his father. He started to walk away and received a hefty shove in the middle of his back. Stumbling, surprised, he turned to find himself facing the blond squire and his companion.

"Know what happens to a cub when it wanders too far from the den?" the blond one asked in a voice straining in the space between boy and man. He drew his knife.

Brunin swallowed and his queasiness increased.

"You think he's afraid?" The stocky boy gave Brunin another shove, a predatory glint in his eyes.

"Of course he is."

"I'm n-not!" Brunin contradicted. Something strange was happening to his bladder, as if the blond squire's blade was sawing through his ability to control it.

The youth thumbed the tip of the weapon and then ran his finger lightly across the edge. "You should be, whelp," he said. "Perhaps I'll cut off your little tail and send you home to your pack with a stump, eh?" He sliced the steel descriptively under Brunin's nose.

Brunin flinched. He knew it wasn't manly but couldn't help himself. He wished he were back at the guest house with his mother and brothers and even his grandmother. He wished he were still with Mark and bored stiff.

The squire in blue grabbed Brunin's arm. "Shall I hold him down?"

"If you like."

Terror shot through Brunin like a molten wire. Drawing back his foot he kicked his captor in the shin and, twisting, bit the hand that was gripping his elbow. The youth yelled and let go. Brunin took to his heels. Winding among the booths, he was as swift and pliable as an eel between rocks, but his pursuers were fast too and there were two of them. Brunin darted toward the stall where he had left Mark supping ale and cozening the girl but, to his horror, the young serjeant was no longer there.

The girl scowled over the counter at the wild-eyed, panting boy. "He's gone looking for you." Her tone indicated that she was furious at having her flirtation curtailed. "You're in trouble, you are."

He didn't need to be told. "Please..." he croaked, but it was too late. The squires grabbed him one either side and held him fast. When the girl looked askance, the fair-haired one winked at her. "Young rascal," he said. Reassured, she turned away, abandoning Brunin to his fate.

He fought the youths with every shred of strength in his narrow body, but he was no match for their adolescent brawn. Their fingers bruised his flesh as they dragged him across the fairground. A hard hand cupped his mouth to stifle his yells, and when he tried again to bite, he felt the cold burn of the knife at his throat. A sudden, shameful heat flooded his braies and stained his hose.

"God's bones, the weakling's pissed himself!" the stocky youth jeered.

His blond companion snorted. "What do you expect of blood like his? The wonder is it's red, not yellow." He showed Brunin his smeared fingers then dragged them down the boy's cheek.

"If you cut out his liver, I'll warrant you half a mark that it would be the color of buttercups."

"Half a mark? Done."

"Boys!" The voice was peremptory and stern. Through a stinging blur of tears, Brunin saw the dark figure of a Benedictine monk blocking their path, arms folded high on his chest, and expression stern. "What are you doing?"

"None of your business," sneered the older youth.

The monk raised one thin silver eyebrow. "I can make it so very quickly indeed," he said coldly. "Let him go and be on your way."

The stand-off was short. Bravado the squires possessed in bucketloads, but they were lads, not grown men. Faced by the charisma and authority of the Church, they grudgingly capitulated and, pushing Brunin to his knees, swaggered off. At a distance, the blond one turned.

"Your liver's mine, piss-hose!" he shouted. "And I'll come back for it!"

Brunin stared at the dusty grass inches from his eyes. A dark drop of blood plopped from the knife wound and ran down the stems to soak into the soil. He could hear his breath sawing in his chest and breaking over his larynx in hoarse sobs. He wondered if he was dying and wished that he were already dead.

"How now, child." The monk stooped and raised Brunin to his feet. "What had you done to them to make them set on you?"

"Nothing," Brunin gulped in a quavering voice and sleeved his eyes. He felt sick and his legs wobbled like a foal's.

The monk gently tilted Brunin's head to one side so that he could see the cut on his throat. "No more than a nick," he said, "but it could have been nasty indeed." He clucked his tongue and spoke more to himself than Brunin. "Every year, with the revenues, this fair brings us these squalid troubles, the more so since men quarrel over who rules the kingdom." He drew Brunin gently toward the abbey precincts. "Come, child, let us find some salve for that scratch and a place for you to sit a moment." His gaze was shrewd. "If you are not a foundling, which I judge not by the cut of your tunic, someone will be looking for you."

❖ ❖ ❖

Fulke FitzWarin, lord of the castles of Whittington and Alberbury and more than fifteen estates in the counties of Shropshire, Staffordshire, Devonshire, and Cambridgeshire, took a drink of wine, rolled it experimentally around his mouth, and swallowed. He handed the cup to his companion. "What do you think?"

Joscelin de Dinan sniffed the brew and, under the anxious eyes of the hovering vintner, set the rim to his lips. "Not bad," he said, wiping his mouth. The creases at his eye corners deepened as he smiled. "Certainly I wouldn't be insulted if you served it to me."

FitzWarin grunted with amusement. "Useful to know I don't have to broach my best wine to satisfy you then." He raised his forefinger to the vintner. "I'll take thirty barrels. You can haggle the price with my steward." He set the cup under the spigot of the sample barrel and refilled it. Around them the crowds ebbed and flowed in rapid tidal surges. The vintners' booths were always busy and it was best to visit them early while there was plenty of choice.

It was good to be out in the sun-soaked morning with no more pressing business than the pleasure of talking to old friends, restocking the wine supplies, and the later prospect of exploring the horse market and weapon booths.

"Your steward?" Joscelin raised his brows. "Not your mother?"

FitzWarin laughed and pushed his heavy hazel-brown hair off his forehead. "Doubtless she'll have her say but for the moment her mind is fixed on buying cloth and thread for sewing. Sometimes there are just more pies than she has fingers." His mother's reputation was legendary among the baronial community of the Welsh Marches. It was said by many, sometimes to his face, that the lady Mellette was a match for any dragon that happened out of Wales. She was five years past three score but had more stamina than FitzWarin's wife who was less than half her age.

The men enjoyed a few more samples. Joscelin wanted some Rhenish and FitzWarin bought a firkin of sweet, potent mead.

"There is something I have been meaning to ask you," FitzWarin said as they sauntered companionably away from the wine booths. His feet were steady, his balance good, but he could feel his tongue wanting to run away with him. Joscelin's cheekbones bore a red flush that made his smoke-gray eyes gleam like polished flints.

"As long as it is not about my daughters," Joscelin said, only half in jest. With two stepdaughters, two girls of his own blood, and no son, Joscelin de Dinan was constantly being petitioned by men who desired a future stake in the strategic castle and prosperous town of Ludlow.

"No." FitzWarin shook his head. "It is about my son...my eldest," he qualified, for he had six. "It is past time that he began his training. The lad's ten years old now. I was wondering if you..."

Joscelin raised his brows, for usually a man kept his heir at his side and fostered the sons of other men as his companions. It was the younger sons who went to other households in the hopes that they would find a niche through marriage or as household knights. "You are not keeping him at Whittington?"

They paused to let a string of pack ponies through, bells jingling on their harness, wicker panniers piled with belts of gilded leather like a tangle of flattened snakes.

FitzWarin sighed and gave the telltale hair-push. "No," he said. "If it was Ralf, or Richard, or Warin, I would do so, but Brunin needs to spread his wings. I can think of no better place for him to receive his training than at Ludlow…if you will have him."

Joscelin looked thoughtful and sought for the meaning in FitzWarin's words. He had no doubt that Ralf, Richard, and Warin would prove engaging lads, easy to train into manhood. However, a boy who needed to "spread his wings" suggested one who was going to be more of a challenge. "It is no small responsibility to raise your friend's heir," he said.

"I trust you."

"And you don't trust yourself?"

FitzWarin glowered. "I was sent away for training because I was a younger son, but it was the making of me…and provident too, since my older brother died and left me to inherit. Brunin is like me. He will have more opportunity to flourish in a different household, and I would like it to be yours."

Joscelin frowned. "Have you discussed the matter with your wife?"

"Eve will do as I say, and I will deal with my mother," FitzWarin said brusquely.

Joscelin thought of his own comfortable domestic situation and knew that, despite Eve FitzWarin's astonishing beauty, he would not change places with his friend for one minute of one day.

"I'm buying Brunin a new pony," FitzWarin added on a lighter note. "Mark's taking him around the fair just now, but we're meeting at the horse market at the sext bell. If you want to see the boy, you are welcome to join us."

"So that I can look in his mouth too as if he were a colt for sale?"

Joscelin's sarcasm was lost on FitzWarin. "Well, yes, if you put it like that...After all, you wouldn't buy a horse without looking it over."

Joscelin was spared from making an answer as a worried-looking young man came hastening toward them from the thicket of cookstall booths. He was wearing the quilted tunic of a man-at-arms and his left hand rested on the hilt of a long hunting knife.

"Mark?" FitzWarin's expression sharpened. "Where's Brunin?"

The young man bowed his head in deference and chagrin. "I do not know, my lord."

FitzWarin's glare could have cut steel. "You do not know?"

The serjeant licked his lips. "We became separated by the crowds, my lord. I was on my way to the horse market to see if he was there. He knew it was our meeting place and I thought..."

"How in God's sweet name did you become separated?" FitzWarin's raised voice boded ill for his serjeant.

"I...One minute he was there, the next he was gone."

"He was where?" Joscelin asked. "Where precisely did you lose him? At which booth?"

The serjeant blenched. "At one of the cookstalls, my lord."

FitzWarin's eyes flashed. "I suppose you were drinking and filling your belly when you should have been watching the boy."

"I only looked away for a moment, I swear it."

"A moment is all it takes." FitzWarin made a terse gesture with his clenched fist. "I have no time for this now; I'll deal with you later. For the nonce, we had better find my son."

Joscelin cleared his throat. "Doubtless your serjeant is right and the lad will make for the horse market. I suppose he has the sense?"

FitzWarin glowered at Mark. "Yes," he muttered. "He has the sense if he chooses to use it...more than this muttonwit here."

The men began making their way among the booths. FitzWarin sent Mark to fetch the other household knights and serjeants and set them to searching. "But don't alert the women," he commanded. "The last thing I need is panic in the hen house."

FitzWarin and Joscelin went straight to the horse fair, but although there were plenty of lads standing at bridles and helping the grooms, there was no sign of the one they sought. Small hand clasped in the protection of a toil-reddened fist, a boy walked past the men with his father. The pair paused side by side to inspect a well-fed dappled pony. FitzWarin looked at the child's earnest, upturned face, then at the father's indulgent smile and knew that God was punishing him. "If anything has happened to Brunin, I will have my serjeant's guts for hose bindings," he muttered through clenched teeth.

Joscelin's initial instinct was to murmur the platitude that the boy would turn up unharmed, but he bit his tongue. Doubtless, if one of his daughters were lost in this vast tide of humanity, he would feel less sanguine. Prudently he said nothing and applied himself to the hunt.

Mark and the other soldiers searched along the banks of the Severn where the traders' barges bobbed at their moorings, but there was no sign of Brunin and no one had seen him. The river, although it looked innocent, was treacherous and deep and would quickly swallow a child if he fell in. Millrace, brook, and pond were investigated too, but without result. FitzWarin had walked the circuit of the fair with Joscelin to no avail and his agitation had increased from simmer to boil when a young monk approached them.

"My lords, I hear you are searching for a lost child?"

FitzWarin's eyes lit up. "Praise God, you have found him?"

"Yes, sire. Brother Anselm has him at the porter's lodge." The monk pointed behind him, indicating a low stone building near the Foregate.

FitzWarin set off at a rapid walk, clapping his hand to his scabbard to keep it still. Joscelin strode beside him. "If he went to the monks for help, that too shows sense," he said.

FitzWarin grunted. "Sense would have been staying with my serjeant," he said. "I'll have both their hides in recompense."

Seated on a bench outside the porter's lodge, a thickset monk of middle years was comforting a woebegone child. Tear tracks snailed the boy's smooth olive skin and his dark eyes were glazed and heavy. Marks resembling bloody fingerprints painted one cheek and a yellow salve had been smeared over a cut on his neck. There was a telltale stain at the crotch of his hose.

FitzWarin slewed to a halt and his eyes widened. "God's sweet bones, Brunin?"

The monk removed his arm from around the boy's shoulders and rose to his feet. If he was disturbed by the use of blasphemy in God's own precincts, he kept it to himself. "The boy is yours, my lord?"

"He's my son," FitzWarin snapped. "What has happened to him?" Striding to the bench he stooped to Brunin and turned his jaw to the light. "Who did this?"

The boy's expression was blank. FitzWarin knew the look of old. Whatever pain Brunin had suffered had been drawn within where he would feed upon it in silence, and it would feed on him.

"Some older youths were making sport with him and it was becoming ugly," the monk said. "I intervened and brought him to the lodge. When I heard from one of my brethren that there was a search going on, I sent Brother Simon to direct it here." He gestured. "He's badly shaken but no lasting harm seems to have been done."

FitzWarin turned to Brunin. "Would you know the youths again?" he demanded and clamped his jaw as he saw terror fill his son's eyes. "Would you?"

"Yes, sir." Brunin's throat rippled.

FitzWarin jerked him to his feet. "Then let us go and find them, and let us see what they have to say when they taste my sword."

"My lord, violence only begets more violence," the monk intervened. "Surely we have all seen enough in this lifetime not to seek out more."

"Save your homilies for church," FitzWarin snarled. "I've

swallowed enough of them in the past to last me a lifetime too!" Turning his back on the monk, he scowled down at his son who was quivering in his clutch. "What did they look like?"

Brunin stammered out a description, his complexion paling until he was ashen.

"It might be best to leave him behind," Joscelin said neutrally. "Look at him. He is in no state to be walking around the fair."

"I can see the state he is in," FitzWarin snapped. "And when I find those who did this, they will pay. Come on, boy, you've the blood of kings in your veins. Show your worth."

Brunin had been clenching his teeth and swallowing convulsively while the men were in discussion, but his body reached a point where his will could no longer control it and, bending his head, he vomited, the spasms heaving through his narrow body until his knees buckled.

"For the love of God, send him back to your lodging," Joscelin said, his expression filled with appalled pity. "He is beyond his endurance. He could be descended from King Arthur himself and it would make no difference just now."

Grimly, FitzWarin swept Brunin into his arms, his strength making nothing of the boy's weight. He felt beneath his fingers the dampness where Brunin had pissed himself and was filled with a deep and tender rage, not least because he was ashamed that his son had been frightened enough to lose control of his bladder. Did such a trait show a predisposition to cowardice? The thought was like a pebble in his shoe. What if Brunin lacked the qualities he needed to guide his family's interests when the time came? It would not have mattered if he were one of the younger boys, but he was the heir. And because he was ashamed, FitzWarin was angry with himself too. He should be thanking God that Brunin was safe, not agitating over the child's lack of backbone. Torn both ways, he hugged his son before handing him abruptly into the custody of two of his knights.

"Guy, Johan, take him straight to my lodging and give him to the women. Tell them as little as you can get away with. I'll deal with it myself when I return."

"Yes, sire." Guy hoisted Brunin across his shoulder like a deer.

Frowning, FitzWarin watched them leave. Then, shrugging his shoulders as if to level and settle a heavy burden, he sent another man to call off the search and turned back toward the fair.

*2*

*Y*OU WILL BE HUNTING FOR A NEEDLE IN A HAYSTACK," Joscelin warned, striding beside his friend. "And if you start a brawl, you will have the sheriff down on you like a stone from a trebuchet."

FitzWarin bared his teeth. "You need not come with me."

"I know."

They walked in silence, eyes darting and assessing the crowds through which they shouldered. Joscelin was the taller, standing a finger's length above two yards; with his thick, garnet-red hair and leonine prowl, he caused heads to turn. The men were followed by their retinues who were out of earshot of the conversation, but close enough to be summoned at need.

"I will understand if you decline to take my son," FitzWarin said as they skirted a tumbler performing handstands on two sword points.

A kitten-pretty girl in a gown that exposed an indecency of ankle twirled up to the men and shook a painted bucket under their noses. FitzWarin glared at her. Joscelin thumbed a quarter penny into the bucket and folded his arms, indicating it was all she was going to get. He had been balancing on sword points of one kind or another for most of his life.

"You say he is like you." Joscelin gave him a sidelong glance.

FitzWarin pushed his hair off his brow and clutched a fistful of the heavy brown strands. "God's bones, I don't know." He sucked a breath through his teeth. "Yes, I suppose, although at his age I had more——" He broke off and grimaced. "I was going to say courage but that is not the right word. Spirit, perhaps. I'm certain he has it within him, but he keeps so much to himself that it is difficult to know where to begin looking."

"And that is why you said he needs to spread his wings?"

"I stand too close and I will only hamper him."

Joscelin nodded. "I make no promises, but I will think on it. First I need to speak with my wife."

FitzWarin eyed him with surprise verging on disapproval. "If I take a squire into my own household, I do not seek permission from Eve. It is my business and she would not dream of meddling."

"But your mother would," Joscelin said with a smile.

FitzWarin shook his head. "Not in such a matter."

"Not directly, but you would soon learn if she objected to your choice. The lady Mellette is not one to hold her peace—I say it with the greatest respect. And it is out of respect that I will first consult with Sybilla. She is lady of Ludlow and even if I do take Brunin into my train, he will spend much time under her supervision—in the early days at least."

FitzWarin continued to look as if he thought Joscelin was being overindulgent, but he nodded. "As you wish," he said.

They left the players behind and kept on with their search, doggedly going from booth to booth, without success.

"Likely they are long gone by now," Joscelin said as they paused beside the shops of the weapon smiths.

"They are here somewhere," FitzWarin replied with the certainty of a terrier with its head down a badger hole. "No one comes to the fair for a single day. Even if they have left the field, they will be lodged somewhere close."

"Sir." Mark spoke up, his voice nervous and eager. He had come up from the river and tagged himself onto the end of FitzWarin's retainers.

FitzWarin followed the serjeant's pointing finger toward another group of knights and squires who were at the far end of the weapon booths. Prominent among them was a tall nobleman with crisp black hair and a neatly cropped beard. He was accompanied by two youths, one flaxen-fair and clad in a red tunic, the other stocky, freckled, and wearing blue. The former had a swagger and an ostentatious knife at his belt.

Joscelin looked too but it was the sight of the noble rather than the squires that sent his right hand twitching toward his sword hilt. Gilbert de Lacy was his wife's cousin, but since de Lacy claimed that Ludlow was his, it was a cause for strife, not friendship. De Lacy's father had been deprived of the fief more than fifty years ago for rebellion, but it had not prevented his son from campaigning vigorously, both through the courts and on the battlefield, to have the lands restored to their branch of the family. Joscelin would usually have sidestepped an encounter with him. While he could handle himself in a fight, he didn't relish a confrontation with the bitter, dangerous competence of Gilbert de Lacy.

Raising his head de Lacy noticed FitzWarin and Joscelin. His own hand went to the hilt at his hip and his angular cheekbones reddened. He checked his stride for an instant before continuing forward to a scabbard-maker's booth. Then he turned his back, deliberately ignoring the two barons. Exchanging swift glances, the squires held close to the shadow of their lord.

FitzWarin lowered his head like a bull and charged straight in to the attack, gripping de Lacy by the shoulder and jerking him around. "My lord, your squires assaulted my son," he snarled, "and I demand redress."

De Lacy threw him off with a fierce shrug and contemptuous eyes. "Boys are boys," he retorted. "If your son cannot fend for himself, you should not let him stray from his wet nurse's tit."

Goaded, FitzWarin lunged.

De Lacy blocked FitzWarin's fist on his muscular forearm and spoke hard into his face. "Were I to intervene in every brawl and skirmish that my squires got into, I'd waste my lifetime, and I have more important matters to pursue." He thrust FitzWarin away. "I would willingly break both you and de Dinan on the battlefield, but I'm not stupid enough to make one of this fairground even if you are. Ernalt, Gerald, run back to my lodging and tell the steward I am on my way and to have wine ready. Quickly now." He stood his ground, barring FitzWarin's and Joscelin's way until the boys had made their escape.

"If I think it necessary to punish my squires, I will do so myself," he said vehemently. "They are mine to discipline."

"Then make sure that you bloody their hides with your whip," FitzWarin said, his teeth bared, "for if you do not, then I will. Rough and tumble is one matter. Using a knife on a child is another."

Surprise flickered in de Lacy's expression.

"A knife," FitzWarin repeated. "Only a coward draws steel on the vulnerable. If you saw it and did nothing, you are a coward too. If you did not, you are as much at fault for letting your squires run wild like a pair of ill-trained dogs as I am for not watching over my son."

A muscle ticked in de Lacy's cheek. Without a word, he spun on his heel and strode away. His retainers followed with several back-cast glances at their counterparts in FitzWarin's and Joscelin's retinue. The taverns were going to be dangerous places that evening.

FitzWarin let out a shaken breath, releasing rage and tension. Joscelin slowly relaxed his hand from his sword hilt. He had clenched the grip so hard that the pattern of the braided leather was imprinted on his palm.

"De Lacy," FitzWarin grimaced. "It would be de Lacy."

Joscelin's right hand was trembling. He had badly wanted to fight and at the same time was vastly relieved that it had not come to that. "Did you notice the men with him?"

"I was more interested in those misbegotten squires of his. What about his men?"

"I saw two of them outside a tavern yesterday, selling their swords."

"You mean de Lacy is hiring soldiers?"

Joscelin nodded. "Yesterday they were unemployed mercenaries. Now they have their fee. And if de Lacy is hiring, then it behooves me to double the guard at Ludlow and send out more patrols."

"You think de Lacy will attack you?"

"I don't think he'll sit down to besiege Ludlow; he doesn't have those kinds of resources, but he can snap at my heels and cause trouble. You'd best look to your walls too. He's not your enemy the way he is mine, but there is no love lost between you, and you are my ally. I would not put it past him to incite your Welsh enemies into raiding your lands."

"They'll receive a welcome that will last them a generation if they do," FitzWarin said darkly.

Joscelin's gaze wandered over the swords, axes, and spearheads displayed at the nearest booth, their edges honed to river-blue. Usually the sight of such beautifully crafted objects lifted his spirits, but today they seemed like a portent and he felt a deep melancholy rushing to fill the space where battle tension had been.

❖ ❖ ❖

FitzWarin returned to his own lodgings in a mood as dark as a thunderstorm. A flagon of wine in one of the taverns had done nothing to lighten his humor. The brew had tasted like piss-vinegar and Joscelin had been taciturn and sunk in his own thoughts. FitzWarin had made his retainers return with him and banned them from drinking in the town. A brawl with de Lacy's men might vent the heat, but the potential cost was too great.

When he strode in the door, a servant was stirring a cooking pot and trying to keep the stew from burning on the bottom. His wife and mother were examining bolts of cloth laid out on a coffer and his sons, except for Brunin, were tumbling on the floor like a litter of puppies, even William, the two-year-old, who kept tripping over his smock.

"Husband." Eve came toward him, a tense, eager-to-please look on her face. He had married her eleven years ago when she was fifteen. The bearing of six sons had slackened once taut muscles, but she was still slender and the bones of her face were such that even in old age she would be a beauty. Her hair shone through its net like a sheaf of wheat and her wide-set hazel eyes were as appealing as a fawn's.

He greeted her with an indifferent mutter.

"Are you hungry?"

He was, but not for overcooked stew. "Bread and cheese will do." Going to the sideboard, he cut a chunk from the loaf that was standing there. Eve watched him, her underlip caught in her teeth.

"Where's Brunin?" he asked.

"In the sleeping loft." She indicated the ladder stairs to the long roofspace above. "Guy told us he'd been attacked." Her voice trembled on the last word.

"Wolves always recognize weaklings." The voice was pitched deep for a woman and as cold as a raw January morning. Leaving the bolts of cloth, the lady Mellette joined her son and daughter-in-law. Although elderly, her spine was as straight as a measuring rod. Her robe of dark blue wool and a tight wimple of bleached linen were fittingly severe. Even in her youth, she had been no beauty, but she possessed the more lasting gift of presence. No one was ever allowed to ignore the lady Mellette.

FitzWarin felt the familiar stab of anger and guilt. "Brunin is not a weakling." His own ambivalence toward his son made his tone harsh. "It could have happened to any child who was in the wrong place at the wrong time."

"As he always seems to be." Mellette's expression was unforgiving. "Guy told us he'd wandered away from his guard. If he had been obedient and stayed where he was, this would not have happened."

FitzWarin dug his free hand through his hair. "Christ on the Cross, Mother, if he were obedient all the time, I'd worry about him more. At least it shows he has a spark to kindle."

"That is like giving a fool a piece of gold and expecting him still to have it at the end of the day. And do not blaspheme at me!"

He did not apologize, but lowered his gaze rather than meet the blaze in hers. "Did Brunin say anything?"

Mellette gave an impatient snort. "As much as he ever does. Anyone would think that he had been born without a tongue in his head. I wonder about his wits too."

FitzWarin swallowed his bread and clung to his temper. "Brunin has both voice and wits when he chooses."

"Which is less than often."

From the midst of the litter, the two-year-old uttered a loud wail as four-year-old Thomas sat down hard on him. Eve went to intervene, plucking her youngest son from the melée and hoisting him in her arms. An instant later, he was clamoring with outstretched arms to rejoin the fray. Mellette watched with a softening of approval then returned her attention to FitzWarin.

"You discovered who did it?"

"Two squires belonging to Gilbert de Lacy."

"Hah, well, that comes as no surprise. His father was a traitor and he's changed beds in this dispute between Stephen and Matilda more often than a whore on the eve of a battle. You have dealt with it, I trust?"

"Yes," he said curtly. "I've dealt with it." Like his son, he did not intend to elaborate on the matter. Lifting the flagon, he poured himself a cup of wine.

His mother's brows drew together. "You should let a servant do that," she said, looking around for one.

"We're lodged in a merchant's house, not at the royal court," he growled. "I can do for myself."

"That is no reason to let standards slip. Remember your blood is the blood of the Conqueror."

Through a more than dubious lineage, he thought, but he managed to clench his teeth on the words. His mother was the bastard daughter of the Earl of Derby, who in turn claimed bastard descent from William the Conqueror, who was himself bastard born. FitzWarin's father was an adventuring mercenary whose fast wits and sword had brought him to the Earl's notice and earned him Mellette's reluctant hand in marriage. The slender, swarthy Warin de Metz had married high and the haughty lady Mellette considered that she had wed far beneath the status of her paternal line. The belief had soured the union from the start and although her husband was long in his grave, she could not let go of her bitterness. Her domain was a royal court; she was the queen and woe betide anyone who forgot the fact.

Mellette clucked her tongue against her teeth in irritation, then sighed. "I have been thinking about the boy."

"Indeed?" FitzWarin grimaced into his cup.

"You have five other sons, all robust and healthy." She indicated the noisy brawl of small boys. "Why not dedicate Brunin to the Church? To have a son in holy orders is useful on all counts and it seems to me that he would be suited to the cloister."

"No," FitzWarin said more loudly than he had intended. The notion had sometimes occurred to him too and her words had touched the raw patch of his guilt. "No," he repeated on a more controlled note as her brows lifted in surprise. "I hope that I have arranged for Brunin's future today. I spoke with Joscelin de Dinan about fostering him at Ludlow."

That silenced her. Behind him, he heard Eve's soft intake of breath.

Mellette moved to a bench by the hearth and perched on its edge, knees pressed together, hands folded in her lap. "The heir is usually educated within his own home," she said. He did not miss the gleam in her eyes, nor the way that they flickered briefly to Ralf.

"Usually, yes, but not always. I hope that experience in a different household will be the making of Brunin."

"And Ralf and Richard, you will educate them at home?"

"Likely they will go for fostering too," he said. "I would not want to break the rules too far."

She gave a contemptuous sniff. "You think that an education by a Breton mercenary will better serve us and Brunin than sending him to the Church?"

"Joscelin de Dinan is more than just a Breton mercenary," FitzWarin said shortly. "He is of the line of the Counts of Brittany, and Ludlow is an important fortress. Indeed, it makes Whittington look like a peasant's hovel."

Mellette flinched at the comparison, her mouth puckering as tight as a miser's drawstring purse.

"He has the warrior skills, but he can play the courtier at need," FitzWarin added. "Brunin's education will be well rounded. Lady Sybilla is a conscientious chatelaine. She does her duty by her husband's squires." He had been laying the bait in a trail of crumbs. Now he set down the remainder of the loaf, tempting her with the prize of Ludlow itself. "Joscelin's heirs are his two daughters. Given Sybilla's age she is unlikely to bear him a son to inherit the lands."

Mellette looked down at her clasped hands, her expression mulish. FitzWarin's resolve hardened. He would send Brunin for fostering whatever she said.

After a moment, she raised her head. "Perhaps you ought to send Ralf to Ludlow. If you have a match in mind, your second son stands the better chance of impressing de Dinan."

"No, Mother. I have offered him Brunin and for good reasons." FitzWarin forced himself not to gulp the wine. He had already drunk more than he should in the tavern, plus the cups at the vintners' booths.

"Name them," she challenged.

"He is my heir," FitzWarin said. "Joscelin will not accept a second son as a mate for one of his daughters, no matter how accomplished the boy might be. And Brunin needs a chance to step out of the shadows. Joscelin de Dinan can give him that chance."

Mellette's jaw rotated as if she were chewing on his words and finding both nutrition and grit. "I suppose that if he goes to Ludlow, we will not have to sponsor him through the priesthood," she grudgingly admitted, "and it may be that Joscelin de Dinan will work a miracle and turn base metal into gold." Her tone said that she was skeptical but willing to see what happened.

Knowing that it was as much agreement as he was going to receive, FitzWarin abandoned his wine and moved toward the loft stairs.

"Husband, do not wake him," Eve said quickly. "He's asleep."

He paused and turned. Eve swiftly lowered her eyes.

"Don't fuss, woman," he said, but in a gentler voice than he had thus far used since coming home. The steps creaked beneath his tread, but he reckoned that if Brunin could sleep through the brawling of his brothers, a few stealthy footfalls would not disturb him.

The shutters were open and FitzWarin paused briefly by the window. Men were still drinking in the taverns—women too, he thought as a particularly piercing cackle arrowed through the window. Lanterns and cooking fires glimmered among the booths as many of the owners sat vigil with their stock. There was a pervasive smell of woodsmoke and onion stew. A horse whinnied and was answered by several others. Sighing, he turned into the twilit room and paced along the row of pallets laid out on the floor.

Brunin was on the end one, his form outlined by a coverlet of striped Welsh wool. He was breathing so quietly that FitzWarin had to lean close and look for the rise and fall of his chest. The child's right forearm was flung across his eyes and even in sleep, the fist was tightly clenched. With great gentleness, FitzWarin lifted Brunin's arm and laid it down at his side. The boy made a sound and the dense black eyelashes flickered, but he did not waken. Exasperated, baffled, assailed by a wave of affection so strong that it was almost grief, FitzWarin watched his firstborn son sleep. He remembered the wild stormy night in March when he had been born, the wind strong enough to uproot trees and flatten hayricks and hovels. The midwife had come from the birthing chamber, a snuffling bundle wrapped in her arms, and presented the men with the next link in their bloodline.

FitzWarin's father had been alive then, and he had been the first to hold the child. Even then, the resemblance between grandfather and grandson had been marked. Not just the coloring, but the shape and symmetry of flesh and bone, one new as a tight-furled hawthorn leaf at winter's end, the other sere and tattered from the long autumn's descent into withered old age. FitzWarin had never seen his father weep, but he had done so that night. Now he was dead, and the spark he had passed on was in danger of being quenched.

Hearing soft footfalls, he turned to see Eve coming toward him. The dusk had leached the color from her skin and hair and made dark pools of her eyes so that she resembled a faery creature from the hollow hills. His Welsh nurse had told him such stories of fey women and he often thought of his wife thus. Much of the time she was like an empty shell and it was as if her true substance walked elsewhere. Their marriage had been arranged to suit ambition and policy, without a shred of romance involved. They performed their marital duties, but it was like a social dance between two strangers. She was attentive, docile, obedient, and abundantly fertile. Since he had never strayed from their marriage bed nor raised his fist to beat her, he considered that he was a good and considerate husband.

Stopping at his side, she too studied their son with a troubled gaze. "He hasn't said a word." Her tone was quiet and expressionless. "Not to me or anyone. Your mother tried to make him speak, but it just seemed to push him further out of reach." She bit her lip. "If I could take his pain, I would."

FitzWarin was surprised into a glimmer of deeper feeling that led him to lament the cramped sleeping conditions and wish for their bedchamber at Whittington. He set his hand to her waist and his tough, swordsman's fingers spread to the upper curve of her buttocks. "Brunin has to learn to stand up for himself," he said gruffly.

She stiffened. "Oh yes," she said. "He has to learn. As all men do." Her expression was blurred by the gathering dusk, but there was no mistaking the bitterness in her usually tractable voice.

"Eve?" The word was startled out of him and he eyed her askance.

Her throat rippled. "In God's name, my lord, send him out of this household before it is too late." Twisting from his embrace, she almost ran from the chamber.

Her leaving caused the boy to stir on his pallet and mutter in his slumber, but what he said, his father could not tell.

FitzWarin washed his hands over his face. A dull ache compounded of an excess of wine and tension was beginning to pound in his skull. He could not face going back down to the women and his yelling boisterous offspring. After removing his boots, he stretched out on the empty pallet beside Brunin and went to sleep, his right arm bent across his eyes and his fist tightly clenched.

# 3

*H*ER HEAD PROPPED ON A BOLSTER, HAWISE DE DINAN LAY on her back in her parents' bed and stared at the canopy. Beside her, she could hear Marion trying not to giggle and that made Hawise want to giggle too. She compressed her lips, fighting the explosion gathering beneath her ribs.

"You're supposed to have your eyes closed. You're badly injured," said Sibbi crossly.

Hawise strained her gaze sideways to her sister who was wearing their mother's second-best green gown, purloined from the clothing coffer, and the matching silk wimple. She was holding a roll of linen bandage.

"People die with their eyes open," Hawise pointed out. Not that she had actually seen anyone breathe their last, but she had been to a vigil in the chapel last year for one of the knights and remembered that they had had to put coins on his lids to keep them shut.

"Well, you're not dying; you're just wounded."

"Can I groan then?"

Sibbi rolled her eyes.

"I'd be groaning in real life, wouldn't I?"

"She would," Marion reinforced, with a vigorous nod of her flaxen head. She had a cushion stuffed up her dress. "I think the baby's coming," she said. "Can I groan too?"

"No, you can't." Sibbi's slate-blue eyes flashed with irritation. "And you can't give birth until I've bound up your husband's wounds!"

The three girls were playing at "sieges." It had been Hawise's idea, for she was a tomboy with a vivid imagination and she had easily projected herself into the role of bold knight saving the castle from assault. Marion had opted to be the lady of the keep and, being just as fond of drama as Hawise in a different way, had added the embellishment of pregnancy to her perils. Sibbi, who was two years older than her sister and Marion, was keener on the nurturing aspect of the game. She wanted to bind the imaginary wounds, make them better, and practice her bandaging skills at the same time. Delivering a baby was somewhat beyond her knowledge, but a cushion was a start.

"Give me your arm," she said to Hawise.

"You're supposed to give me lots of wine and get me drunk first," Hawise said knowledgeably. "When Papa fell off his horse and broke his collar bone, Mama made him drink three quarts of Welsh mead before she tended him."

"Well, you'll just have to pretend," Sibbi snapped.

Hawise screwed up her face and tried to remember the incident. Her father had spoken a lot through clenched teeth and been very bad-tempered. The mead had improved matters but when he had started singing a song about two lusty maidens, a wayfaring man, and a ginger cat, her mother had bundled Hawise from the room. A tremendous pity. She would have liked to know how the song ended.

Hawise submitted to having her arm bandaged and pinned against her body, uttering a few moans to improve the authenticity and even daring her father's favorite curse of "God's sweet eyes," until Sibbi clucked her tongue and Marion threatened to tell on her.

Hawise sighed. "How long do I have to lie here?"

"Until you're better."

"Papa didn't. He was on a horse the next day."

"Can I have the baby now?" Marion asked querulously. She kneaded the bulge beneath her gown with small clenched fists.

Sybilla de Dinan appeared in the doorway that led through to the day chamber for the castle's women. She was winding a length of spun wool onto her spindle as she regarded the girls with amusement. "Sibbi, Hawise, your father's home from Shrewsbury," she said. "I've just seen him ride in." Advancing to the beds, she paused before Hawise. "Very accomplished," she said, tucking the spindle in her belt and examining Sibbi's handiwork. "I could not have done better myself."

Sibbi blushed with pleasure.

"Although Hawise had best take it off, lest her father think she has met with an accident..."

"Will Lord Joscelin think I'm with child?" Marion piped up.

"Of course he won't," Hawise sniffed. "You're not married. Anyway, it takes a long time to grow a baby...doesn't it, Mama?" She turned so that Sybilla could unpin the bandage.

"Yes, three seasons." Sybilla's expression was still warm with amusement, but a guarded look had entered her eyes. She turned to Marion. "You'll need some braid to decorate that new gown of yours. Do you want to come and choose the colors now?"

Marion chewed her underlip and thought about the offer. Then she nodded and having solemnly tugged the cushion from beneath her dress, cast it on the bed as if she were suddenly afraid of it and ran to clutch Sybilla's hand.

Hawise unwrapped the bandage, threw it down in an untidy tangle, and dashed for the door, her heavy auburn braid bouncing against her spine like a bell rope, the soles of her shoes flashing.

With a sigh and a head shake, Sibbi picked up the snarl of linen strips and began rolling them back into a neat coil.

Hawise pelted down to the hall and out into the bailey where the men were dismounting. Her papa had only been gone for two days, but she was wild to greet him. He had promised to bring her some bridle bells for her pony and a set of leather juggling balls from the fair.

By the time she reached him, he had dismounted from his roan cob and was talking to a couple of his knights. A long train of pack ponies was clopping away toward the undercroft. "Papa!" she cried and flung herself at him.

He caught her in mid-run and swung her around in his arms, making her shriek with delight. Then he kissed her soundly on the cheek and set her down.

"Did you remember my bridle bells and juggling balls?" she demanded, hopping from foot to foot.

"Your what?" He rubbed his hand over his stubbled jaw and Hawise felt a jolt of apprehension at the blank look on his face. Just as the apprehension was about to become panic, he winked. With another shriek, she threw her arms around his waist and hugged him.

Laughter rumbled in his chest. "How could I forget them when I know the terrible consequences of doing so? You can have them when I unpack my baggage." He glanced down and, with a smile, tugged the leather belt at her waist. A wooden sword in a cloth sheath was thrust through it. "What's this?"

"We've been playing sieges," she said. "And I was the lord of the castle."

His lips twitched. "I hope you fought off the enemy."

She nodded. "But I was wounded and Sibbi had to look after me. And Marion was having a baby."

Her father made an interested sound in his throat and she could tell, from the vibration that ran through him, he was silently laughing. Behind them, she heard the chuckles of the knights, but it was a comfortable sound and she felt indulged rather than ridiculed.

"I might have another surprise for you soon," he said as she grabbed his hard, callused hand and began pulling him toward the living quarters.

Hawise frowned up at him. Her imagination scurried, but she could think of nothing she particularly wanted beyond bridle bells and juggling balls…unless perhaps a pair of stilts. "What sort of surprise?" she asked.

He squeezed her hand. "I'll have to talk to your mother first."

Hawise squeezed him back, exerting all her pressure until he screwed up his face in mock agony and she giggled.

"Tell me, Papa," she demanded.

"On the morrow." He tweaked her auburn braid.

"Is it a toy?"

He shook his head. "Wait and see," he grinned.

She was intrigued and mystified but knew her papa and the boundaries he set well enough to realize that he wouldn't say until he was ready and that neither cajolery nor stamping and tantrums would work. Indeed, the latter would merit the flat of his hand. Besides, despite her high spirits and impulsive streak, she was a stoical child who could be patient when the occasion arose. "Promise you'll tell me first."

"I'll think about it." He gave her another wink.

❖❖❖

Replete with spiced chicken stew, white bread, and an obscene quantity of honey and rose-water tart, the girls were preparing for bed. Gowned in their chemises, their hair combed and their prayers said, they sat on their beds and chattered like sparrows as they waited for Sybilla to come and snuff the candle.

"I don't know what sort of surprise," Hawise said. Having imparted the information, she was now the center of attention. She tossed three of the five leather balls in the air and for a moment succeeded in keeping them in rotation. "Papa said it wasn't a toy, though." The balls fell around her and she picked them up to begin again.

"Perhaps it's some cloth for a new dress," Marion predictably suggested as she flicked back her hair. The strands shone like a field of barley, pale gold and silky under the breeze.

Hawise shook her head, her own thick curls glowing like dark wine. "I thought of that, but Papa's not interested in clothes or buying them."

"A puppy then," Sibbi offered.

Hawise thought about that. Her papa had several large hunting hounds that followed him around the keep and slept across his chamber door. Their mother would pat the beasts in passing but, although she was kind to them, was largely indifferent to dogs. She probably wouldn't object if worn down by pleading. "No," she concluded with a regretful shake of her head, "because Papa would have brought a puppy with him and he wouldn't have asked her about it."

The girls mulled the problem over in silence for a while, Sibbi sitting in contemplation, hands folded neatly in her lap, Hawise casting and dropping her juggling balls, and Marion stroking her already smooth hair with the antler-work comb that Joscelin had brought her from the fair.

"Perhaps he wants her to have another baby," Marion said at length. "That would be a surprise."

Hawise dropped the balls and Sibbi's head jerked up. Both girls stared at Marion.

"Yes." Marion nodded decisively. "They don't have a son and everyone knows that boys have the best claim to family lands." She continued her grooming like a cat washing itself, her air feline and knowing.

"They would have had one sooner than now," Sibbi said doubtfully.

Marion shrugged. "Ask them. I bet it's true."

"All right, I will." Hawise dropped her juggling balls, scrambled to her feet, and ran into the main chamber.

Marion's eyes widened as if she hadn't expected quite so immediate a result.

Hawise found her mother putting away her sewing. Sybilla had removed her wimple and hairnet. Her curly hair was tamed into two thick braids, the sable-black stranded here and there with silver. She had changed from her ordinary dress of brown wool to the crimson one with the deep neckline broidered in gold. It was Hawise's favorite of her mother's gowns, and her father's too, for she had often heard him say so.

"I was just coming to kiss you good night," Sybilla said, and then her gaze sharpened. "What's the matter?"

"Marion said that Papa wants you to have another baby."

Her mother straightened. A look of complete astonishment crossed her face. "Where did she get that notion?"

"Papa has a surprise for us, and Marion said that was it."

"It certainly would be a surprise," Sybilla said with a shaken laugh. "I think, failing a miracle, we can safely say that Marion is wrong." She latched her sewing basket and, taking Hawise by the hand, turned toward the small anteroom where the girls' beds were arranged.

"He said that he had to talk to you first."

"Well, it won't be about babies, I can promise you that." She brushed Hawise's red curls tenderly with her palm.

Later, when the girls had been kissed and settled and the lantern snuffed, Marion's mattress rustled. "Well, if it's not a baby, then it'll be a betrothal," she whispered knowingly. "One of us will be given a husband."

"Go to sleep," Hawise hissed, "or else I'll tell Mama, and she'll be cross this time." Hawise had already been unsettled by Marion's talk of babies and wanted no more threats of disruption to the security of her life.

"Tell her. I don't care," Marion said, but fell silent after that.

Hawise closed her eyes and, as she waited for sleep, wondered what the surprise was, her previous anticipation now tinged with more than a little apprehension.

❖❖❖

Sybilla moved quietly around the bedchamber, tidying clothes, pouring wine into two cups, lighting the beeswax candles that for thrift had been left until now. Joscelin sat in the cushioned window seat, watching the first stars prick the twilit sky. Now and again, he cast his glance to her work, but he said nothing and the silence between them was companionable.

Sybilla finished what she was doing and brought the cups

of wine to the window. She stood looking out for a moment, enjoying the sight of the evening light against the castle towers. She had lived here for most of her adult life and every stick and stone of Ludlow was as familiar as her own hand. Joscelin took a swallow of the wine and leaned his head against the wall. "Good," he said.

"It's from a new barrel." She looked at him mischievously. "Knowing your taste, I thought you'd appreciate it."

He gave her a sleepy smile that made her cheeks grow warm. "You know my tastes well."

"I should do by now." She sat down beside him and he pulled her close so that she was leaning against his chest rather than on cold stone. His palm rested at her waist, the gesture light but possessive.

Joscelin had been eight and thirty when they had wed, and she a recent widow whose husband had died in sudden violence during a war with the Welsh. Her first marriage had been a political arrangement as most matches were, but they had made a success of it and she had been grief-stricken when Payne had been killed. Almost immediately, without respect for mourning, King Stephen had forced her remarriage to Joscelin, one of his most experienced mercenaries. Those first months had been difficult, but although he was a soldier first and had long been a bachelor, Joscelin had a courtier's polish and an innate liking of women. She knew her good fortune and its limitations—as he knew his.

"So," she said, "what is this surprise of yours?"

"Surprise?"

"You told Hawise that you had one for her."

"Ah, yes." He grinned.

"And Hawise told the other girls. Marion seems to think that we are to have another child."

She felt his snort of amusement, although the comfortable atmosphere developed a strained quality. Sybilla bit back the apology that sprang instinctively to the fore. She was nine and forty and her flux had not come in a seven-month. Nor had she proved a prolific breeder of offspring in her fertile years. As Payne's wife, she had borne Cecily and Agnes. Since her remarriage she had only quickened twice, each time with a daughter.

"Marion is still fascinated by the matter?" he asked.

Sybilla sighed. "I think a little less than of yore, but still too much for comfort. Whenever the girls play, she is always the lady of the keep and about to give birth. It is as if by acting out the part, she tries to heal herself, or make the outcome different."

"You have great patience."

"I need it," Sybilla said ruefully and took a long swallow of her wine. "I could kill the fool of a maid who let her wander into the birthing chamber when her mother was bleeding her life away in childbirth." She folded her arms with indignation, remembering the day when Joscelin had brought Marion to Ludlow from her home—a wan little thing of five years old, peering fearfully over the edge of his fur-lined cloak. Her father, who was one of Joscelin's knights, had died in a fall from his horse and the shock had sent her heavily pregnant mother into labor. There had been complications, and the woman and baby had died, leaving Marion an orphan. Sybilla had taken her under her wing and was raising her with Sibbi and Hawise, but it was no easy task.

She took her mind from the thought and concentrated on her husband. He might have inquired out of politeness, but she was not sure that he would understand or be particularly concerned. "Your surprise," she prompted.

"Well, in a way it does concern a child," he said, "although not as small as Marion might be anticipating. And it will involve you to an extent."

"You have another orphan for me?" She kept her voice light, but behind her smile, she braced herself.

"Not as such." He told her about his meeting with FitzWarin at St. Peter's Fair and the request that had been made. "I said that I would consult with you first."

"Providing that he is house-trained, I have no objection." Her eye corners crinkled with humor.

"Then you will take him?"

She had seldom met the FitzWarin family. Occasional weddings and marcher gatherings had brought her into passing contact with the womenfolk. Eve FitzWarin possessed the beauty and responsiveness of an effigy. Mellette Peverel was an autocratic matriarch with a sword for a tongue. FitzWarin himself had sometimes visited Ludlow and had campaigned often with Joscelin in the war between Stephen and Matilda. He was not at ease with women the way Joscelin was and more than a little dour. But she had seen him laugh once and it had changed his face.

"Yes," she said, "I will be glad to take him." She studied Joscelin. "What are you not telling me?"

"Nothing." He avoided her gaze. "The boy will need gentle handling."

She sat up and faced him. "As Marion needs gentle handling?"

"No, not quite like that. But..." He made a gesture. "He needs encouragement from me...and the tenderness of women from you. He's not had much of either in his own household. FitzWarin did not put it in those terms exactly, but I know what he meant, and after what happened at the fair..."

Sybilla raised a questioning eyebrow and Joscelin gave her an abbreviated account of Brunin's ordeal. As she listened, her indignation grew. "The poor child," she said. "Even if FitzWarin is your friend, he is a dolt."

"Sometimes," Joscelin conceded, "but you were not there to see the undercurrents. Whatever else, he loves the boy. I'll have a scribe draft a letter on the morrow and send a rider to Whittington."

She nodded. "You had better tell Hawise about him, because I am not sure that she believed me. Marion certainly didn't."

He chuckled. "I promise I'll do it in the morning, straight after mass." Draining his wine, he set his cup aside.

Sybilla gave him a considering look. "You don't think FitzWarin is inveigling a match between his son and one of our daughters?"

"Of course he is," Joscelin said easily. "In his place, I would certainly have an eye to the future, but it is the secondary reason for his request. We can observe the boy's progress and measure our decisions as the future dictates. I am in no hurry to betrothe our girls, and I think you are of the same mind?"

"Indeed," Sybilla said. "I want them to be content with the choice we make when the time comes, and for that they need to be old enough to have a say in the decision."

He took the end of her braid in his hand and ran his thumb over the wiry silver and dark strands. "You want them to have the choice that you did not?"

"Yes." She covered his fingers with hers, thinking that sometimes his perception was too keen for comfort. "That is not to disparage you or Payne. Perhaps you also would have preferred a choice...a younger wife, for instance?"

He gave her that sleepy smile again. "I have no complaint with my lot," he said. "Younger wives bring their own burden of troubles and there is much to be said for experience." His hand left her braid and, with slow deliberation, he unpinned the brooch that fastened the neck of her gown. Leaning into his body, Sybilla closed her eyes and raised her face to his.

❖ ❖ ❖

Usually he would fall asleep after they had made love, but this time he did not. "The squires that attacked the boy...they belonged to Gilbert de Lacy," he murmured as his heartbeat slowed.

Sybilla held her breath. Her cousin's name was one that had echoed down the years of both her marriages as he continuously pressed his claim to Ludlow. Payne and Joscelin had thwarted him at every turn, but that had not deterred him. Rather his persistence had grown until it was a constant, nagging pressure. A knot of apprehension replaced the languor of good lovemaking.

"To be fair, he did not know about the assault on Brunin. I could see the surprise in his eyes."

Sybilla raised up on her elbow and, by the light of the candles, gazed at her husband. His expression gave little away, but she knew how to read him by now. The tightness of line at his mouth corners, the taut eyelids that should have been lax with sleep and satisfaction: all spoke of his unease. "You came face to face with Gilbert?"

"Beside the weapon booths, of all places." He gave a humorless laugh. "FitzWarin stepped straight in like a loose bull and I thought we were going to have a battle then and there."

Sybilla's eyes widened in dismay. "You didn't fight?" Mentally she shook herself. Of course they hadn't fought. It would have been the first thing she would have heard about on his return and there were no marks on his body.

"No…but we came close." Remembered anger flickered across his face. "He looked at me as if I were a turd stuck to the sole of his shoe."

She tossed her head. "Looks count for nothing. He is not strong enough to come against Ludlow, and neither King Stephen nor the Empress will recognize his claim." Her voice had strengthened with indignation as she spoke. Although Joscelin was its lord, Ludlow was hers by the right of her blood and she was fiercely protective of that right.

"Yes, I know, I know." Joscelin sighed and pillowed his arms behind his head. "But between them, Gilbert de Lacy and Hugh Mortimer of Wigmore still cause a deal of trouble." He spoke the names of the two largest thorns in his side with a suitably pained expression.

Sybilla studied his long bones, the fluid strength of his muscles, the tufts of auburn hair in his armpits. Despite being close to fifty years old, he still had the honed physique of an active warrior. "Nothing we cannot handle," she said by way of faith and encouragement. Leaning over, she kissed him. The "we" was telling.

"No," he agreed. "Nothing we cannot handle." But it was a long time before either of them succumbed to sleep.

❖ ❖ ❖

Seated at the dais table in the great hall, Joscelin broke the bread that his chaplain had blessed and dipped it in the small bowl of honey at his side. His wife and daughters followed suit. Joscelin chewed, swallowed, and licked honey from his thumb.

"I have something to tell you," he said to the girls and was amused at the rapid communication of glances between them before they looked warily at him. He gestured to the two squires serving at the dais table. "Hugh and Adam are growing into men," he said, "and it is time that I took a younger squire into my household for training. A friend has asked me if I will foster his son and, after discussion with your mother, I have agreed."

A brief silence ensued, busy with more unspoken exchange between the girls. Hawise was the first to speak.

"How old is he?"

"About your own age," Joscelin said. "And his birth name is Fulke, although he is known as Brunin."

"Is he going to marry one of us?" Marion wanted to know.

Taken aback, Joscelin blinked and it was his turn to exchange looks with Sybilla.

"Child, he is coming here to learn to be a knight, not a husband," Sybilla replied firmly. She gestured to the bread and honey. "Eat your food."

Marion dropped her gaze to her platter, her lower lip developing a pout.

"When is he coming, Papa?" Sibbi asked.

"As soon as it can be arranged. I want you to welcome him and treat him as you would a brother."

Sibbi nodded. "Does he have any sisters at home?"

"No, only brothers. He's not used to girls, but I'm sure you'll help him grow accustomed." He managed not to look too wry.

"Yes, Papa." Sibbi tucked a stray wisp of dark hair behind her ear and resumed eating. Her cheeks were rosy and there was a gleam in her eyes.

"She will mother him to death," Sybilla muttered from the corner of her mouth so that only Joscelin could hear.

He smothered a grin behind his hand. "It won't do him any harm."

"Marion will need extra attention so that she doesn't feel left out...and perhaps Hawise too," Sybilla added shrewdly.

He considered the two girls. Marion was picking at her food, but then she had always had the appetite of a sparrow. Hawise, who usually devoured her meals, was toying with her second piece of bread, a thoughtful look on her face. After that first question, she had said nothing.

"Marion will want to bear his babies," Joscelin murmured. "And Hawise will lead him into more scrapes than a hound pup off the leash."

Sybilla eyed him. "And that is not cause for worry?"

He laughed softly and closed his hand over hers. "Oh, yes indeed," he said, "but of the kind that I am glad to have."

"Since it will likely be me dealing with them," she retorted, but she was smiling.

They finished breaking their fast. Sybilla took Marion and Sibbi with her to the women's chambers to cut out some linen tunics. Usually Hawise would have gone with them, but her father beckoned her to accompany him instead.

Mystified, but delighted, she dusted breadcrumbs from her gown, hastily dabbled her hands in the fingerbowl, and joined him. "Where are we going?"

"Just a ride out," he said. "I want to look at the horses."

Hawise gave a little skip. She loved going with her papa to view their horses. The mares and geldings that made up the herd grazed together with the common saddle beasts. There were separate paddocks for his destrier and his hunting courser, both stallions.

The grooms had saddled Rouquin for him and in minutes had tacked up Hawise's barrel-bodied chestnut pony, Sorelle. She was a competent rider and, with a boost up, settled herself in the saddle and drew the reins through her fingers. Her father smiled his approval. Surrounding them, his bodyguard and squires waited attendance.

"So," he said as they rode across the bailey and over the bridge beyond the gatehouse. "What do you think of having a 'foster' brother?"

Hawise pondered the matter. She had been little more than a babe in arms when her father's younger squire, Adam, had arrived in their household and still a little child when he had entered adolescence. She had never played with him as such, and he had never encroached on what she considered her territory. "I want him to come," she said slowly. "I'd like a boy to be my friend... but..." She bit her lip.

He bent his head and looked at her from under his brows. "But what, sweetheart?"

"But how do I know that he'll be my friend? What if I don't like him?"

Her father covered his mouth with the palm of his hand. She couldn't tell if he was thinking or smiling. The former it proved, for when he took his hand away, his mouth was straight. "Brunin will need some time to adjust to our ways," he said. "Think of how it would be if you had to leave home and go and live among strangers. For the first few days everything would be different and unsettling—yes?"

"Yes," she said with a frowning nod.

"Just remember that when you meet him and do not expect too much at first. But I see no reason why you and he cannot be friends." He winked. "It would be good to have a companion in arms when you play at sieges, hmm?"

Again Hawise nodded. It would indeed and she felt a spark of excitement at the notion. But she would hate it if she was relegated to the role of admiring onlooker or binder of wounds. She had seen how the boys of the keep played and what they expected of their sisters.

"When I go to fetch Brunin from Whittington, I want to take him the gift of a pony."

Hawise gazed up at him in surprise. "Doesn't he have one?"

"Yes, but he's almost outgrown it. His father was going to find him one at St. Peter's Fair, but for one reason and another, by the time he came to look, there was nothing suitable. I said I would see what I had among our own herd...and I thought that you might like to choose."

Hawise brightened at the thought and swelled a little with pride, for she recognized that the task was an important one, and he had entrusted it to her, not Sibbi or Marion.

After much deliberation, she settled for a sturdy Welsh cob, built on the same lines as her father's Rouquin, but a pony, not a horse. Its hide was the hue of sweet black cherries, its tail almost swept the ground, and its mane entirely covered one side of the proud, arched neck. It was the one she would have chosen for herself, had she not possessed her own adored Sorelle.

Her father smiled his approval. "An excellent choice," he said. "I have no doubt that young Brunin will look well on his back." He tilted his head. "What's the scowl for, sweetheart?"

"I hope he's not faster than Sorelle. I don't want to lose too many races."

Throwing back his head, her father laughed. "I am sure you can hold your own in any situation," he said.

# 4

*STAND STILL,"* MELLETTE SNAPPED. "I'VE KNOWN A BASKET OF live eels to wriggle less." She turned Brunin by the shoulders to face her, her grip bony and hard.

Behind a blank expression, Brunin mentally grimaced. He was being made ready for his departure to Ludlow and was heartily sick of the fuss. A thorough head-to-toe scrubbing in the bathtub earlier that morning meant that his black hair gleamed with the rainbow sheen of a crow's wing. His smooth olive skin was marred at the cheekbone by a scabbed-over cut caused by a branch-whip while riding in the woods. He would have liked to be in the woods now with nothing but the hoofbeats of his outgrown pony and the flicker of falling leaves for company. But since Lord Joscelin of Ludlow was expected at any moment, his place in the scheme of things was strictly preordained.

His grandmother snatched a comb out of the hands of a maid and drew it through his hair until he felt the sharp antler teeth scraping his scalp.

"Same mop as your grandsire," she muttered. "Never looks tidy. In my day, the best men wore their hair like King William. Shaved and short. None of this long nonsense." Standing back she considered him with narrowed eyes. Brunin's stomach churned with the sudden fear that she was going to send for the shears and barber him as bald as a June sheep.

"That will have to do," she said. "There's no making a silk purse from a sow's ear, but at least you're halfway presentable." She tugged at his new tunic of dark-red wool, aligning a fold. The cuffs, neckline, and hem were embroidered with a design of green and gold scrollwork that had taken his mother and her women several days to stitch. His chausses were made of expensive double-dyed blue Flemish cloth and bound with braid that matched the colors in his tunic. This outfit would see him through feast days and formal attendance in Joscelin's household. His mother had packed plainer garments in his baggage for everyday wear.

"Remember," his grandmother said. "You are a FitzWarin by name, but your great-grandsire was Earl of Derby and his sire was the Conqueror himself. You must not disgrace your blood...do you hear me, boy?" Her voice sharpened a notch.

"Yes, madame." Brunin knew that his silence was annoying her, but he could think of nothing to say. Her lecture was an old one. Every day he and his brothers had their bloodline dinned into their heads. Besides, whenever he opened his mouth, he displeased her, so what was the difference? There was even a kind of painful satisfaction in watching her mouth purse and her knuckles clench.

"I still say it is a pity that your father is not sending Ralf to Ludlow," she muttered with a glance toward Brunin's nearest brother. Ralf too was dressed in his finest tunic for Joscelin de Dinan's visit, and the sky-blue wool was a perfect foil for his fair coloring.

Brunin said nothing. That opinion had been overruled by his father. It did not matter how many times his grandmother voiced it, she had still been defeated.

"Brunin will do his best, *Belle-mère*," his mother said quietly.

"Well then, let us hope it is good enough," the older woman snapped, as always getting the last word, before she stalked from the chamber to see how matters were progressing in the great hall.

Eve laid her hand on Brunin's head. "I would say pay her no heed," she said softly, "but that is both disrespectful and hard to do. She is, after all, your grandmother and her blood is in you."

Her voice shook, then steadied. "But the road you take from here is your own. I know that your best is good enough." He felt her fingers in his hair, combing it off his brow as tenderly as his grand-mother had not. It was an awkward caress and Brunin stood still beneath it, unsure what to do. A part of him yearned to reach out and respond, but, aware of the presence of his brothers who would scorn such a thing, he remained still.

His mother stifled a sob. Her hand descended to his shoulder, squeezed hard and briefly, and was gone. When he had mastered the stinging of his own eyes and dared to look around, she was engaged in conversation with his infant brother's nurse.

Ralf sauntered over to him. He was large for his age. Brunin topped him by a head but the difference looked less because of Brunin's slender darkness and the younger boy's much stockier build.

"When I go for fostering, *Belle-mère* has promised me it will be with an earl, not a common mercenary," he taunted. "My training will be better than yours." Ralf made it sound like a sneer, although in truth he was consumed by jealousy. Even if he was pleased at the thought of being the eldest son left at home, he deeply desired the position that Brunin was taking up because it was a step on the road to manhood.

Brunin shrugged. "What if Lord Joscelin was a mercenary? He has had to fight for what he has."

"So?" Ralf thrust one foot forward and placed his hands on his hips, attempting to intimidate Brunin the way he intimidated the younger ones.

Brunin stared him out. "So he will be able to teach me how to fight too...and better than an earl who hires men to do it for him. Besides, our grandsire was a common mercenary, so it's in our blood too."

Ralf's chest swelled. "You'll never learn; you're no good at fighting," he jibed. "I wouldn't have pissed my hose if I'd been attacked by two older boys."

"How do you know you wouldn't?"

"Because I'm not a coward."

The last word was too much for Brunin. His foot swept out and neatly hooked Ralf off his feet. He planted his right boot firmly on his brother's sleek tawny hair, as close to the scalp as he could.

"You whoreson!" Ralf gasped, and his eyes filled with tears for the pain was not the dull bruise of the wrestling matches which he usually won anyway, but sharp and stinging, and he was effectively pinned down and rendered helpless. "Richard…Richard, get him off me!"

Ralf's accomplice came running. Without lifting his foot, Brunin pivoted and elbowed his oncoming brother in the midriff. Richard went down with a choking gasp.

"Boys!" Eve started toward her sons, her hands outstretched in supplication. Brunin looked at her and removed his foot from Ralf's hair. It was a mistake, for Ralf leaped on him like a young wild boar, his fingers grappling for Brunin's windpipe. Ralf's weight brought them down and Brunin banged his chin on landing and his teeth snapped together. He tasted blood as he rolled and slammed his knee into the softness of Ralf's groin.

"Boys!" Eve cried again, wringing her hands. "Stop it, stop it now!"

"That will do!" This time it was a masculine voice that thundered the command. FitzWarin strode forward, seized Ralf by the scruff of the neck and hauled him to his feet. Ralf immediately doubled over, clutching his groin and retching. Richard was gingerly sitting up, one arm across his stomach. FitzWarin spared him the flicker of a glance before grabbing Brunin's arm and raising him too, and not gently. Then he stopped and stared.

"Christ on the Cross!" He laid his fingers over the livid marks at Brunin's throat. Brunin could feel blood dribbling down his chin from his bitten tongue and sleeved it away on the cuff of his new tunic, staining the painstaking embroidery.

FitzWarin rounded on his wife. "Is it beyond you to keep order for even a moment?"

Eve flushed. "They were at each other before I knew it. I do not even know how it began."

"He started it," Ralf croaked, pointing at Brunin.

Brunin said nothing. He looked at his cuff and then at Ralf with a gaze that was like dark water—anything could have lain under the surface.

FitzWarin glared at his sons. "Then I will finish it," he snapped. "Joscelin of Ludlow has this moment ridden in and I want you in the bailey to greet him. One step out of line from any of you, and you'll wear the stripes of my horsewhip for a month. Understood?"

"Yes, sir," Brunin said. Ralf and Richard echoed the response with subdued murmurs and downcast lids. The younger boys looked on in round-eyed silence.

FitzWarin gave a brusque nod. "Make yourselves presentable and come straight down." He shook a warning fist. "I mean what I say, and don't think I will stay my hand because we have a guest." He strode from the room on a rush of angry air.

Brunin spat bloody saliva in Ralf's general direction. Huddled over his bruised testicles, Ralf could only glare murder. Richard prudently sidled out of the way and took charge of the little ones.

"Let me see." Eve FitzWarin tipped back Brunin's head and looked into his mouth. "A bitten tongue," she said with relief. "The bleeding will stop in a moment." Hands shaking, she used a length of clean swaddling band dipped in the water jar to wipe the blood from his face. "Here, put on your cloak; it will hide those marks at your throat." She fussed around Brunin, draping him in his outdoor cloak of double-lined wool, fastening it with a pin of heavy silver, pushing his hair off his brow. Brunin endured her fretting with the same stoicism that he brought to most trials and tribulations.

"I feel sick," Ralf said, fishing for sympathy despite all.

"So do I," said his mother, tight-lipped. "Every day."

❖❖❖

Joscelin de Dinan dismounted from Rouquin and handed the reins to a waiting groom. A stiff autumn breeze whipped around him, blowing his cloak against his legs, threatening to pluck his cap from his head. Removing his shield from its long strap at his back, he gave it to one of his squires. Behind the youth, the rest of Joscelin's entourage dismounted in a rattle of weapons. It was a common sound these days, even when the visit was a social one.

Turning, Joscelin faced Whittington's bailey and the stout timber service buildings, gleaming with lime wash.

"Welcome!" FitzWarin stepped forward to greet Joscelin with a strong handclasp. "I am glad to see you!"

Joscelin grinned. "And I you. I am looking forward to broaching a barrel of that wine you bought in Shrewsbury!"

"I think I can find better than that for so honored a guest," FitzWarin replied, his color high. "You had a good journey here?"

It was obvious to Joscelin that FitzWarin was ill at ease. In Shrewsbury, on neutral ground and with only his immediate retainers to hand, he had been relaxed. Now, he was trying too hard to play the affable host.

"We went unmolested and it did not rain," Joscelin said with a smile. "That is as much as any man can hope for in these troubled times." He looked around at Whittington's walls. Unlike Ludlow, which was stone built, Whittington was mainly timber, but well protected by the surrounding marshy ground. The main threat was from the Welsh, who were not masters of the siege, and unless a castle could be taken with sudden onslaught, were not inclined to attack it. Here the "sudden onslaught" would be straight across a bog, and that would bring any attacker to an ankle-deep standstill.

"Welcome, my lord. Will you come within and unarm?"

Joscelin turned to face the lady Mellette. Although she smiled in greeting, it was a mere stretching of her lips without genuine warmth. The carriage of her head and the set of her jaw told of pride and an authority that it would take a brave man to flout. Her daughter-in-law, who should have been the one to step forward and speak, remained in the background with the children, her eyes modestly downcast.

"Thank you, my lady." Joscelin bowed his head and returned Mellette's smile. He could play the courtier's game when called upon to do so and he had encountered women of her ilk before, the Empress Matilda being one of them. "Perhaps I could request the services of my newest squire in helping me to remove my mail?" His glance flickered briefly to the line of boys waiting with their mother and descending in increments from Brunin to the toddler who was holding his nurse's hand and sucking his thumb.

She looked taken aback, but almost immediately rallied. Like an experienced swordsman, he thought with grim humor. "As you wish, my lord, although how much help he will be, I do not know."

Joscelin leaned a little closer to her than was polite, but it meant that his words did not carry beyond his lips and her left ear. "It does not matter how much help he is or isn't at this stage," he said with emphasis. "Only that I should speak to him and put him at his ease, and that he should speak to me."

Mellette took a step back. "You will be fortunate to get him to speak at all, my lord, but if you desire him to attend you, then by all means take him."

He inclined his head and moved to stand before Eve FitzWarin and the children.

"My lady," he said.

She curtseyed and murmured obligatory words of welcome. Joscelin felt as if he were standing before a house with a light in the window but the occupant long gone.

"My wife sends her greetings," he replied, "and says to tell you that she will look after your son as if he were her own. You know that you are welcome to visit Ludlow whenever you choose."

Eve's eyes were smudged as if with exhaustion or tears, but nothing could detract from their wide beauty. The warm hazel tints put him in mind of the autumn forest beyond the keep. "Thank you, my lord, that is kind."

She spoke the words as if there were not much of that kindness in her life. Joscelin turned to the boys. Brunin was staring straight ahead like a well-drilled serjeant under the inspection of his lord. In the stiff breeze his heavy raven hair fluttered like the feathers of a bird. His cloak was pinned high at his throat and showed a lining that matched his tunic.

"So, Brunin." Joscelin laid a firm hand to the boy's shoulder. "If you are to be my squire, we might as well begin. I want you to help me unarm."

"Yes, sire." A tinge of color flushed the boy's olive complexion. Joscelin's grip had flattened the lie of the cloak and what he saw on the boy's throat gave him pause for thought. He said nothing though, merely stored the sight in his mind for further investigation.

❖ ❖ ❖

Feeling as if he might burst with the emotions roiling through him, Brunin led Joscelin de Dinan to the guest chamber. In anticipation of Joscelin's arrival, the room had been swept out and aired. An embroidered frieze depicting a hunting scene had been hung at eye level along the back wall and the bed was spread with his mother's best coverlet of Flemish wool lined with coney fur. A ewer of water and a deep brass bowl had been set out on a coffer in case Joscelin should desire to wash, and beside it stood a flagon and cups.

Brunin stood waiting, trying not to breathe hard. The climb up the stairs had not winded him, but he felt sick with apprehension. What if he did something stupid and shamed himself and his family at the first test? What if Lord Joscelin said that he was useless and he did not want him in his household? What if he asked to take Ralf instead?

Lord Joscelin stood with his hands on his hips gazing around the room, a half-smile on his lips, his expression one of amiable curiosity. He didn't look as if he was about to be angry, but Brunin had learned never to take anything or anyone at face value.

Joscelin reached to his scabbard and unfastened the thongs

binding it to his swordbelt. "Here," he said to Brunin, "lay this carefully on that bench, and don't put your fingers on the steel."

Reverently, Brunin took the sword from Joscelin's large, hard hands. "I know about not touching the blade," he said, to show his new lord that he wasn't ignorant.

"I am glad that you do," Joscelin said gravely. "A squire must learn how to handle and look after all weapons. It is one of the first lessons of his training."

Brunin walked carefully over to the coffer, pacing as if he were involved in an important ceremony. The sword had a shiny round pommel and a grip of braided leather that spanned more than two of his hand-widths. With great reverence, he laid the scabbarded sword on the coffer and turned around.

"Now then." Joscelin indicated the two youths who had come to stand at either side of him. "This is Adam and this is Hugh. They will soon finish their training, although, like you, they are my squires. If you are not sure of something and you need to ask when I am not by, then you need not fear to approach one of them."

Brunin nodded dutifully to show that he understood, but he was wary. Although the youths, who were old enough to show beard stubble, gave him encouraging smiles, he did not smile back.

Joscelin held his gaze while he unlatched the gilded swordbelt and passed it across. As Brunin took it, Joscelin's hand stayed a moment on the strap so that he and the boy were connected by the leather. "I truly mean you need not fear," he said. "I know what happened at Shrewsbury Fair, but I promise that you will come to no harm beneath my rule. I expect swift service and obedience, not miracles." He glanced briefly to the elder of his squires. "How often have I beaten you, Hugh?"

The youth rolled his gaze heavenwards as if the answer was written on the roof beams.

"The truth," Joscelin said with both humor and warning in his voice.

Hugh lowered his eyes and fixed them on Brunin. "Not very

often, my lord. And only when I deserved it…even if I did not think so at the time." He winked at Brunin and ducked the playful cuff that Joscelin aimed in his direction.

"That is not to say that I am as soft as new butter," Joscelin said. "If I treat you fairly, I expect the best in return. And the same goes for everyone under my rule."

Brunin nodded and tried to look knowing, although he felt out of his depth. The easy attitude between Joscelin and his squires was like a new language…one that he very much desired to learn, but was not sure how to go about doing so.

Joscelin released his grip on the swordbelt and again directed Brunin to the coffer. Brunin laid it beside the scabbard and lightly touched the gilding on the pattern of stamped lozenges. When he became a knight, he wanted a belt like that.

When he turned again, the squires were helping Joscelin to remove his hauberk, the weight of which would have been too much for Brunin. Between them, the youths carried and draped the mail shirt over the coffer near the window. Brunin received Joscelin's spurs and placed them beside the sword and belt while the squires dealt with the quilted undertunic that Joscelin wore beneath his mail.

Now Joscelin was down to his tunic proper, of green wool with detailed embroidery of red and blue. A fabulous round brooch closed the neck opening, amber and garnets glowing like honey and blood amidst the gold.

"Well, young man, am I fit to face your grandmother, do you think?" Joscelin raised his hands and raked them through his hair, leaving deep feather marks in the glossy russet. His variegated gray eyes were agleam and Brunin was unsure whether to smile or not. Playing safe, he murmured a dutiful response.

"You need not wear your cloak inside," Joscelin said. "Take it off and put it over there with mine."

Brunin raised his hand to the pin, and then remembered why he was supposed to keep it on. His throat didn't hurt, but from the reaction of the adults, he knew that it must look worse than it was. "I'm...my mother said..."

"And I know why she said it. I have seen the bruises; there is no point in hiding them from me."

Slowly, a little unwillingly, Brunin removed the garment and the good humor vanished from Lord Joscelin's eyes as he studied the marks. "They are fresh," he said. "How did you come by them?"

Brunin shrugged. "I had an argument with my brother," he said reluctantly. His natural reticence had been exacerbated by both his grandmother, who never listened to his side of a story, and a subtler conditioning that suggested only weaklings told tales.

"Your brother did this?" Joscelin lifted his brows. "Which one?"

"Ralf, sire. But it doesn't matter."

"It doesn't?" The eyebrows remained aloft.

Brunin shook his head. "Not now, because I kicked him in the stones."

Joscelin rubbed his hand over his mouth. "Ah, now I understand why he was hunched over in the courtyard like an old man."

Brunin compressed his lips. Behind Joscelin, Hugh and Adam were openly grinning and their expressions were so infectious that Brunin almost choked.

"Well," said Joscelin, "it seems to me like tit for tat. Doubtless if someone was trying to throttle me, brother or not, I'd kick him in the stones too. Once you start your training, we'll deal with all the things you can do to protect yourself against an opponent bent on killing you...although it seems to me that you have made an excellent start."

The door opened and FitzWarin strode into the room in his usual vigorous manner that made him look as if he was being blown from behind. Then he stopped, hands to his belt, and looked at the rare smile lighting his son's face and the humor glinting in Joscelin's eyes.

"Is everything well?" he asked.

"Very well indeed." Joscelin gave Brunin a conspiratorial look. "I think my new squire is going to be a great asset to my household."

❖❖❖

"Of course," said Mellette, "the boy is not without some training. He might not be able to carve meat and cut trenchers, but he can pour wine well enough and set the high table."

Joscelin nodded. "From what I have seen, he is quick to learn," he said. "He does not chatter like a magpie, but perhaps that is all to the good. His silence does not mean that he is dull-witted. Far from it." He was seated at the dais table in the great hall with Mellette one side of him and Eve FitzWarin the other. An appetizing aroma wafted from the dishes set at intervals along the board. There was boiled wheat delicately flavored with almond milk, soft white bread, and a spicy fruit and venison stew. FitzWarin's chaplain had blessed the food and folk were setting to with a will.

Mellette gave him a narrow look. "None of my grandsons is dull-witted," she said.

"Indeed not, my lady. Only sometimes a quiet child is seen as being thus, when in fact he is absorbing knowledge like a cloth soaking up water."

"When he was smaller and just learning to talk, he would ask questions faster than I could answer them," Eve volunteered in her soft voice. "'What' and 'why' were constantly on his tongue." She glanced almost wistfully at Brunin where he sat at a side table on the dais between Joscelin's two squires.

Joscelin chuckled. "My youngest daughter is still like that."

Mellette's lips pursed. "Would you serve me with some of the venison, my lord," she said, changing the subject, reminding Joscelin of his manners.

Joscelin applied himself to sweetening the older woman. Probably her face would crack before she allowed a genuine smile to cross it, and he did not attempt that far. But he pandered to her desire to be treated like a lady of the royal court rather than a dowager living in a timber keep on the edges of Norman rule. Under his deference and subtle flattery, she thawed a little. The lines between her brows relaxed. She preened and made elaborate hand gestures as she spoke, emphasizing the wealth of gold on her fingers. Joscelin silently hoped that the meal was not going to be one of those interminable affairs that lasted all night. He could do without that particular aspect of court life. He was biding his time, waiting the moment when he and FitzWarin could sit in the private chamber, cups in hands, feet pointing toward the fire, and discuss business not appropriate to the dinner table.

Finally the meal drew to a close and Mellette signaled for the fingerbowls and napkins to be brought. She beckoned peremptorily at Brunin, indicating that he should perform this task for his parents and their guest.

Brunin had been lulled into a false sense of security by the presence of Joscelin's squires. They had been talking to him cheerfully throughout the meal and sharing dishes with him as if he had long been of their number. Hugh had been telling him all about Ludlow and what his duties would entail and Adam had been adding amusing asides and remarks. He was never to leave Lord Joscelin's shoes on the floor because one of the dogs had a habit of chewing them to pieces. If he saw Mistress Sibbi approaching with a pile of bandages, he was to run for his life. Ela the cook's wife baked the best griddle cakes along the Marches and if you were nice to her, she'd give you one.

"Hah, if you're nice to Wulfrun, the laundry wench, she'll give you one too," Hugh said.

Adam nudged him. "Yes, but he's too young yet. Save that for when he's got the wherewithal to do something about it."

The way the youth's eyebrows were waggling, Brunin knew that they weren't really talking about griddle cakes. Kissing probably, which wasn't on his agenda of interests.

"I think your grandmother wants you," Hugh murmured, sobering.

"Looks as if you're getting fingerbowl duty," Adam said. "That's one of the first ones. If you spill it, it's only water—it's not as if you're wasting good wine."

The warm feeling abandoned Brunin as if someone had snatched off his cloak on a midwinter day. He rose to his feet and approached a trestle on the edge of the dais where bowls of clean water and napkins were laid out. He could feel his grandmother's eyes boring into him like hot needles and knew that she was expecting perfection of him. The pressure of such knowledge made his hand tremble as he draped a napkin over his arm and lifted the bowl of beaten silver.

Approaching the high table he walked with deliberate care, certain that at any moment the contents of the bowl were going to slop over the sides, or the napkin drop from his arm into the floor rushes. His heart was racing and he felt queasy. The journey from trestle to table seemed to take forever, but finally he stood before his grandmother.

"Guests first," she said, her eyes censorious. "Surely I do not have to tell you that."

Stiffly, Brunin presented the fingerbowl to Joscelin, who washed his hands and dried them on the proffered napkin. "You'll have plenty of occasion to learn," he said easily. "There will come a time when you can handle the ceremonies without even having to think about them...Your grandmother now." With a smile he indicated the frowning old woman.

Courage bolstered, Brunin picked up the bowl and took two paces to the side to offer it to Mellette. Unfortunately, the second of those paces was over the rump of one of the hounds that had settled under the table to wait for scraps, its presence concealed by the drape of the cloth. Brunin tripped forward, his midriff connecting with the edge of the table. The water in the fingerbowl flew toward his grandmother in a bright silver arc, drenching her bosom and lower face in a great wet slap. She sucked a breath over her voice in a crow of shock, her eyes widening and her mouth working like a trout's. The dais table became a tableau of people staring in frozen horror.

Spinning on his heel, Brunin fled, thrusting past the servants, ducking and avoiding a steward who tried to seize his scruff, pushing past the startled usher, and bursting out into the cold autumn air. The duty guards looked at him in surprise as he exploded from the hall. In panic he ran away from the domestic buildings toward the storage barns and stables in the bailey. There were plenty of hiding places and, if he was lucky, they might not find him for hours.

Hens scattered before his flying feet. A pair of doves clapped skyward, winging for the safety of the shingled cote roof. He ducked into a barn near the palisade that protected the ladies' garden from the depredations of the bailey's poultry and fowl. Lord Joscelin's horses were stabled there and the animals lifted startled heads from mangers and hay nets to watch him run past into the deepest shadows at the end of the barn and there bury himself under a mound of bedding.

His breath roared in his ears and, beyond that sound, he could hear the movement of the horses, the swish of their tails, the stamp of their hooves. He bent his head against his upraised knees, his eyes screwed shut. There was a superficial darkness, but behind it, in merciless clarity, he could see the moment when the contents of the fingerbowl had dashed across his grandmother's face. He imagined the sting of her rod across the backs of his hands, but that didn't matter as much as the fear that Lord Joscelin might not want him now and that he would be forced to stay at Whittington and shamed into the bargain.

One of the horses gave a low nicker and his stomach clenched as he heard a man's voice speak softly in response. Peering through the hay, he saw Joscelin de Dinan standing beside the roan cob, his hand on its neck. He appeared to be alone, and his expression was calm. Brunin deliberated. Should he stay where he was, hold his breath, and hope that the man would go away, or should he stand up and make a clean breast of it? The lord of Ludlow glanced briefly at the bedding pile, but his gaze did not linger. He sauntered over to a large black pony and clicked his tongue to it, acting as if he had all the time in the world and that it was usual to spend it in a stable.

Summoning his courage, Brunin unfurled from his hiding place and emerged in a small eruption of hay.

"I wondered how long it would take," Joscelin said. "When I was a boy I used to lie for hours outside my father's warren, waiting for the coneys to poke their noses out of their burrows."

Brunin swallowed. He did not know how to respond, or even if he was expected to.

"There is no need to look so worried," Joscelin continued in the same easy tone. "I have no intention of dragging you back to the hall. That would be the worst thing to do in the circumstances. I told them that since you were going to be my squire, I would deal with you."

"Are you going to whip me?"

"What?" Joscelin's gaze widened. His eyes were the opaque gold-gray of field flints. "God save you, child, of course I am not going to whip you. What happened was an accident...I hope."

Brunin licked his lips. "I tripped over my grandmother's hound. It always hides under the tablecloth."

"Well then, it is not your fault." He looked to be almost on the edge of laughter. "Unfortunate, I grant you, but not your fault. Come here."

As wary as a cat, Brunin approached. When Joscelin reached out to pluck stalks of hay from his hair and tunic, he almost flinched, and Joscelin's levity vanished.

"You have suffered rough handling, haven't you?" he said. "I can see it's going to take longer than a day to alter things. If I were your father I'd..." He shook his head and seemed to change his mind about what he had been going to say. "I suppose I have that chance now, don't I, and so do you. No use crying over a spilled fingerbowl."

Brunin gave him a questioning look. He wasn't going to be whipped, that much was obvious, but he was not sure what Lord Joscelin was talking about.

"Tonight you will sleep on a pallet in my room with Hugh and

Adam, and I will talk to your grandmother. She will have nothing further to say to you about the misfortune just now." His expression hardened. "I give you my promise on that."

"Thank you, sire," Brunin said, feeling relieved and grateful, but still uncertain of his ground.

Joscelin nodded firmly to show that the matter was dealt with and changed the subject. "While I think on it, and while we are here, I have a gift for you. I understand your father was unable to find you a new mount at Shrewsbury Fair."

"Yes, sire." Once again caution entered Brunin's eyes. The reason they had not found a mount was that owing to the incident with Gilbert de Lacy's squires their choice had been very limited by the time they came to look. All the best animals had been sold.

"I thought I might have a fitting beast among my herd. My daughter Hawise is your own age and I asked her to choose." He indicated the black pony. "His name is Morel and, if he suits you, he is yours."

If innate caution had held Brunin back before, now he was lost for words and could only stand and stare. Joscelin watched him, his eyes creasing with humor. "I take it that he does."

"He is mine?" Brunin echoed, tearing his gaze briefly from the pony to look at Joscelin.

"Have I not just said so?"

Somehow, Brunin stammered out a thank you. The pony regarded him out of long-lashed eyes, stalks of hay protruding either side of its whiskery muzzle, jaws champing. Brunin stretched out his hand, palm flat so that the pony could grow accustomed to his scent. The small cob stretched its neck and lipped at his tunic.

"You probably smell of new hay," Joscelin said with a smile.

Brunin smiled in return, but all his attention was on the wonderful gift. While the dream lasted, he was going to enjoy it to the last drop. He ran his hands over the sleek, black neck, working back until he found the spot on the withers and scratched. The pony leaned blissfully into him. Brunin admired its short, glossy back, the rounded hindquarters, the raven cascade of tail. He had wanted either a pied pony, or one as black as midnight shadow—and, in a roundabout and strange way that he was not going to think about too hard, he had got his wish. He spoke softly to the cob, unlooped its tether and, grasping a handful of mane, threw himself across its back. The pony responded with a startled snort, but answered the grip of Brunin's thighs and the tug on the rope.

A thoughtful expression on his face and satisfaction at his core, Joscelin watched boy and pony circle the barn and then trot out into the yard. FitzWarin was right about the child. Out of his element, Brunin was as awkward as a grounded swallow, but give him the open sky and he had the potential to soar.

❖❖❖

"You see now why I asked you to take him," FitzWarin said.

Joscelin fondled the ears of the deerhound curled beside his chair and took a drink from his cup. It was Welsh mead, sweet, potent, and dark. "Yes, I see," he said. And I am glad to have him…truly glad. His light may be hidden under a bushel, but I saw it glow as bright as day when I gave him the black pony."

"That was generous of you."

Joscelin shrugged. "I knew you had found nothing suitable at Shrewsbury. The boy rides as if he and the beast are one."

A spark of paternal pride lit in FitzWarin's eyes. "He was on a pony before he could walk," he said. "I have done the same with all my sons, but it is Brunin's particular skill."

Perhaps because it was one of the few areas where he could be free, Joscelin thought. And a horse might act up, but it was never judgmental.

A brief silence fell between the men, punctuated by the settling of the logs in the hearth and the soft snoring of one of the dogs. The women had retired to their chamber and the children were abed. In the hall, folk were laying out their sleeping pallets along the side aisles. Joscelin drained his mead. "I heard some interesting news last week," he said casually.

"Oh yes?" FitzWarin refilled Joscelin's cup and tipped the remainder of the flagon into his own. "Where from?"

"Family connections."

Ah." FitzWarin rubbed his chin. Joscelin's relatives held land in Devon and in Brittany and they had strong ties with Empress Matilda's Angevin faction. Joscelin frequently heard snippets of information long before they became common knowledge.

"Prince Henry is crossing from Normandy in the spring."

"With an army?" FitzWarin grimaced. "Last time he came, he was a whelp of fourteen with grand notions and naught in his coffers."

"I do not know what will be in his coffers this time," Joscelin said slowly, "but he is to be knighted by King David of Scotland and, of course, all those who wish to see him achieve manhood will be present to wish him well."

FitzWarin gave him a piercing glance. "The knighting will take place in Scotland?"

"Carlisle, so I am told. My son-in-law is to be knighted too."

FitzWarin nodded. Joscelin's eldest stepdaughter, Cecily, was married to one of Prince Henry's staunchest supporters, Roger, the young Earl of Hereford, so such a privilege was to be expected and welcomed. "I assume that the gathering will be more than just a muster of celebrants and witnesses."

Joscelin said nothing. He didn't need to.

Sighing, FitzWarin pushed his hair off his forehead. It was thirteen years since King Henry had died, leaving his throne to his only surviving legitimate child, his daughter Matilda, widow of the German Emperor and remarried to Geoffrey, Count of Anjou. Many barons had refused to be ruled by a woman...and, what was worse to their Norman sensibilities, by a woman with an Angevin husband, Anjou being Normandy's traditional enemy. They had opted instead to bow the knee to Matilda's cousin, Stephen. War had ensued as the opposing factions had battled for supremacy.

The FitzWarin family, itself dominated by a strong woman, had sworn loyalty to the Empress from the beginning. That loyalty had remained staunch through every day of thirteen traumatic, bloody years.

Joscelin had been one of King Stephen's hired mercenaries at the start of the dispute, but soon after becoming lord of Ludlow he had revoked his oath and sworn instead for the Empress. There had been triumphs that burned in the blood like new wine and defeats that had left grown men broken and weeping. The land had burned under summer skies and winter's starving gray. The price of life had become both as cheap as straw and as valuable as gold.

"When Empress Matilda left England in January, many said that she would never return." Joscelin warmed his goblet between his hands. "Perhaps they are right, but with her eldest son almost grown to manhood, it does not matter. In truth," he added softly, "many will be glad to see Prince Henry steering the ship."

"Let's hope he can keep it steady in a storm," FitzWarin muttered. "He's perilously young."

Joscelin gave him a quizzical look. "Are you having doubts at this late stage?"

"Jesu no!" FitzWarin choked. "Even if I were sympathetic to Stephen, I'd not bend the knee to him, knowing that that son of his would inherit the crown. Eustace is about as fit to rule us as a whore to be an abbess. Young as he is, Henry has more of the spirit of kingship in his little finger than Eustace has in his entire body."

Joscelin nodded. "Many who would follow Stephen to their last drop of blood will not spill so much as a pinprick for his son."

"I suppose they think it will be easy to manipulate a raw youth to their own ends." There was a cynical note in FitzWarin's voice.

Joscelin's laugh was devoid of humor. "What they will do when they realize that Henry is as easy to manipulate as a mountain of granite remains to be seen."

FitzWarin quirked an eyebrow. "And just what are we supposed to do with a mountain of granite?"

Joscelin contemplated his mead before lifting his gaze to FitzWarin. "Build ourselves a fortress that will keep us and our families safe."

"What if Gilbert de Lacy comes courting Prince Henry too?"

Joscelin's wide, generous features grew closed and hard. "Possession is nine-tenths of the law," he said grimly.

## 5

$\mathscr{B}$RUNIN HAD NEVER BEEN TO LUDLOW AND, ALTHOUGH HE was accustomed to the sight of stout castles such as the one at Shrewsbury, nothing had prepared him for the imposing proportions of the massive stone walls rising out of the smoky autumn mist.

The fortress stood on a ridge with steep slopes descending to the river below. Where the river did not guard, a deep, dry ditch had been cut, spanned by a timber bridge leading to a passage through a heavily defended gatehouse.

"There's not another to touch it in the Marches...not even Shrewsbury," Adam said, his eyes alight with pride.

"I doubt that the people of Shrewsbury would agree with you," Joscelin replied drily as he joined his squires. He was relaxed in the saddle—a contrast to his earlier tension. Although Brunin had not been told anything in great detail, he knew that Lord Joscelin had been worried about being ambushed or attacked on the road by the men of de Lacy and Mortimer, who were his enemies. Hence, the knights had ridden in close formation with shields at the ready and hands never far from their scabbards. Now they were almost home and there was a perceptible lightening of the atmosphere.

The thought of encountering a troop led by Gilbert de Lacy had churned Brunin's stomach. He didn't want to meet up with the baron's squires ever again and the fear of doing so had haunted his dreams ever since Shrewsbury Fair. The anxiety dwelt at the back of his mind like a small, vicious rodent, spending much of its time asleep, but occasionally rousing to bite him hard.

"But do *you* agree with me, my lord?" Adam pursued. Of Joscelin's two squires, he was the more garrulous and familiar.

Joscelin smiled. "Of course I do, lad, but then I'm not of Shrewsbury. Just now, I have never seen a sweeter sight in my life than those walls. I cannot wait to be rid of the weight of this thing." He grimaced at the mail shirt encasing his body from throat to knee.

Brunin thought that Lord Joscelin looked rather splendid in his hauberk and was anticipating the day when he could be a knight and wear one himself. From his child's perspective, the weight seemed a small price to pay.

They rode over the timber bridge spanning the ditch. Brunin listened to Morel's hooves beat on the wood and straightened proudly in the saddle, imagining that he was a lord returning from a day's deeds in the field and that the knights and men-at-arms surrounding him were his own.

The guards on duty at the gatehouse saluted Joscelin and his troop through into the bailey. To the right were the timber dwellings of the guards' quarters, the laundry, and sundry storage buildings. Straddling the thatched roof of one of them was a girl of about Brunin's own age. Much of her curly, dark-red hair had straggled loose from its braid and coiled around her dirty, tear-streaked face in eldritch tangles. A rip in the side seam of her dress exposed her chemise and an orchard ladder was skewed at the foot of the shed as if it had been climbed and then fallen awry.

Astonished, Brunin stared at her. Catching his eye, she stared defiantly back, as no peasant's daughter would have dared. Beneath the grime, her complexion flushed campion-pink. She scrambled to her feet, balancing precariously on the dusty, chopped reeds of the thatch.

"God's bones!" Joscelin muttered and spurred Rouquin over to the store shed.

"That's the lady Hawise," Adam side-mouthed to Brunin. "Lord Joscelin's youngest daughter and the apple of his eye." The squire gave a low chuckle. "I wonder what scrape she's got herself into this time."

Brunin was incredulous. That disheveled dirty girl was Joscelin's daughter? The one responsible for choosing his mount? He had been carrying the hazy vision of a demure, tidy girl with a sweet smile, but that now dissipated faster than smoke in a brisk wind. This one had the sinewy wildness of a young vixen.

Joscelin drew rein under the shed. "Jump down," he commanded and spread his arms.

The girl drew her sleeve across her eyes. With trembling chin, but not a shred of hesitation, she did as he bade, leaping from the thatch with absolute trust. He caught her cleanly, but with a loud whoof as his breath was forced from his lungs. The roan sidled once and then stood firm. The girl embraced her father's neck in a stranglehold and buried her face against his mailed breast.

"What were you doing up there, child?" Joscelin asked. To Brunin, who, in the interests of self-preservation, was accustomed to listening for every nuance in adult speech, his lord's tone carried inquiry, amusement, and only a hint of reproof.

The girl wriggled. "Nothing."

"A strange place to be doing it. Where is your mother?"

She shrugged and raised her head, appraising Brunin with a bright gray stare. He hastily looked away. "Marion threw one of my juggling balls out of the window because I wouldn't play midwives with her," she said indignantly. "So I pushed her and she fell over and banged her head." She held out the ball of red leather she had been gripping tightly in her fist. "Look, it's split."

Joscelin bit his lip and Brunin saw that he was fighting not to laugh. "Just like Marion's head then," he said.

"She only bumped it, but she screamed as if she was dying, and Mama was angry with me because she didn't see what happened." Hawise's voice rose with grievance.

"So you judged it best not to stay?"

She nodded and rubbed her cheek against Joscelin's mail.

"That still does not explain what you were doing on the store-shed roof."

"The ladder slipped," she said, as if surprised that he should ask.

"Hawise..." A warning note entered Joscelin's voice.

"I was playing." She drew back to look at him. "You said that when you came to a siege here before you wed Mama, there were ladders up against the keep wall and that men climbed them and fought on the battlements."

Joscelin sighed and, shaking his head, tweaked a tangled strand of her hair. "Perhaps I did, but that is no call for you to re-enact the event. You saw what happened to your ball when Marion threw it out of the window. What would have happened if you had slipped off this roof?"

"I wasn't frightened."

"That is not necessarily a good thing," Joscelin said. "I certainly was."

"I am sorry, Papa." She looked down as if contrite but Brunin had his doubts.

Her father sighed and gave her a little shake. "All right," he said. "But I want you to go straight away and make your peace with Marion and your mother." He prepared to let her down off the horse.

"Can't I stay with you?" She looked around him at Brunin. "Do you like Morel?"

Brunin opened his mouth, but was unsure what to say or how to address her. Nothing thus far in his life had prepared him to respond.

"Child, where are your manners?" Some of the indulgence left Joscelin's expression. "That is not the kind of question to ask of a gift you have given, and especially not before introductions are made. Nor," he added wryly, "are you fit to be introduced at the moment. You look like a hoyden out of a gutter. Now go, do as I say, and when the time is right you can ask Brunin all the questions you want."

She hesitated as if she might further argue, but then seemed to think the better of it and relaxed so that Joscelin could set her down. Shaking out her dress, she looked again at Brunin and gave him a smile.

"I hope you do," she said. "I chose him." And then she was gone, lifting her skirts above her ankles to run long-strided like a boy, her wild auburn hair bouncing at her shoulders.

Joscelin sighed. "What am I to do with her?" he said, and then he gave a reluctant chuckle. "I am her father and I ask that?" He turned to Brunin. "One rule to remember is always judge on your instincts, never on first appearances."

"Yes sire." Brunin said neutrally. He was still struggling with his astonishment. He didn't have a sister, but if he did, he dared not imagine what punishment such appearance and behavior would merit at Whittington. Rather than feeling censure, he sympathized with her plight, although his own instinct would have been to hide in a corner rather than climb conspicuously onto a roof. Judging with one's instincts was not as simple a matter as Lord Joscelin made it sound. First, you had to trust those instincts.

❖ ❖ ❖

Hawise held her breath and screwed up her face as her mother attempted to comb the tangles from her hair. It was her father's color, but possessed Sybilla's curly wildness and the only time it was calm was when it was wet, or so severely braided that it hurt her scalp.

Sybilla clucked her tongue. "I've never seen such knots." Delicately she plucked out a broken stalk of straw and a pigeon's breast feather, evidence of Hawise's scramble onto the store-shed roof. Not that Hawise had told her mother anything about that—she had just let it be assumed that she had flounced off to the stables.

"She should have been a boy," Marion said with a superior

sniff. "Then she could wear it short." She was sitting on the coffer swinging her legs. Her own butter-gold hair shone in two neat, silky braids, twined with blue ribbons that matched her immaculate gown of Flemish wool. The hectic spots on her cheeks and another red mark slightly higher on her temple bore mute testimony to earlier traumas.

Hawise glowered at Marion, who smiled sweetly. Hawise had made her apology, albeit a forced one, but she had only done so to please her father, not because she was truly sorry. As far as she was concerned, Marion had deserved the thump...and was in danger of receiving another one.

"Welsh women have shorter hair too," Marion said. She wound one of her braids around her forefinger and examined the smooth, golden gleam. "So do nuns."

"Well, I'm not Welsh, or a nun."

"Your papa might betroth you to a Welshman or make you take vows."

"Marion, enough. Pass me that length of braid, the green one," Sybilla said with labored patience. Marion hopped off the coffer and meekly did as she was asked. Gathering Hawise's hair, Sybilla expertly wove the braid through and around, taming the wayward mass into a semblance of order.

"There," she said. "No one would ever think that you had been any further than the bower door this morning, hmmm?"

Hawise reddened beneath her mother's knowing scrutiny and fiddled with her belt. It was woven in the same pattern as the braid on her hair and the ends were weighted with delicate silver fillets. Her ripped gown had been consigned with a sigh from Sybilla to the mending basket, along with the split juggling ball, and Hawise was now wearing her second-best dress of green wool with yellow embroidery.

She thought about the boy; how fine he had looked astride Morel, his black hair and dark eyes a perfect match with his mount. His face had been unreadable and her question to him had elicited no response, save perhaps a tensing of his fingers on the bridle. She wasn't sure that she was going to like him; by the same rule, he probably wasn't sure about her either.

There was a brief warning of footsteps outside the chamber door and her papa entered, bringing with him the pungent aroma of hard travel. His three deerhounds bounced at his side, tails swishing like whips, pink tongues lolling. She cast a covert glance toward the squires who had followed him into the room bearing sundry items of equipment. Brunin had her father's helm, arming cap, and mail coif and was panting from his climb up the stairs thus encumbered.

Her mother hastened to greet Joscelin with a kiss on the mouth and a murmur of welcome, then turned to Brunin. "Put those down in that basket in the corner," she said.

"Yes, my lady." Eyes lowered, he did swiftly as she bade him. When he returned, her mother laid one hand lightly on his shoulder and with the other tilted his face on her palm.

"Look up, child," she said.

He lifted his lids. From her position a little to one side and behind her mother, Hawise was struck by how dark his eyes truly were. Not the usual hazel or mild amber-brown, but a color that was much closer to sable.

"That is better. Always look me in the eye when I am speaking to you."

Hawise gnawed her underlip and shuffled her feet at that remark. Sybilla gave a satisfied nod and dropped her hand to his shoulder. "I am Lord Joscelin's wife, Lady Sybilla, and I welcome you into our household. I know everything will seem strange for a time until you have grown accustomed to us, but I want you to feel that Ludlow is your home."

"Yes, my lady."

His flat response gave nothing away. Hawise tilted her head to one side while she absorbed the nuance. It might be useful to learn how to do that, she thought.

"These are my daughters." Her mother turned Brunin gently

with the palm of her hand. "Sybilla, whom we call Sibbi, and Hawise. Marion, like you, is being fostered as one of our own."

His gaze lingered briefly on Sibbi before passing to Marion who was fluttering her lashes like an afflicted heifer, making Hawise want to kick her. Then he looked at Hawise. She drew in her breath and held her stomach tight, afraid that he was going to give her away and mention the store-shed roof. However, he said nothing.

"Welcome." Sibbi smiled compassionately like a Madonna as she tried to ape their mother. Hawise had to stop herself from making a face. Obviously ill at ease and unsure of his ground, the boy bowed in Sibbi's direction. Hawise remembered her papa telling her that it would be strange for him in the early days and that, as he only had brothers, he wasn't used to girls. She was longing to ask him about Morel, but not in front of Marion.

"Can you juggle?" she asked, blurting out the words before she had time to think better of them.

The sable eyes widened. "Juggle, Mistress Hawise?"

He had remembered her name and he spoke it with formal propriety. Hawise was torn between wanting to continue and wishing that she had never opened her mouth. "I just wondered."

"No, mistress." He shook his head and she saw his glance go to the nearby sewing basket with her torn dress and the split ball. "But I could learn." She thought she saw the hint of a smile at his mouth corners.

"You never know when you are going to need the skill," Joscelin agreed. While the older squires had been divesting him of hauberk and gambeson, he had been listening with amusement and, like his wife, studying the subtle undertones at play. "If you have finished your introductions, I am in sore need of a bathtub, and there's fetching and carrying for the lad to do."

"By all means." Sybilla removed her hand from Brunin's shoulder. "I expect you'll want food brought up?"

Joscelin nodded. "Enough for all of us," he said. "We might as well dine in the private chamber tonight."

Laying a table had been part of Brunin's early training at Whittington. With his grandmother's strict tuition and insistence on the etiquette of the court, he could have prepared a trestle for a feast, let alone a simple family meal. He straightened the cloth of embroidered linen and began setting out the cups at intervals. Further into the room, Lord Joscelin was bathing in a barrel bathtub and murmuring to his wife who was listening to him with folded arms and nodding now and again. Once or twice she laughed, the sound throaty and warm. Brunin couldn't imagine his own parents ever talking in so informal and relaxed a manner, and his mother never laughed.

The atmosphere at Ludlow had overwhelmed Brunin. It had swept out to engulf him like a huge, joyous embrace, and he was still struggling to regain his balance. He kept thinking that it was a dream and, in a moment, he was going to awaken and discover himself back at Whittington, placing bread trenchers beneath his grandmother's gimlet stare. Indeed, when he looked up from his task, he was being stared at—but with nothing more hostile than intense curiosity.

"I'm fostered too," said the kitten-featured fair-haired girl who had been introduced to him as Marion.

"Yes, I heard Lady Sybilla say so," he murmured as he set the decorated salt dish directly in front of the lord's place.

"My mama and papa are dead." She adjusted the salt dish an inch to the left and crumbled a pinch of the grayish crystals onto her tongue. "Yours aren't though."

"No," he said, unsure how to respond. The intensity of her hyssop-blue gaze was unsettling. He wondered what would happen if he pushed the salt cellar back to its original place.

"My papa fell from his horse and broke his neck, and my mama died the day after in childbirth, so I had to come and live here."

"Oh."

When he didn't say anything else, she put her hands behind

her back and tilted her head coyly to one side. "Do you think I'm pretty?"

Brunin looked around, but everyone was busy and he couldn't abandon his task. "Yes," he said. It was true. She was as dainty as a daisy.

She smiled and dimples appeared in her cheeks. "Truly you do?"

He nodded and moved away to fetch the trenchers that a servant had piled up on a side table. He was aware of her scrutiny and it made him fumble and almost drop one.

"Are you betrothed?"

Wordlessly Brunin shook his head.

"I'm not either…but I will be one day." She wrapped one of her silky braids around her forefinger. "Will you sit next to me when we eat?"

He dealt the trenchers along the cloth. "That is for Lord Joscelin to say."

"Don't worry, he'll let you." Her smile deepened. "I'm glad you're here."

Hawise arrived from the other end of the room where she had been helping to sort through her father's baggage. "Mama says you're not to pester Brunin," she said with an irritated glance at Marion and, taking a pile of trenchers, began setting them at the places that Brunin had yet to do.

Marion looked affronted. "I'm not." She gazed toward Sybilla who was still talking to her husband. "She wouldn't send you to tell me anyway."

"I heard her say to Papa that she hoped you weren't going to pester his new squire to death."

Marion turned her huge blue stare on Brunin. "I'm not pestering you, am I?" Her lower lip drooped.

Brunin shook his head and mumbled a disclaimer. Marion cast a triumphant glance at Hawise. "He's going to sit next to me at the table," she said possessively.

Hawise placed the last trencher and dusted her crumby hands on her gown, causing Marion to grimace. Brunin thought that they were like cat and dog—one fastidious and elegant, the other boisterous and open. He didn't want to be the morsel over which they fought lest it jeopardize his position. Lord Joscelin might decide that his new squire was causing more trouble than he was worth.

Hawise shrugged. "I don't care," she retorted. "I'm going to sit with Papa." She lifted a dish of dried figs from the side table and set it on the trestle near the lord's chair—near where she would be sitting. "I like these," she said. Taking three in her hand, she juggled them.

Brunin pressed his lips together, but it was too much and suddenly, despite his best effort, he was grinning. Hawise grinned back and, catching the figs in her right hand, returned to her father, nibbling one.

Marion sighed and shook her head. "She has no manners," she said in a tragic voice.

# 6

*B*RUNIN BREATHED ON THE SHIELD BOSS AND BURNISHED IT
vigorously with the rag until he could see his reflection in
the iron. Not entirely satisfied, he repeated the action. The body
of the shield had been resurfaced with a new leather skin and the
latter painted with the design of a mythical winged creature called
a wyvern, in fire-red.

Bright spring light poured through the tower window into the
chamber, making Joscelin's mail shirt gleam on its pole. Clustered
around the base were various items of baggage and weaponry.
On the morrow, Lord Joscelin was setting out for Prince Henry's
knighting at Carlisle and the household was in a turmoil of preparation. Like everyone else, Brunin was full of tension and excitement, and although it was near the dinner hour, he wasn't in the
least hungry. As the youngest squire, he had thought that Joscelin
might leave him behind with the women, but Joscelin had said
that it would do him good to see the world outside the Marches.
The knighting of a prince was not something that happened every
day. Brunin's father was attending the muster too and Joscelin said
it was an ideal opportunity for him to measure his son's progress.

Joscelin seemed to think that his father would be pleased.
Brunin hoped so too, but was a trifle uncertain. His father was
not as tolerant as Lord Joscelin; nevertheless, he was looking
forward to seeing him. While Brunin had not been homesick

these past seven months, there had been occasions when he felt the lack of FitzWarin's dour, solid presence. He missed his mother too—sometimes. Lady Sybilla was kind and maternal, but she did not have the same way of pushing his hair from his brow as his mother did, nor was she bound to him by the ties of the womb. His grandmother he did not miss at all, except in the way of relief from a pain long endured. Nor in truth did he have many regrets about leaving his brothers behind. There had never been any love lost between him and Ralf and what nostalgia there was had been overwhelmed by all the new experiences and challenges provided by life at Ludlow.

After his initial distrust, he had come to enjoy spending time in Hugh and Adam's company He would sit with them to polish Lord Joscelin's mail and weapons. He joined them on errands into Ludlow town and began to grow familiar with the area and its inhabitants. The youths built on his rudimentary battle skills and he practiced for several hours each day. Sometimes Lord Joscelin would be on hand to supervise and give tuition, usually where sword and shield skills were involved. He was taught archery by a one-eyed Breton serjeant named Judhel, who could hit the target more cleanly than any whole-sighted man in the castle. Brunin played vigorous ball games, skinned his elbows and knees, blacked his eyes, bloodied his nose, but accepted all such scrapes and grazes stoically. Indeed, the worst part of being injured was the tending. As the squires had warned him, Sibbi was a zealot with the bandages and unguent and in desperate need of patients on whom to practice. She treated his skinned knees as if they were serious battle wounds and bathed a cut lip with a lotion that was so foul it almost made him vomit…and then, because he was heaving, she said that he ought to stay in bed for the remainder of the day. Fortunately, Lady Sybilla had rescued him and declared him well enough to run errands for her.

A portion of Brunin's time was spent in the household under Lady Sybilla's tutelage, for there were skills beyond the military ones to be learned and honed: conversing, etiquette, the correct table manners for the court and grand occasions. Usually Marion was his partner at the dining table when such lessons were conducted. She enjoyed the drama of playing the elegant court lady, turning up her nose if she considered that he had served her in a clumsy fashion, thanking him graciously when he succeeded. He rarely shared his trencher with Hawise, for she had a tendency to giggle and not take matters seriously. Once he had dropped a pigeon breast in her lap and, in the end, she had been sent from the room, tears of laughter pouring down her face and a large gravy stain on her dress. Marion had looked utterly horrified and Brunin had had to struggle to master the mirth that had surged through his own chagrin. Sybilla had laughed too, but she had not set Brunin beside Hawise again. However, Hawise partnered him when they went riding, or practiced their skills with the hawks in the mews, for Marion had small interest and aptitude in those areas; and it was Hawise who lent him her juggling balls and cajoled him out of his natural reticence…and taught him to laugh.

The shield boss finished to his satisfaction, he turned his attention to Joscelin's spurs and helm. Dearly as he would have liked to polish sword and dagger, that was a task left either to Joscelin himself, or Hugh, and would not be entrusted to him until he began full weapons training.

Entering the room, Hawise saw him at his toil and wandered over. The expression on her face was almost a scowl.

"What's wrong?" he asked. The fact that he spoke first was testament to the changes that two seasons at Ludlow had wrought.

"I wish I was going with you," she said moodily. "It's going to be boring when you've gone."

He knew that she wasn't referring to him alone, but to her father and the other squires. There would be fewer opportunities to ride out and her freedom would be curtailed. "It won't be for that long," he said, although he wasn't sure how many weeks they would be absent.

"It will seem like forever." She flounced down on the stool at his side. "I'll have to sit and do sewing with Marion and Sibbi while you'll be watching Prince Henry knighted."

Brunin shook his head. "The ceremony will only be for the barons, not their attendants. The squires will be standing out in the rain holding the horses."

That raised a half-smile.

"And there'll be so much mud that we'll have to spend all our time grooming and polishing."

"Would you rather stay here?" she challenged.

"No," he admitted.

"Well then." She sulkily kicked the floor rushes.

Brunin draped the cloth over the rawhide top of the shield. "We could go riding now if you want," he offered. "I've polished all the equipment I'm allowed to touch, and no one has given me other tasks yet."

For a moment he thought she was going to refuse, although she was not usually given to fits of pique. That particular trait belonged to Marion. Then she nodded grudgingly. "It's the last chance I'll have all summer," she said, a note of accusation in her voice. However, by the time they had saddled their ponies, she had brightened. Since no grooms or serjeants could be spared to escort them, they were only allowed as far as the sward beyond the castle walls, but there was enough space to canter their mounts and indulge in short races. Hawise forgot to sulk and her laughter rang out. Brunin found himself grinning in response and realized that he was going to miss her too.

❖❖❖

Joscelin lay in bed and, in the soft light from the night candle, played with his wife's hair, repeatedly lifting the strands to release the clean, astringent scent and letting them fall against her shoulders and spine. Her back was to him, but she wasn't sleeping. He could feel her consciousness, and her breath had none of slumber's measure.

"I have a fear," he said softly, "that when I return you and Ludlow will be gone. That I will find it has all been a dream and I am naught but a penniless knight."

The bedclothes rustled as Sybilla turned over and the scent of her body flooded his senses. "Even when you had nothing, you were always more than a penniless knight," she said, touching his face with her palm. "What has brought this sudden mood upon you?"

He brushed his lips against her skin. "Ah, I do not know," he said, irritated with himself. "Probably the lateness of the hour and length of the journey I've to make on the morrow when I would rather lie abed with you."

She gave a throaty laugh. "Flatterer."

"I mean it," he groaned. "Earl Ranulf of Chester and the King of the Scots are no substitute for you and Ludlow."

"And Prince Henry?"

"That is the reason I must go. I would be a fool not to secure his favor. He may still be a youth, but one day he is going to be our king, and he will remember who has served him faithfully and who has not." Joscelin sighed. "I am gambling hard and the stakes are high. Sometimes I wonder what will happen if Henry does not prevail and Stephen secures his line to the Crown. What happens if his son Eustace takes all?"

She was silent for a time. Then she said, "You cannot change your allegiance. It is hard to ride two horses without falling between."

"Some do," he said darkly. "Some men have no difficulty in leaping from one saddle to another."

Sybilla traced his jaw with her forefinger. "But not you. I well recall how long you dragged your conscience like a shackle when you renounced your oath to Stephen."

He didn't want to be reminded of that. Stephen had been his paymaster and had expected him to hold Ludlow against the Empress. But his loyalties had been strained even then, and his new wife had been an ardent supporter of a woman's right to inherit.

In a way, his change of horse had been inevitable. "I did not say I was going to renege my allegiance to Henry," he answered a trifle testily. "What I said was that I was gambling hard. I hope for our sake that Henry prevails. And as to men who leap saddles to their own advantage…if you were to ask me what troubled me the most, it is not knowing where Gilbert de Lacy stands in this broil."

Her finger stopped on the point of his chin and he heard her breathing catch, then resume. "Gilbert de Lacy rides his own ambition," she said. "His loyalty is self-serving."

"I realize that. What I meant was that I do not know whether he will present himself in Carlisle, ride to join Stephen, or stay here and make trouble. Which strand will he choose? I doubt Carlisle, because Hugh of Wigmore is his closest ally and he is firmly for Stephen…but the other two is any guess. I am worried that he might make an attempt on Ludlow when I am not by to thwart him."

"You have left sufficient good men to guard the place," Sybilla said, "and I am no ninny. He will not have Ludlow from me." Her voice, usually low-pitched and serene, now rang like a man's.

Pride surged amidst Joscelin's anxiety. He had been warned when he married her that she was a handful. She might not storm and stamp like the Empress Matilda, but her will was forged of the same indomitable iron. She just went about achieving her goals in a different way. Honey instead of gall. "I know that, love, and I have every faith in you and my men. But that still does not prevent my imagination from conjuring troubles out of wisps of smoke."

"Ludlow will be here when you return, every stick and stone. And so will your wife and daughters." She leaned over to kiss him. "I am counting on you to come home to me with your hide intact. You are not the only one to conjure troubles in the smoke."

"I can look after myself," he said and cupped his hand at the back of her neck to feel the warmth of her skin and the coolness of her hair.

"See that you do." Her tone was husky, beguiling him into

desire. As he moved with her and within her, Sybilla hid her face against his shoulder and tried unsuccessfully to forget that her first husband had told her not to worry as he made love to her on the eve before he rode away to be killed in a skirmish with the Welsh.

❖❖❖

Brunin was astonished when he saw Prince Henry. He had expected someone tall, imposing, and of regal bearing. The reality was a stocky youth, whose eyes were on a level with Lord Joscelin's chest. His hair was lighter than copper and redder than gold and looked as if it hadn't been combed in a week. He had the fair, freckled complexion that accompanied such coloring, sandy lashes, and a bright gray gaze that was as sharp as a new sword. Although his clothes were embroidered and of the finest weaves and richest dyes, he wore them carelessly as if unaware and uncaring of their cost.

The Prince paused in his energetic meeting and greeting of the supporters that were streaming steadily into Carlisle to drink a measure with Joscelin and FitzWarin. Brunin was given the task of pouring wine for their royal guest and his companion, a slender, serious-looking young man with fine mouse-brown hair and a sparse tawny beard. Serving from a flagon was a skill Brunin had been practicing for seven months and, although he was under his father's scrutiny and in the presence of royalty, he accomplished the task without mishap.

"My eldest son, Fulke, though we know him as Brunin," said FitzWarin, a gleam of pride in his voice as Henry took the proffered goblet and Brunin bowed deeply.

"It is good to see such youngsters in the ranks," remarked the youth, who was barely sixteen himself. He gave Brunin a quick smile of acknowledgment and then brought the conversation into more serious fields. A squire was expected to stay in the background, pour wine, and keep his mouth shut.

The quieter young man at Henry's side proved to be Lord Joscelin's son-in-law, Roger, Earl of Hereford, who was wed to Sybilla's eldest daughter from her first marriage, Cecily. Accepting his cup of wine from Brunin, he went to stand by the brazier that was warming Joscelin's camp tent.

"…go to Lancaster and then advance on York," Brunin heard Henry say.

"Ambitious, sire," Joscelin replied, his tone mild, his fingers clenching around his cup.

Henry lifted his shoulders. "I must use whatever opportunities are given to me. You have not attended my knighting purely because you like to feast and make merry."

"No, sire. I came to offer you my sword and my fealty," Joscelin said.

"You doubt the wisdom of advancing on York?"

"No, sire…"

"But…?" Henry's brows lifted.

"York is loyal to Stephen and has no love for the Scots you bring in your train. It will not be an easy nut to crack."

"Then you do doubt the wisdom."

"No, sire, but every man will have to play his part to the hilt and we will have to move swiftly."

Henry drank down the wine and handed the cup back to Brunin. "I think you will be surprised at how swiftly I can move…and so will Stephen." He flashed a perfunctory but confident smile and strode from the tent to continue with his visiting. Roger of Hereford remained a while to talk, although he added nothing to what Henry had already said about the immediate plans.

"How is Cecily?" Joscelin asked. "Enjoying the Norman court?" His tone was carefully neutral.

The young man's complexion flushed. "Yes, my lord. She bids me greet you and her mother, and I have letters and gifts in my baggage. The Prince's mother is very taken with her."

Joscelin grunted. "That is good to hear. Naturally her own mother worries about her and misses her."

Roger left shortly after that and Joscelin gave a hard sigh and pushed his hands through his hair.

FitzWarin handed his cup to Brunin for a refill. "You're not easy with him," he said gruffly. "Even a blind man like me can see it."

Joscelin rubbed the back of his neck. "He's not the same as his father. I could say anything to Miles. We drank and fought and hunted together—wenched as well. You know the way of it."

FitzWarin made a wry gesture of acknowledgment. "All I remember are the skull-crushing headaches afterward."

Joscelin grinned briefly, but was not sidetracked. "Miles was my friend," he said. "Roger's my ally, my stepdaughter's husband, and Prince Henry's confidant, but I do not think we will ever be bosom companions." He rubbed harder at his neck until the skin reddened. "For Sybilla's sake I wish we were closer. Cecily may have flown the nest, but her mother is still concerned about her and anything that worries my wife worries me. It's like having a sore in the middle of your back that you can't reach to anoint."

FitzWarin gave him a chiding look. "You are too tenderhearted for your own good."

Joscelin smiled. "Is that why you gave me your son?"

FitzWarin shook his head, but his own lips curved. "You have me there, and I have to admit that you are doing a fine job with the lad...but when it comes to women, believe me, you give them too much leeway."

"It pleases me to please them, and I may be tenderhearted, but I am not a fool. My household is comfortable and so am I. Love's rule is as strong as the rod...stronger perhaps," he added with a glance toward Brunin.

❖ ❖ ❖

Prince Henry was knighted on Whitsunday and a great feast held to mark the occasion. King David and Earl Ranulf of Chester formalized their truce and put behind them the quarrel over land that had long made them enemies. Now Henry had an army and he prepared to turn it on York.

As one of the youngest members, Brunin stayed back with

the pack ponies and wains of the army's baggage train. Ranulf of Chester had gone to Lancaster to bring more troops, but still Brunin had never seen so many men gathered in one place at one time. Although not a large army, it seemed so to him, for he had never ridden in a company greater than the personal troop belonging to his father or Lord Joscelin.

The Angevins and Normans of Henry's bodyguard, gleamed in mail from head to foot, their accents at subtle variance with the Normans who had laid down roots in England. Mercenaries from Flanders and the Low Countries bolstered the ranks and also men from Brittany where Lord Joscelin's family had originated. For the first time, Brunin heard Joscelin speaking in rapid, fluent Breton, a language somewhat akin to Welsh, and it made him realize that there were facets of his lord that he did not even know existed and that the genial, easy manner was but the surface polish.

Brunin was also fascinated by King David's Scottish troops. The wealthier ones were mail-clad and French-speaking, with little to distinguish them from their Norman counterparts. The middle ranks and footsoldiers went bare-legged and carried either small round shields not much bigger than trenchers, or ones as huge as cartwheels—of the kind that Lord Joscelin said had been popular with the Saxons at the great Battle of Hastings. For the most part they spoke English, but in a guttural manner that Brunin could not begin to understand. Their staple fare was oatcakes and heather ale, occasionally enlivened by some sort of boiled meat pudding or salted herrings. While their leaders rode warhorses as fine as any in the army, the lesser troops made do with scrawny ponies. The little beasts looked as if they were on their last legs, but their stamina could outdo the fittest oat-fed destrier.

Brunin alternated between riding Morel and resting him by tying the pony to the back of a baggage cart while he rode on top of the sacks of fodder and oat flour. When they stopped in the evening, he had to help Adam and Hugh to pitch Lord Joscelin's tent. There was a cooking fire to set up, pallets and blankets to sort out, horses to be rubbed down, fed, and watered, harness and armor to be checked over and cleaned. Brunin was so weary that he collapsed on his pallet each evening like a poled ox and slept without dreaming until kicked awake at the first paling of the sky. There was water to fetch and horses to prepare for the day's march. Breakfast consisted of flat bread or oatcakes cooked in the ashes of last night's fire and served with fatty slices of gray ham.

"Christ, now I remember why I hate going to war," Joscelin groaned as he took the cup of wine that Brunin handed him. Outside a watery dawn was rising out of last night's rain. Drizzle, fine as cobwebs, hung in the air. He pressed the heel of his hand into his lower spine. "I feel as if I've been trodden on by a giant."

Brunin wasn't sure how he felt, other than exhausted. The rain had woken him in the night because there was a spark hole in the top of the tent through which water had dripped onto his face, but by the time he had struggled through the swaddling layers of sleep, the water had seeped down his neck and soaked into his tunic, making him feel as clammy as a frog.

Joscelin took a mouthful of the wine and sprayed it back out. "God's bones, boy, what's this, cat piss? Fetch me something I can at least drink!" He sloshed the cup back into Brunin's hand.

Brunin beat a hasty retreat and found Adam saddling the horses. It had started to rain harder and the drops could be heard hitting the ground. Smack, smack, smack.

"He says I'm to find him some decent wine."

Adam peered at him around the hood of his cloak. "Then you'll have to go searching in York. There's naught but Scottish ale and that vinegar in your hand." Adam turned back to the horse and gave it a shove. "Stand still, you brute."

Brunin swallowed. Lord Joscelin was always so even-tempered that to see him in a foul mood and directing his anger outward was as much a shock as hearing him hold forth in rapid Breton. Summoning his courage, he sidled back into the tent.

"Please, my lord, this is all we have…unless you want ale," he said, holding his voice steady, but feeling the familiar tightening in his gut. He braced himself to be shouted at again...perhaps even struck.

Joscelin straightened up from donning his quilted tunic. His gray eyes were as threatening as the sky. Brunin met them and quickly looked down.

"Oh, give it here." Joscelin snatched the cup, drank down the contents with a shudder, and tipped the sludgy lees on the tent floor. "I should know what to expect."

Brunin felt as if his stomach were touching his spine. He clenched his jaw. Joscelin turned, saw his face, and made an exasperated sound.

"Christ, boy, I wasn't referring to you. I meant I should know what to expect on campaign. You'll grow a thicker skin before this is out, I promise you." He tousled Brunin's hair. "I suppose the morning's bread is about as appetizing as a dried cowpat too."

Brunin dared to look at Joscelin. Behind the impatience, behind the irritation, a glint of the customary sangfroid still shone. "Yes, my lord. Do you want me to bring you some?"

Joscelin never replied, for FitzWarin billowed aside the tent flap. He was clad in his mail, his helm tucked under one arm and his sword girded at his hip. The look in his eyes sent Joscelin reaching for his own swordbelt.

"Get the tents down and saddle up fast," he said. "The scouts have just reported that Stephen's here and ready to do battle."

"What?" Joscelin's expression said that he had heard perfectly well but didn't want to believe it. "That's impossible!"

"No, it's not. He's here with more mercenaries at his back than the crowd on the first day of St. Peter's Fair." FitzWarin waved his arm. "And there's no sign of Ranulf of Chester with his troops from Lancaster. We're caught with our braies around our ankles."

Joscelin swore. "Does Henry know?"

"Yes. He's already given the order to break camp. There's not a hope on God's earth that we can take on Stephen and win—not without Earl Ranulf's contingent. King David's turning back to Carlisle. The Prince says that he's heading to Bristol...and that means we ride with him, at least as far as the Marches. I have to go." FitzWarin turned to Brunin. "Do as Lord Joscelin tells you." He curled his hand over the boy's narrow shoulder and gave it a firm shake. "God keep you; I'll talk to you tonight." He nodded stiffly and ducked out of the tent.

Joscelin stood for a moment as if turned to stone, then shook himself and began issuing rapid orders, all thoughts of breakfast, palatable or otherwise, forgotten.

❖❖❖

Brunin's experience of an army on the move now became one of an army on the run. Without the presence of the Scots, the baggage train was considerably smaller. Carts were abandoned in favor of the swifter-moving pack ponies. Joscelin's master-at-arms purchased two sturdy Scots hobbies to add to their string and lighten the load. They hastened south, using every hour of daylight and the gray times of dawn and dusk. Stephen remained in Yorkshire to consolidate his hold on the north, but he sent soldiers in pursuit of Prince Henry: fast troops with a brief to waylay and put an end to the Angevin threat before it could take deep root. But Henry's scouts were good, discovered the ploy, and the Prince changed direction, taking his army along pack routes and rough byways where they would be least expected to go.

It was a deadly game of hide and seek. Stephen wanted Henry at all costs; and, at all costs, Henry could not afford to be caught. Men ate and drank in the saddle and slept in their armor. Brunin would remember the nightmare journey for the rest of his days. The constant tension that made men act as if a layer had been peeled from their skins; the stumbling exhaustion of horses and soldiers pushed beyond their limit but forced to go on. Through it all, Prince Henry proved that he had stamina akin to one of the Scots ponies. He was the first up in the morning, the last to his bed at night, his energy and determination as fiery as his hair—and, even though he was on the run, the notion of losing was not one that he was prepared to entertain.

Once Brunin fell asleep in the saddle and awoke to find himself being carried in his father's arms, a fur-lined cloak tucking him against the pommel and the stars shining like salt crystals as the army rode by moonlight.

Finally they came to Hereford, and the yellow glow of torches replaced the white fire of moon and stars. In a state that was still half-dream, Brunin ate pottage and bread in the great hall and then lay down on a straw pallet pushed against the wall. Within minutes he was asleep.

❖❖❖

In the private chamber beyond the hall, Joscelin slumped on a cushioned bench and took a cup of wine from an attendant. In typical fashion, while other men had taken the opportunity to sit, Prince Henry was on his toes and pacing the room like a caged young lion. "At first light we ride for Monmouth," he said, flashing a bright glance around the room. "Roger has heard from his scouts that Eustace has troops out looking for us now."

Joscelin grimaced wearily. Stephen's son Eustace was like a vicious dog and enjoyed nothing better than to be unleashed and given license to bite.

"They need to destroy you at all costs, sire," said Roger. "If they do not do it now, then their time is over."

"And mine is just beginning." Henry prowled to the end of the room, gazed at an embroidered wall hanging, and turned back. "They won't prevail. Ranulf of Chester intends to create a diversion that will keep Stephen in the north, and Hugh Bigod will bait him in the east." His gaze flicked to Joscelin and FitzWarin. "You, my lords, will hold down the Marches."

Joscelin felt a surge of relief. He would have followed Henry to Bristol—so would FitzWarin, for that matter—but, in doing so, they would have left their own castles vulnerable to the assault of barons like Hugh of Wigmore and Gilbert de Lacy, not to mention opportunist raids from the Welsh. Now they had reached Hereford, the guarding of Henry's person could be left to fresher men.

"As you wish, sire," he said and relaxed as he spoke. On the morrow, Henry would head for Bristol and he could go home to Ludlow, Sybilla, and his daughters. At one time a battle campaign had been a source of adventure and satisfaction to him. These days the pleasure rusted with more speed than mail in a downpour.

# 7

TWENTY MILES LAY BETWEEN HEREFORD AND LUDLOW: A comfortable distance that could be covered in less than a day when it was high summer.

Henry had departed the city while the sky was scarcely gray with first dawn, hastening toward Bristol and reinforcements.

"To be sixteen again, eh?" said FitzWarin as he gained the saddle in the full light of day and gestured his squire to take up his banner.

Joscelin grinned. "It has its advantages," he said. "Then again, there's value in experience." His eyebrows flashed with innuendo before he turned to Brunin, who had just mounted Morel. "Feeling better this morning, child?"

"Yes, my lord." Brunin gave a brisk answer to Joscelin's query. A night's slumber within the security of stone walls and two hot meals with as much wheat bread as he could eat had done much to restore him.

"Good. Then, if you are up to it, you can bear my shield for a time. Certainly you'll handle it better than Adam." Joscelin's tone contained both humor and asperity. Brunin followed his glance to his second squire, who was mangling an attempt to mount his black and white cob, Pie. Adam's complexion was green and, as he finally gained the saddle, his throat bobbed convulsively.

"Young idiot," Joscelin growled. He looked at Brunin. "Just

remember when temptation comes your way that a boy will drink beyond his means and a man will know when he's had enough."

"Yes, sir," Brunin said dutifully. Inside he was grinning from ear to ear, for the task of shield-bearer was important and would not usually have been given to the youngest squire. Not wanting to gloat at Adam's expense, he did his best to conceal his delight. Taking up Joscelin's red and gold wyvern shield, he set it by its long strap at his back. It was heavy, but bearably so, and his pride lightened the burden.

"By rights I should let Adam take his punishment and bear the shield anyway, but, as your father is always saying, my heart is too tender." Joscelin cast a laughing glance over his shoulder. "We've all been boys when we should have been men and how else is a boy to become a man, save by performing men's tasks?"

FitzWarin made a rude sound at the speech, but it was good-natured. He was as glad as Joscelin to be going home—even if it was to prepare for storms to come.

They rode out into morning sunshine and took the road toward Ludlow. Now and again, Joscelin or FitzWarin would make a comment and the other would laugh. It was not so much the humor that caused the mirth as the release from tension. Ludlow was only twenty miles away and each stride of the horses brought them closer to home. Hugh had a good voice and struck up a bawdy song that was taken up by some of the others. The sunshine was hot and the morning was filled with the creak and smell of leather, the jingle of harness, the hollow clop of shod hoof on dusty road. Adam had to keep diving from his horse to retch into the verge. The older men laughed and teased him mercilessly.

The weight of the shield began to make Brunin's spine and shoulders ache, but he endured the discomfort, determined not to show it lest his father or Lord Joscelin take the task from him. He wanted to bear the shield all the way to Ludlow and ride proudly into the bailey with it still at his back for everyone to see. He counted Morel's strides along the road and envisaged how much ground they were covering. When Joscelin inquired if he was tired, he shook his head and set his jaw.

As they began the final stretch of their journey, the forest closed in at the roadside. It was supposed to be cut back to make it difficult for outlaws to waylay travelers or ambushes to be set up, but the summer's growth and a recent lack of diligence meant that the greenery was thicker and darker than it should have been. Frowning with displeasure, Joscelin murmured to FitzWarin that he would have sharp words with the men responsible and make it a priority to have the woodland shorn away from the road.

Adam had to scramble down from his mount and dive into the bushes again as his bowels added their protest to his malaise. Good-natured jeers followed him, but were cut off as an instant later he sprinted from the bushes, clutching his unlaced braies at his waist.

"Ware arms!" he cried. "Soldiers in the woo—" The end of the warning was cut off in a grunt as an arrow slammed into his spine and he fell forward on the road at Morel's hooves.

Brunin's eyes widened in horror. A second arrow thudded into the wyvern shield and the force of the blow almost punched him from the saddle as Morel canted sideways with a startled snort. Instinctively, Brunin gripped with his thighs and tightened his grip on the reins.

He heard Joscelin roaring orders, but later was not to remember what they were. Two knights dismounted, ran to Adam, hauled him up and threw him across his horse. Amid a hail of arrows, the company spurred up the road to outrun the archers, but, beyond the bowmen, mounted troops and footsoldiers were waiting.

Brunin swallowed. The same terror he had felt at Shrewsbury Fair surged over him, but this time, conditioned by training and new experience, his reactions were different. Every sense was poised on a knife-edge, keen and sharp as he kicked Morel forward and brought the arrow-pierced shield to Joscelin. The faster everything became, the more time seemed to slow down. His father bellowed at him to get back, and the command was like a shout echoing in a cavern. He reined Morel about and peeled back into the ranks of men. Above his head he saw the banners snapping on the enemy lances and heard the battle shouts of Wigmore and de Lacy. The clash of weapons was hard, fast, terrifying; in a dreadful way it reminded him of a full dining hall on a feast day, save that the aggressive roars were not of laughter, but of fear and fury and effort, and the assault of blades was upon human flesh, not haunches of venison. He saw Joscelin's stallion rear, forehooves pawing, and the wyvern shield smash down into a footsoldier's face. He saw the FitzWarin banner plunge and come back up, blood running down the point and staining the bright silk, and his father's bay stallion shouldering into an opponent's mount.

A gap opened in the fighting and one of Joscelin's serjeants yelled at him to gallop through it. Brunin slammed his heels into Morel's flanks and the pony surged forward. He felt Hugh beside him, his fist around the bridle of Adam's horse. Adam was bent over Pie's withers, the arrow protruding from between his shoulder blades. There was no blood from the wound itself, but it dripped steadily from the squire's open mouth into his mount's silver mane.

A low-hanging branch whipped at Brunin and he ducked low over Morel's straining neck. Behind them he could still hear the clash of battle, but it was fading, as if they were out of the dining hall and into the vestibule.

"Don't slow!" the serjeant bellowed. "Not for anything!"

Brunin didn't, not until Morel began to labor, and then he sat up and slackened the rein to ease the winded pony. Through the thundering of his heart, he heard hoofbeats drumming fast from behind and his gut twisted. The serjeant drew his sword and turned, grimly. Then he slumped. "Thank Jesu!" he gasped.

Brunin saw his father's bloodied banner and Joscelin's battered wyvern shield. The rest of the troop followed them at a hard pace and Joscelin was gesturing wildly.

"Ride on!" he roared. "Don't stop, you fools, ride on!"

Brunin dug his heels into Morel's flanks and the pony gamely gave him a burst of speed, but was soon blowing hard. After a mile of this punishing pace, Joscelin hauled on the bridle and slewed his stallion to face the road behind. It was quiet save for the ticking sound of settling dust. Sunlight dazzled down, for now the trees were cut back the requisite distance, and the woods were a silence of green-gold leaf dapple.

"There's no sign of pursuit, but that does not mean they have drawn off." He reined hard about, kicked his mount's heaving flanks. "We won't be safe until we're behind Ludlow's walls."

With as much haste as the flagging horses could muster and the injured men stand, the company hastened on to the castle. The guards had seen their approach and the gates were already flung wide. Word had gone speeding to the lady in her chamber.

As the gates closed behind them and the great walls embraced them like the arms of a mother, Brunin began to tremble. A familiar wave of nausea hit his belly. He swallowed and swallowed again, determined not to shame himself. He watched them take Adam down from his horse, the arrow protruding from his back like the stalk on some strange fruit, his chin crimson with blood, the front of his gambeson and his horse sodden with it. Joscelin knelt by him, propping him in his arms, murmuring words of comfort while the youth fought for breath and his lifeblood gushed from his open mouth.

"Brunin, run for the priest," Joscelin commanded over his shoulder in a cracking voice. "Make haste!"

Brunin slipped from Morel's back and sprinted toward the chapel. On his way he caught sight of Lady Sybilla running from the living quarters with her women, the smile of greeting on her face already changing as she realized something was wrong.

Father Ailred was sorting through a wooden chest near the chapel door and looked up in myopic surprise as Brunin gabbled out Lord Joscelin's command. For an instant the little priest stood frozen in shock, then, shaking himself, hastened outside. Brunin ran after him, his heart drumming and his stomach pushing into his chest. The heat of the afternoon sun was hot enough to bake bread; the sky was as blue as enamel and the smell of blood like the day of a pig-slaughter.

Father Ailred fell to his knees at Adam's side, speaking in swift Latin, doing what had to be done with haste while the soul still occupied the body. Joscelin held the youth, bracing himself to absorb the shudders of imminent death. Sybilla knelt too, clasping Adam's hand so hard that her knuckles were white. Brunin stared, his eyes locked on the scene.

"Jesu...Jesu..." Hawise came to Brunin's side, her eyes huge, the back of her hand pressed to her mouth.

Close by, Marion stood as rigid as an effigy. "Look at all the blood," she whispered. "There was a lot of blood when my mama died."

Father Ailred sat back on his heels, his fingers glistening red. His voice rose in a prayer for the dying, powerful with the breath that was denied the young man. Adam arched in Joscelin's arms in a final paroxysm as he strove to live and then slumped, eyes staring blankly at the sun. Joscelin's hands were red to the wrists, the rims of his fingernails black with blood. He bent over the dead youth and his own body shuddered.

Hawise gave a small, wounded whimper. Marion said nothing, but swayed from side to side as if in a trance. Sybilla's senior maid, Annora, came belatedly to her senses; setting her arms around the girls like a mother hen, she hustled them away toward the living quarters. Sibbi remained, but turned her face into Hugh's breast. He raised his arm and set it around her shoulders, drawing her in close. He clenched his hand around her braid like a man clutching a lifeline.

Brunin watched Joscelin slowly relinquish his hold on Adam and rise to his feet, his movements slow and stiff as if he had been repeatedly kicked. A litter was fetched and Adam placed gently on it—face down, for the feathered shaft was still lodged deep in his flesh. For the rest of his life, Brunin was never able to view the arrow-shot carcass of a deer without feeling sick.

❖ ❖ ❖

He was in the stables rubbing the caked sweat from Morel's hide with a twist of straw when Hawise came to find him, her face tear-streaked and swollen. She had unbound her hair, as girls and women did in grief, and it framed her face in wild auburn spirals. Brunin had not cried. The shock and the pain had channeled inward, not out. He kept reliving the moment when the arrow had struck. He kept seeing Adam die and the desperation in Lord Joscelin's face. Henry's difficult campaign had seasoned Brunin to some of the brutal realities of warfare, but today had been the difference between wading in a stream and being swept away in a red torrent. That was why he was lurking in the stables, seeking solace from Morel's solid bulk and solitude for himself.

"I knew you would be here," she said.

Brunin gave a defensive shrug. "I had to gallop Morel hard. He needs tending."

She sat down on a heap of straw and wrapped her arms around her raised knees. "Papa said it was Hugh Mortimer and Gilbert de Lacy and that they were far too close to us. I wasn't supposed to hear...but I did." A shiver rippled down her spine.

Brunin compressed his lips; turning back to Morel, he groomed the black hide with long, forceful strokes. Most of the sweat had gone, but there was comfort in the motion of his arm—in a different kind of repetition to that occupying his mind.

"Do you think they'll come for us?"

The frightened misery in her voice made him turn. He knew her fear for he could feel it crawling through his own bones. It was all too easy to imagine an army of mail-clad men gathering outside their walls, intent on slaughtering everyone within. "No," he said, more bravely than he felt. "Ludlow is far too strong for them to take. Your father says so, and it's true." He threw away

101

the twist of straw and, wiping his hands on his hose, sat down beside her. "They are desperate because Prince Henry is here and they know their time is slipping away. Even if we were ambushed, we managed to fight our way out, and they didn't chase us because we had wounded too many of their men." He found comfort in comforting her and, as he spoke the words, realized that they were true. De Lacy and Mortimer had not pursued them because they were matched and dared not risk riding closer to Ludlow where the balance would have tipped in Joscelin's favor.

She gnawed her lower lip. "Were you frightened when they attacked?" she whispered.

Brunin grimaced. He didn't know what to say. It had been drilled into him that only a coward admitted to fear...that only a coward felt fear. His grandmother in particular was adamant on that issue, and, since the incident at Shrewsbury, his father too had been vehement on the subject. And now Hawise wanted to know...and he was afraid to answer. Was that cowardly too?

"I don't remember," he said.

She looked disbelieving. "You don't remember?"

Jerking to his feet, he returned to fussing with the pony so that his back was to her. It was easier that way. "Well, only bits of it," he said. "It was as if none of it was happening to me." He laid his hand flat against Morel's side, taking courage from the glossy black flank. "But afterward I felt sick." He preferred not to tell her about the initial surge of terror, so huge that it had numbed him. He didn't have the words to describe it, nor truly the comprehension.

"I was frightened," she admitted in a small voice. "Mama said everything would be all right, but I could see she was afraid too." She rubbed her chin against her upraised knees. "Papa wasn't scared," she said on a more vibrant note. "But I've never seen him so angry. I think there's going to be lots more fighting. He says that de Lacy and Mortimer will pay." Her voice shook. She was in desperate need of reassurance.

"They will," Brunin said awkwardly

Hawise rose and came to the pony. Leaning against the opposite side to Brunin, she pressed her face into Morel's hot, black neck and wept. Unsure what to do, Brunin stood rooted to the spot. When his mother cried, his father would stalk out of the room, growling about the weakness of women. He had never seen his grandmother weep. Marion and Sibbi always ran to Sybilla for comfort. Hawise usually went to her father, or else, like him, sought a corner alone.

Uncertainly he came around to her and set his arm across her shoulders. He didn't know what to say, but the act of going to her and touching seemed right and when she turned and cried against him, rather than against the pony, he felt his vitals knot with pain and his eyes start to burn.

❖ ❖ ❖

That night, a vigil was held for Adam in the castle chapel. His body had been washed and tended by Sybilla and the women, the arrow that had killed him drawn from the wound and burned on the fire. He had been gowned in his best tunic, and a sword had been placed between his clasped hands. Grim-faced, Joscelin stood guard before the bier upon which the youth lay. FitzWarin and Hugh stood with him...and Brunin, who had begged to be allowed to keep vigil too. Beeswax candles burned on the altar and in every sconce and niche, so that although there were shadows, none were deep, and the air in the chapel was scented with honey.

Sybilla brought the girls, each bearing a lighted candle, and for a time they prayed at the bier. Sibbi wept quietly throughout. Hawise and Marion were dry-eyed, but the former's face was a swollen testimony to all the tears she had shed, and the latter looked so pale and wraithlike that Brunin fancied he could almost see through her.

After a few hours, Marion began to sway on her feet; Sybilla made the girls leave their candles and took them away to bed. But later she returned and knelt to keep vigil with Joscelin.

Several times during the night, Brunin almost fell asleep. The need to close his eyes crept over him like a slow, warm blanket. Despite his preoccupation, Joscelin noticed and nudged him awake. On the third occasion he murmured that Brunin should lie down for a while. No one would think less of him. But Brunin shook his head and adamantly refused. Joscelin gave him several sips of sweetened wine and sent him to duck his head in the rain barrel outside the door. After that, Brunin stayed awake until the cockerels began crowing on the dung heaps and a new day brightened in the east. It seemed a lifetime since yesterday morn when they had set out from Hereford. In a way it was, and although he could not fathom the difference yet, Brunin knew that he had changed.

❖ ❖ ❖

Joscelin rubbed his hands over his gritty eyes and poured another measure of wine into his cup. In the two days since the ambush on the road, he had barely slept. There was too much to do, or so he kept telling himself. He dreaded the time when he had to stop and allow thoughts beyond the practical into his mind. He dreaded having to face Adam's father when he rode in to claim the body of his son. Wine, he hoped, would grant him an interim oblivion tonight.

FitzWarin was drinking with him, but not as fast. His mood was somber and, although he was keeping Joscelin company, he was saying little.

"I will understand if you choose to take the boy back to Whittington with you on the morrow," Joscelin said, summoning his voice from the dregs of his cup.

FitzWarin shifted in his chair and patted one of the deerhounds as it raised its head. "You do not want him anymore?"

"No, of course I want him. But after what has happened, perhaps you would rather keep him at your side." Joscelin looked down into the murky lees in his cup. "Perhaps I am not to be trusted with other men's sons."

FitzWarin gave a rude snort. "I never thought to hear you

talking from wine and self-pity. You're supposed to be the one with the clear head."

"It doesn't feel clear at the moment," Joscelin said bleakly. "Indeed, I'm not even certain that it's my head."

"And that's a good reason for me to ignore everything you say." FitzWarin leaned forward and opened his hand. "Christ, man, there was nothing you could do. If not Adam, someone else would have taken that first arrow. We were riding in good formation; we fought them off and gave them a hiding into the bargain. Your patrols should have been more diligent in keeping that undergrowth cut back, but that's one mistake and, since you have spent the summer away, not your fault. God knows, if you are going to wallow in guilt, you're a weaker man than I took you for."

Joscelin tried to feel anger, but it wouldn't come. "Then perhaps you should indeed take your son," he said.

"Perhaps I should rattle your teeth in your skull," FitzWarin retorted impatiently. "I watched the way you dealt with Brunin on campaign and I have seen the difference in him that time with you has wrought. He is as likely to fall down a well at Whittington or get trampled by a horse as he is to be struck by an arrow. You take too much blame on yourself. I can think of no man who is a better master to his squires." Finishing his wine, FitzWarin rose to his feet and stretched. "I'm for my bed," he said. "And you should be too."

Joscelin grimaced. "I doubt I will sleep."

"You've got wine; you've got your wife. Never fails for me."

Despite himself, Joscelin found a laugh…and realized that what FitzWarin said was true. Perhaps, mercifully, he would find a brief respite in the remedies suggested.

❖ ❖ ❖

At Wigmore, Gilbert de Lacy was also suffering a fretful lack of sleep. A sword blow had reached past his shield in the skirmish with de Dinan's troops, and he was nursing not only a cracked collar bone, but dented pride and frustrated ambition. He had picked his moment, chosen his place, and attacked hard—to no avail except to sound a warning at Ludlow that would set it even further beyond his reach. He had retreated with three dead men and a passel of wounded ones who would take days and in some cases weeks to heal.

"That bastard has the luck of the devil," he muttered to his ally, Hugh Mortimer, lord of Wigmore and ardent supporter of King Stephen.

"Of which bastard are we talking?" Hugh asked. "Henry of Anjou certainly has it, since he's slipped through all our traps like a fox and managed to reach Bristol."

De Lacy shifted on the settle, trying to ease the nagging ache in his damaged clavicle. He had little interest in whether Henry of Anjou had avoided the traps or not. Nor did he care about Stephen and Eustace. They were all cut from a similar cloth. His main reason for forming an alliance with Hugh of Wigmore was their mutual objective of wresting Ludlow from Joscelin de Dinan, and everything else was little more than the backcloth on which to sew his stitches.

"Let Prince Eustace deal with Henry of Anjou," he said. "I was talking of Joscelin de Dinan."

Hugh tugged a fleshy earlobe. "Luck plays its part, I agree, but he's no novice at war. He was a field mercenary before he took command of Ludlow, and field mercenaries are not given castles like that unless their abilities are exceptional."

"Not that exceptional," Gilbert grunted sourly and glanced to his squires who had no tasks for the moment and were engaged in a game of dice. "Ernalt, more wine," he snapped.

The blond youth rose and went to the flagon. A healing cut striped one cheekbone where a tree branch had whipped him during the fight. He had been supposed to stay back with the archers but had ignored the order and engaged in a skirmish with one of de Dinan's footsoldiers. As it happened, he had wounded the man and come out of it with his own hide intact. Gilbert had whipped him for disobedience, but, in acknowledgment of his courage, not too hard. Besides, whipping seldom had any effect on Ernalt. The youth's mental hide was as tough as boiled leather.

"Ludlow is mine," he said as he took the wine from the squire's hand and dismissed him. "I will not rest until it is in my family's possession again."

Hugh ran his forefinger across his upper lip. "To which de Dinan would answer that it does belong to a de Lacy. His wife is one by blood, if not by name."

"But not in direct male line," Gilbert growled. "Sybilla is my cousin out of my father's sister…the distaff line twice over." He jutted his jaw. "I will have it, I swear. One day, I will ride under that gate arch, climb its tower, and plant my banner on its walls."

"Amen to that," Hugh said. "But you must acknowledge that that day will not be tomorrow, or the next one, or even next year…and perhaps never if we do not drive Henry from England."

Gilbert snorted down his nose. "Henry or Stephen, what's the difference? I have ceased to have faith in the word of rulers and kings. The only honor I trust is my own."

De Mortimer narrowed his eyes. "You drink my wine and tell me that?"

"I am never less than honest with any man," Gilbert said with a bleak smile. "For now we are allies because we have a common enemy. I am not impugning your own honor, but neither am I foolish enough these days to have blind faith…except in the matter of my God." He made the sign of the Cross.

De Mortimer returned the smile with an equal lack of warmth. "Well then," he said, "shall I withdraw my aid and leave you to your own war?"

"Only a man too foolish or too proud refuses a boost into the saddle," Gilbert replied. "Let us say that we are both looking in the same direction but at different objects."

De Mortimer conceded the point with a brusque nod. "I have

to go south to aid Eustace, but you are welcome to use my lands to launch raids on Ludlow. If you can keep de Dinan pinned down, so much the better." Rising to his feet, he stretched. "I'm for my bed. I've a fair distance to ride on the morrow."

Gilbert bade him good night and stayed awhile to finish his wine and gaze into the fire. De Mortimer's loyalty was to Stephen, and his interest in Ludlow that of a man with a thorn in his side. Should de Dinan suddenly declare for Stephen, then Hugh would immediately become Ludlow's ally. But for Gilbert the matter was more than a thorn. It was a barbed spear in his heart.

From childhood it had been dinned into him that Ludlow rightfully belonged to his branch of the family. He was the eldest son of the eldest son. The castle had been taken from them when his father had been involved in a rebellion and given instead to his uncle whose loyalties were not in question. The latter had died childless and instead of passing Ludlow to Gilbert, who was the next in line, King Henry had bestowed it upon Sybilla, whose claim was through the distaff line. Gilbert's side of the family had always considered it an unjust decision. The rebellion had not been against Henry; it had taken place before he had become king, and it had been in an honorable cause. When old Uncle Hugh had died and the lands had become vacant, Gilbert had expected to inherit, but King Henry had said that he would not give the lands where he could not trust and that it was the end of the matter. Far from it, Gilbert thought with an unconscious frown. It would never end until a de Lacy of the true bloodline sat in the great hall at Ludlow and dispensed his justice from there.

Draining his wine, he considered retiring, but he was not sleepy. His mind was still churning and no amount of wine or fire-staring would settle him down. From long experience he knew that the only solace to be found was in prayer. Beyond the driving desire to regain his birthright, another flame burned with almost as much vigor. Three years ago, many men had answered the call to go and protect the Holy Land from a renewed infidel onslaught. Gilbert had thought about taking the Cross, but the ties of family duty had kept him in England. However, he had sworn to himself that once he had secured Ludlow for his bloodline, he would take holy vows, become a Templar knight, and end his days in military service to God.

He rose to his feet and his squires followed suit. He thought about bringing them with him for the good of their souls, but he desired solitude and he knew that the youths would only pay lip service at this time of night. Sometimes he suspected that Ernalt in particular paid lip service all the time.

"Go to bed," he told them and bent a warning look on Ernalt, who had recently been caught with his hand up the skirt of a garrison knight's daughter. "Your own, unless it's your ambition to be gelded."

The boys smirked. Gilbert increased the ferocity of his glower until their faces fell. Turning on his heel, he left the chamber and sought the calming solace of the chapel.

## 8

INGERS RED WITH COLD, BRUNIN MOLDED THE SNOW IN HIS hands into a compact ball and hurled it. Hugh ducked, but the edge of his cloak caught a starburst of white crystals.

"You've got the aim and eyesight of a girl!" Hugh jeered. His words were cut off in a splutter as a large snowball smacked him in the mouth.

"No, he hasn't!" Hawise cried with glee, sending a second snowball whirling after the first. One of her father's dogs leaped up and intercepted the missile in its jaws, then capered around the ward, shaking its head and sneezing.

Hugh snatched up a fistful of snow and ran toward Hawise, furrowing through the ermine whiteness like a plow. Shrieking with laughter, she fled. Marion clung to Brunin, hiding behind him, hampering his aim. "Don't let him get me!" she squealed. She floundered, lost her footing, and fell, dragging Brunin down on top of her.

"Ouch!" she cried. She wasn't really hurt but knew that big eyes and a quivering lip were sure ways of getting attention. If it was masculine attention and stolen from Hawise, so much the better. The dog flurried around them, barking and wagging furiously.

"Are you all right?" Brunin rolled over and, thrusting the dog aside with his forearm, scrambled to his feet. Glancing across at Hawise and Hugh, he grinned as the latter caught his prey and started stuffing snow inside her hood. Marion flashed him an upward glance, saw that his attention had wandered, and gave a gasp. "I don't know." She screwed up her face.

Turning back to her, Brunin grasped her hand and helped her to her feet. Marion looked down at their linked fingers and imagined her own adorned with a betrothal ring. She would be Lady FitzWarin and have a castle of her own and a dozen different gowns to wear like the ladies in the troubadours' stories.

"Can we go within and get warm?" she asked plaintively, leaning against him and fluttering her lashes. "I am so cold."

Brunin didn't want to go in. His hands were numb and tingling, but he was exhilarated and raring for more sport. Lady Sybilla had sent them out because she said she didn't want them under her feet, and Lord Joscelin had given him and Hugh leave from their duties to hold a snow-fight. Indoor tasks could be left until darkness fell and, with the snow this thick, it wouldn't harm the horses to spend the day in their stalls.

Hugh helped Hawise to her feet. Removing her hood, she set about tipping the mountain of snow from inside it. Her braids had come loose, her hair streamed down her back in a curtain of garnet twists, and she was red-lipped and laughing.

"Please," Marion said, insistently pathetic now.

"Why don't you go and stand by the guards' fire and warm your hands?" He indicated the wrought-iron brazier in the corner of the bailey where several soldiers were standing around the blaze of logs it contained, hugging themselves in their cloaks, stamping their feet.

Marion tugged his arm. "You come with me."

He was spared such purgatory by a shout from one of the guards manning the wall walks above the gatehouse. Hugh ceased beating snow crystals from his cloak and looked apprehensive. Brunin suddenly felt as if he had swallowed a snowball and that it was slowly melting, filling his stomach with freezing water. Ever since the ambush at the end of last summer, Ludlow had been held in a state of high tension. There hadn't been any serious attacks, but there had been several skirmishes between patrols sent out to secure their boundaries and test those of the enemy. Herds had been driven off, hamlets raided, grain stores burned. Not all of it was the work of de Lacy and Mortimer. Prince Eustace's mercenaries had played their part in some of the more savage raids. Joscelin had retorted in kind for he too had once been a mercenary and he knew the movements of the dance as well as his enemies—if not better.

No one went on serious campaign in January, Brunin told himself, as the guard replaced his shout with three rapid blasts on the horn at his belt. There was no fodder for the horses and the weather was too cold for the men. The horn rang out again, but this time on one long, sustained note.

Brunin's taut shoulders relaxed. Hugh exhaled a long cloud of breath. "Friends," he said with a self-conscious laugh of relief.

The guards were making haste to open the gates that led onto the bridge.

"Must be a large troop," Hugh added, joining Brunin and dusting snow crystals from his hair. "The guard wouldn't shout for a handful of men."

The gates swung inward and moments later mail-clad riders entered the bailey, riding two abreast. The banners proclaimed Hereford and FitzWarin. Brunin felt a surge of pleasure and pride as he saw his father's silks rippling on a spear end. At the end of last October, having strengthened the garrison at Whittington, his father had ridden to join Henry's army in the south. The threat from Mortimer and de Lacy was less to him and the Welsh had been quiet during the autumn and winter; thus he had been free to aid Prince Henry's cause.

FitzWarin dismounted from his stallion, tossed the reins to an attendant, and, with a gleam in his eye, crunched through the snow to greet his son.

"Christ, boy, every time I see you, you've grown!" He thumped a gauntleted hand down on Brunin's shoulder. His glance flickered to Marion who was still clinging to Brunin's arm. Immediately she dipped him a curtsey and lowered her eyes, displaying that she knew her manners and how to mind them before guests. FitzWarin absorbed the detail with approval and in the same glance dismissed her from his mind.

"What are you doing out here, lad?"

"We had some free time," Brunin said. "We've been having a snowball fight."

"Hah, when I was a squire, I never had any free time," FitzWarin said gruffly, but he was smiling. "Where's your lord?"

Brunin led his father across the ward to the domestic buildings. News had already gone ahead and Joscelin and Sybilla were on hand to welcome their unexpected guests and furnish them with warmth and wine. For a while Brunin was busy with flagon and cups, helping to remove mail and surcoats, and fetching warm water to thaw frozen hands and feet. The conversation ebbed and flowed around him and he had small opportunity to listen. Not that he missed much, for most of the talk was conventional pleasantry to begin with. By the time the men settled down to the meat of the matter Brunin had more leisure to take notice of what was being said. Sybilla remained with the men. While most women would have retired to their sewing, or the overseeing of feeding the multitude, Sybilla delegated those tasks and remained firmly at the center of discussions. She was lady of Ludlow and it was her right and her intention to know everything. Her daughters had stayed too, although they were expected to sit, observe, and say nothing. Like Brunin, the larger part of their duty was to listen and learn.

"What news of Prince Henry, my lords?" Sybilla asked, the pitch of her voice low and pleasant.

FitzWarin lifted his shoulders. "What news had you last heard?"

Joscelin glanced to the young Earl of Hereford. "Roger sent us the message that the Prince had narrowly escaped defeat at Devizes but was whole and still strong of purpose."

"So he is," Roger said. "He knows that his time is coming and Stephen knows that his own is running out."

Sybilla leaned forward, a frown between her brows. "But there is more to this matter, or you would not be avoiding my gaze."

FitzWarin cleared his throat. "There is no point in sweetening the truth, madam. Prince Henry is returning to Normandy. Indeed, he has probably sailed already."

"Returning to Normandy?" Joscelin sat forward too, looking alarmed. "Was his cornering at Devizes more serious than we thought?"

FitzWarin shook his head. "It was a damned hard fight," he said, "but no worse than some I've been in, and the Prince has played a man's part throughout. But he needs more money and men, and they are better to be found across the Narrow Sea. His resources are so stretched that the best he can obtain from the situation is to be chased from pillar to post while Eustace and Stephen follow him, burning all in their wake. For England's sake, as much as his own, he has to leave."

"And how long will it be before he returns with reinforcements?" Sybilla's generous mouth pursed with displeasure. "How much longer do we have to live on promises and watch the smoke rise from our burning fields?"

FitzWarin narrowed his eyes at Sybilla's forthright remark.

"The Prince is not abandoning us; he will return as soon as he can," Roger said emphatically. "These are the final throws of the dice. Men have seen that Henry is no green boy, but has the maturity to govern like a king."

Sybilla raised her eyebrows and Roger flushed beneath her stare, but held his ground.

"Henry has been in England for almost a year and Stephen has been unable to destroy him. Nor will he now."

Joscelin sighed in resignation. "In truth I had expected as much. If nothing else, we are well prepared. All I hope is that Mortimer and de Lacy do not see Henry's leaving as a signal to redouble their attacks on Ludlow."

"They will not dare when they have the full might of Hereford to contend with," Roger said. "Before, my troops were split between those following the Prince and those in my garrison, but now I can bring the full brunt to bear on anyone who dares to think us prey for the taking."

Joscelin grunted assent and looked a trifle more sanguine. Sybilla's expression remained tense, but she allowed the subject to lie for the moment.

"I have some good news to take home to my wife and mother," FitzWarin announced as Brunin went around replenishing the cups. His gaze lingered on his son. "Before he left, Prince Henry enfeoffed me with two estates in Gloucestershire to hold of him in chief. Only a quarter the size of Whittington, but fertile and bringing rich profit." Pride and pleasure filled his voice—as well they might. In addition to being an acknowledgment of his loyalty, each acquisition was another step up the rung of FitzWarin ambition. He waited for the murmured congratulations to finish before adding, "And Eve sent word that she is again with child—due at midsummer."

Joscelin smiled. "That too is good news," he said, "although you will need to obtain lands hand over fist to support your brood."

FitzWarin grinned agreement. "At least I have had no dowries to find thus far, but my mother seems to think that it will be a girl this time and daughters are always useful for making alliances through marriage." He looked at Brunin. "Would you like a sister, lad?"

Brunin tilted his head and wondered if he should jest. The news was no great surprise to him. For most of his life his mother had either been expecting a child or recently delivered of one. "Better than a brother," he dared and was relieved when his father and Lord Joscelin laughed.

❖❖❖

In the bedchamber, Hawise opened the shutters and peered out on the moonlit ward. The churned snow resembled hard-beaten egg-white and deepening frost glittered on the surface. It looked beautiful and eerie and she had half a mind to sneak out and walk through it. The other half knew it was nonsense. She would never win past the maids, and the deep cold would shred her lungs.

"Close the window; you're bringing a chill into the room and the night air is bad for you," Sibbi said querulously. She had recently begun her fluxes and at the time of her bleeding was irritable beyond belief for one of usually so sweet a nature. With a sigh, Hawise drew in the shutters and latched them. The candle guttered at the sudden puff of air, then steadied.

Marion was sitting on her bed, humming softly to her straw doll. It was swaddled with strips of linen left over from the cutting of a gown and its face was made of more linen sewn around a ball of compacted fleece. She didn't play with it as often these days, but still indulged in a nightly ritual of singing it a lullaby. Her expression was thoughtful.

"Brunin's father will be a rich man now," she broke off her singing to remark as she laid the doll in a small basket lined with sheepskin.

Hawise sat on her own bed. "What of it?"

Marion half shrugged. "If I marry into a rich family, I can have lots of jewels and dresses and drink from silver cups."

"You want to marry Brunin, don't you?"

Marion lifted her chin. "I might."

The idea of a betrothal between her father's youngest squire and Marion filled Hawise with dismay. She knew that in the fullness of time all of them would be betrothed, but her mother had always said that they need not worry about such things yet. She said that she wanted them to be women when the choice was discussed, not little girls. Hawise occasionally thought about it, but it was something far off and adult. When Sibbi had begun her fluxes, the matter had resurfaced, but not with any urgency.

"You can get married when you are twelve years old," Marion added. "And I was twelve last month."

"Yes, but boys have to be fourteen," Sibbi pointed out.

"Besides, you haven't started your fluxes yet. Mama and Papa won't think of marrying you to anyone for a long time."

Marion thrust out her lower lip and looked stubborn.

"You've plenty of dresses now," Hawise said frostily. "And you drink out of silver cups on special days. There are lots of families richer than Brunin's."

"Yes, but he's related to King Stephen and Prince Henry," Marion said grandly. "He's got royal blood."

"Well then, his family can do much better than you," Hawise snapped, feeling both pleasure and guilt at her own spite.

Marion flung her a murderous stare through narrowed lids before turning her back with a flounce.

When Sybilla came to bid the girls good night, it was to a room that bore the chill of a squabble. She had encountered such atmospheres before and thought little of it...but it was several days before there was a thaw between Hawise and Marion, and it left its mark. As they were growing up, the small rubs of childhood were becoming harsher frictions.

# 9

*B*RUNIN PEERED INTO THE CRADLE AT HIS NEW SISTER. TODAY had been her official christening, although she had been baptized at her birthing a month earlier. Her name was Emmeline, and like him, she was dark of hair and eye.

Joscelin had taken advantage of a lull in the skirmishing along the Marches to attend the festivities at Whittington. A christening, being a celebration of life, was a perfect opportunity to renew hope for the future.

Brunin had no particular interest in babies; they belonged to the world of the bower and the nursery, which he was rapidly leaving behind. However, since this was his first sister and since everyone said that she resembled him, he had paid more attention to her than he would have done a new brother—although he still could not understand why the visiting women and girls were so dewy-eyed. Sibbi and Lady Sybilla were adoring and Marion positively obsessed. Only Hawise had shown some sense of balance and even she had been utterly fascinated when the wet nurse had arrived to put the baby to suck and change her swaddling.

Marion joined him. She had been keeping vigil by the cradle for most of the day and had only yielded her watch when a visit to the garderobe became a necessity. "I wish we could take her back to Ludlow," she said wistfully.

Brunin grimaced at the notion. "She would probably cry all the way."

"Don't you like her?"

He shrugged. "Yes," he said, but without strong conviction. A baby was a baby. It slept, it bawled, it sucked from the tit, it shat itself and bawled again.

Suddenly Marion bowed her head and sank in a demure curtsey. Turning, Brunin found himself eye to eye with his grandmother. Following a recent stint of growth, he was now taller than her, but her blue stare still cut him down.

"The girl knows not to bandy looks with her elders," she said. "So why do you still dwell in ignorance?"

Brunin studied his feet and muttered an apology.

"Joscelin de Dinan seems to think you are making good progress, but then perhaps he is easily satisfied."

Brunin clenched his fists. She had paid him little attention thus far and he had hoped to escape the visit without wounds from her tongue. Now he realized that such a hope was futile. She would have her say, and it would be all the more acute for nigh on two years of waiting.

Mellette turned to Marion. "You, child," she said sharply. "Are you one of Joscelin de Dinan's daughters?"

"No, my lady. Like Brunin, I am being fostered," Marion said in a sweet, deferential voice.

"Indeed?" Mellette looked her up and down. "What's your name?"

"Marion de la Bruere, my lady."

Brunin's grandmother considered the reply with a speculative look in her eyes, said, "Hmph," and went on her way.

Brunin breathed out and unclenched his fists. His stomach felt as if it was full of cold marrow jelly.

Marion was gazing in Mellette's wake, her own expression thoughtful.

❖❖❖

"Girls with red hair are unlucky," Ralf taunted.

Hawise glared at him. She had taken a hearty dislike to Brunin's brother, who had returned from his training with the Earl of Derby for the baby's christening. He was tall and fair, his looks and nature reminding her of a young mastiff. "That's not true."

"It is, everyone knows it. They're full of temper and not to be trusted."

"Prince Henry's got red hair. So has my father."

Ralf flicked a glance toward the dais table where Hawise's father sat at his ease, talking with FitzWarin and other male guests. "Yes, but they're men. You're just a girl..." He turned to the younger boy at his side for support. Richard FitzWarin looked uncertain, but gave a half-nod.

Hawise drew herself up. "And you are a mannerless lout," she snapped. "No wonder Brunin was glad to come to Ludlow if he had to suffer you at home."

"Hah, we all had to suffer him," Ralf sneered. "He's useless."

"He's worth ten of you," Hawise retorted, her complexion brightening with anger. "If my father could hear you, he'd take a whip to your hide."

"And how's he going to hear? I suppose you are going to carry tales to him like a spoiled little milksop?" His lip curled with contempt and his gaze flashed to Brunin who had just walked within earshot. "Has he told you yet about the time he pissed his hose in terror of Gilbert de Lacy's squires?"

Hawise could sense Brunin resonating like a plucked bowstring, although his expression was blank. "You are not worth the storm it would raise to teach you a lesson, Ralf," he said indifferently.

"You'd never best me in a fight."

"You have a short memory for some things." Brunin sat down on the bench beside Hawise; taking a small loaf of bread from the basket in the middle of the trestle, he broke it in two.

Ralf flushed. "Come outside now and we'll see."

"This is a celebration. I don't want to fight you."

"Because you know you'd lose."

"Because you're my brother." Brunin broke the bread again and began to eat as if he were indifferent to Ralf's belligerence. "Surely our family has enemies enough without squabbles between ourselves."

Ralf opened his mouth, but no words emerged. Glowering, he shoved away from the table and stalked off. After a moment, Richard gave Brunin a look of hangdog apology and shuffled after him. Warin and the younger boys remained where they were, their unease apparent. Nevertheless, none of them rose to follow Ralf and Richard.

Brunin stared at the bread in his hands as if he did not know what it was; with a tremendous effort, he swallowed the morsel he had been chewing. Hawise noticed that his hands were trembling. He had told her about his brothers and had mentioned Ralf as his particular *bête noire*, but he had never gone into detail. Now she thought she understood.

"If you had taken up his challenge, he would have come off worse," she said stoutly.

He forced a smile and pushed the remainder of the loaf aside. "Perhaps."

"I don't believe what he said about you and de Lacy's squires."

He hunched his shoulders and looked down at the trestle. "Oh, that part's true. He likes to taunt me with it, but he wasn't there to know what it was like. If he had been, he'd probably have helped them hold me down." He breathed out hard as if pushing the memory from his body.

Hawise bit her lip and wished she had not spoken.

"I heard what he said about your hair," Brunin said into the awkward silence. "I hope you paid as little heed to Ralf as I did."

She curled a tangled tress around her forefinger. She knew the prejudices against folk with red hair, especially girls and women. It was said that they were hot-tempered, quarrelsome, and false. Ralf had probably only been repeating what he had heard at his nurse's knee. If Hawise had not been so certain of her parents' love for her, and had she not been so proud to take after her father, her confidence might have been knocked.

"No," she said with a defiant shake of her head. "I paid him no more heed than I would a buzzing fly." She brought her hand down on the table in a swatting motion and Brunin smiled.

❖ ❖ ❖

"I must thank you for the changes I see in my eldest son," Eve FitzWarin murmured to Sybilla.

The men were still drinking in the hall, and the women had retired to the chamber above. Two musicians played a harp duet in the corner, the notes hanging sweetly amid the soft layers of hearth smoke in the air. Eve's eyes were dark-circled and Sybilla thought that she did not look well. By all accounts the birth of her daughter had been difficult, and Mellette's constant presence in the bower did not lend itself to domestic tranquillity. Nor did the tense situation in England yield the kind of peace essential to a breeding woman. Sybilla was glad that she was no longer of child-bearing age. That worry at least was behind her. Instead she had her daughters to watch through the trials of young womanhood.

"The changes are of his own making too," Sybilla said. "I have done nothing beyond that which any lord's wife would do for her husband's squires." The speech was graceful and formal. She was aware of Mellette FitzWarin lurking in the background, her ears cocked like a terrier's.

"Nevertheless, you have my gratitude."

"It is early days," Mellette commented. "Has he started full weapons training yet?"

"You would have to ask my husband, Lady Mellette," Sybilla said quietly but with an edge to her voice. She would respect the old woman's age and status, but she would not be browbeaten or yield to bullying. "Brunin gained much useful experience when they were on campaign last year...and learned some harsh lessons too. My husband is delighted with his progress, and I enjoy his presence in my household."

"And your girls, do they enjoy his presence too?" The sharp blue glance darted to Sibbi, Marion, and Hawise, who were sitting a little apart from the older women, playing a game with dice and counters.

Sybilla frowned, wondering what meaning to ascribe to the question. "I hope so, madam. Why do you ask?"

"Are any of them betrothed?"

Ah, so that was the way the wind blew. Sybilla straightened her spine and folded her hands in her lap, her posture a direct echo of Mellette's. "Not yet. They are too young. We will make no decisions until each one reaches the age of fifteen."

"I had been wed a full year by the time I was fifteen," Mellette said.

"So had I, but, given the choice, I would not have married so young."

"Choices are dangerous for girls. Their eyes will light on men unsuitable and their bodies will lead them into sin and disgrace. Better to yoke them to a husband than to let them stray."

Sybilla blinked. She looked at Eve, but her eyes were downcast as if the sheen on her silk gown was fascinating. "I would hope and trust that my daughters have more sense," she said with dignity. "And surely it is better to 'yoke' them to a man for whom they have an affinity rather than to one they dislike. The second is just as likely to lead them to stray, do you not think?"

Mellette made small chewing motions. "Not if they have had a sense of duty dinned into them by a strict upbringing," she said. "I knew my duty when I married Warin de Metz, as doubtless you knew yours when you were wed to your husbands."

"Yes, I knew my duty," Sybilla answered. "But I wish I had been given a choice. I came to be fond of Payne, and you have seen that there is a deep bond between myself and Joscelin, but at times it was very difficult, especially when he was Stephen's man. I intend to give my daughters—and Marion—more say in the matter of choosing their mates than I was given."

Mellette shook her head. "Then I say that you are storing up trouble for yourself. What if one sets her eyes upon an inappropriate man?"

"That could happen anyway." Sybilla bent a firm gaze on Mellette. "I give my daughters leeway, my lady, but I do not let them run wild."

Mellette cast her glance toward the girls. They had obviously been half listening to the conversation for three pairs of eyes looked back, Hawise's through a loose tangle of hair.

"So you say."

Sybilla bit her tongue with difficulty for Mellette's comment was downright rude. Everyone else was supposed to have impeccable manners, but the family matriarch appeared to be exempt.

"The fair one…what kind of bloodline and dowry does she have?"

Sybilla had had enough. "I doubt it will be of concern to you, my lady," she said with icy civility.

"Oh, but it might be one day," Mellette said. "I have a brood of grandsons and some of them at least will marry."

"Marion has a good bloodline and a comfortable dowry. I am certain that if she were a horse, she would sell for an excellent price at Shrewsbury Fair."

Sybilla's response had been bitingly sarcastic, but Mellette seemed to find it amusing. A smile would have been too much, but a gleam lit in her eyes. "The seller always expounds the worth of the goods," she said.

"And this particular one would be very careful about the buyer."

Mellette nodded. "That much we agree upon."

The conversation ended there. It was like a sparring match where the partners had withdrawn to consider their opponent's strengths and weaknesses. There was no liking between them, nor even much respect, but there was an acknowledgment that they were two of a kind. Women of strong will, who, in their different ways, ruled the roost.

# 10

JOSCELIN AND HIS FAMILY RETURNED TO LUDLOW AND MATTERS continued as before. There were occasional spats between Ludlow and de Lacy, but no outright warfare. Henry's adherents waited for his return and the country held its breath. It was like a still, autumn day; everything waiting for the first blustery gales to blow away the tired debris of the previous season, to bring on winter and prepare for spring.

Plenty of news sailed across the Narrow Sea, but no Henry, for he had other concerns. It both interested and disconcerted Joscelin to see Prince Eustace cross to France at the invitation of King Louis and attempt to take on Henry on Norman soil.

"There speaks desperation," he said when they heard the news from one of Hereford's messengers. "If he cannot catch him on English ground, what makes him think that he can take him on in Normandy?"

It came to nothing, a mere ripple of breeze that drifted a few leaves from the trees. But other strands of fate were strengthening the wind. Suddenly and unexpectedly, Henry's father died and Henry, at eighteen, became Count of Anjou as well as Duke of Normandy. Stephen's queen died too—and King Louis of France divorced his.

The tidings of the divorce and its aftermath blew into Hereford on the same day. Joscelin had been lodging there overnight while patrolling the road between Hereford and Ludlow. He rode homeward in thoughtful mood, digesting the news, saying little to anyone. Brunin did not disturb him, but rode close to his left shoulder, bearing his shield. He had trained fiercely to earn the privilege that had once been Adam's, and he carried the shield proudly in Adam's honor. He was now tall and strong enough to bear it as a matter of course rather than a burden. Although he was still as slender as a colt, adolescence was beginning to lengthen bone and develop muscle. His voice had deepened, but had yet to break, and there was a smudge of dark down on his upper lip.

Brunin was fast outgrowing Morel too, and Joscelin had said that, come next Shrewsbury Fair, they would see about obtaining a full-sized horse for him so that he could concentrate on his mounted battle training. Currently he was borrowing Hugh's brown stallion for tilting at the ring and the quintain, but it would be better to have his own destrier and such an acquisition would be another marker on the road to manhood.

They came to the place where Adam had been killed nearly three years ago. The woods had been fiercely chopped back on either side of the road so that there was nowhere for ambushers to hide or for archers to make a killing shot. Even so, Brunin's shoulder blades twitched and his muscles tightened. Beneath him Morel caught his tension and sidled his haunches.

Joscelin emerged from his reverie. "You feel it too, lad?"

"I remember it as if it were yesterday, sir." Brunin crossed himself. The place was not marked but he knew it was here. Sweat moistened his palms and he rubbed them on his hose.

Joscelin nodded. "As if it were about to happen again." He was biting the inside of his cheek. "We have had little war since that time. Only brawls and tit for tat. But I feel as if something is gathering."

Involuntarily, Brunin set his hand to the strap of the shield. "Perhaps it is the wait for Prince Henry," he suggested.

Joscelin made a face. "You are probably more right than you

know—and, given what has just happened, God knows when that will be." His fingers clenched on the reins in frustration. "We need Henry here now, while Stephen is still reeling from the death of his wife. She was his backbone."

"Yes, sire," Brunin said dutifully.

Joscelin bent him an astute look. "Never underestimate the importance of women in the scheme of things," he said. "It is a mistake too often made by men, and I include your father in that. A woman can make, but she can break too, and when the pieces shatter, they are difficult to pick up and reassemble. Remember that."

Brunin thought of his grandmother and the strewn debris of all the people she had broken beneath the rod of her will. There were some parts of himself that he would probably never find because he dared not go looking for them in the shadows where she had cast them.

"I suppose Prince Henry is going to find that out soon enough," Joscelin added with a sudden wry grin and flicked a warning glance at Brunin. "I would counsel you never to tangle with older women—except that I married one myself…They can be tricky, but I promise you'd never be bored."

"No, sire."

Joscelin chuckled. "You have no idea what I'm talking about, do you, and I do not suppose I would have done either at your age."

Brunin studied his reins. He had an inkling, but he wasn't going to tell Joscelin about one of the maids at Hereford and the exciting, disturbing propositions she had put to him. He had been rescued by the crone employed to keep the fire going in the solar…which had been both a relief and a pity. Another moment and the maid's hand would have reached its intended destination and he might just have plucked up courage to touch her breasts.

Joscelin's grin became a deep, reluctant laugh. "I won't ask," he said. "The answer might disturb my notions of your innocence."

❖ ❖ ❖

"So, what news do you bring from Hereford?"

Joscelin sat down on the cushioned bench in the private chamber and took the wine Sybilla gave him. "What makes you think I bring any news?" he asked nonchalantly.

"You have that look about you—like a hound waiting to be taken out for a walk."

Joscelin laughed. "That's not very flattering."

"You asked." She sat down across from him and drew forward her braid-weaving frame. Cupping the numerous small wooden squares in her palm, each one threaded at the corners with embroidery silks, she gave them a quarter-turn and pulled the weft thread tight. "Has Henry finally been persuaded of the importance of returning to England? Is that what you are waiting to tell me?"

Joscelin made a face. "Not precisely," he said.

Sybilla's mouth drew tight. The expression might have been caused by her concentration on the pattern she was weaving, but, given her interest in the political machinations and power struggles that surrounded them, Joscelin suspected not.

"You would have thought," she said, "that when he receives a plea from his own uncle to make haste, he would heed it."

"He did." Joscelin stretched out his legs and winced as his knees creaked. "There was a council held at Lisieux and detailed plans made for his return. Roger had his scribe read the letter to me."

Sybilla turned the threaded tablets, creating a pattern of red and white chevrons. "Then what has changed?"

Joscelin studied her over the rim of the cup. "King Louis divorced his wife…"

She looked up from her weaving, her eyes filled with surprise. "What does that—"

"And Henry had her at the altar with a new wedding ring on her finger before the old one was scarcely off," he concluded with a wolfish grin.

Sybilla's gaze widened into astonishment.

Joscelin laughed. "Yes," he said. "Eleanor of Aquitaine.

Eleanor of Poitou. In one fell swoop, Henry has become lord of an empire and the most envied husband in Christendom…and of course Louis loves him not. He might not have wanted his wife, but he hardly expected the likes of Henry to snap her up like a starving hound." His mirth subsided into thoughtfulness, and he raised one forefinger in amendment. "Although from what I heard, she was as keen to wed as he was. I suppose it spites Louis, and while Henry may not be a handsome man, he is certainly an energetic one. And, of course, he has red hair." He smoothed his own with deliberation.

Sybilla smiled at the joke, but with no more than a token curve of her lips.

"Henry sends word that he will come as soon as he has sorted out his few difficulties across the Narrow Sea. Louis is saying that it is an offense for a vassal to marry without his overlord's permission, and since Henry owes him fealty for Normandy, he is in breach of feudal law."

"And meanwhile we wait and pray."

Joscelin shrugged. "Yes," he said. "We wait and pray."

Sybilla sighed heavily. "Oh, the color wearies my eyes." She pushed the weaving frame aside with unwarranted force for one whose actions were usually steady and measured.

Joscelin looked at her askance.

She bit her lip. "Why did Louis divorce her?"

"Consanguinity."

"That's the excuse, not the reason," she said, and her voice was unsteady. "It has taken him a long time to realize that he and Eleanor were related beyond the permitted degree."

"I do not know what is in the French King's mind," Joscelin said uneasily. He knew where this was leading and that it was inevitable.

"Yes, you do. There have been rumors aplenty for some time."

Joscelin waved his hand. "Very well. Louis divorced Eleanor because he couldn't get a son on her and she was proving too mettlesome for him to handle both in bed and out of it." Leaving the bench, he went to Sybilla and pulled her roughly into his arms. "Which has no bearing on our marriage. For one thing we're not related within a prohibited degree, for another I don't have Louis's monkish tendencies—and mettlesome suits me well."

She gave him a challenging look "And if it didn't?"

"Then I'd be as foolish as Louis and justly served." He made an exasperated sound and kissed her. "I knew you would respond like this. Did it never occur to you that in my turn I might worry about you fleeing our marriage bed for the arms of a young suitor?"

She pushed at him. "That's preposterous."

"Yes," he said. "As preposterous as you suggesting that I'd divorce you in the same wise that Louis divorced Eleanor. I waited a long time for a place like Ludlow and a woman like you." One arm held her trapped, the other plucked at her wimple pins. "Loose your hair for me."

"It's gray...I don't..."

"Like a waterfall...Loose it."

Slowly she raised her hands to her head, removed the wimple and the net that held her braids. They tumbled down, each as thick as his wrists, silver and black entwined, bound with red ribbons, scented like honeysuckle.

"Forget Louis and Eleanor," he said, untying the ribbons and combing his fingers through the plaits until all that was left of them were undulating waves in her sea-wash curtain of hair. "Forget Henry and Eleanor too. They have no place in our bedchamber. That belongs to us alone."

YOUTH AND MAIDEN

## St. Peter's Fair, Shrewsbury, August 1152

*D*ESPITE THE CONTINUING WAR, SHREWSBURY CLAD ITSELF IN festive garb and prepared for the annual fair. There were winter supplies to be bought in, bargains to be struck, secrets to be whispered to the highest bidder, alliances to be made and broken while the silver grease of coin kept the wheel of trade ponderously turning.

Sybilla arrived in Shrewsbury with her household and a tally of required purchases as long as her arm. When Joscelin groaned that she would empty their treasure chest, she retorted that she was a thrifty housewife and had she been frivolous, the list could have been twice as long. Of course, if he wanted to see his daughters dressed in sackcloth…Throwing up his hands in capitulation, Joscelin had abandoned his squires and serjeants to the mercies of the women and had gone in search of fellow husbands with whom to commiserate and share a flagon.

On escort duty to Sybilla, Brunin leaned against a mercer's booth, facing outward, arms folded, dagger sheath prominent at his hip. Hugh stood beside him, hand on sword hilt, gaze restlessly prowling the crowd. Hugh had been knighted at midsummer, and within the last month, negotiations had opened between his family and Sybilla and Joscelin over a match between himself and Sibbi. Taking his new responsibilities seriously, Hugh was being determinedly grave and mature. Brunin hadn't seen him smile all morning. Not that there was much to smile about when escorting a handful of women around the clothing and haberdashery booths. Even Hawise, who was usually sensible about the matter of shopping, seemed captivated by the array of cloth and was as avidly engaged as her companions. Brunin fervently hoped that the cookstalls were next on Sybilla's formidable list for it was almost noon and his stomach was rumbling more loudly than a charge of destriers on a battlefield.

He wanted to go and look at the horses, but for that he had to wait for Joscelin. With the memories of his childhood burned into his brain, he had no intention of wandering off anywhere on his own—even with a dagger at his belt. He knew that Gilbert de Lacy was in Shrewsbury for he had glimpsed his entourage across the Foregate yester eve, including his two squires, now almost grown men. To his great relief and continuing apprehension he had not sighted them today but they were bound to be in the throng somewhere.

"Show me the gold wool." Sybilla pointed to a bolt of cloth. The mercer lifted it from his shelf and created a fan of pleats on the counter. "Hawise, this will suit you; what do you think? Good and thick for winter."

In previous years, the sight of bolts of fabric rowed on the shelves of the mercer's booths at Shrewsbury Fair would have glazed Hawise's eyes with as much boredom as the men's. Today, however, the cloth exuded a fascination. Her fingers itched to pinch and rub; to smooth over cold, glossy silk; to crumple linen and test for softness. "I like it." She picked up the end to hold it against herself.

Sybilla considered and gave a satisfied nod. She gestured to her steward, giving him permission to haggle a price. "Enough for a dress and a length over for alterations and patching," she said. "Now show me that blue."

Hawise moistened her lips with greedy pleasure as the next bolt thudded onto the counter. This was for her too, and also for Sibbi.

She heard Brunin heave a deep sigh and pretended not to hear. He was as bad as her father. Marion watched the mercer's apprentice measure and cut with envious eyes.

"I wouldn't want to wear the gold, or the blue," she said loftily. "They're too dull."

"For your fairness, perhaps," Sybilla said. "But not for Hawise and Sibbi. I was thinking of the light blue up there for you, or that rose-pink." She pointed out a couple of bolts.

Marion's eyes brightened and she leaned on the counter to scrutinize Sybilla's suggestions.

Sybilla had the mercer bring out his chemise linens for her perusal.

"Finest weave of Cambrai," the trader said proudly. "Only shipped in a fortnight since."

Hawise set her hand beneath the fabric and fancied that she could almost see her fingers through it.

"If you've a bride in the family, it'll be fit for the wedding night," the mercer said, eyeing the girls. Sibbi blushed and glanced quickly over her shoulder at Hugh, but he was watching the milling crowds. "And if not, it's still a dainty thing to wear against the skin. Almost as fine as silk, but a deal less costly."

Hawise willed her mother to be swayed and was delighted when Sybilla bought sufficient for an undershift each.

Finally, when every shelf of the mercer's booth had been inspected and plundered, Sybilla announced that they would visit a cookstall to fortify themselves for the afternoon ahead. Watching Brunin stifle a yawn and unfold himself from his leaning post, Hawise was reminded of the rangy stable cats at Ludlow.

"Never mind," she said with the sympathy of one whose own appetites were temporarily sated, "you'll get to look at the horse fair soon and we've bought enough linen to make you a new shirt too."

He gave her a sidelong look in which she was surprised to read irritation. "I am not a child to be cozened by promises of rewards for patient behavior," he said stiffly and turned away with Hugh to forge a way through the crowds.

Hawise gazed after him in astonishment.

"Pay no heed," Sybilla murmured with a smile. "No male's temper is proof against accompanying women around the merchants' booths. Why do you think your father has delegated the task?"

Two squires clutching hot pasties eased past the women. One youth was of ordinary looks: brown-haired, snub-nosed, and stocky. His companion, however, caused Marion to inhale sharply and Hawise to stare, her stomach wallowing. He had wheaten hair, eyes of deep woad-blue, and features of the kind that adorned her imagination when the minstrels in the hall sang of bold and handsome knights.

His gaze traveled over the women and for one liquefying moment paused on Hawise. Then it moved to Marion and held for longer. In the instant before the press of the crowds and the angle of direction separated the parties, he smiled and closed one eye in a knowing wink.

"Who do you think he was?" Marion whispered, agog.

Hawise craned back over her shoulder, but to no avail for the young men were already out of sight.

Brunin stared after the squires too, but he already knew their identities. He tightened his fist around the hilt of his knife, reassuring himself with the solid presence of the leather grip, knowing that this time he was not defenseless, but his mouth filled nonetheless with the bitter taste of fear.

❖ ❖ ❖

It was late afternoon by the time Brunin was relieved of his duties with the women and finally able to go with Joscelin to look at the horse fair. Since it was high summer, the latter was set to continue into the late dusk.

Joscelin grinned and slapped the youth across the shoulder blades as they walked toward the lines of tethered horses. "So how has your lesson in patience been, lad?" he asked. "I hope you know your sarcenet from your samite and your twill from your wadmal by now."

Brunin looked pained. "I do not know about that, my lord, but my brains have certainly gone wool-gathering."

Joscelin threw back his head and laughed. Brunin laughed too, but the sound had a hollow ring. He was remembering the fear that had jolted through him when he saw de Lacy's squires. He wanted to speak out and rid himself of the moment but, reluctant to sound unmanly, tightened his lips and pressed the emotions down, as if weighting a floating corpse with stones.

Brunin, Joscelin, and the Ludlow men set about examining the beasts for sale with as much pleasure and concentration as the women had perused their cloth. And, like the cloth, there were all kinds to consider, from the coarse workaday to the refined and magnificent and all qualities between.

Joscelin looked in the mouth of one and shook his head at Brunin. "Teeth have been filed to make it seem younger," he said.

They moved on from that particular seller and avoided another whose horses had whip scars on their rumps. Brunin admired a large gray stallion with arched crest, rounded rump, and restively stamping hooves.

"Ideas above your station," Joscelin chuckled. "That's not a training mount; that's a warhorse in every sense of the word. He'd battle you all the way to Normandy and back."

Brunin had not thought for a minute that he would be able to have the stallion, but it still gave him wistful pleasure to look. A training mount, he told himself and, with an inward sigh, turned from the highly bred beasts to more prosaic fare. Hugh pointed out a handsome chestnut and Brunin tried him, but despite being young, the horse already had a hard mouth and its muscles shivered nervously as if constantly attacked by midges. Joscelin liked the look of an older dun, and the horse was sound of wind and limb, but Brunin was not as enthusiastic.

"It's like women," chuckled one of the knights. "Either you want them enough to burst your braies, or they're as appealing as skin on cold pottage."

Joscelin flashed a smile. "You can live on cold pottage skin," he said. "'Bursting your braies,' as you call it, creates more trouble than it's worth."

Brunin ignored their banter and approached a raw-boned gelding standing near the back of a horse line. It was a bright bay with black mane and tail and its two hind legs were white to the gaskins, making it look as if it were wearing hose. A white blaze straddled its cobby face and slipped to one side, covering one nostril and giving the horse a comical appearance. When he set his hand to its neck, it breathed on him gustily and immediately set about searching his garments as if expecting to find a hidden tidbit.

"This one," Brunin said.

Joscelin lifted his head from examination of the dun and stared with widening eyes. Hands on hips, he wandered over to Brunin's find. "Jesu! He looks as if he was made out of all the bits God had left over when he'd finished!" he scoffed. "Why in the name of St. Peter should you want him?"

Brunin flushed beneath Joscelin's scorn, but stood his ground. "Not all that is plain is dross," he said. "He's got a strong back, and his coat's in good condition. See, no mange. And he's young— only about six or seven. He's been well handled in the past too."

Joscelin arched his brows. "I am relieved to see you are not a complete fool," he said. "A halfwit rather than a lack-wit, but he's still a nag."

"I could try him..." Brunin willed Joscelin to say yes. He could see that the matter hung in the balance, that Joscelin was wondering whether to humor him or have done. Brunin stared at Joscelin and set his jaw. The older man's gray-hazel eyes filled with a smile.

"I once said to Sybilla that you were the most obedient and biddable squire I had ever trained and she replied that one day you would find your feet and surprise me." He waved his hand. "Oh, go on. Put your saddle on him." He turned to the coper who had been watching the exchange with alert eyes and the scent of a sale in his nostrils. The man scuttled with alacrity to help tack the horse up.

"How did you come by the beast?" Joscelin wanted to know. "I doubt you bred him yourself. No one would be that foolish."

The coper looked affronted. "He is a fine mount, sire. I would have been proud to have bred him, but you are right, I did not. He was sold to me by a knight who owed a debt to the Jews."

"By a knight…?" Joscelin stared at the horse in fresh appraisal. Brunin efficiently cinched the girths, working swiftly, horribly afraid that at any moment Joscelin was going to change his mind.

"Yes, my lord. Said he were a destrier, full trained."

A rude snort erupted from Joscelin's nose. "If that's a destrier, then I'm a priest's catamite! Good Christ, no one rides a gelding into battle. I've seen better donkeys in my time!"

Brunin set his foot in the stirrup and swung astride. The horse's head came up and it pricked its long, mulish ears.

"There's a quintain post over there if you want to try your hand with a lance." The coper nodded obligingly at a short run of churned grass and a post with a crossbar. On the end of the crossbar was a ring fashioned of woven withies. "Has the lad started tilting at the ring?"

"He has, but he's not having that horse," Joscelin said.

Brunin drew the bay out of the line and leaned to take the blunted lance that the coper had propped against the side of his booth for clients to use. Brunin was aware of Joscelin shaking his head and looking skeptical, but it only made the youth more determined. He dug his heels into the bay's flanks and urged him toward the quintain run. The bay responded to the lightest touch on the reins and canted his haunches sideways at the dig in the side. His long ears waggled and as Brunin turned him to face the quintain, he felt a ripple surge through the horse.

Couching the lance, Brunin set the gelding at the target and immediately realized what he had found. The bay's stride was short because of the shortness of the run, but smoothly controlled, and he brought Brunin straight as a die to the target. As the youth neatly lifted the ring off the hook, the bay turned away on a right lead and brought them back to the start of the run. Brunin pulled the lance head back to his body and tipped the ring off into his hand. The horse coper waddled up, took it from him, and replaced it on the quintain. Again Brunin made a run and again the horse did everything except put the lance on the ring.

Joscelin rumpled his hair. "I'm a priest's catamite," he said softly as Brunin reined about and returned to the line, his eyes shining.

Joscelin looked in the horse's mouth, sounded its wind, tested its legs. He kept repeating the word "nag" and "mule" to himself. Brunin held silent, his throat dry with apprehension. He couldn't say why he so badly wanted the bay, only that it was an instinct that came from the gut.

"How much do you want for him?" Joscelin asked. The coper named his price and Joscelin choked. "Hell's teeth, I'd expect to get a Spanish stallion for that, not a spavined hobby like this. I tell you what. I'll give you five marks. Take it or leave it."

The coper looked affronted and said he would leave it; the horse was worth four times that amount.

Brunin knew desperation, but he fought not to let it show on his face. He knew that much about buying and selling. He willed Joscelin not to walk away.

The coper looked around. Other customers had arrived to look at his wares. After a lull in the late afternoon, the evening crowds were beginning to throng the fair while the light lingered—and some of them, made careless by drink, had a lighter grasp on their purses. He named a lower price and Joscelin increased his in the time-honored fashion. Finally a deal was agreed and a tally stick notched, recording the sale. Brunin's chest swelled with joy and gratitude.

"No, do not thank me," Joscelin said, holding up his hands. "I still cannot believe what I have done. And when your father sees what I have bought to carry his son to knighthood, I'll be fried alive."

"He looks nothing, sir," Brunin said. "But that doesn't mean he is nothing. He'll prove his worth."

"He had better do," Joscelin said ruefully.

A shout from the quintain caught their attention and they turned to see Gilbert de Lacy's fair-haired squire tilting at the ring. He was mounted on the gray stallion that Brunin had admired earlier and the pair were a glorious sight. Brunin narrowed his eyes and watched the young man perform the maneuver with flawless precision. He used thighs and heels to turn the horse, showing off his considerable equestrian skills and muscular strength as he mastered the stallion. Brunin willed the horse to stumble or the rider to make a clumsy mistake, but neither happened.

A smiling Gilbert de Lacy arrived to watch his squire's performance and cupped his hands to shout words of pride and encouragement. The wry humor faded from Joscelin's face, leaving it taut and grim. De Lacy looked up and across. An air-scorching stare passed between the two men.

"Come," Joscelin said to Brunin, without taking his eyes from de Lacy. "We are done here and the light's fading."

Brunin grasped the bay's bridle close to the headstall and, with a click of his tongue, followed Joscelin and his retinue from the horse fair. He heard laughter at his back, and his ears burned. Although he knew it unlikely that he or his new horse were the object of the mirth, his imagination was raw.

"It will look as if we are running away, my lord," muttered Hugh, who was flushed with chagrin.

"But we had finished our business," Joscelin replied evenly. "If we linger with no more purpose than making a show, he will have driven us to respond. I do not fear him. That is all that matters."

"But—"

"Enough," Joscelin said curtly. "I will hear no more."

❖❖❖

On returning to their lodgings, Brunin's new mount was greeted with reserve by the women. Sybilla said little enough, but her expression made it clear that she would be having words with Joscelin later on. Sibbi was too interested in Hugh to pay much attention to the new purchase. Marion took one look at the horse and, turning from Brunin, flounced off to the sleeping loft above the main room. Hawise regarded the new mount with narrowed eyes and folded arms.

"You gave up Morel for this bag of bones?" she asked as Brunin, somewhat dismayed by the women's reactions, led the bay toward the outbuildings where the rest of Joscelin's mounts were tethered.

"I haven't given up Morel," he snapped. "My feet almost touch the ground when I ride him now. You knew that I was going to buy a bigger horse for weapons training at the fair. William de Cressage is having Morel for his son Meric—he's a good lad. Your father's going to take him for a junior squire next year."

She trailed after him, continuing to look sulky. Someone had been dressing her hair and for once it was tidied into a neat braid, with smaller braids plaited into the main one. The laces of her gown were drawn tight at the sides, emphasizing the curve of developing bosom and narrow waist. Brunin glanced once and then gave his attention to the horse, which was slobbering at his right shoulder.

"He's not a nag," he said quietly. "A man does not have to be handsome to make a fine warrior—just efficient and skilled."

Hawise shrugged, as if physically discarding his words. "But you do not know if the horse is good or not and ugly men can as easily make bad warriors as handsome ones."

"The trader said he was trained to the tilt."

"The trader would." Her tone was cynical.

Brunin swallowed his irritation. "I tried him myself and he knew what he had to do. Indeed, he was eager to do it. Whatever my pleading, your father would not have bought him had he considered him dross."

She followed him into the barn. Having tethered the horse, he fetched a pile of hay from the stooks in the corner and a pail of water.

"Does he have a name?"

Brunin could tell from the change in her voice that she was trying to make amends without having to apologize. Her nature might be generous, but he had discovered that she found it difficult to admit to being in the wrong. "No," he said. "What about 'Ugly'?"

Her eyes flashed and her color rose. "Yes," she said. "That would indeed be appropriate."

He gave his attention to the horse, hoping that she would go away, but she ignored the hint.

"Well, you cannot call him 'Beauty.'" Advancing to the horse, she laid the palm of her hand against its smooth bay neck. "'Jester' perhaps?"

Brunin rather liked the name but responded with a grunt that could have meant anything.

"You know that Marion won't talk to you for a sennight now." Reaching on tiptoe, she scratched the horse behind his ears and the gelding turned to butt her with his comical white-snipped nose. "You won't be her 'knight' anymore."

Brunin filled his hand full of oats from an open sack and offered his palm to the gelding. "Her opinion matters not to me," he said curtly. It wasn't true, although he would never admit it to Hawise. He took pleasure in the admiring glances Marion fluttered at him from beneath her lashes, in the way she curled her arm around his in the great hall and smiled up at him as if he were her world. She was often querulous and demanding, but she had a sweet, playful side that could melt most male hearts at a hundred paces. He knew that she was sizing him up as a future bridegroom, especially in the light of Sibbi's betrothal, but he viewed such notions as foolish play of the kind indulged in by girls as they chattered over their embroidery in the domestic chambers.

Hawise smiled. "It matters not to me either," she said. "Except when I want to smack her."

Brunin had to swallow a grin. Giving his new horse a final pat, he turned toward the lodging. Hawise walked beside him, her stride long and confident, almost masculine. She didn't fold her arm around his, nor did she bat her lashes at him. And, despite their recent argument, he was far more comfortable with that than Marion's clinging adulation.

❖❖❖

Sybilla handed Joscelin a cup of wine. "You are going to tell me you knew what you were doing," she said. "That you weren't swayed by a boy's whim."

Joscelin gave her a preoccupied smile. "Rather say that the boy knew what he was doing, love. There's a good beast hiding within those raw bones and untidy markings."

"If you say so."

"I do." He took his wine and went to the embrasure. Swallows swooped in the gloaming over the river, their cries a poignant reminder of a summer that was past its zenith. Another month and they would be gone to wherever they went in the winter months. The grain was ripe in the fields and the harvest imminent...if it didn't burn. He thrust his shoulder against the wood and sighed. There was melancholy in the air tonight. "I have been thinking." He turned around to Sybilla. Beyond her the girls were seated in a semicircle trying out different ways of braiding each other's hair. Giggles and snatches of whispered conversation drifted over to him and echoed the cries of the birds preparing to fly the familiar roost...as Sibbi would fly soon enough.

"About what?" Sybilla was smiling but her gaze was wary.

Joscelin chewed his thumbnail. "About Gilbert de Lacy."

"What of him?"

"I was wondering whether I should bargain with him for a truce, at least until the harvest is gathered in and the winter months past."

"A truce?" Sybilla's voice remained level but her pinched expression left him in no doubt that she thought he had lost his wits.

He gave a defensive shrug. "Other men are making pacts while they wait to see in which direction the balance will ultimately lean. Ranulf of Chester has made alliances with Ferrers and Derby and yet they fight on opposing sides. Your son-in-law flirts with Robert of Leicester."

"Why should you think that my cousin Gilbert will even consider a truce?" she demanded. "All of his life has been one long striving to take Ludlow. If you sue for peace, he will think you are wearying of the fight—that you are weakening."

Joscelin's gray eyes flashed. "He knows that I will never yield him Ludlow," he snapped. "But I believe he will welcome a period of truce to gain breath."

"And why do you believe that?" She put down her wine, her action as precise and controlled as her words. He knew that language. The beginning of their marriage had been fraught with it.

"Because he too has harvests to bring in; because he too has lost men. He might be fighting for his own gain, but he needs to take stock and decide whom to support: Stephen or Henry. Sooner rather than later it will end and those who are wise will not be caught with their braies around their knees."

Sybilla frowned at him. "When were you thinking of calling this truce?"

"Now, since he is in Shrewsbury for the fair."

"And if I ask you not to?"

He met her gaze and was not reassured by the emotions it contained. Anger, hostility, hurt. "Do you not want to spend a winter at peace and see the people fed because the harvest has been vouchsafed?"

Her lips thinning, she turned away from him. He hardened his resolve. Sybilla was fiercely possessive over Ludlow and distrusted her cousin Gilbert with every bone in her body. Joscelin had always viewed Gilbert as his sworn enemy, but had sufficient pragmatism to see the advantage of talking peace as well as war.

"Would you see us fight ourselves into the ground this winter?" he demanded. "Would you see the harvest fields on fire and the flames reflected on the blade of my sword?"

Her back remained to him, but he saw her flinch at his words and perhaps their tone. "He won't agree to talk with you," she said stiffly.

"That is up to him. At least I can say I have tried."

Sybilla sighed heavily and threw up her hands. "Do as you please," she said. "But if, by some remote chance, he does want to talk, do not expect me to welcome him with open arms."

"I promise I won't." Relieved at her yielding, glad to relinquish his own harsh stance, he went to her and embraced her from behind, leaning around to kiss her cheek and finding it half turned from him.

"Men and their promises," she said and did not relent into a smile.

❖ ❖ ❖

Taking Joscelin's invitation to Gilbert de Lacy was a task that Brunin would rather have forgone, but he was not given a choice.

"You'll never overcome your fears unless you face them," Joscelin had said as he dismissed Brunin with an impatient wave of his hand. "Make haste now."

Brunin had never felt less like making haste, but since Joscelin had commanded with an irascible look in his eyes, he strode out briskly toward de Lacy's lodgings, which were situated over the bridge from the abbey in the town. When he arrived, de Lacy's squires and grooms were preparing to exercise their lord's string of horses. Observing Brunin, the fair-haired squire turned the powerful dun stallion he was riding and came over.

"What do you want?" he demanded, looking Brunin up and down with hauteur but no recognition.

Brunin cleared his throat and forced himself to look up into the hostile, woad-blue eyes. He tried not to think about the dagger resting in the sheath at the young man's right hip. Even after several years, he could still feel his belly tightening and shrinking. "I have a message for Lord Gilbert de Lacy," he said.

"Give it to me. I will make sure he gets it."

Brunin tried to breathe slowly and not show how intimidated he was. "I was told to deliver it in person."

"I doubt that Lord Gilbert will want to trouble himself." The squire nudged the dun forward, forcing Brunin to give ground as the stallion pawed the air with a powerful foreleg.

"Even so, I am charged with the duty." Brunin's throat was tight and it made his voice husky, but at least the words did not emerge as a squeak.

The young man looked irritated. "You'll have to wait," he said. "There's no one to take you to him."

Above them a door opened. A brindle greyhound clattered down the outer stairs, followed at a more sedate pace by Gilbert de Lacy, who was dressed in a split-front riding tunic. The Baron reached the foot of the stairs, opened his mouth to speak to his squire, and stopped as he saw Brunin.

"He says he has brought you a message, my lord," said the young man in a tone that conveyed his contempt for Brunin. "I told him he would have to wait."

Brunin scowled at his tormentor before bowing to Gilbert de Lacy.

"A message?" said de Lacy. "You're de Dinan's squire, are you not? I saw you at the horse fair yester eve trying out that bay nag."

"Yes, sire." Having dropped his gaze for sufficient time to be courteous, Brunin looked up again. The hound thrust its moist nose into his hand and licked his fingers.

"De Dinan bought him too."

The squire sniggered. "Handsome is as handsome does, Ernalt," de Lacy said, waving him about his duties.

Ernalt. Committing the name to memory, Brunin watched him ride off, the dun's muscular haunches flexing and clenching.

De Lacy turned back to Brunin. "I wouldn't have bought the bay myself," he said. "But then I stand on my dignity and that is something that Joscelin de Dinan has never done."

Brunin stiffened at the remark. "The horse will prove himself, sir."

De Lacy looked amused. "Well, either that or he'll prove what an ass his buyer is." He clasped one hand lightly around the hilt of his sword. "So, what message does your lord have for me—aside from 'rot in hell'?" His smile developed a sour edge. "I can think of nothing he could say to me that I would find of interest, unless he is offering to surrender Ludlow."

"My lord requests that you meet with him to talk of a truce between you."

The smile became one of bared teeth. "Indeed?"

"Yes, sire." Brunin watched the pulse beat hard in de Lacy's throat and the ruddy color flow into his face.

"He's a Breton mercenary. I should not be surprised at his gall," de Lacy growled, "and yet I am. Or perhaps there is more to it than that. Why should he want a truce? Are the steps of the dance too fast for him these days?" He spoke above Brunin's head, his eyes narrow and speculative.

Brunin understood that no answer was required. He waited quietly—something that was easier to do now that de Lacy's squires had ridden off.

"Tell him I will come to him when I have finished my business at the fair," de Lacy said. "Perhaps around the hour of noon." He gave Brunin a hard smile. "But tell his wife not to wait the dinner hour for me." He nodded in dismissal and moved to where a lad of about Brunin's own age was holding a copper-colored stallion. Mounting in one smooth motion, he reined about and whistled to the dog.

Brunin closed his eyes, exhaled hard, and took the message back to Joscelin on legs that were suddenly as unsteady as a drunkard's.

# 12

THE YOUNG MAN WAS STANDING IN THE COURTYARD MINDING the horses while Gilbert de Lacy took wine in the house with Joscelin and Sybilla. Perched on his wrist, clinging to a thick leather gauntlet, was a peregrine falcon, a crimson hood covering its fierce gaze. Made allies and rivals by their fascination, Marion and Hawise peered around the corner of the house at the object of their desires.

"I wonder if he's betrothed." Marion ran her hands over her gown, the lacings of which were pulled tight to emphasize her budding breasts and tiny waist.

"I thought your interest was in becoming Lady FitzWarin," Hawise muttered, wishing she had changed her own dress, which had a mud stain on the skirt and a frayed sleeve.

"Your mother said we should have a choice," Marion said sententiously.

Hawise didn't think Marion's interpretation was quite what Sybilla had meant but, given the circumstances, could hardly say so. "What makes you think he'll be interested in you?" she sniffed instead.

"Watch," Marion said in the tone of a master to a particularly inept pupil. Leaving their hiding place, she walked directly toward the young man. Despite her bold approach, her steps were small, coy, and feminine. He looked up from the hawk and the way his gaze widened and filled with appreciation made Hawise burn with jealousy. Marion flirted with him through her lashes. She pointed to the hawk, and he smiled at her and said something, his finger gently stroking the bird's breast feathers. Marion giggled in response and played with her braids, the small gestures she made drawing attention to her throat and the pert curve of her bosom. Hawise ground her teeth. Unable to stand by and watch Marion building a huge advantage, she stepped out to join her.

The squire stared. "Is this your maidservant?" he asked Marion.

Marion giggled with horrified delight. "No," she said, her hand to her mouth. "Hawise is Lord Joscelin's daughter."

The young man bowed to Hawise. "Forgive me, mistress, I should have known," he said, slowly appraising her from head to toe. "There is a strong resemblance."

Hawise reddened, unsure if he was being complimentary or not, although his tone was courteous enough. The way he was smiling created a whirlpool in the center of her pelvis. "And who are you?" she asked imperiously.

He continued to gentle the hawk and the sensual movement of his hand made her shiver. "My name is Ernalt de Lysle, and I am senior squire to Gilbert de Lacy."

"Are you betrothed?" Marion's question was as direct as her gaze was artless.

"Not yet, mistress. Are you?"

Marion shook her head. "I'm Lord Joscelin's ward, and he will not seek a match for me until I reach my fifteenth year day."

"And how far away is that?"

"A little over a twelve-month," Marion said, giving him another of her flirtatious glances. "Lady Sybilla says that girls should marry for love as well as land."

"Does she indeed?" Ernalt thought the girls diverting. He had noticed them watching him and had wondered how long it would take them to approach. Most young women of rank were heavily chaperoned but it did not prevent them from giving their mothers, maids, and sometimes husbands the slip to make assignations. Marion, as she had told him she was named, was as pretty as a kitten, and the manner she had of looking through her lashes was provocative and promising. The de Dinan girl resembled a servant on first glance, but beneath the smirched gown, the outline of her breasts was tempting and that eldritch hair would look magnificent tumbled about her naked body.

These were the women of an enemy household, but that knowledge only added piquancy to the notion of seduction. To snatch and despoil one of de Dinan's chicks would be immensely satisfying. Marion was the prettier and more flirtatious, but she wasn't the daughter of the house. The redhead was wary, but he could sense her hunger, and he had not missed the competitive atmosphere between the girls.

"Is that your hawk?" Marion wanted to know.

"No, mistress, she belongs to Lord Gilbert, but you can stroke her if you want."

Biting her lip, Marion extended her hand and timidly touched the bird. As if sensing the girl's nervousness, it bated its wings and she flinched with a frightened little cry. Observing her response, Ernalt thought that it would be exciting to be the first to touch her, to bruise that pink petal mouth and watch her eyes widen like a wild thing in a snare.

"Would you like to stroke her too?" he asked Hawise de Dinan.

Her red plait rippled with the scornful toss of her head. "I handle hawks all the time," she said. "Give me your gauntlet and I will hold her."

He saw the dagger look flashed at Hawise by the daintier girl and swallowed a smile. Rivalry indeed. Removing a spare gauntlet from his mount's saddlebag, he handed it to Hawise. "Go on then," he said.

She donned the glove with a determined set to her lips and a tiny frown between her eyes. When she took the bird from his hand, it bated its wings, but she soothed it with a gentle voice and a steady touch. "I spend much time with my father's hawks," she said complacently.

"That's true," Marion retorted. "Lady Sybilla is always telling her that she smells of the kennels and the mews." She raised her sleeve to her face as if to protect her nose from a lingering aroma and gave him a look that egged him to agree with her.

Above them a door opened and Ernalt watched de Dinan's squire descend the external stairs, a wine jug in his hand. There was something vaguely familiar about him, which Ernalt was unable to place. The youth's expression was impassive, but the dark eyes were not and, despite his own bullish confidence, Ernalt felt the hair rise on his forearms.

Hawise de Dinan flushed as if she had been caught with her hand down his braies. Marion brazened it out by smiling and waving. The youth let his gaze linger on the trio for a moment, then continued toward the kitchen with the jug.

"Your father's squire is a sour fellow," Ernalt remarked with a laugh to dissipate his unease.

"Don't worry," Marion said. "Brunin won't say anything. Can I hold the hawk?" She pointed at his gauntlet. "I'm not very good, but I'm sure you could teach me."

"His name is Brunin?" Ernalt removed the gauntlet and stared after the squire. Memory hesitated on a brink.

"His father's lord of Whittington," said Marion. "Do you know him?"

"Oh yes," Ernalt said, relief brightening his eyes. "I know him. Scared him half to death when he was a pup. He still looks terrified now." He shrugged one shoulder, to show the girls how insignificant he considered Brunin to be.

Marion gave an excited giggle, her gaze full of admiration. "The hawk," she said breathlessly. "Show me how to hold the hawk."

"You've been shown many times, but you don't like the feel," Hawise said waspishly.

"Perhaps I haven't had the right teacher."

With great reluctance, Hawise transferred the peregrine to Marion's wrist and with satisfaction watched it flutter and flap its wings. Marion leaned away, a frightened look in her eyes.

"No, no. Gently, like this." Ernalt moved to soothe and correct. It was an excuse for his hand to touch Marion's spine solicitously, to linger. For his head to dip toward hers. The hawk danced on its jesses and slowly settled.

"There," he said. "See, that's not so hard is it?"

❖❖❖

"A truce." Gilbert de Lacy sampled the word as if it were some strange food he had been asked to taste and was unsure whether he liked it or not. "I ask myself why you should suggest one now? What do you have to gain? What do I have to lose?"

Joscelin dug his hand through his hair, caught himself in the nervous action, and lowered his arm. "We both gain a breathing space. As to what you have to lose—only you can decide that." He met de Lacy's stare. The blue eyes and the straight dark brows were disconcertingly like Sybilla's but there the resemblance ended. Her cousin's mouth was thinner, his bones sharper and close to the surface like overgrazed pasture, his nose a bony blade.

"You know what I want from you, de Dinan, and it is not a truce," de Lacy growled. "I think that you desire to keep yourself whole until Henry FitzEmpress returns to make yet another attempt on his thwarted inheritance—and you believe it will be easier without me salting your tail."

"Think what you will," Joscelin said with forced indifference. "I have made the offer. It is yours to take or leave."

De Lacy's glance flickered to Sybilla. "What does my fair cousin say?"

She returned him a flat stare. "That you will want in vain, but if you have any sense in your skull you will accept the offer."

He smiled sourly. "Madam, you remind me of the Empress Matilda—a lady now living in exile."

"I take the first as a compliment and the second as a cheap jibe." Sybilla looked to the door as Brunin returned, a replenished jug in his hand. "More wine, my lord?"

He shook his head. "It is not that I do not trust present company, you understand, but that I do not trust myself. Who knows where my tongue might stumble while slackened by drink…and while there is truth in wine, there is danger too."

Joscelin watched Brunin set the jug on the sideboard. The youth's movements were precise, but Joscelin could sense a tension similar to his own. "Whatever happens in the near or distant future, at some point you will have to make your allegiance," Joscelin said. "Or will you gamble on fence-sitting and hope you can bow low enough to the victor when the time comes?"

"Why should it matter to you?" de Lacy asked suspiciously.

"It doesn't. I was suggesting a reason why you might consider my offer generous."

"That depends on the terms." De Lacy leaned back and chewed on his forefinger. "There are truces and truces."

❖ ❖ ❖

"You won't say anything, will you?" Hawise said urgently to Brunin.

It was early afternoon and Gilbert de Lacy had recently left with his handsome squire. De Lacy and her father had agreed to keep peace with each other until the first day of the new year and review the situation then.

Brunin gave her a dark look. "About what?" He was grooming his new horse, although its coat already gleamed like a wet hazelnut.

"You know 'about what,'" she said tersely.

He swept the brush along the gelding's flank. "If you and Marion want to make fools of yourselves, that is your own business."

She reddened. "We were just talking to him."

"Then why ask me to watch my tongue?"

"Because he's de Lacy's squire and my parents wouldn't approve—even if a truce has been agreed."

"And with good reason." He ceased grooming the horse and

turned to look at her. "Hawise, have a care. I've tangled with him before and he is not to be trusted."

"He said that he had frightened you once. Perhaps you still hold a grudge."

"Perhaps you would too if he had held a knife to your throat."

"He was probably just teasing you," she said defensively.

Brunin's stare was contemptuous. "Oh yes," he said acidly. "How stupid of me. Teasing was all it was, even while the blood was running down my neck."

She turned her back on him with an abrupt movement, not wanting to hear.

"Did you not see the way he was playing you and Marion against each other for the pleasure of it? With his looks he can have any woman he wants. Why should he settle for two foolish little girls?"

"I'm not foolish and I'm not a little girl!" she shouted at him.

He looked at her.

"I hate you!" Hawise spun on her heel and stamped from the stables, vowing that she would never talk to him again. Ernalt wasn't like that; she knew he wasn't. No one who stroked a hawk with such gentleness would threaten a child with a knife. Probably Brunin had done something to annoy him and then been oversensitive to Ernalt's retaliation. With equal determination she dismissed Brunin's remark about Ernalt playing her and Marion against each other. Marion was a dreadful flirt. Ernalt was bound to respond to her; that didn't mean he had been encouraging rivalry between them. He had said that he hoped to see them around the fair on the morrow and that now his lord was at truce with her father, perhaps there would be more opportunity to talk. He was nice and Brunin was the one being foolish.

❖❖❖

On the third day of the fair, Brunin's father arrived to make some belated purchases. He had left his womenfolk at Whittington and was accompanied only by his retinue. "Trouble over the border," he said succinctly to Joscelin as the men drank wine at one of the vintners' booths. "Iorwerth Goch and the sons of Wrenoc ap Tudor have been raiding and I have had to put a deal of effort into protecting my boundaries." His tone was morose. "Ap Tudor claims Whittington by right of birth because his grandsire once held the land of the Earls of Mercia, but they lost that right a long time ago, before the death of the first King William."

"Losing a right doesn't stop the loser from trying to regain it," Joscelin said, with all the bitterness of personal knowledge.

"I will give them the ground to bury their dead," FitzWarin said savagely. Then he shook himself and found a smile of sorts. "I hear you have been using diplomacy to make your eyrie a safer place from your own would-be predators."

"For the time being." Joscelin looked pensive. "If I am fortunate, it will last until the harvests are in."

FitzWarin swirled the wine in his cup. "Think you that Henry will come soon? Does your son-in-law at Hereford hear anything?"

"Only that preparations are in place. Louis of France and that fool Eustace are chasing Henry around Normandy to no avail. He has the measure of both of them."

"If he misjudges, we could end up with 'that fool Eustace' as our next king," FitzWarin said grimly.

"I doubt it. The Church won't let Stephen confirm him as next in line to the throne, and even those who would follow Stephen to the ends of the earth would turn their mounts aside from tipping over the edge with Eustace."

FitzWarin gave a snort of bleak amusement. "You are right about that," he said. The humor froze on his face and he stared. "God on the Cross, what is that?" His eyes bulged.

Joscelin turned. Brunin was leading his new horse toward them. While the men had engaged in conversation, he had been told to run back to the lodging and fetch him.

"That," said Joscelin hastily, "is a bargain disguised as a disaster. I know what you are thinking, but reserve your judgment until you have studied his paces." He drained his wine and stood up. "Right." He clapped his hands together. "I had better find my wife and daughters before they bleed my coffers dry. You have seen little enough of the lad recently. You'll want some time alone with him."

"If I did not know you better, I would say you were absconding before the storm," FitzWarin growled.

"It is well you know me then," Joscelin retorted and departed with a wave, pausing only to slap the bay gelding on the neck in passing and wink at Brunin.

❖❖❖

Ernalt de Lysle was buying a new strap and buckle for his belt at one of the lorimer's booths when Sybilla and her retinue drew near upon a similar purpose. It seemed like chance, but it wasn't. He had been watching and awaiting his opportunity for some time. He spoke the women fair, and Sybilla, although cool in her greeting, was disposed to allow him to stroll with them awhile. Hawise's stomach fluttered almost as much as Marion's lashes. He was impeccably polite toward the girls, but now and again, when Sybilla's back was turned, he would return Marion's flirtatiousness with a wink, or smile at Hawise in a way that made her bones melt.

He accompanied them to the cookstalls and further ingratiated himself by holding a hot pie with his hawking gauntlet while the women broke pieces off. Then Sybilla met an old friend, and de Lacy's second squire arrived.

"Lord Gilbert's looking for you," he said breathlessly. "Best make haste. You know what he's like if he's kept waiting."

Ernalt nodded. "A moment." Carefully removing the gauntlet so as not to spill the portion of pie still resting in the palm, he presented it to Hawise. "I'll return for it later," he murmured, his voice so low that it carried no further than the short breath between them. "Meet me at your stables at compline."

She stared at him, heat flooding her face, but he had already turned away and was following the other squire through the crowds.

Marion narrowed her eyes. "What did he just say to you?"

"I...nothing." Hawise's heart was hammering so loudly that she was certain everyone would hear. She swallowed. "Nothing," she repeated. "He just said to be careful not to drop the pie." Her, he wanted to see her, not Marion. Her body sang like a plucked harpstring.

"I don't believe you."

Hawise set her jaw and prepared to brazen it out. "Believe what you want," she said. "You are jealous because he gave the glove to me and not you."

Hawise had hit the mark: Marion pouted and put her nose in the air. "He gave it to you because you remind him of a servant," she retorted spitefully.

Once the pie was finished, Hawise dusted the crumbs from the glove and folded it through her belt. She spent the rest of the afternoon in a daze, taking scant notice of the spice-vendors' booths, the hose-sellers, the cages of brightly colored finches, exotic coneys, and striped cats. She responded to her mother's exasperated questions with vague replies, until Sybilla threatened to have her examined by a physician. Marion too came in for the sharp side of Sybilla's tongue, with a warning that if the wind changed, Marion would be left with a bottom lip to stand a cauldron upon. Only Sibbi escaped the scolding, and she regarded the other two with bewilderment.

Once back at their lodging, Hawise lovingly cleaned the grease from the glove with fuller's earth and dusted it off with a brush made of badger hair. Marion flounced away to her pallet, complaining of a stomachache. At first she rejected Sibbi's offer of a soothing rub, but as Sibbi made to leave her alone, grabbed her hand and made her stay. Any attention was better than none.

The evening meal was an impromptu one of goods bought from the stalls at the fair. There were large mushrooms stuffed with breadcrumbs and cheese, chicken pasties, griddle bread, tangy smoked sausages, honey cakes, and spicy fruit loaves. Hawise, who would usually have devoured such fare and looked for more, pushed the morsels around her dish, feeling as if her stomach were clamped to her spine.

"I hope you are not sickening for something," Sybilla said, looking concerned. "There are often foul airs at large gatherings like these."

"I am all right, Mama." Hawise took a drink of wine to wash down the mouthful of bread that would otherwise have stuck in her throat. "I'm just not hungry."

Sybilla was plainly unconvinced. Her glance went to Marion who was lying on her pallet and had said she was not hungry either.

Joscelin paused chewing. "It's probably shopping sickness," he jested. "I'd have it too, after three days of wandering the stalls out there." He smiled at Hawise and then at his wife. "You worry too much. There is nothing wrong with them but the tiredness of excitement. Early to sleep, ready for the morrow's journey home, will soon sort them out." He reached for another sausage. "These are excellent."

Hawise felt a jolt of alarm. She didn't want to be sent to bed… not yet at least, but she knew better than to make a huge protest. Circumspection was called for.

Following the evening meal, her mother set about packing their traveling chests for the journey home. Helping her and Sibbi, Hawise felt the time crawl by like a beetle up a long blade of grass. Hugh went out to fetch a new pair of shoes that a cordwainer had promised to have ready by dusk. They heard his tuneful whistle fading as he ran down the solar steps and crossed the yard.

The compline bell rang out from the abbey, the sound sweet and plangent on the evening air. Hawise secured the hasp on the chest containing fabric for new winter cloaks and, murmuring that she needed to visit the privy, left the room. Her mother was too busy trying to fit all their purchases into the inadequate space available to reply with more than an absent wave of the hand.

Relieved to have escaped so easily, Hawise opened the door and descended the outer stairs to the courtyard. The shadows had begun to lengthen and the wash of sun on the side of the stable wall had shaded from the afternoon's primrose to deep rose-gold. Hawise glanced rapidly around, her heart thumping. Would he come to the tryst? If he did, what would she say? Would they just talk or would he try to kiss her? The thought was frightening and delicious, and she had to steel herself to go on and not run back up the stairs.

Cautiously she entered the stables. The light was muted and fragrant with the aroma of hay and horses. There was no sign of the grooms and stable boys who were away in the alehouses, enjoying the last evening of the fair. The horses dozed in their stalls, loose-hipped, tails swishing. He wasn't here. Relief and sharp disappointment coursed through her.

"Aha, you managed to escape then?"

Hawise stifled a scream as Ernalt stepped out of the shadows. His hair gleamed in the darkness like the palest barley straw.

"I…Yes…I…" She struggled for coherence. "I cannot stay long," she whispered. "My mother thinks I am visiting the privy." His closeness made her feel giddy.

"Well-thought-of, nonetheless."

"I've…I've brought your glove." She tugged it from her belt and held it out to him.

He took it from her, using the moment when he grasped the fingers to pull her toward him. "I have been thinking of you all day," he said and his hand touched hers over the plush, talon-scarred leather.

Hawise swallowed. "I doubt that," she said, trembling like a foal with fear and excitement.

"It's true, I swear it. To distraction and the shirking of my duties."

"What about Marion?"

"What about her?" His right hand held hers. His left moved stealthily to encircle her waist.

"I thought you liked her too."

"She is pretty, for certain, but I prefer women who are capable and daring." He moved closer. She felt his breath on her cheek and equal proportions of pleasure and panic jolted through her body. "It's you I want," he said and kissed her.

Hawise responded tentatively, but when his tongue entered her mouth and began making small thrusting motions, she drew back sharply.

He gave a sleepy smile, his predator's gaze calculating, and pressed his mouth to her throat instead, sucking there until she shivered. Taking her hand, he pushed it down between them. "See what you do to me?" he murmured.

Hawise knew enough from whispered discussions with Sibbi and Marion and from snippets garnered elsewhere that a man's member grew stiff when he was aroused, in order that he could mate, but she had never seen one in such a condition, much less touched one. Even separated from her hand by his braies, the feel of it was thrilling and terrifying—the latter in ascendance, especially when he groaned. She tried to snatch her hand away, but his grip tightened and he moved it back and forth with his own. "That's it," he said. "Like that."

"I have to go," she gasped. "My mother will be wondering where I am…"

"Not yet. Stay awhile…just a little while," he cajoled. "Be sweet to me."

Hawise had once heard one of the guards at Ludlow inveigling a tavern wench to "be sweet" to him as he plundered her unfastened bodice and pushed her against the castle wall.

"I can't. I thought we were just going to talk a little…"

"Talk?" He grinned. "Who comes to a tryst in a stables at dusk to talk?"

She struggled in his grip, beginning to panic. "Let me go."

He held on to her, his left arm an iron band around her waist, his right hand still trapping hers at his crotch. "I promise I won't despoil you if that's your worry. I know ways…"

Thoroughly alarmed, Hawise dug her fingernails into the bulge in his braies and was rewarded by an agonized yelp. She thrust away from him and tried to run, but he stuck out his foot, tripped her, and brought her down hard in the straw. The wind flew from her lungs and as she lay stunned he climbed on top of her, pinning her with his weight, grinding his hips against her buttocks. "I can be as gentle as a dove or as savage as a hawk," he muttered beside her ear. "Which is it to be?"

Hooves clopped in the yard, a horse snorted, and a shadow darkened the doorway. Raising her head, Hawise saw Jester's comical blaze and pricked furry ears, and Brunin standing at the bridle, his eyes widening in astonishment and then filling with rage. Ernalt started to rise but was only halfway up when Brunin leaped at him, knocking him sideways into the straw. A well-aimed fist drove the air from Ernalt's body and a follow-through blow caught the squire square in the mouth. An oath of shock and surprise sprayed bloodily from the squire's lips and even though he was wounded, he pounced on Brunin. The latter blocked the descending blow with his forearm and tried to kick and roll, but Ernalt was athwart him and, being several stones heavier, was not going to budge. Sobbing, Hawise grabbed the gauntlet lying in the straw, where it had fallen during their struggle, and set about belaboring Ernalt with it. The hard leather fingers whipped across his cheek and caught him in the corner of the eye. His arms came up in defense and Brunin was able to dislodge him, throw him, and reverse their positions.

"In the name of Christ, what's all this?" demanded Hugh, striding into the midst of the fracas. Casting aside the pair of boots, which had been tucked under his arm, he seized Brunin and hauled him off his adversary.

Ernalt struggled to his feet, his tunic and hose stuck with straw. Blood dripped steadily from his cut lip. A red weal striped one cheekbone and vanished at its upper edge into the puffy flesh around his right eye.

Hawise whimpered, knowing that she was in the worst trouble of her life, her reputation in tatters.

"It's my fault. I started it," Brunin panted, one arm bent across his midriff. He sent a glare toward Ernalt and a warning look at Hawise. "I had an old score to settle."

Hugh's brows rose into his thick brown fringe. "An old score?" His tone was incredulous.

"My own business," Brunin answered stiffly.

"Not when it involves a squire of Gilbert de Lacy's, it isn't." Hugh's usually mild hazel eyes were aglitter as he looked between the three of them.

"I came to fetch my hawking gauntlet," Ernalt said, pressing the back of his hand to his bleeding mouth. "The ladies borrowed it from me at the cookstalls, and I need it early on the morrow...Then this dolt set upon me like a wild beast." It was a plausible version of the truth with major omissions...omissions that Hawise dared not contradict unless she wanted to be ruined, and he knew it.

Hugh looked at Brunin. "Is this true?"

Brunin glared at de Lysle. "The bastard has owed me this for four years," he said in a smoldering voice.

"Go piss your hose," snarled de Lysle.

Brunin lunged, and Hugh had to brace his forearm and thrust him back. "Get out," he said curtly to de Lysle. "And stay away if you value your life. A truce is not friendship." He laid his hand to the hilt of his sword to emphasize his meaning.

"No, it isn't," Ernalt retorted. "You had best look to yourselves in the hour that it ends." He spat a mouthful of bloody saliva into the straw. Head down, he started from the stable, then paused before Hawise and held out his hand. "My gauntlet, demoiselle."

She pushed it at him, her chin trembling and her eyes blazing with revulsion.

Hugh exhaled hard into the silence following de Lysle's departure and slowly uncurled his fingers from his sword grip.

Hawise swallowed. "Hugh, I…"

He held up his hand, the palm and fingers imprinted with the mark of the hilt binding. "Say nothing," he warned, his expression grim. "I knew there would be trouble the moment he joined us at the fair." He curled his lip and his voice thickened with contempt. "Taking an interest in booths of women's fripperies, sharing pasties indeed. He had only one thing in mind, and I'm certain it wasn't collecting his hawking gauntlet."

Hawise fiddled with the long end of her belt and flushed bright red with chagrin.

Hugh shook his head. "Best return to the chamber and say nothing of any of this," he said to her. "Brunin, see to your horse. I trust you to keep your mouth shut in the guardroom."

Brunin nodded and, without looking at Hawise, went to fetch Jester, who was snatching at some weedy grass poking up beside the stable's outer wall.

Hawise shook out her skirts and on wobbly legs headed for the sanctuary of the upstairs chamber, but, as she set her foot on the steps, Hugh caught her arm. "If I see him near you or Marion…or Sibbi again, I'll nail his balls to Ludlow's gates and go straight to your father. Understood? I mean what I say."

Chastened and ashamed, Hawise nodded. "Yes," she whispered. "Thank you, Hugh."

"Go on." He released her with an abrupt wave of his hand and turned back to Brunin who was tethering Jester in the stables. "God's life," he growled, digging his fingers through his hair, "that's one truce almost broken before it's born. What really happened?"

Brunin gave him a level look. "I think you have guessed the biggest part of it for yourself," he said. "She thought it was innocent play but he wanted bloodsport…and he got it, but not as he expected." He examined his grazed knuckles. "What I said about an old score was true, though."

Hugh rubbed his hands over his face. "Better get one of the

men to look at your fist," he said. "You don't want it going septic."
Stooping, he retrieved his boots from the straw and smoothed his
hand over the new leather.

"It won't," Brunin said. "Not if there's any justice in the world."

"In that case you had better offer up some prayers too," Hugh
said wryly.

❖ ❖ ❖

Brunin was in the undercroft where the soldiers had made their
beds when Hawise appeared bearing her mother's box of salves
and remedies. He surmised that she must have seen him leave the
stables and cross the yard from the upper window and that she had
been waiting her moment.

"Is not one escapade in a day enough for you?" he demanded
curtly as he set about unrolling his straw-stuffed mattress.

"I have my mother's permission. I told her that I had met
you in the stable yard and that you had hurt your hand." She
sat down on the low wooden campstool beside the mattress and
unfastening the satchel withdrew a small earthenware jar. "Honey
salve," she said.

Brunin knelt back from his pallet. "It's no more than a graze,"
he said without looking at her. "One of the men can tend it."

"No, please. I want to do it."

"Why? To make your guilt go away?"

"You were right," she said in a small voice. "I should not have
trusted him."

"No, you should not."

Hawise turned her head away, but he heard the choked sound
she made. She raised one hand and rubbed it swiftly across her
eyes. Brunin didn't know what to do. Weeping was Marion's art
and preserve.

She turned back to him, her face so rigid with control that she
looked like her father when he went into battle. "He left his glove
behind," she said, her voice wobbling with strain. "He made me
laugh and was so kind that I saw no harm in meeting him to return

it. I thought he wanted a few moments to talk to me in private—away from Marion. I wanted it to be a sweet tryst, not…" She made a gesture and he saw her mouth twist with revulsion. "You were right. I was being a simpleton."

He thought of the rough, masculine talk between the grooms, squires, and knights of Joscelin's company. He had learned much from keeping his mouth closed and his ears open. Women expected "sweet trysts" and those men who had the art of persuasion could often talk a woman into the bedstraw. Those who didn't, or who found their partners unwilling despite cajolery, had either to resort to rougher kinds of wooing or remain frustrated. The men exchanged the best lines of love talk as if they were passwords into the place between a woman's legs. There were crude names for the women who yielded and equally crude ones for those who slapped faces and refused, all of it far distant from the wooing that women craved and seldom received.

"Here," he said and gave her his right hand with its raw, scraped knuckles. "Since you have brought the salve especially."

Taking it, she composed herself with a loud sniff and another wipe of her eyes. "Thank you," she said with a watery smile.

Brunin shrugged. "I needed little excuse," he replied, thinking of hard hands pinning him down, of a knife's cold burn at his throat and the hot sting of urine down his leg. The debt wasn't paid yet by half.

# 13

CROWMARSH, BANK OF THE RIVER THAMES, AUGUST 1153

*M*OVING SWIFTLY AND QUIETLY, BRUNIN POURED WINE FOR Joscelin, his father, and Earl Roger of Hereford. Beyond the sheltering canvas, the August sun blazed upon the tents of Prince Henry's army and dazzled like millions of coins on the surface of the Thames. It also magnified the stink of recent battle. The particles of settling dust reeked of blood, excrement, and sweat. An attempt to take the siege tower guarding the bridge to Wallingford had just failed.

"Well," snarled FitzWarin. "That was a waste of time." Blood-stained saliva dribbled from the corner of his mouth. A blow above his shield rim had knocked out a tooth.

"We had to try," gasped Roger of Hereford. "And it might have worked." He gulped down the wine and signaled Brunin for a refill. His hand was trembling and his thin face streaming with sweat. He had been unwell throughout the spring and early summer with a persistent low fever, and although he had improved during the last month, the exertion of battle had taken its toll. "A siege will take longer, but the outcome is not in doubt."

"How reassuring," Joscelin said acidly, holding out his own cup for a refill. "Do Stephen's men in their tower know that?"

Roger grimaced. "They will," he said.

Unobtrusively, Brunin set out a bowl of new cheese seasoned

with herbs and a basket of bread. The latter was going stale, but was not bad for army rations grabbed on the move.

Henry had arrived in England in the middle of a raw, wet January and immediately set about making his presence felt. His invasion force had been small, no more than a hundred and forty knights and three thousand foot soldiers, but his ranks had immediately been swelled by the English barons who had rallied to his banner. Brunin had been living an interesting and itinerant life for the past seven months as Henry moved from town to town, laying claim, besieging, taking; sometimes being embraced with open arms; on other occasions having to fight for every inch of ground.

Brunin and Joscelin had made sporadic returns to Ludlow or Hereford, but these were mere days of respite while they changed horses and garnered fresh supplies. Henry and Stephen had circled each other warily like two hostile dogs. In the early days there had been the threat of a major battle at Malmesbury, but the swollen River Avon had separated the two armies and Stephen had stepped away from the confrontation.

"Losing the control and support of his men," Joscelin had said, and in his gaze there had been a mingling of pity and satisfaction.

Losing control or not, the skirmishing and circling had continued throughout the spring and summer. Henry had celebrated Easter at Gloucester in grand style, as if already king, but the fact remained that vast areas of England still held loyal to Stephen and nothing was resolved. Now Henry had come to the rescue of a beleaguered Wallingford, but first his army had to get past the guard tower that Stephen had built to prevent passage across the river.

"I hate sieges," FitzWarin complained. "The men sit about on their arses and grow quarrelsome. There's only so many you can post to man the trebuchets or send foraging. They drink, dice, and whore. They fill up the latrines and get siege-belly from the miasmas. Worse than that, they start killing each other instead of the enemy."

Joscelin raised his cup in toast. "The voice of experience," he said and looked at Brunin. "I hope you're listening to your father, lad."

"Yes, sire," Brunin said.

"Aye." FitzWarin gave a harsh bark of laughter. "Especially about the drink, dice, and whores, if I'm any judge of his years."

"I train my squires better than that, and besides, I lead by example," Joscelin said righteously. "If he knows about those things, it is not from me."

FitzWarin snorted and looked at his son. "You have nothing to say, boy?"

"No, my lord. I listen and learn," Brunin answered with a gleam in his eye that made the older man give a reluctant chuckle before waving him away.

The men returned to the serious business of discussing how long the siege would take; how many engines to use; whether they should try a night sortie to fire the timbers of the siege castle walls. And Brunin listened and learned, absorbing all and storing it for future use.

In the morning, Brunin went to help Roger of Hereford's trebuchet team assemble one of the siege machines that had been brought to Crowmarsh in dismantled sections. It was hard work positioning and nailing the timbers. The stone-thrower worked on a counterweight system: the long, stone-laden arm drawn down by a sturdy winch at the center of the structure and released by a trigger at the back.

"Won't be ready until the afternoon at least," said the foreman, blotting his forehead on his sweating brow.

Stripped to his shirt and braies, Brunin took a swig from his water costrel and squinted through the sun dazzle at the upright posts they had nailed together. "What about ammunition?"

"Stones in that cart behind. Some of the serjeants can go for-aging for more. Of course, we've got to get the range first. That'll take a couple of attempts."

"How do you—" The question went unasked as the sound of a horn blared across the river and was answered by more horns from the soldiers trapped in their siege tower.

Brunin shaded his eyes and stared across the water. Amidst a churn of dust, he saw the familiar glint of armor and ripple of banners.

"Looks as if the stakes have just risen," the trebuchet foreman muttered.

Hearing a snort and the clink of harness, Brunin turned to see Gilbert de Lacy drawing rein beside the trebuchet, Ernalt de Lysle following close behind.

"Well, well," said de Lacy to no one in particular, a half-smile on his lips, "now we arrive at the crux."

The truce between him and Joscelin had held until January and then had been renewed as Henry landed and made his play for the crown. De Lacy had opted to throw in his lot with Henry and had used the decision to needle Joscelin at every opportunity. He might not be raiding Joscelin's lands, but he could and did keep prodding him verbally. Now, he studied the growing dust cloud of men across the river before turning his stallion toward the tents. His gaze fell on Brunin among the trebuchet team, and he inclined his head as he rode past.

"Tell your lord that a reckoning comes," he said. "Perhaps sooner than he thinks."

Sending a silent snarl in Brunin's direction, de Lysle followed his lord, but rode his horse so close to Brunin that he was forced to leap aside before he was trodden on. Brunin had no intention of telling Joscelin anything, but he went in search of him nevertheless. If there was indeed an army across the river, then the game was afoot.

❖❖❖

"Leave that," Joscelin said as Brunin picked up the wyvern shield to check it for battle readiness. "There won't be any fighting today or tomorrow, or the next one." He pointed to the flagon.

"Sire?" Brunin fixed him with a questioning gaze. Abandoning the shield, he poured wine. Joscelin had just returned from a meeting of the barons in Henry's tent, and lines of strain furrowed his brow and tightened his mouth corners.

"We're striking camp." Joscelin took the wine and gulped it down.

"But…but what about Stephen's army? What about the relief of Wallingford?"

"What about them?" Joscelin stood up, took the flagon from Brunin, and poured himself a second cup. "Stephen wants to fight Henry because he thinks that he can win. Eustace wants to fight Henry because he knows that defeating and killing him in pitched battle is the only way he's ever going to get a sniff of the crown. Henry wants to fight them because he thinks he can defeat them outright—he's already trounced Eustace in Normandy." He gave Brunin a glance from beneath his brows to see if the youth was following him. "But no one else desires a battle, myself included. There is too much to lose."

Brunin nodded but looked uncertain.

"Archbishop Anselm and the Bishop of Winchester are trying to negotiate a lasting settlement. Why should we risk it all now on a single throw of the dice?"

Brunin frowned. "So why are we in the field at all?"

"Think about it." Joscelin said. "While the main armies are apart, they can dare small bites at each other's territory without too much risk. But bring them face to face and it becomes all or nothing. A different prospect entirely." He grimaced. "Prince Henry didn't see it in those terms, of course. His face turned redder than his hair and he threatened grief to us all if we didn't do as he said, but it's just the same in Stephen's camp. None of his lords wants to fight."

"So what happens to Crowmarsh and Wallingford?"

"It has been agreed that the siege tower will come down and both armies will leave and seek other targets."

Brunin controlled his response, but not well enough.

"What is it?" Joscelin demanded. "Do not tell me that your belly is full of fire for a fight?"

"No, my lord."

"What then? Come on, out with it."

Brunin sighed. "It seems so...so..." He wrestled with the word. "...dishonorable," he said at last. "To come to the point of battle and then to shirk away because of too great a fear of loss."

"I see," Joscelin said in a biting tone. "So, you agree with Henry and Stephen; you would risk your all rather than settle for a negotiated peace? You would risk seeing your men slaughtered and all your plans perhaps brought to naught? Indeed, you surprise me."

Color branded Brunin's cheekbones and he drew himself up. "Indeed I would settle for a negotiated peace above battle," he said. "But that is exactly what it would be. I would not ride away and attack some lesser target because I thought it was easy plunder."

Joscelin sighed wearily. "You ride a high horse, lad. When you have lived in this world as long as I have and been on as many campaigns, you will see wrong and right in subtle and patterned shades. If the truth were known, I suspect much of your irritation stems from the fact that you're not going to see that trebuchet launch a stone after you've spent all morning erecting it."

Brunin's flush darkened for Joscelin was not far off the target.

"Well, that's the way of war too." Draining his second cup, Joscelin went to the tent entrance. "It will doubtless suit your notion of honor that I am not accompanying Prince Henry in search of softer targets."

"Where are we going, my lord?"

"Where do you think?" Joscelin answered over his shoulder. "Home to Ludlow."

Brunin's expression brightened.

"Best go and help them dismantle that trebuchet," Joscelin said.

He watched Brunin run between the tents until he was lost to sight and chewed on his thumb knuckle. Gilbert de Lacy had been at the meeting of the barons, and he had offered to ride into battle at Henry's side. Not subtle in the least. Hoping that it would tip the scales.

"Should I have done the same?" Joscelin murmured.

"Sir?" Hugh, who was returning from a conversation with some of Hereford's knights, gave him a questioning look.

"Nothing." Joscelin tipped the cloudy wine dregs onto the ground outside the tent. "I was thinking aloud." He stared at the red puddle for a moment, then shook himself out of his ill humor and smiled at Hugh. "Time to return home and celebrate a marriage," he said to the young man.

❖ ❖ ❖

Silver pins poking from between her folded lips, Sybilla worked on the hem of Sibbi's wedding gown. The fabric was a heavy, deep-red wool damask that suited Sibbi's black hair and fair skin. "You look just like your mother did on her wedding day to Lord Payne," said Annora, her mother's chief maid, her expression misty. "All that curly black hair and those blue eyes. If that boy isn't smitten beyond all recovering, then he's a stone."

Sibbi blushed with pleasure. Hawise thought that her sister did indeed look beautiful, but even without the bridal gown Hugh was besotted. Since his return from Wallingford, they had scarcely been able to take their eyes off each other. Folk were always stumbling over them hand in hand, or kissing in corners.

Brunin came into the chamber from battle practice, bearing Joscelin's wyvern shield. Hawise could remember a time when the shield had been bigger than he was and too heavy for him to bear for longer than a dozen heartbeats. He carried it casually now, his fist curled lightly around the inner strap. His hair was dripping with sweat and hung in his eyes and there were damp patches on his shirt. A pungent aroma coiled about him. His whalebone practice sword hung in a sheath at his hip, its weight and balance the same as a steel blade.

"Hugh isn't with you?" Sybilla said, casting around swiftly for a cloak to cover the wedding gown.

"No, my lady. He knew you were making wedding preparations, so he stayed in the hall."

Sybilla relaxed. "You hear that?" She smiled at Sibbi. "You have a treasure beyond worth there. A man who thinks before he treads—rare as hen's teeth. I hope you are listening too, Brunin."

"Yes, my lady…and learning," he added graciously as he went to prop the shield beside Joscelin's coffer. Marion's nose wrinkled fastidiously. When he turned back into the room, she exaggerated the expression and folded her arms.

"A knight would not enter a lady's presence stinking like a hot horse," she admonished.

Brunin halted. "A lady would not call attention to the fact," he retorted, flourished her the bow of an accomplished courtier, and left the room.

Marion clucked her tongue and looked affronted. Hawise giggled. "You asked for that," she said.

"There are worse things in a man than the smell of honest sweat, believe me," Sybilla said as she finished pinning the hem of Sibbi's gown and stood back.

"You could always offer to bathe him," Hawise said mischievously.

"Don't be foolish," Marion snapped. "I couldn't do that unless I were betrothed to him."

Hawise bit back a smile. Marion's eye might wander over the various squires and young men who visited Ludlow, but she still considered Brunin to be "her" property and had made it known that barring a marriage offer from royalty, she expected to become Lady FitzWarin. No one had ever agreed with her, but neither had she been contradicted and it was the latter which mattered in Marion's mind.

"The way you spoke to him, he probably thinks it is a good thing you are not," Hawise said artlessly. "Still, I do not suppose you'd want him when he has no notions of finesse."

"Hawise, stop teasing and pass me that roll of gold braid," Sybilla said with a warning glance.

Marion pouted, but quickly forgot her pique when Sybilla bid her fetch the jewel casket so they could decide whether to decorate Sibbi's belt with pearls or garnets.

Hawise handed her mother the braid and was not surprised when Sybilla sent her on an errand to summon the chaplain with whom she wanted to speak. Hawise knew it was a pretext to separate herself and Marion for a while. Of late, they could not share each other's company for more than a few minutes without bickering. The petty squabbles of childhood had changed as their bodies changed, becoming more complex, more wounding, less easily forgiven and forgotten.

Her father was in the hall talking to Hugh and several knights. She passed them by and went out of the door into the bailey, intending to cross to the chapel. Brunin was standing by the well housing. Stripped to his braies, he was vigorously washing himself in a horse pail, using a linen rag and a jar of soap. His skin was darkly tanned on face and hands where it had been most exposed to the sun. The rest of his torso was a pale, smooth gold. Hawise stared at his flat, taut belly and the stripe of dark fuzz disappearing into his braies as he stooped to the bucket. The wet, black strands of his hair against the nape of his neck. She felt as if her lungs had plummeted into her stomach for suddenly it was impossible to breathe. He was Brunin. She had romped with him and teased him, treated him as a brother, a friend, and a nuisance. A short while ago she had watched him walk into her mother's chamber and had laughed at his exchange with Marion, her awareness of him casual and unthinking. But gazing at him now, she felt as if she were staring at a stranger.

He looked up from his ablutions and his gaze met hers, dark as sable. However, he seemed to sense none of her tension and his grin flashed.

"You think she'll find me presentable now?"

"Who?" Hawise asked vaguely.

"Marion, of course. The soap's only what's used on the

linens—not scented. But I suppose smelling like a tablecloth is better than a hot horse."

Hawise found a smile from somewhere. His words seemed to be going in one ear and out of the other. With an effort she tore her eyes from the line of hair running down into his braies. "You want to impress her?"

His grin broadened. "Marion's never impressed," he said. "But she was right. If I'm to stand attendance, I need to sweeten myself. Your father pushed us hard today and it's been harvest-hot." He glanced toward the sweltering blue of the sky and thrust his wet hair off his forehead in a gesture that made Hawise feel hot too. Then he looked at her again.

"What is it?" he asked. "What's wrong?"

"Nothing," she said in a flustered voice. "I'm on an errand for my mother. I can't stop." But she did not move and the moment stretched out.

His brows drew together in a look of puzzlement, and then his eyes broke contact with hers as a courier galloped into the bailey and flung down from his sweating horse. The beast's flanks were pumping like bellows and its nostrils were as wide as red goblet-rims.

The tension that had been gripping Hawise dissipated as she focused on the messenger. No one rode a horse like that in this heat unless he had vital news and, in this uncertain climate, that news could be either joyous or devastating.

Throwing down the washcloth, Brunin slung his shirt over one shoulder and ran toward the man, Hawise hard on his heels, the chaplain forgotten. Her father arrived and thrust his own wine cup into the man's hand. The messenger grabbed it and drank in deep, grateful gulps.

"King Stephen's son Eustace is dead!" he gasped out when he had finished and, although he tried for gravity, there was a joyous light in his eyes.

"Dead?" Joscelin repeated. "How? In battle?"

"No, my lord. He choked on a fish bone after he had desecrated the lands of the abbey of St. Edmund. Men are saying it is the retribution of the saint." The messenger crossed himself and bowed his head in a pious gesture that was spoiled by the grin tugging at his mouth corners.

"God have mercy on his soul." Joscelin murmured and crossed himself too; those around him followed suit, but everyone's eyes were gleaming, for they all knew that it brought an end to war that bit closer. Stephen's eldest son had always been ambitious to inherit the crown and it was his refusal to concede his right that had been delaying the negotiations for a peaceful settlement. With Eustace gone, the path was open and King Stephen isolated.

"There is more," the messenger declared as a groom arrived to walk his horse around and cool it off. A broad smile lit his face and he raised the dregs of his cup on high in toast. "Prince Henry's Duchess Eleanor was delivered of a son on the same day that Eustace died. He has been christened William, and he thrives!"

Loud whoops and cheers followed his words. Turning, Joscelin slapped Brunin on his bare, sun-hot shoulder. "Go and tell the butler to broach a cask of the best wine," he said with a new-moon grin. "It might be in bad taste to dance at tidings of Eustace's death, but a birth must be celebrated in the proper fashion."

"Yes, sire!" Brunin departed with alacrity.

Joscelin hugged Hawise to his side and gave her a smacking kiss on the cheek, then turned toward the outer stairs. "Let us go and tell your mother the news!"

❖ ❖ ❖

Although Hawise's reaction to the sight of Brunin in his braies had been a revelation, it was one that she did not have time to think about. The double news of birth and death threw Ludlow into a turmoil of celebration and she was kept busy helping her mother organize an impromptu feast. By the time she saw Brunin again, she had more than spurious errands to the chaplain to think about, and he was fully dressed in a clean shirt and summer linen tunic, with tasks of his own.

Later, when she did have leisure to ponder the matter, Brunin had been relieved of his duties and, in the way typical of young males let loose at a feast, had joined the younger knights and attendants to enjoy the celebration with a drinking game. Watching his folly, Hawise could not summon an echo of the way she had felt that afternoon. It was like that other time she preferred not to remember: when she had longed for the sweetness of romance and discovered the violence of lust.

One of the knights started up a song, and the others, including Brunin, joined in. They all knew the words by rote and Hawise realized that it was the one about the maidens and the ginger cat that she had once heard her father slurring when he was drunk and having an injury tended. She had never heard the denouement of the song because her mother had been too swift, but there was no help for it now. It involved days and nights of non-stop copulation, the women's appetites so insatiable that the hero had difficulty satisfying them.

Hawise listened in fascination. Her father, although not joining in, was chuckling. With narrowed eyes her mother declared that it was time for the women to withdraw from the hall and duly saw to the evacuation.

"Are you angry?" Hawise asked her.

Her mother sighed. "No," she said. "God knows, when you have fighting men gathered together in one place and you let the wine run freely, you do not expect them to behave like monks...and they need the release." She gave an exasperated smile. "The trick is to know when to yield and when to hold your ground." She looked at Hawise, whose lips were moving silently. "And you can forget the words to that song!"

Marion said thoughtfully, "A hundred and eighty-eight is a lot." She gave Sibbi a speculative, slightly pitying look.

"A hundred and eighty-eight is an exaggeration by a hundred and eighty-seven, I can assure you from experience," Sybilla said severely. "And that is enough on the subject."

# 14

$\mathscr{B}$RUNIN PLACED THE FINGERBOWL IN FRONT OF HIS GRAND-
mother. Neither the surface of the water nor the muscles
of his face moved beyond a glimmer. She gave him one of her
looks and he felt it jab straight to his vitals, but he maintained his
composure, pretending that she was nothing to him but another
wedding guest.

Sibbi's marriage had drawn a mass of friends and allies from all
parts of the Welsh Marches and beyond. Gilbert Foliot, Bishop of
Hereford, had performed the blessing and officiated at the mass.
Roger, Earl of Hereford, and Sibbi's half-sister Cecily had come
to the wedding, Roger from Henry's side, Cecily, slender and
resplendent in a gown of blue samite, fresh from her attendance
on Duchess Eleanor. The light from sconces and candelabra shimmered on silks and wool brocades and the glossiness of exotic furs:
arctic bear, miniver, beaver, marten. Brunin was wearing a new
tunic of blood-red wool that enhanced his dark hair and eyes. A
round brooch of gold and garnets closed the deep neck opening.

He took the towel and fingerbowl and, having bowed to her,
moved along the trestle. He could feel her stare boring into his
spine and separating the vertebrae. When he paused before his
mother she smiled at him.

"Life in Lord Joscelin's household suits you," Eve said. "I am
glad your father sent you here."

"I am glad too," Brunin replied with a veiled glance at his grandmother. She was no longer looking at him, but talking to another woman guest.

His mother said softly, "Pay no heed."

"I don't," he lied, managing to sound indifferent. A lord farther down the board was beckoning and Brunin went to serve him.

The dancing had begun in the center of the hall and those guests who had not eaten to bursting point were linking hands and turning circles, men in one direction, women in the other. The strident sound of a bagpipe replaced the harp music that had played throughout the various courses of the wedding feast. Sibbi and her sisters led the women, Hugh and the young males of his family the men. It was more than just the pleasure of the wedding that made the steps exuberant; it was the hope for the future. A peace treaty was soon to be signed; the affairs of the kingdom settled, and men could think about raising their families in the knowledge that they might live to see their sons inherit and their daughters marry.

Leaving the dais to fetch a fresh fingerbowl and clean napkin, Brunin encountered his father returning from the garderobe. FitzWarin clapped him on the shoulder with a moist and heavy hand. "If you see one you like, lad, let me know," he said, nodding at the turning circle of girls and women. "It's time we began considering your betrothal. I've already had two fathers approach me and ask if I have plans for you." FitzWarin's breath was wine-laced and his complexion ruddy, but he was not yet in his cups...just loose of tongue.

Brunin was taken aback. He looked toward the dancing women as they wove through and under the arms of the men so that the outer circle became the inner one. "Who?" he asked.

"William Pantulf was wondering if you'd suit one of his girls, and I've had an inquiry on behalf of the Dover Peverels." He gripped Brunin's shoulder in a man-to-man squeeze. "You're growing into your looks, lad, and the girls are beginning to take notice. Since you're my heir, the parents are looking too. That's half of what weddings are about, eh?"

"Yes, sir," Brunin mumbled. The Pantulf daughters were part of the circle of female dancers. The older one looked like a horse and had a laugh that set his teeth on edge. The other was about eight years old and an inveterate thumb-sucker. He had no idea what they were like beyond the superficial—although what mattered most were their dowries and whether they would enhance the lands that Brunin would eventually inherit from his father.

"I say you can do better than the Pantulfs and Peverels," his father said, and his gaze fell briefly on the dancers, although Brunin could not tell if he was looking at any girl in particular. There were a dozen likely candidates. "Much better." With another squeeze of Brunin's shoulder and a wink, his father made his way back to his place on the benches.

Brunin continued thoughtfully on his errand. He had no particular interest in looking for a future wife; his main concern was with his training and the camaraderie of the other young knights and squires in Joscelin's household. Of course there had always been the good-humored teasing about himself and Marion, but he knew it wasn't serious. He gazed again upon the dancers as the women threaded through to the outer ring again and his eyes chanced upon Hawise. The tight lacing of her gown emphasized her figure. Against the fabric, her hair gleamed with tints of garnet and copper beech. Her head was thrown back in laughter, exposing the creamy line of her throat. What had his father said? That he could do better than Pantulfs and Peverels?

"Come on, lad, you're on duty. Don't stand around like a tent pole." Joscelin's steward, who was overseeing the feast, gave him a warning nudge. "Go and swill the grease out of that bowl and make haste."

Chastised and brought down to earth, Brunin bowed and

hastened to do the steward's bidding, the notion of wife-finding cast completely from his mind.

❖❖❖

"Promise you'll tell us what it's like," Marion whispered to Sibbi.

The women had retired to the bedchamber to prepare the bride for her wedding night. Sibbi's beautiful red dress had been carefully brushed and hung on the clothing pole, and the pearl and garnet belt locked away in her personal coffer. She stood barefoot in her linen chemise, the throat and cuffs tied with delicate ribbons of crimson silk.

"I won't tell you anything," Sibbi whispered back fiercely, her cheeks flushing with indignation. "It's no concern of yours."

"But I want to know if it's nice, or if it hurts," Marion said in an injured tone, as if her demand were quite natural and Sibbi just making a fuss. "It must hurt if there's blood—"

"Leave her alone," Hawise snapped. "Have you no sense?"

Marion pouted. "I was only asking…"

"Well, don't. How would you like such talk on your own wedding night?"

Marion flounced away in a huff and Hawise gave her sister a hug. "Don't let her upset you," she said.

"I'm not upset." Sibbi looked speculatively in Marion's wake. "But I think she is."

The older women fussed around Sibbi, combing her hair until it crackled and the filaments floated on layers of energy. It wasn't particularly glossy, but like Sybilla's it was thick and strong with a life of its own.

"She's a healthy mare," Hawise overheard Lady Mellette mutter to Brunin's mother. "Her father's blood could be better, but she'll likely produce some sturdy offspring and the dowry she brings is useful indeed."

Hawise turned to glower at Lady Mellette and was met by a gaze as sharp as broken glass. Eve FitzWarin looked cowed, her eyes downcast and her hands folded in front of her like a nun...save that her knuckles were white with pressure rather than clasped in serenity.

The groom arrived, borne into the wedding chamber on a tide of bawdy jests by the male guests. He too had been stripped to his undergarments, in this instance no more than a long shirt that came to his knees. There was much robust teasing—a traditional part of the wedding night ritual, but something of an ordeal for bride and groom. Everyone had crowded into the chamber to witness the couple being put to bed so that they could do their duty. The Bishop of Hereford solemnly blessed the bed, the bride, and the groom, after which the women drew back the covers and settled Sibbi between the sheets. The moment of decorum was abruptly terminated as Hugh's companions picked him up between them and threw him in with his bride. The mattress bounced and several feathers flew out to the accompaniment of a loud jangling sound. A swift examination revealed that someone had tied numerous packhorse bells to the ropes supporting the mattress.

Hawise turned accusingly to Brunin. "Now I know why you went into Ludlow yesterday," she hissed.

Brunin looked the picture of wounded innocence. "I was on an errand for your father, and I bought a couple of spare bells for my hawk's jesses."

"Don't lie, I know it was you."

He gave her a sly grin and she poked him. He sidestepped to avoid her and trod on Marion, who immediately squealed and made a show of being hurt. Brunin had to escort her to the window seat where she could sit and rub her foot. Then she got him to rub it for her. Hawise rolled her eyes in irritation—as much at Brunin as at Marion. The latter just had to bat her lashes and act like a helpless ninny and men fell for it every time.

Arms wide, Joscelin began ushering the wedding guests out of the room, leaving the bride and her tousled groom to their bed. As Sybilla wished them well and drew the hangings to shut the couple away from the world, more bells rang in the folds of the heavy fabric.

"I have been giving you far too much free time," muttered Joscelin to Brunin with a mingling of annoyance and mirth. "Remind me on the morrow to increase your workload." Inclining his head to Lady Mellette, he stood aside to let her and Eve precede him. The older woman's eyes had sharpened at the sight of Brunin and Marion in the window splay, but she said nothing. Hawise left with Cecily, but threw an exasperated look over her shoulder at the couple.

"Shall I carry you?" Brunin asked Marion, for the bedchamber was emptying swiftly now.

She shook her head. "No, I can manage…just let me lean on you."

Brunin was certain he hadn't trodden that hard on Marion's foot, but the way she was looking up at him, as if he were big and masculine and she were a dainty, easily bruised kitten, soothed emotions wounded by his grandmother's scowls. She pressed her lithe, slender body against his and the scent of sandalwood rose from her gown. Biting her lip, she took several cautious steps, and then tugged him to one side to let others pass and go down the stairs ahead of them.

"Do you think Sibbi will have a baby after tonight?" she asked.

Brunin gave an uncomfortable shrug. "That is up to God." He hoped that Marion was not going to start down her usual track.

She turned, laying both her hands upon his chest, and looked up at him. Her pupils were as wide as a hunting cat's, almost obliterating the blue iris. "One day it might be us in that chamber," she whispered huskily. "There has been a lot of wedding talk in the hall tonight. Your grandmother likes me; I know she does."

"I doubt my grandmother likes anyone," Brunin replied and swallowed as she stepped closer. He felt the swish of her gown against his thighs; the merest hint of her leg within the fabric and almost immediately he was hard. Locking her arms around his neck she stood on tiptoe and licked his neck like a cat. "Do you want to kiss me?" she whispered. "You can if you like." Closing her eyes, she raised her face.

Brunin knew that this was dangerous—that they were playing with fire—but knowing with the rational part of his mind was one thing, and resisting her allure and the urges of his developing young body another. He brought his hands to her waist, and it was so slender that his fingers almost linked at her spine.

Tentatively he lowered his mouth to hers. Marion's eyes widened and for a moment she froze. Then it was as if a barrier gave way and everything within her opened and melted. Her lips parted beneath his, her body undulated, and she made a soft sound in her throat. Her lips tasted of the sweet wine she had been drinking and they were cushion-soft. Stealthily Brunin took his hand up her side. He could feel the swift rise and fall of her rib cage against his palm, the warmth of her flesh through the thin layers of chemise and gown. He had no great experience with women, but he was not entirely ignorant. A maid at Hereford had been sweet on him and there had been a laundress on the Wallingford campaign who had shown him a trick or two. Only boys, she had said, grabbed like unmannerly dogs snatching at a bone. Experienced men understood the pleasure of taking their time.

"Oh," said Marion. "Oh." And her hands tightened against his spine.

The sound of brisk footsteps on the stairs caused them to break apart hastily and face the intrusion with guilty expressions and rapid breathing. It was Hawise and she too was panting—in her case from her swift climb. The look on her face quashed Brunin's lust with more efficiency than a pail of cold water.

Raising her chin, Marion gave Hawise a smug, almost pitying smile. "Were you looking for us?" She licked her lips.

Hawise's gaze could have made a clean cut through glass.

"Brunin's grandmother was asking for him, and I said I would fetch him," she replied stiffly. "And you shouldn't be lingering here anyway."

Marion sighed as if she were dealing with an imbecile. "Don't look at me like that; we've done nothing wrong." Lifting her gown above her ankles so that it would not hamper her on the stairs, she squeezed past Hawise and began making her way down, her step light with no sign of an injury. "Brunin, you had better make haste," she called back sweetly. "Your grandmother wants you, and her anger probably matters more than Hawise's."

"I'm not angry," Hawise snapped. Turning abruptly she made to follow Marion, but she was not as adept at handling her gown, which, being her best one, had yards of fabric in the skirts. She caught her toe in the hem, tripped, and would have fallen head over heels had Brunin not lunged and caught her. He gripped her arm with bruising force and thrust her against the side of the stairway, holding her there with his weight while he regained balance for both of them. Chest heaving, he stared down into her eyes and she blazed up into his. Suddenly he was as hard as a rock again, but this time he had the good sense to draw away.

"Thank you." Not looking at him, she straightened her gown and rubbed her arm. "You were kissing her, weren't you?"

"What of it?" he said defensively. "Everybody kisses at weddings."

"Yes, but there is already speculation about you and Marion."

"No...there is jesting."

"And jesting leads to speculation and rumor." She descended the stairs with him following in silence. At the foot, she swirled to face him. "Do you truly want her for your wife?"

"I never said in the first place that I wanted her to wife," he said with growing exasperation.

"Then why kiss her?"

"Because it suited the moment," he snapped. "After what happened between you and de Lysle in Shrewsbury, you censure me over a simple kiss?"

She flushed crimson. "I suppose you are going to belabor me with that mistake at every opportunity?"

"No, but you were being unfair."

She fumed at him through narrowed lids but after a moment her expression relaxed and she almost smiled. "Perhaps I was," she said, "but I'd hate to see you make as much of a fool of yourself as I did." Turning from him, she went into the great hall.

Brunin shook his head in bemusement. He felt as if he had been buffeted by several small, violent storms, one after the other…and suspected that there were more to come. Bracing his shoulders, he entered the hall where the roar of wine-fueled conversation competed with the hefty music of tabor and bagpipe and sought his grandmother.

What Mellette wanted of him was not unconnected with what had just happened and her questions echoed those Hawise had asked. He managed to fend them off in a similar wise, his reticence increasing to match the level of her probing. Yes, Marion was pretty and biddable (when she chose). No, he was not courting her. He had merely been solicitous after he stepped on her foot. No, Lady Sybilla and Lord Joscelin had not hinted at a union.

"She seems to have made a remarkable recovery," Mellette observed narrowly as Marion skipped past the dais in the midst of the circle of dancers. Her gaze fell on Hawise, who had also joined the dancing. True to form, ruddy tendrils of her hair had escaped her braid and whirled about her as she stepped and turned. "Girls like that are trouble," she said, but the direction of her stare made her words decidedly ambiguous.

❖ ❖ ❖

"My mother wants to know more about the de la Bruere girl," FitzWarin said to Joscelin. "She's wondering whether she would make a suitable wife."

It was the third evening of the wedding celebrations and, having returned from a day's hunting, the men were easing their tired muscles before the hearth in the great hall. The women were above stairs in the domestic quarters, chattering over their needlework, listening to the minstrels, and regaling the bride with all manner of well-meaning advice.

"For whom?" Joscelin stretched his legs toward the fire and plucked a burr from his hose.

"She has one of my younger boys in mind."

Joscelin shrugged. "Her lands are modest but profitable and she has good blood."

"And the girl herself?"

Joscelin suddenly looked wary. "You would do better to ask my wife."

"And so I will, but what do you say?"

Joscelin was silent for a while and when he spoke he measured his words. "Marion will either make a superb consort for one of your boys, or be his ruin, depending on how she develops. She has passed her fourteenth year day and is of an age to be betrothed if you follow the law, but still a child if you are talking in terms of her maturity. And it would depend on Marion herself. As you know, Sybilla wants to involve all the girls in choosing their mates."

"Dangerous."

"No more so than not involving them," Joscelin countered. "If there is some attraction at the beginning, then it has the potential to grow. If you sow your seeds in the right soil, you will reap a better harvest than planting them where they do not suit. As the sower, you have to observe and be diligent. We thought that Hugh de Plugenet would be ideal for Sibbi. We nurtured, we guided, but we did not force." He smiled. "And of course we had an eye to the lands the Plugenets had set aside for her."

FitzWarin studied some loose stitching on his boot. "Then for the nonce that soil is fallow, but holds possibilities," he said, but more to himself than Joscelin. He contemplated his cup for a moment and then put it down. "I have been wondering about Brunin's future, though. I know you are fond of the lad, and from what I have seen of his progress, he has come as far from the frightened coney I sent to you for training as a pilgrim going from here to Jerusalem."

Joscelin's eye corners crinkled. "I know what you are going to say."

"And I know what you are going to answer...that she is your youngest daughter, that she is not old enough, and that when the time comes, the choice is hers."

"If you have developed the ability to read my thoughts, then I need to guard them better," Joscelin laughed. "All the words you have put in my mouth are true, and you will not persuade me to exchange them for others."

"I know that. Nevertheless, I will ask you to consider a match between Hawise and Brunin. Not a moment since you said that you and Sybilla might not force, but that you nurture and guide."

Joscelin looked pensive. Brunin and Hawise were easy together. They treated each other with tolerant, irreverent camaraderie. Even when they quarrelled, which was not often, they were swiftly reconciled. But that was boy and girl, not man and woman. Of late, however, he had sensed a certain tension between them. It might be no more than part of their growing to maturity, but Sybilla had the better instinct on such a matter. Besides, there were other factors involved. Hawise had a half-share in considerable lands. Brunin would rise in status if he married Hawise, but her rank would remain the same. Countering this was the matter of alliance and friendship...and the fact that Brunin's grandmother had royal blood.

"I will think on it," he replied, "although that is as much as I can offer for the now."

"Then for now I am content," FitzWarin said, refilling his cup.

# 15

## MAY 1155

*J*OSCELIN HAD SPENT A DAY HUNTING IN THE WOODS surrounding Ludlow and was riding home replete with pleasant weariness. It was a long time since he had felt so optimistic. The trees were just opening into full spring leaf, a pale, tender green contrasting with the enamelled blue of the sky—a day to swell the heart and fill it with song.

Stephen had died the previous October and Henry had been crowned King at Christmastide. He was two and twenty, had all the vitality of his youth, and, from somewhere, all the wisdom and cunning of a man thirty years his senior—and wisdom and cunning it was to bend the Church and the barons to his will. Making a peace treaty was one matter, ensuring that its tenets were carried out was another. It was early days yet, but Joscelin had pinned his hope to the line of brightness on the horizon and allowed himself to believe that he could grow old in peace.

Joscelin and his company rode down toward the bridge over the river, but before he crossed, Joscelin paused to look across the water at Ludlow. The stone glowed in the sunlight, soft gold, mellowing and changing with the shadows and angles of light. Scaffolding caged the south side where he had begun some improvements. He felt secure enough to do that. Gilbert de Lacy and Hugh of Wigmore had been very quiet of late. Lying low, he suspected, while they waited to see what Henry would do about the various measures of the peace settlement now that he truly was King.

A fish leaped, plundered the haze of mayflies, and splashed back down in a dripping sparkle. Upriver, small boys from the town were throwing stones in the water and wrestling, trying to soak each other. Joscelin smiled at their play and, clicking his tongue to the horse, rode on to the castle.

Once in the bailey, he saw that they had visitors. A groom was leading away a striking pale gold mare, her saddle cloth decorated with a double row of small silver bells. Some of the pleasure departed Joscelin's expression. He wanted to stretch out in his chair and doze in his wife's company, a cup of wine to hand, but he recognized that horse and knew that such an indulgence would have to be put aside.

"The Countess of Hereford is here," said Brunin, a question in his voice as he dismounted from Jester. He too had recognized the mare.

"Yes." Joscelin concealed a grimace. Cecily had not sent word that she was intending to visit. Roger wasn't here, or there would have been more horses.

"Take the deer to the kitchens," he said to Brunin, "and then come and find me."

"Yes, sir." Brunin took the pack pony's bridle and headed across the bailey. The two dead roe deer swayed from side to side on the felt saddle pad. Suddenly they didn't seem so much the fruits of a successful day's hunting, but as portents of trouble on its way. Sighing heavily, Joscelin pushed his hands through his hair and went to find his wife and stepdaughter.

❖❖❖

The solar was filled with women: those of his own household and those who had accompanied Cecily, all chattering and bustling as they unpacked chests and sorted out sleeping spaces. Reminded of a flock of hens running into the coop at dusk, Joscelin noted the industry with a sense of foreboding. This wasn't just a visit on a whim, but looked as if Cecily had arrived for a long stay. The bedchamber door was firmly closed when usually during the day it was wide open to allow traffic between the two rooms. Joscelin halted before it, assailed by a foolish urge to heel about and return to the men in the hall. Then he rallied. It was his chamber too, and where else could a man have authority, if not in the heart of his private quarters? Squaring his shoulders, he set his hand to the latch.

Hawise was kneeling by the hearth, simmering a pot of spiced wine on the edge of the flames. Sybilla sat on their bed, her arm curved around a weeping Cecily.

"What's wrong?" He closed the door and the sound of bustle diminished to a background mumble. "What's happened?"

His question prompted a fresh onslaught of sobbing from his stepdaughter.

Sybilla's gaze met his above her daughter's bent head. "There's trouble at Hereford," she murmured. "Hawise, is that wine ready yet?"

"Almost, Mama."

"What sort of trouble?" Instinctively Joscelin set his hand to the hilt of his sword.

"Not the sort to be solved with a blade unless you want to go to war with the new King," Sybilla said, a bitter note in her voice.

Cecily gave a loud sniff. "Roger's been ordered to give up…" She gulped. "…to give up his castles at Hereford and Gloucester to King Henry."

Joscelin's jaw dropped. "He's been what?"

Cecily shook her head and buried her face in a linen square already saturated with tears, and it was Sybilla who repeated the words. "It's supposed to be in accordance with the treaty everyone signed at Winchester," she said. "All lands are to revert back to those who held them in the time when the King's grandfather was on the throne, and fortresses built since that time are to be pulled down."

"I know the terms of the treaty," Joscelin said tersely. "But surely there's room for a little leeway. Roger and his father were Henry's staunchest allies throughout the darkest period of the war. Henry can't take them away from him." His tone rang with indignation.

Cecily blew her nose. "It's not just Roger..." she quavered. "Hugh Mortimer's been ordered to surrender his castles too—Cleobury and Wigmore and Bridgnorth. Roger says...Roger says that he will make a pact with him and they will fight the King." She looked at her stepfather with swimming eyes. "I have never seen him so angry. He was throwing cups and stools...he even took his sword to our marriage chest."

Sybilla made an appalled sound. "He was out of his mind with rage," Cecily continued, shaking her head. "It could have been any furniture...and then, because of his exertion, he started to cough and we had to summon the physician."

Joscelin strode to the window and looked out on the normality and bustle of the castle bailey. He imagined how he would feel if a royal letter arrived demanding that he yield Ludlow into the King's custody and ice ran down his spine. What price loyalty? he wondered grimly, and how ironic that Roger and Hugh Mortimer should suddenly find themselves with a common cause after all these years.

"He swears he is going to go to war," Cecily whispered. "But I fear for him. He is not well, and he has enemies enough from the old days who will be all too willing to ride against him."

Sighing deeply, Joscelin went to pour himself ordinary wine from the flagon on the coffer. He took a sip. It had the faintest taint of vinegar, as if it were on the turn. "I will ride and speak with him if you wish," he said.

Cecily flashed him a glance brimming with gratitude. "Please," she said. "He might listen to you."

"You should not have left him," Sybilla gently reproved her daughter.

"I had no choice, Mama." Cecily's voice descended toward tears again. "He ordered my chests packed and the horses saddled.

I'm not like you. I'm no good at standing my ground…If you had seen his temper…"

Sybilla tightened her lips and patted Cecily's back like a mother soothing a colicky infant. "Hush now," she said. "Done is done." She looked again at Joscelin and he read her unspoken anger and concern. He could almost feel her willing the wine down his throat so that he could be on his way.

"It might be different if we had children," Cecily wept. "I know that he's fond of me but no more than he's fond of his dogs or his favorite horse…I can bind him neither with love nor with duty to his offspring. He won't see it. He says that if war comes to Hereford, I will be better protected at Ludlow."

Joscelin turned back to the window so that she would not see the narrowing of his gaze. If Roger of Hereford was not safe, then no one was.

❖ ❖ ❖

Following Joscelin into Roger of Hereford's chamber, Brunin was hit by the sour stench of sickness and sweat. Roger was on his feet, but looked as if he should be abed. His red tunic was a match for the burning crimson stars on his cheekbones. The rest of his face was the pasty hue of bread dough.

"Roger, dear Christ, man!" Joscelin slewed to a halt, his expression appalled.

"I will thank you not to take the name of the Lord God in vain," said a mellifluous voice and a priest rose from a chair set to one side of the hearth.

"My lord…" Joscelin hastened to the cleric and, dropping to one knee, kissed the episcopal ring. Recognizing the thin, sharp features of Gilbert Foliot, Bishop of Hereford, Brunin swiftly followed suit. The Bishop inclined his head, showing that he was disposed to forgive, and reseated himself.

"I suppose Cecily sent you," Roger rasped, his chest heaving.

"No, she didn't, but you should know that making your wife pack her baggage and return to her mother is sufficient insult to bring me down on you as fast as my courser can gallop," Joscelin said brusquely. "Not that you're in a fit state to answer for the dead. I've seen better-looking corpses. You should be abed!"

Roger leaned against a painted chest with a deep gash of raw wood in its side. Brunin could see his body trembling with the force of his heartbeat and the heat was coming off him in waves. "I should," Roger agreed, "but I'll be damned if I let Henry take away my lands!" Sweat glistened in the hollow of his throat as he swallowed. "It is better for Cecily to be with her mother now. I meant no insult."

"So what will you do, Roger?" asked the Bishop, his gaze piercing. "Take up arms and go to war? Have you not had enough yet?"

"If it comes to that, yes. I haven't held out these past years to be stripped of everything like a common thief."

Exasperation flickered in Foliot's face and was then tucked away in the firm line of his mouth. "You are not being stripped of everything," he said. "Henry desires the return of the castles of Hereford and Gloucester, which were held in royal domain before Stephen took the throne. By the peace treaty of Westminster, he is entitled to claim them. It does not mean that he has turned against you."

Roger bared his teeth. "It certainly seems that way to me."

"If he let you keep them while he took estates from others who fought for Stephen, how would it look?" The Bishop spread his hands as if ministering from the pulpit. "The King has to be seen to be even-handed."

Roger looked feverishly at Joscelin. "Tell me that you have come to give me your support," he said. "Tell me that you will be fried in hell before you let Henry's officials come within ten miles of Hereford."

Joscelin gnawed on his thumbnail. Brunin recognized the habit. There were times during the weeks of campaigning in the field when Joscelin's flesh had been bitten bloody. "You are my son-in-law and my ally," he replied. "Of course I will offer you support…but not to rebel against the King."

Bishop Gilbert had stiffened at the first part of Joscelin's answer. As the sentence finished, he exhaled with relief. Roger gave a choking splutter.

"Look at you, man," Joscelin said brusquely. "You're burning up with fever. You couldn't fight your way out of a flour sack just now, let alone organize the defense of this place. If you go to war, you will lose everything. I like what Henry is doing no more than you...but I won't defy him."

"Hah, and what if he made you sacrifice Ludlow?" Roger snarled with glittering eyes. "After all, it wasn't yours in the first Henry's day, was it, and Gilbert de Lacy's claim is perilously strong."

"Playing at what if is futile," Joscelin snapped, beginning to flush. "As is this conversation. Were you not out of your wits with fever, I would shake you until your teeth rattled in your skull."

Roger started forward with raised fists, but took no more than two steps before his knees buckled and he went down like a shot deer. Joscelin leaped to catch him and braced Roger's weight with his own body. "Brunin, run and find the physician," he commanded.

"I am all right," Roger wheezed. "There is nothing wrong with me."

"And I'm Helen of Troy," Joscelin retorted as he carried Roger to the bed. "My dogs' old beef bones have more flesh on them than you have. You can't defy Henry, you're too sick, and I won't do it for you. Douse your anger and your pride, or they will destroy you."

Roger closed his eyes. His lashes were gummy and clumped with pus. "You think that matters to a dying man?" he croaked.

"Christ, you're not dying, and even if you were, it's the living that matter," Joscelin snarled and felt fear and helplessness sear through him as Roger turned his face to the wall and refused to respond.

❖❖❖

Dosed by the physician, made to drink gingered wine, and wrapped up in the bedclothes like a caterpillar in a cocoon, Roger finally slept.

"I am glad you have come," said the Bishop as he and Joscelin sat down before the hearth in the antechamber. "I have been trying to talk sense into him for two days but he would not listen to me."

"He did not sound as if he was listening to me, either," Joscelin said grimly.

"Oh, he was. I think he expected you to take his side in his affairs—half the reason he sent you his wife. I think he was hoping that you would come roaring in here like a wild bull and insist that he take up arms against Henry. I am eternally grateful that you did not."

Joscelin grunted. "Even if I were thus inclined, I would hope to have more sense. There are many who are unhappy at having the influence they have built up diluted. Roger is only one tree in the forest. But if we are to have peace, then we need to compromise."

"I am glad that you see it in such terms, my lord," said the Bishop.

"Perhaps I can afford to." Joscelin looked bleak. "As Roger said, if I were commanded to yield Ludlow, then perhaps I would not be so reasonable."

The Bishop gave him a considering look. "You do know that Hugh Mortimer has been ordered to surrender Cleobury, Wigmore, and Bridgnorth?"

"Yes, Cecily told us. She was afraid that Roger was going to join with him and begin a rebellion."

"It was my concern too," said the Bishop, "but aside from you thrusting a broomhandle into the cogs—for which I am grateful—Roger's own body will not let him defy the King."

Joscelin met Gilbert Foliot's gaze. Neither of them flinched from what they saw in each other's eyes.

"He is fighting the inevitable," the Bishop said gently. "He knows what he will not acknowledge, although he must come to terms with it soon. And perhaps that too is one of the reasons that he has sent his wife to Ludlow." Foliot stroked the dark wool of his habit. "Roger's estates will go to his brother since he has no heirs of his body to inherit, but I believe that the King will not transfer the earldom with the titles."

Joscelin raised a brow. Gilbert Foliot had a far-reaching web of spies and intelligence-gatherers. Joscelin knew that asking him how he knew about certain matters was futile. The response would be a gentle, steely smile and a change of subject. "Are you not moving too fast?" Joscelin asked.

"No," Gilbert said somberly, "I do not think that I am."

# 16

*HAWISE HAD NEVER BEEN CLOSE TO CECILY. WHEN HAWISE* had been born, Cecily was already married to Roger FitzMiles. Now, they were walking together, the oldest and the youngest of Sybilla's offspring, returning from Hereford Cathedral where they had been giving thanks for Roger's miraculous recovery. Against all expectations, he had revived and was preparing to go and make his obeisance to King Henry.

Behind them, Hawise was aware of their mother murmuring quietly to Marion and one of the other women. Sybilla had insisted that they came to Hereford. She had no intention of allowing Roger to dispose of his wife in such a cavalier fashion. On arriving and discovering the seriousness of her son-in-law's illness, she had taken over the running of the keep with the same brisk efficiency that she brought to the task at Ludlow, thus leaving Cecily free to nurse her husband.

Hawise ran her prayer beads through her fingers as they walked toward the castle. "Will you stay at Hereford now?" she asked Cecily.

Her half-sister made a pensive face. "That depends upon Roger." She glanced quickly over her shoulder as if checking that their mother was not listening.

Hawise frowned at her. "You mean he might send you away again?"

Cecily sighed. "It is likely. Mother has known him since he was a babe in arms and he respects her. He respects my stepfather too, but I am not sure that it is enough to stop him."

"And what about you?" Hawise asked, for Cecily had left herself out of the reckoning. "Doesn't he respect you?"

"In his own fashion," Cecily said bleakly. "He has never beaten me, nor has he reviled me because I have failed to conceive. He doesn't lie with whores—or at least not under the same roof as me—and he affords me every courtesy in the great hall when all eyes are upon us. But he is indifferent. His dogs receive more affection than I do—and in similar wise, I do my duty by him and compensate myself with the fact that I am Countess of Hereford and can wear silk at my whim." Her hazel eyes filled with desolation.

Hawise thought of their mother's determined insistence that she and Sibbi should have a say in selecting their future mates. "Didn't Mama let you choose your husband?"

Cecily shook her head. "My father wasn't soft in those matters like yours. Sometimes she could argue him around, but once he had made up his mind there was no moving him…and he wanted me to marry Roger because he was his best friend's son and had a rich inheritance." She gazed pityingly at Hawise. "Even with choice it is the way of the world—you'll discover that."

The guards saluted them through into the castle. At the gate a priest was doling out bread to a line of beggars and unfortunates and Cecily scattered a handful of quarter pennies among them, exhorting them to pray for their lord. "Roger is still not well," she murmured to Hawise, "but he is determined to go to the King at Wallingford."

"Will he give up his castles?"

"He has no choice, save to have them taken away by force. The King might give them back to him for his lifetime, but not by right of inheritance." Cecily set her jaw. "He has been talking about taking the cowl. But where does that leave me? I have no desire to become a nun. If he puts me aside for the cloister, I cannot stay at Hereford, and I don't want to be pitied at Ludlow."

"You wouldn't be pitied!" Hawise said with widening eyes. "Indeed you would not!"

"No?" Cecily gave a cynical smile. "Then perhaps I need to fight my own pride instead."

"What does Mama say?"

Cecily gave another swift glance over her shoulder. "I haven't told her. I don't need to. Unless Roger changes his mind, it will be common knowledge soon enough."

"I am sorry." Hawise felt completely out of her depth.

"So am I," Cecily said.

The bailey was busy with knights and soldiers making preparation to leave and join the King, and Hawise saw Brunin among them. One of Hereford's older squires wanted to spar with him, but Brunin was shaking his head and refusing to cooperate.

"Come on," the squire laughed, raising his voice. "It's good practice and the ladies like a show!" He cast a look toward the women. He was a handsome young man, blond-haired, brawny and strong.

Brunin's glance flickered and a grimace crossed his face. The squire grabbed a spear from a stack leaning against the wall and tossed it at him. Brunin caught it and reluctantly took up a quartering stance. The squire leaped at him with a cry. Brunin's blocking of the assault was clumsy and he received a sharp rap on the knuckles.

The two serjeants of the women's escort paused to watch the contest with folded arms and judgmental expressions. "It's a pity about the lad," remarked one after a moment, nodding at Brunin. "You wouldn't think he had a grain of ability to look at him now, but I've seen him train with my lord and he's faster than a swallow on the wing."

"I heard a rumor that he was originally intended for the Church," his companion muttered. He pointed as Brunin took a blow to the side. "Look at that. I could understand it if he'd never fought with the staff before, but not at this stage."

The men shook their heads. "You'd think he was frightened."

"Likely so. I've seen fear make men as clumsy as bears with burned paws."

Hawise watched Brunin duck out of the squire's way. His mouth was grim and tight, his eyes blank. Having taken a couple of blows to the hands and body he had dodged out of the way but was being relentlessly pursued and backed toward the castle wall.

Hawise wondered if the serjeant's words had a ring of truth. She too had seen Brunin train with her father and knew what he was capable of...but that was with her father and at Ludlow. She could not make a guess at why his performance was so clumsy now, for she was no longer certain of him. The easy camaraderie of their childhood had become awkward with adolescence. His physical presence made her stomach jolt, but these days he was not often in the bower. As maturity and knighthood approached, he spent most of his time in the company of men. She only saw him in close proximity at the dinner trestle, or if he were attending on Joscelin in the women's chamber. And even then he was distant and polite. She suspected that it had much to do with the incident at Sibbi's wedding, for he was distant and polite with Marion too. It irked her; made her want to kick his shins. Once she might have done, but they were no longer children.

Brunin withdrew from the bout by tossing the spear to another squire, who caught it with a startled look.

"Coward!" the blond youth panted, angrily. "You spar like a clumsy child!"

Brunin absorbed the taunts with a neutral expression. "Then there's no gain to you in fighting me," he said and, inclining his head, walked away, leaving the blond squire opening and shutting his mouth.

There was a moment's silence. One of the serjeants muttered

under his breath with disgust and the other gave a snort of contemptuous disbelief. The other squire hastily returned the spear to the stack before he became Brunin's surrogate. The blond youth shook his head in disgust, his hands to his hips. "Remind me never to fight at your side in a battle!" he called in Brunin's wake. Ignoring him, Brunin kept on walking.

Hawise felt as if she had been struck in the soft part under her heart. She wanted to shout at Hereford's squire that he was wrong, but she held back, afraid that his perception was perhaps sharper than hers.

❖❖❖

"Brunin?" Joscelin folded his arms and leaned against the door of the small antechamber that had been allotted his squires while they were at Hereford.

Brunin had emptied the straw from his pallet and was folding up the linen canvas ready for their departure. "Sire?" His heart sank because he knew why Joscelin was here.

"What happened this afternoon on the sward? Look at me."

Reluctantly Brunin raised his gaze to Joscelin's flint-bright one. "I am not a coward, my lord," he said tautly.

"I know very well that you are not, but I need to understand what is wrong with you. Sybilla says you were like a green boy in the first days of training; so did my serjeants, yet I know you can hold your own against any of the grown men in my retinue. If the truth be admitted, sometimes you press me hard."

Brunin flushed at the mingling of praise and censure in Joscelin's speech. "I didn't want to fight him, sir." He arranged the pallet on top of his bundle of gear.

"So I was told." Joscelin frowned at him, perplexed. "It's not the first time that you have drawn back. The men say they've noticed it in you during training of late. What is binding you?"

Brunin grimaced. "Nothing, sir."

"Then think." Joscelin seated himself on the narrow bench cut beneath the window-slit. Hands folded between his knees, he contemplated the young man. "I have done as much as I can for you out of my own store. I cannot help you unless you help yourself."

"No, sir."

The silence stretched out, but Joscelin continued to wait. "What happened with Roger's squire?" he repeated in a level voice.

Brunin gnawed his lower lip. "He reminded me of my brother...and of Ernalt de Lysle," he said slowly.

"Who?"

"Gilbert de Lacy's squire," Brunin mumbled, feeling his ears begin to burn with shame as Joscelin compressed his lips. "They are both of a kind, tall and fair and boastful...At first..." He swallowed. "At first I didn't want to fight because I...I was afraid." It took all of Brunin's will power to make the admission and meet that intense gray stare.

Joscelin nodded. "Go on."

"I..."

"You said 'at first.'"

"Then...then my fear of him went away and I knew I had to stop."

Joscelin folded his arms and waited.

Brunin hesitated. "Because instead of being afraid of him, I was afraid of myself," he said. "I knew what I would do to him if I let slip the leash. He called me a coward...I walked away rather than risk killing him."

"I see." Joscelin thumbed his jaw. "And is this the same reason you hold back against your own training partners at Ludlow? Because you are afraid your rage will get the better of you?"

Brunin shook his head. "No, my lord." His expression brightened. "It is not the same, and none of them remind me of Ralf or de Lysle."

"What then?"

"Well, I know most of their moves. Thomas never holds his shield tight enough into his body and Rob always does that backhand swipe at the legs but leaves himself wide open." He demonstrated with his arms. "I could hurt them if I wanted. It has become too easy." He looked anxiously at Joscelin. "I never pull my blows with you, my lord. I know I don't have to."

Joscelin narrowed his eyes. His palm crossed his mouth. From the look in his eyes, Brunin guessed that he was hiding a grin he did not consider appropriate to the occasion. "I haven't entirely lost my edge then," he said drily before he sobered. "It seems to me that we need to move your training up a notch in that area. But it also seems to me that you need to tackle your demons. I can only do so much. What is in here," he tapped his head, "is yours to deal with."

"I know that, my lord."

Joscelin nodded briskly, indicating that the discussion was at an end, and, placing his hands on his knees, eased to his feet, grimacing slightly as his joints cracked. "Good then," he said. "When you have finished here, come down to the hall. I've plenty of tasks for you." He gave Brunin a perceptive look. "Of all the squires I have trained down the years, you've been the greatest challenge... and in all likelihood the best. Remember that."

"Yes, my lord."

Joscelin left and Brunin finished packing his baggage. He didn't go straight down to the hall though, instead he spent several moments staring across the room at the plastered wall, absorbing everything that had been said.

❖❖❖

Brunin stood in the shadow cast by the keep at Bridgnorth. The sun was so hot that it had bleached the sky and every footfall raised a powdering of dust from the baked cart track. Henry had sent an army against Hugh Mortimer's defiance and the land surrounding the castle was clumped with tents and cooking fires, with horse lines and the raw wood of trees new felled to make siege engines. Older and wiser now, Brunin was not holding out hopes of getting to operate either a perrier or a trebuchet. If they had been part of the besieging troop at Cleobury, he might have done so, for there had been some stiff skirmishing before the castellan had yielded. Wigmore was being invested too and there were bets being taken on which would fall first. Brunin had put a shilling on Cleobury.

"Mortimer will have to dismount from his high horse and negotiate," Joscelin said. "Thank God that Roger agreed to yield up Hereford. He would never have held it…and I would have had the nightmare of choosing between loyalty to my kin or loyalty to my King."

Brunin nodded, folded his arms on his breast, and tried to look wise. He did not know what he would have done and was glad that it had not come to the crux with Lord Joscelin.

Roger of Hereford had yielded to Henry, but from necessity, not choice. They had all expected Roger to die of the fever and congestion that had attacked him six weeks ago; none had expected him to rally, but rally he had. Not only that but he had swallowed the unpalatable and submitted on bended knee to Henry, handing Hereford Castle into royal custody.

It was obvious that Roger was still seriously ill and that surrendering the right to hold his earldom as a hereditary title had broken his spirit. His cheekbones were like knifeblades, his eyes sunken. He had never possessed a robust build, but his wiry strength had been in proportion to his frame. Now his body was cadaverous with deep hollows beneath his rib cage and limbs where muscle and sinew were no more than string attached to the underlying bone. He talked constantly of becoming a monk and even now was closeted in his tent, praying with his chaplain.

Brunin glanced toward the laced-up canvas flap and squeezed his fist to feel the strength and vitality flowing through his own young body. Despite the burning heat of the day and the sweat dripping from the tips of his hair, a shiver ran down his spine. Footsteps on his grave, as there had been footsteps on so many others. While his flesh was still tingling, a horn sounded three sharp blasts, and men turned their attention away from the keep and fixed it on the road where a dust cloud billowed the horizon.

❖❖❖

"I cannot believe Hugh Mortimer is surrendering." Ernalt de Lysle's mouth twisted as if it were full of vinegar. He gave his horse a bad-tempered kick, and then had to tighten the reins as the beast plunged. Ahead of them, the banners of Mortimer were carried on dipped lances in token of submission as the rebels rode into the royal camp to make peace with Henry.

De Lacy turned in the saddle to look at him. "What choice does he have?" he said with a hint of impatience. "Cleobury has fallen and it is only a matter of time until his other castles fall too. Only a madman would continue to hold out against the King. Pride makes poor bread to live on when all else is taken away; believe me, boy, I have done it."

Ernalt flushed. "We will have to ride past the men of Ludlow," he said in a mortified tone. "I don't want to be mocked by them."

De Lacy gave the young knight a speculative look. "Joscelin de Dinan may be satisfied at today's outcome but I doubt he'll mock," he said. "Not when his son-in-law has been stripped of the greater part of his authority. Besides, from what I hear, Roger of Hereford is not long for this world. De Dinan knows very well that he's balancing on a knife-edge."

"But he still possesses Ludlow."

"For the moment, but that will change." De Lacy had known that taking up arms with Hugh Mortimer would set back his claim to Ludlow. Yet he had been honor bound to answer Mortimer's call for aid, and since a man without honor was detestable, there had been but one choice.

Ernalt scowled. "Hugh Mortimer should help you to take Ludlow in recompense."

De Lacy had been thinking along similar lines himself, but to hear it from the mouth of his knight made him pause to wonder at Ernalt's fervor for the de Lacy cause. There was more than just loyalty involved, he was certain. Ernalt seemed to harbor a personal grudge against de Dinan. While Gilbert could justify his own grudges, he had no inkling of what goaded Ernalt. "The idea has its merits," he said, "but it would be necessary to move with care. To do it straight away would not be wise."

"No, my lord, but with the Earl of Hereford ailing and stripped of much of his authority, de Dinan has no one of any weight to take his part. The FitzWarins may have royal connections, but wield no true power." A sneering note entered his voice.

De Lacy had no love for Fulke FitzWarin of Whittington, although mostly his antipathy consisted of feelings of superiority. Judging by his tone, Ernalt had a more active grudge against him. A vague memory flickered at the back of de Lacy's mind and was gone before he could grasp it. "No," he said, "FitzWarin is nothing to me."

De Lacy remembered what the grudge was as they were conducted through the siege camp under their banners of truce. In the course of avoiding Joscelin de Dinan's neutral gray stare, his gaze fell on the squire standing at his left shoulder. Fulke FitzWarin the younger, known as Brunin. Ernalt made a sound in his throat and muttered something that sounded like "whoreson." The FitzWarin youth raised his head and fixed his sable-dark gaze on Ernalt and it was plain that Ernalt's sentiments were reciprocated in full measure.

"It was at Shrewsbury Fair, wasn't it?" said Gilbert as they rode beyond the contact and the tension dissipated.

"What was?" Ernalt looked wary.

"Don't play games. You know of what I speak."

"My lord?"

"That incident—three years ago, was it?—when you came home looking as if you'd been trampled on by a warhorse. I never got much sense or reason out of you at the time, but I heard from other sources that you and de Dinan's squire had had a fight over a girl."

"It was nothing." Ernalt raised the back of his hand to his mouth for a moment, as if touching a wound.

"And that is why you look at him as if you would carve out his liver and feed it to the crows. There is more to it than that, I think."

Ernalt shrugged his broad shoulders and said nothing. After a moment, Gilbert looked away and let the matter drop. It was of no real concern, after all.

# 17

HAWISE HAD DISCOVERED THAT SHE ENJOYED EMBROIDERY. As a child she had possessed little patience, but now she found that there was something soothing about sitting in a quiet corner and ordering her thoughts to the movement of her needle. It was satisfying to see a pattern take shape on the fabric, to watch delicate leaves and scrolls curl and coil upon the stretched linen. She also had sufficient vanity to be aware that her hands were one of her best features, the fingers long and graceful, adorned by rings of braided silver and gold. The act of embroidery gave them prominence to an observer and became one of the first things they noticed about her.

Her mother joined her on the bench by the window and took a silver needle from the pin cushion in the sewing casket. Beyond the open shutters, October sunshine clothed the keep and bailey in light the color of falling leaves. Sybilla selected a hank of amber-colored thread and carefully pared off a strand. "It is time and past time we considered the matter of your marriage," she said after a moment. "I have been remiss, and so has your father."

Hawise concentrated on her stitches while her stomach gave a sudden wallow. Discussion of her future had been deferred several times over the past year, for although Henry was firmly entrenched on the throne, their position at Ludlow was still uncertain. There had been Mortimer's rebellion at Wigmore and de Lacy had continued to claim vociferously that Ludlow was his. Thus far his protests had landed on deaf ears, likely because he had joined Mortimer's defiance, but there was no safeguard for the future. Then there had been the tragic matter of her brother-in-law's death. Although they had been prepared, the end had still come as a shock. Roger's earldom was to lapse and her father had lost his most powerful ally.

"You say nothing, daughter? Does the thought disturb you?"

Hawise frowned and shook her head. "A little," she said, "but I know that you and Papa will not force me to anything that is not of my will."

Sybilla's lips twitched. "I see you have listened well to my homilies on the matter, but it will be up to you to help us decide."

Hawise glanced out of the window. Cecily was walking in the bailey with Marion, the stiff autumn breeze swirling their cloaks and fluttering their veils. Her half-sister had returned to Ludlow to mourn. Even if Cecily's heart was not broken, it had been scarred, and she needed time to recover before the subject of her own future "choice" was raised.

"Do you have anyone in mind?" Sybilla pressed gently.

Hawise continued to stare. "Do you?" she countered.

"One or two, but I was going to ask if you had a preference first."

Hawise heard the prick of her mother's needle through the taut linen, her stitches measured and precise. "No," she said neutrally. "I have no preference."

"Hmmm," said Sybilla, not making it clear if it was a sound of thoughtfulness or doubt. She took several stitches in silence, then rested her needle and looked at Hawise. "A messenger came from Whittington today and that is part of what has prompted me to speak with you. Fulke FitzWarin has asked officially if we will consider a marriage between you and Brunin."

Hawise flushed crimson. It had been a possibility for some time, albeit among many possibilities, including an offer from a northern baronial family.

Sybilla watched her. "What do you think?"

Hawise gave a panic-stricken laugh. The difference between possibility and certain offer was terrifying. "What does Brunin say? Does he know?" She thought that he must do, for he was spending a month at Whittington with his family and it was inconceivable that he had not been involved in the discussion.

"That I cannot say, since the offer was couched in formal terms." Sybilla smiled. "Judging by the way he looks at you some-times, I doubt he has objections. Indeed, if your father thought for one moment that he had, he wouldn't entertain his return to Ludlow. As far as your father is concerned, no man will ever be good enough for you, but it is you I am asking. There are many eligible young men who would be glad to have you to wife. You may not have the kind of beauty that the troubadours sing about, but you have an allure of your own that is perhaps more attrac-tive." Sybilla reached out a tender hand to stroke Hawise's thick auburn braid.

"An allure called Ludlow," Hawise said, lips thinning. "That's all Robert le Vavasour could talk about when he came courting!"

"Perhaps," Sybilla said with amusement, "but his eyes did a lot of looking."

Hawise sniffed indignantly. "Yes," she said. "I almost had to fish them out from between my breasts!"

Sybilla spluttered, and then compressed her lips to quash her mirth. "I take it you are not enamoured of Robert le Vavasour."

Hawise shook her head. "He was too fond of listening to himself." She was aware of the sidelong looks cast at her by the young men of the keep and guests who visited with their eligible sons. Their glances left her feeling breathless, vulnerable, and flat-tered. She could not recall Brunin ever eyeing her like that; to her face he was more likely to laugh and tug her braid but perhaps he was different when her back was turned. More than once she had studied him and speculated. The memory of him swilling down at the well in the bailey a couple of summers ago was still one that burned in her imagination. "I do like him," she said, her voice slow with consideration. "And I know that I will have to make a choice soon…but…"

"Is there anyone you would prefer? The Earl of Leicester's second son perhaps?"

Hawise made a face. "He was good company, but no more than in passing and all he wanted to talk about was hunting. If I married him, there would be hounds all over the bed."

Sybilla bit back a smile. "And Brunin is more than in passing?"

Hawise sighed. "Perhaps it is just that I have known him for longer. I've had time to quarrel with him as well as be polite."

Sybilla studied her thoughtfully. "Then perhaps you should try to imagine your life without Brunin in it. If he should be knighted and leave Ludlow for pastures new, how then would you feel?" She laid her hand upon Hawise's wrist to emphasize her point. "Lost? Indifferent? Relieved?"

"I do not know…" Hawise rubbed her temple.

"Use your heart, not your head," Sybilla said quickly. "Give me the answer you feel inside."

Hawise laughed. "Is that not the opposite of what you are always telling us? Look before you leap is what you usually say."

Sybilla answered the laugh with a reluctant one of her own. "Yes, it is what I usually say, but this time, no. You have to go beyond the mind and make your choice from the heart too. Otherwise, your father and I might as well have selected a husband for you at birth."

Hawise looked down at her mother's insistent hand. The flesh was slick over the bones, the veins prominent, a few brownish spots adding evidence of years, but the nails were well tended and the several gold rings were a display of wealth and power and feminine vanity despite the onset of years.

"How do you feel about sharing a bed with Brunin?" Sybilla asked. "About bearing dark-eyed sons and daughters with his mannerisms?"

Hawise reddened at the words and felt a pang somewhere in

her mid-section. Almost without knowing, she laid her palm to her belly. She saw her mother take note of the action and was flustered. She didn't want to think intimately about Brunin in her mother's presence. "Again, I do not know," she said stubbornly.

"But the notion does not revolt you?"

"No." Her face burned as if she were standing in front of an open forge.

Sybilla nodded and a look of satisfaction entered her eyes. "You do not have to make your decision now," she said. "You have some leeway to think on it."

Hawise bit her lip. "What if I refuse? Will you and Papa be angry?"

"Bless you, child, of course we won't!" Sybilla gave her a reassuring hug. It was a release from strain and Hawise leaned briefly into the embrace. She had always known that this moment would come, but until today, it had been a matter on the horizon, not under her nose. A part of her was excited at the notion, which had sent a new kind of energy tingling through her body; but another part still wanted her juggling balls, her toy sword, and her mother. If Hawise had to run a household on her own, she knew she would never be as wise and capable as Sybilla, and the idea was daunting.

She raised her head from Sybilla's bosom. "How long would the betrothal be?"

"That would be decided if the negotiations went forth in earnest," Sybilla replied. "I do not think that the wedding would be for a couple of years at least."

"Would we still live at Ludlow?" There was anxiety in her tone. Sibbi and Hugh had gone to live on his family lands with only occasional visits to Ludlow and she never saw her other married half-sister, Agnes. She jutted her chin. "If I have to live under the same roof as Lady Mellette, I'll refuse here and now."

Sybilla nodded in acknowledgment of the point. "You would have to visit her from time to time and spend part of the year on FitzWarin lands—after all, Brunin is the heir—but it will not be the greater part of your life. The FitzWarins hold more than just

Whittington, and there will be your dower estates too. There is no reason for you and the gracious Lady Mellette to cross paths more often than duty requires."

"No, Mama." Hawise looked relieved.

"I do not doubt you can hold your own should the situation arise."

Hawise screwed up her face. "I do not doubt it either, Mama. But I'm not sure about the consequences."

Sybilla chuckled softly and rose to her feet. "Any birds that came home to roost would do so in Lady Mellette's belfry," she said. "I'll leave you to think and return later." She began to draw away.

"You don't have to leave me, Mama," Hawise said. "I can give you my answer now. I will be glad to accept Brunin for my husband."

She spoke with such a resolute thrust of her jaw that Sybilla frowned. "You look as if you are bravely swallowing medicine that you dislike."

"No, Mama. I truly wish it," Hawise said steadily. "I will not change my mind."

An expression—relief?—crossed her mother's face and was gone. "Even so, leave it until the morrow," Sybilla murmured. "All decisions should be slept on for at least one night if possible."

Hawise forced a smile. "I don't think I'll sleep very much," she said.

❖ ❖ ❖

"You broached it to her then?" Joscelin looked at his wife and rubbed the back of his neck.

Sybilla studied him in amusement. He was still apt to see his youngest daughter as a little girl, when the truth was that she was fast blossoming into a young woman. He was also fiercely protective and thought that no male, even one he knew and trusted, was worthy of her. "Yes, I broached it," she said, the asperity in her tone revealing what she thought of his cowardice in abjuring the discussion.

"And?" His palm remained on his neck and his brow wore pleats of anxiety.

Sybilla pursed her lips, deliberately extending the moment. She didn't see why she should be merciful. She considered telling him to go and ask Hawise himself, but she tempered the inclination. "She says that she likes him, that there is no one she prefers, but she does not know if she loves him."

"You assured her she did not have to wed if she did not want?"

Sybilla's blue gaze darkened. "I did, but not in a manner that tempted her to seek a way out. I was the one who said she should have a choice, and I stand by that, but she is of an age now when that choice has to be made."

Joscelin cleared his throat and went to the window. He lowered his hand from his neck to clamp it around his belt. Sybilla watched him and her irritation softened into tenderness. Going to him, she slipped her arms around him from behind.

His hand left his belt and pressed down over hers. "She is our youngest," he said in a low voice. "It is hard to let her go."

"You won't be letting her go...well, not immediately. She and Brunin will only be betrothed at first and for much of the time they will dwell at Ludlow." Sybilla rubbed her cheek against his spine, feeling the rough warmth of his linen tunic against her skin. "I hope that she will cleave to Brunin and he to her, but that does not mean to the exclusion of all else. She loves you dearly and you have taught her to love generously too. There will be room for all."

He faced her and lifted her hands to his lips. "Ah, you see through me so clearly that I might as well be made of glass," he said wryly. "Did she have anything to say about the others?"

"Enough for me to know that she leaned toward neither le Vavasour nor Leicester's son...and in truth I am pleased. Brunin is the better match in every way...or he will be when he comes into his own."

Joscelin's gaze sharpened. "Meaning?"

"Meaning that he has yet to achieve his full potential—as has she. Each has it within them to coax the best out of the other. He learns fast and he absorbs knowledge like a wash leather, but he doesn't always do himself justice. Hawise will give him that backbone of confidence. And in his turn he will ride her lightly with free rein instead of ruining her life with bit and curb."

"You make her sound like a prize mare," Joscelin said curtly.

Sybilla shrugged. "When it comes to marriage, that is precisely what women are," she said, and then relented as she saw his eyelids tighten and his lips compress. He knew the truth as much as she did, but there were some things that were best left unsaid. She laid her hand against the side of his face in a tender gesture and after a moment felt him smile.

"Well, I'm still chasing you with my saddle over my arm," he said wryly.

Sybilla laughed and bestowed him a suggestive glance through her lashes. "I could always mount you."

Joscelin narrowed his eyes and gave her one of his sleepy looks. "And ride me all the way home?" His palm flattened against her side and smoothed the fabric of her gown. He drew her hip to hip against him.

She set her hands to his chest and gave a small push. "Go to," she said, but breathlessly to show that she was not unmoved. "You have a scribe to see, if the FitzWarins are to have a formal acceptance, and I have things to do of my own…"

Joscelin sighed and dropped his hands. "I suppose…" he said, but the sleepy look remained. "Later then."

"I promise." She raised one eyebrow. "I'll even rub you down afterward."

Joscelin swallowed a chuckle, made a gesture of dismissal, and headed for the door. "I'll hold you to it."

Smiling and frowning, Sybilla watched him leave. Men were easy to handle…if you knew how and you got the right one. The former knowledge could be taught and she hoped she had educated her daughters sufficiently well; but the latter ingredient depended more on the whim of fortune and she could only hope Hawise would be lucky.

❖❖❖

Marion sat on her bed, her back turned to the world, her head bent, and her shoulders hunched defensively.

"Marion," said Sybilla softly.

The figure vibrated in response but did not turn around.

"Marion, sweetheart…" Sybilla moved closer, one hand outstretched in compassion.

The girl twisted to face her, revealing eyes puffed from weeping and a blotched complexion. "I hate you!" she sobbed. "I hate you all. Go away!"

A pang shot through Sybilla, and some of it was guilt, for she and Joscelin were partly to blame for what was happening now. It had been comically amusing to hear Marion lisp as a child that one day she would marry Brunin. But what had been a game of childish nonsense to the adults had been a matter of deadly earnest to Marion. They should have nipped it in the bud.

"I know how you feel—"

"You don't, and even if you did, you wouldn't care! I'm not your real daughter. I'm just a worthless fosterling!"

"Marion, that is neither true nor fair!" Sybilla advanced to the bed. "You may not think it just now, but you are as dear to me as a daughter. I know you are disappointed, but Brunin was never promised to you. If we were at fault, it was in letting you pretend that he was." She tried to curve a compassionate arm around the girl, but Marion shrugged her off and jumped to her feet.

"You knew I wanted him, but you gave him to Hawise!" she blazed. "She always takes things away from me!"

"I gave him to neither of you," Sybilla said with severity. "The offer was made by the FitzWarin family and they were specific in their choice. Hawise's inheritance is a half-share in Ludlow and that is at the heart of the issue. I have always said that marriages should be compatible for the couple involved, but compatibility involves many aspects."

"You think I am not good enough for him—"

"No, child, that is not true. But I do believe that you are not right for him, which is a different thing…and neither is he right for you."

Marion lowered her tear-spiked lashes. "Lady Mellette liked me better than Hawise," she said with sulky spite.

Sybilla mustered her patience. "Lady Mellette likes the thought of half of Ludlow better than either you or Hawise," she said briskly. "There is no point in taking this conversation further. I can see you are deeply hurt and I am sorry for it, but rail as you will, it changes nothing. Lord Joscelin and I will do our best to find a suitable match for you. Brunin is not the only young man in the world, after all, and I have seen your eyes settle elsewhere on occasion. I have sometimes thought that you considered Brunin your bulwark—a notion to fall back upon should you find nothing better."

Marion's lower lip quivered.

"Oh, child." Sybilla rose from the bed and before Marion could dart out of the way, drew her into her arms. "As you stand here now, it may seem the end of everything, but I promise you it isn't."

At first Marion stood rigid within Sybilla's embrace, but then slowly, like a fist unclenching, some of the tension left her body, and her forehead touched Sybilla's breast.

"I know it is no substitute," Sybilla murmured, "but I was thinking that perhaps you would like to have a new gown and ribbons for your hair."

"To stand at Hawise's betrothal?" Marion asked in muffled tones that implied she would rather die first.

Sybilla stroked the silky barley-gold braids. "No, sweeting," she murmured. "To make ready for your own when the time comes…and I do not think it will be long." Sybilla's voice was soothing, but she had wagered with her intellect not her heart that Marion could be cozened by the prospect of a new gown.

Marion gave a loud sniff and wiped her eyes. "A blue one," she said in a watery voice. "Blue silk and a white veil."

"If that is your wish," Sybilla replied, managing not to make a face at the notion that Marion had chosen the colors of the Madonna.

# 18

RUNIN WAS OUT RIDING WITH RALF. IN THE PAST HE WOULD not have chosen to go anywhere with his brother, but he was making a concerted effort to bridge the chasm between them. They might never want to dwell in each other's bosoms, but setting aside the petty quarrels of childhood and wiping the slate seemed a sensible and mature thing to do. If Henry had been able to make peace with Stephen, then Brunin reasoned that he and Ralf could at least come to an understanding.

Early morning mist wreathed between the trees. At their backs, Whittington was a castle besieged in the ghostly vapor rising from the marshy ground surrounding its walls. The bridles jingled and the horses' hoofbeats thudded on the woodland path, the sound made dull and solid by a carpet of early fallen leaves, moist and mulched from recent rain. Both youths carried bows and wore hunting knives at their belts. Their cloaks were short in the manner that King Henry had made fashionable, and they were wearing tough calfhide boots.

Ralf eyed Jester with disapproval. "Have you no pride?" he asked. "What will folk think of you, riding about on a nag like that?"

Brunin swallowed his irritation. "He will walk all day and still be fresh enough to run a straight, fast tilt at the end of it," he said. "He doesn't snap or cause disruption among the other horses.

There is more in the world than appearance." Leaning forward, he tugged on Jester's long, furry ears.

Ralf drew in the reins on his dappled half-Spanish courser, making the horse arch its neck and champ the bit. "Yes, there is respect, and you won't receive it riding that thing."

"Respect has to be earned," Brunin retorted. "You can obtain it by the way you look, it is true, but it is like limewash. There had better be solid foundations beneath the paint, because in time it will flake away."

His brother grunted and for a moment looked as if he might argue the point, but then made his own concession to brotherly relations by keeping his mouth shut.

They rode on through the woods, their breath clouding outward to join the mist. Cobwebs netted the brambles with gray droplets, and the smell of damp forest was almost powerful enough to be seen. Each youth was intensely aware of his brother but, for a while, neither spoke, for they were not at ease with each other and at a loss for words.

Ralf should still have been at his training with the Earl of Derby but the latter had fled the country, accused of the murder of Ranulf, Earl of Chester, and his lands had been seized by the Crown. Ralf had returned to Whittington to finish his education at home and Brunin did not know if Ralf was pleased or embittered by the fact. Indeed, he did not know anything about Ralf, except that in their childhood and early adolescence there had been resentment, bordering on hatred, on both sides.

It was Ralf who finally broke the silence. "You're going to marry the de Dinan girl," he said.

"That depends on whether she and her family accept the offer. It is more to my benefit than theirs, after all."

"They'll accept," Ralf said. "Whatever else you were born lacking, you've always had the luck."

Brunin bit the inside of his mouth, seeking the control not to retort in kind.

"Not that I'd want to marry the wench," Ralf sneered. "She needs teaching some manners, and you cannot do that when you're under her father's roof. That red hair's a bad omen. Like as not she'll give it to your children."

Brunin looked at the trees, at the turning leaves in all their burnished beauty, and he smiled. "Good," he said.

"Do you think she's red between the thighs too?"

"Most likely," Brunin said evenly, determined not to give Ralf the indignant response he was seeking.

"And as hot as a furnace." Ralf's eyes gleamed salaciously.

"You take a keen interest to say that you'd not wed her."

Ralf shrugged his broad shoulders. "Aye, but I might bed her," he said with a grin. "I warrant she'll be hot to handle."

Brunin said nothing. If he lost his temper, he would have failed.

"Surely you've thought about what it will be like to lie between her thighs?"

"She is my mentor's daughter. I cannot afford to."

"But you can if he accepts your offer." Ralf looked at him curiously. "You must have done. Or don't women interest you?"

Brunin could see the way this was going: a verbal sparring match about sexual prowess and aimed at displaying Ralf's broad experience. Brunin had no doubt that his brother had futtered his way around half the serving girls in Derby's household. If he hadn't done similar at Whittington it was because their grandmother kept a sharp eye on the wenches and disapproved of fornication outside wedlock because it might result in bastard offspring.

"Of course they interest me," he said with an indifferent shrug, hoping that Ralf would grow bored and abandon the subject.

"Ever fucked one?"

Brunin clenched his jaw. "That's my business."

"I'll bet you haven't." There was a gloating note in Ralf's voice.

"And you have had…" Brunin raised one eyebrow. "…let me guess: at least a dozen, and all panting to get their hands up the leg of your braies."

Ralf grinned. "More than their hands," he said. "I had one and she sat over me. Straight up." He took his hands off the reins and held them out in front of his chest, cupped as if to hold overflowing bounty. "There was another, you should have seen the size of her—" He broke off as they heard the cracking of branches and rustle of undergrowth to their left. Jester threw up his head and whinnied. Ralf's gray canted sideways and Ralf had to grab swiftly for the reins. He unslung his bow.

"Perhaps it's a boar," he said, his voice pitched high with tension.

"There haven't been boar in these woods since our grandfather's time," Brunin answered. "Probably just the swineherd with his pigs." He narrowed his eyes to peer into the smoky mist. Ahead of them lay one of the many forest tracks used by charcoal burners, villagers, and woodsmen. Here the trees did not grow as densely and the trunks were younger.

Brunin could make out the dim shapes of animals trotting along the path and, as he and Ralf rode closer, realized that they were indeed the demesne swine. But they were being driven not by Hob the swineherd with his red hood and his two spotted terriers, but by barelegged men mounted on ponies; men with spears and knives and bows. Brunin inhaled, but it was as if his lungs had no strength. He drew rein and felt the familiar, devastating flood of fear. Everything inside him tightened, including his bladder, which he held under conscious command. But he could not control the saw of his breathing or the galloping of his heart which was running as he was not.

"The Welsh," Ralf whistled through his teeth. "It's the Welsh and they're stealing our pigs, the sons of whores!" He set an arrow to the nock, aimed and released. The shaft went wide and thrummed into a tree beyond the man he had intended to hit. The latter gave a yell of consternation and warning and unslung his own bow. His companions turned about.

There were at least a dozen of them and it wasn't only swine they had raided. Brunin recognized some of the ponies as pack beasts belonging to the castle, and there was a cow as well. Four of the Welsh drew swords. Arrows flew in retaliation, flashing out of the mist like deadly rain. Brunin's stomach wallowed. Ralf was reaching to the dagger at his hip. Brunin batted his hand away.

"No!" he cried. "We cannot fight them. We have to ride back and alert the guard!"

"I'm not a coward!" Ralf spat, with flushed face and glittering eyes. "I won't run from them!"

"Christ, then you'll die!" Brunin reined Jester around and dug in his heels. The gelding gave an indignant grunt at the sudden rude treatment, but sprang from his hocks into a gallop. Brunin risked a glance over his shoulder and saw that Ralf had turned his own horse about and was pounding in his wake, his expression purple with fury. The four Welshmen had broken from their companions and were giving chase. Brunin swallowed and swallowed again, feeling sick. The ground flashed beneath Jester's hoofs in a swirling pattern of brown and gold. Brunin could feel muscle, sinew, and tendon reaching for the next stride and the next. The stiff black mane whipped his mouth and cheeks. He could hear the gray galloping at his heels, or at least he hoped it was the gray. The trees closed in and then opened out; they became sparse and the rutted village track was suddenly underfoot. Feeling Jester stumble, Brunin eased up on the reins and again turned in the saddle. Ralf overshot him on the sweating gray and slewed the beast around to a violent halt that must have hurt its mouth. There was no sign of their pursuers.

"You stinking coward!" Ralf bellowed. "You're not fit to be the heir to...to...a dungheap!"

"They would have killed us and flung our corpses in the undergrowth. We're alive to raise the alarm and that's what matters—not the glory!" Brunin snarled in retort, his chest heaving. "And until you realize that, you're a hindrance at anyone's side! We're wasting time." Reining Jester around Ralf's agitated mount, he galloped on toward the castle. Ralf came after him, drawing level.

"You haven't heard the last of this," he bellowed above the thunder of hoofbeats. "I'll show you up for the craven you are!"

Brunin and Ralf raised the alarm and their father immediately assembled his knights and serjeants and set out after the raiders. Ralf loudly demanded to accompany them; Brunin grimly collected a lance, donned a gambeson, and joined the soldiers.

They found the Welsh trail, but the Welsh themselves had a good head start, even herding recalcitrant swine. The border was only four miles away and soon the men of Whittington were trespassing into Powys. By this time, the raiders had melted away into the autumn mists with their prize and there was nothing FitzWarin could do but turn for home in a foul mood.

If FitzWarin's temper was frayed at the edges, Lady Mellette's was bound in place by her will, held down, stitched over, given greater strength and danger by the fact that it was contained.

"You should have ridden faster and harder," she told FitzWarin. "You'd have caught them then."

"I doubt it, Mother." FitzWarin gulped the wine that Eve had unobtrusively handed to him. "The Welsh know how to slip away like wraiths. They do not take the beaten tracks where our horses can follow with ease."

"It is the same every autumn. They come to steal our fattened animals for their winter supplies. You should have been better prepared."

FitzWarin's jaw muscles tightened. "Hindsight is wondrous, Mother. I do my best."

"Hah, not good enough."

"Nothing ever is." He drained the wine and stalked away to unarm.

Mellette stared after him, lips thin, eyes narrow.

"I wanted to fight them until help came, but he ran away," Ralf said with an accusing look at Brunin.

Brunin felt the hair rise at his nape. He had been about to follow his father out of harm's way, but there was no help for it now. Ralf had cast the glowing coal into the dry tinder. "They were a dozen to our two," he said curtly. "There is a difference between courage and foolhardiness."

"We could have held them." Ralf bared his teeth. "They were only Welsh rabble and you were on a warhorse...or so you insist on calling that nag. Christ, King Henry was less than our age when he led an army."

"Yes," Brunin snapped, "he led an army. He didn't go skirmishing in the woods with his brother at odds of a dozen to two. And with what would we have fought them?" He made a casting motion with his fist as if physically throwing Ralf's words aside. "Bows are no use at close range and they had swords and spears. All we had were hunting knives and no bodily protection— neither shield nor gambeson. What a coup it would have been for the men of Powys. Not only the demesne swine, but the heads of the two eldest sons of Fulke FitzWarin."

"Enough." Mellette thumped her walking stick twice on the floor, a token blow for each grandson. "You spar like two pups in a litter and yet you would think of yourselves as grown men." She fixed her gaze on Ralf and leaned forward in her chair. "You eat too much fire, and it burns up your common sense," she told him, although there was a gleam of approbation in her eyes. "But at least I cannot call you wanting in courage. If my grandsire had lacked for such, then his fleet would never have left the Norman shoreline. As for you..." She turned her stare on Brunin who was ashen as he strove to show her nothing. Beneath the weight of her disapproval, he was a child again, and all the years between then and now might as well not have been. "Your father should have done as I said and given you to the Church. You will never make a leader of men when the only target your enemy sees is your back."

He wanted to heel around and leave, but her words pinned him to the spot. If he turned away, he would only confirm her image of him. He was aware of the smirk edging Ralf's lips. He could have protested; could have said that he had been into battle with Joscelin de Dinan, that he would rather use his head to think with, than as a target, but knew that it would only prolong her assault. So he faced her like a statue, saying nothing, his teeth clenched so tightly that his jaw muscles ached.

"Oh, away with both of you," she snapped with an impatient wave of her hand. "The sight of you wearies me."

They bowed from her presence. Ralf shook off the experience like a drake scattering water from its oiled feathers, but Brunin was trembling. Fury and shame rolled over him in deep, nauseating waves. Ralf's smirk was open now and to stop himself from punching it off his face, Brunin turned aside from his brother and headed rapidly toward the stables.

"Going off to cry in the hay?" Ralf taunted.

Brunin swallowed and clenched his fists. He told himself that a good battle commander had control and restraint. If he responded, it meant that Ralf's words had the power to wound, and he would not give his brother that satisfaction. Brunin knew he had been right to do as he did. There would have been no chance against a dozen. He continued walking and ignored the taunts that followed him like flung clods. It was telling, though, that Ralf seemed to know just how far he could push and made no attempt to follow with more than his voice.

Rounding the corner of the stable block in search of a moment's sanctuary, the sight of a sweating chestnut cob led by one of Joscelin's messengers swept the morning's events and all brooding thoughts to one side.

"Ulger?"

The man's lugubrious features lit with a smile. "Master FitzWarin." He inclined his head, baring a bald pink island ringed by gray curls.

"What are you doing here?" The anger in Brunin's belly was replaced by a different kind of wallow. There could be only one reason why Ulger had been sent to Whittington, and he wouldn't be smiling unless...

"I've a message for your father, but being as it concerns you, you might as well be the first to know. Lord Joscelin and Lady Sybilla have accepted your father's offer concerning the marriage between you and Mistress Hawise." The smile became an outright grin. "Great news, is it not? You'll be returning to Ludlow."

Brunin stared. For a moment the balance between the misery of a few moments since and the joy of the new tidings held him numb. And then the numbness gave way and the relief rushed through him, weakening his knees, stinging his eyes. "Great news," he repeated, his voice cracking, although it was the thought of returning to Ludlow as much as the thought of Hawise that overtook him—then, at least.

# 19

HAWISE PRESSED HER HAND AGAINST THE SHUTTERS IN THE domestic chamber, unsure whether to open them wider or close them on the view of the bailey and the castle gates. She was remembering the days when she had sat on a store-shed roof awaiting her father's return, her gown kilted through her belt, her legs bare almost to the knees, and her hair a wild straggle around her shoulders. It seemed long ago, yet still close enough to touch, but whatever the distance, everything had changed.

Today she was waiting not for her father to ride through that entrance, but her future husband. The guards had sighted the Whittington party from the battlements and heralds had been sent to escort it in. Soon she and Brunin would be pledged to each other in Ludlow's chapel in the presence of a priest and witnesses for both families. Last time she had seen him, he had been leaving for Whittington: her father's squire on the verge of knighthood, her childhood friend, her adolescent companion. Occasionally her loins had weakened at his closeness, at his scent, at the sight of his hard, whipcord body, but such times were balanced by others when she had been oblivious of his physical presence. She had grown up with him but was unsure how she was going to make the transition to being his wife…

Hearing a fanfare from the battlements, her breathing quickened and her heart began to thud, like rowers picking up the beat on a galley.

"They are here." Sybilla laid a calming hand to her shoulder.

Hawise gave a broken half-laugh. "Too late to change my mind now."

"Do you want to?" There was gentle concern in Sybilla's voice.

Hawise shook her head. "No, Mama, but I wish it were over instead of just beginning."

Sybilla kissed her cheek. "It will not be as awkward as you think. Doubtless Brunin is wishing it over too. Come, we had best go down and receive them. Lady Mellette might not set store by her own manners, but she expects everyone else to polish theirs, and we would not want to disappoint her, would we?"

Sybilla's arch tone of voice brought a smile to Hawise's lips. "No, Mama," she said. "We wouldn't."

❖❖❖

By law all that was required to make a betrothal binding were four witnesses, two for the bride, two for the groom, but in this case that number was far exceeded: by family members, retainers from both households, and sundry servants and castle folk who had squashed inside Ludlow's chapel to watch. More than one matron grew misty-eyed over the slender, darkly avised young man and his betrothed with her garnet hair curling to her slender waist. If the Lady Mellette had her reservations about girls with red hair, today she kept them to herself as she watched her grandson betroth himself to a half-share in Ludlow.

Joscelin grasped Hawise's right hand in his. Giving it a gentle squeeze in reassurance and farewell, he conveyed it to Brunin's right hand and removed his own, leaving the young couple joined. It was a symbolic gesture, a transferring of masculine authority. From now on, it was Brunin's task to protect and discipline Hawise, as it was hers to cherish and obey him. The betrothal was a pledge as binding as marriage; indeed it was the first part of the marriage ceremony. The concluding part would be the wedding itself, confirmed by a further witnessed oath and consummation. The date set for that had been tentatively placed as the midsummer after next.

Hawise sensed the weight of the witnesses' stares bearing down on them, laden with expectation. She could feel a constriction in her throat. She would not panic; there was nothing to be afraid of. She met Brunin's gaze. Beneath the level black brows, his eyes were darkest brown, but held too a reflection of the red from his tunic. There was intensity in them and concentration, and a flicker of something unsettling that both attracted and frightened her. They exchanged a kiss of peace to seal the pledge, but it was a formal salute and there was no pressure to the gesture. The symbolism was everything and the physical sensation naught. It was the first time she and Brunin had ever kissed, and she realized with an inward grimace that Marion had more knowledge than she.

The couple turned and walked from the chapel back to the hall, pacing in formal procession. The hem of her gown whispered over the ground; his boots made no sound on the hard, beaten earth. He kept his gaze on the middle distance. Hawise's own glance flickered to the thatched roof of the store shed. The memories of her childhood seemed far more real than her current situation.

Marion congratulated Brunin and Hawise with a blinding smile and blank eyes. "I will do better for myself than you," she said loftily to Hawise. "You'll see." She walked away, head carried high and the sun shining on the blue silk of her new gown.

"I suppose I should speak to her and set things to rights," Brunin murmured reluctantly.

"As long as it is not in a dark stairwell," Hawise said, only half in jest.

His eyelids tensed. "No," he said and hesitated as if he were going to say more.

She waited, but he did not speak. Instead he tightened his mouth. She did not push him lest it was something that she did not want to hear.

Indeed, it was for that very reason that Brunin refrained from speaking. He was not sure that it would be courtly to blurt out that he wished he were in a dark stairwell with Hawise. Nor did he want to say something so personal when they were surrounded by a crowd of family and retainers, agog for every sign or nuance of emotion the betrothed couple might display. It was an intimate thought in a less than intimate moment. He was awed at the changes wrought in Hawise during the time he had been away. The territory had altered and even landmarks that remained familiar had undergone a subtle shift. She was still his lord's daughter, she was still his friend, but now she was also his future wife. That oath of betrothal had bound them with ties that could only be sundered by death. Furthermore, she looked ravishing in that gown. He would have to be made of stone for his thoughts not to turn in the direction of dark stairwells…or indeed of feather beds. Yet with those thoughts came anxiety. He did not have to scratch far beneath the surface to find his insecurity. Marion had exposed it like a sharp fingernail tearing flesh when she'd said that she would do better than Hawise. He felt a fraud. He wasn't worthy of this match. There were too many expectations being heaped upon him. The burden was so heavy that he could not understand why he was still on his feet; he anticipated that at any moment he was going to fall flat on his face. Unwilling to articulate such fears, especially to Hawise who was so changed, he held the emotions within and said nothing.

❖❖❖

Toward the end of the betrothal feast, when the guests were relaxed and the atmosphere had grown less formal, Brunin sought out Marion. He slid into the empty position on the bench at her right side. Cecily had been sitting there until a moment ago, but had retired, pleading that she was still in mourning for her husband.

"I am sorry," Brunin said.

Marion gazed at him through wine-bright eyes. "Sorry that you have to be betrothed to her?" she asked with a jut of her chin. "Or sorry for me?"

Brunin winced. "Sorry for what went before," he said. "Everyone treated it as a game—as a whim. But it was serious for you, wasn't it?"

"Treated what? Can you not even say it?" She bared her teeth. "Was it a game and a whim when you kissed me on the stairs at Sibbi's marriage?"

Brunin shifted uncomfortably on the bench, made uneasy by her virulence. "As I remember, you made the first move," he said. "You asked me."

Her expression grew bitter. "But you were eager enough to follow."

He looked down at the board. "I thought you were playing with me. That was what I meant about it being a game and a whim."

"What would you have done if the 'game' had gone further than a kiss?" she demanded. "Would you have stood by me, or would you have seen me branded as a slut and packed off to a nunnery?"

Brunin flushed defensively. "Matters didn't; there is no point talking about it." He started to rise to his feet, suddenly knowing that it had been a mistake to try and make his peace while wine was simmering in her blood and her hurt still sharp.

She laid her hand on his sleeve and gripped his forearm. He felt the dig of her nails through tunic and shirt.

"As I said before, I am sorry…deeply sorry, the more so since it has come to this."

"You will be. I swear to you on my mother's grave that you will be."

He gazed down at her hand and then lifted his eyes to hers. What he saw in them raised the fine hairs at the nape of his neck. Marion gave a short gasp, released her grip, and, thrusting away from the bench, stumbled for the sanctuary of the stairs.

Rubbing his arm, Brunin returned to Hawise. He shook his head when she leaned toward him. "Do not ask," he said. "Let the dust settle." But privately, he doubted whether settling was possible in the storm he had seen in Marion's eyes.

# 20

## Spring 1157

$\mathcal{G}$ILBERT DE LACY GAZED ACROSS WOODS AND FIELDS STEEPED
in spring sunshine. The trees were in bud and early leaf, their
delicate green filtered with gold. Across the cliff, across the river,
Ludlow Castle shone as if dipped in honey. From this vantage point,
he had seen it in all its seasonal incarnations: snow-clad and brown
through frost-fronded branches; silvered in mist like a faery palace
from a romance of King Arthur; concealed like a stag in the woods
by dark summer green. The longing cut into him, and the frustration. No matter how many bandages of truce and reason were laid
upon the wound, the bitter sense of injustice and loss bled through.

Like a sharp pain in flesh, his gaze was drawn to the scarlet
and gold wyvern banner rippling from the battlements. "Henry
promised to restore the lands of the dispossessed," he said in a
bitter voice to de Lysle who was riding at his left shoulder. "But
he has not kept his word. It seems that he would rather sweep the
matter under a bench than deal with it. If I wait his pleasure, my
grave will come to me before Ludlow does." He drew the reins
through his fingers and his horse jibbed at the pressure on the bit.
"Whatever Henry says, possession is nine-tenths of the law."

"So how do you intend to unseat Joscelin de Dinan if the King
shows no interest?" de Lysle asked.

"The King must be made to show interest." De Lacy turned his
stallion about. "I have been patient for too long."

❖❖❖

A week later, Joscelin rode out of Ludlow, intent on visiting a tenant who wanted him to witness a grant to the monks at Wenlock.

"I am fit to accompany you," Brunin protested, when ordered to stay behind, but Joscelin shook his head and would have none of it.

"So you say, but I would rather you took another day's rest than ruin yourself and the horse."

"But—"

"No arguments." Joscelin raised a forefinger. "You can sort out my weapons chest if you want something to do and see about sharpening up my spare sword."

"Yes, my lord," Brunin said with resignation. Three days ago, while Brunin was exercising the gelding, Jester had put his foot in a coney hole and taken a fall. The horse had escaped with a strained foreleg, but Brunin had struck his head and been knocked out of his senses. Although he recovered his wits within the hour, he had been able to see two of everything, had been white as sifted flour, and sporadically vomiting. Three days later, he was still suffering from a persistent headache. Jester had been rested up in the stables and tended by the head groom who had declared the horse to be fit as soon as his master was.

Sybilla had muttered darkly about the coneys. They had been introduced to Ludlow by Gilbert's branch of the family and kept within an enclosure, their meat and fur a valuable addition to the castle's domestic supplies. However, some of them had burrowed their way out and spread to the surrounding countryside where their nibbling and digging caused havoc.

Brunin watched Joscelin ride out. He glittered as he rode, for he was using the occasion to break in his new hauberk, the old one having seen out its better days during three decades of hard strife.

Brunin sighed and turned to his duties. A headache threatened in the background, but he pushed it aside, determined to ignore it. If the women thought he was suffering, they would have him back on his bed, and after three days of sleep and inactivity, his body was twitchy with excess energy. He climbed the stairs to the domestic chamber and asked Sybilla for the key to Joscelin's weapons chest.

"You are feeling better?" she asked as she unfastened the key from the ring at her belt.

"Yes, my lady." He made a face. "I would have ridden with my lord this morning, if he had not ordered me to rest another day."

"Well, the task he has left you should keep you gainfully occupied until noon…and I can find plenty for you to do after that." Sybilla gave a soft laugh at his expression, pressed his shoulder, and left him.

Although he had been a part of the family since his arrival at Ludlow, it astonished Brunin how much deeper that involvement had become since his betrothal to Hawise. Before he had been like a piece of trimming attached to a garment. Now he was part of the garment itself, woven so firmly among the other strands that any attempt at removal would cause a destructive tear.

The weapons chest was stored in a corner of the main bed-chamber that Joscelin had marked for his own territory. Here stood his hauberk pole, currently occupied by his old mail shirt. The garment was supported by an ash stave thrust through the sleeves. The leather of the ventail section was black with grease and sweat. A close inspection revealed that some of the rings were slightly different in shade and shape and indicated where the hauberk had been repaired in the aftermath of battle and altered to fit its wearer as he grew from slender youth to wide-shouldered man in his prime. Brunin lightly touched the oiled rivets. He was to be knighted before he was wed, and he would receive his own hauberk then, and a pair of silver spurs in token of his transition from youth to man. Perhaps then, garbed like a knight, he would feel more like one.

He knelt before the chest, a solid affair crafted of carved oak and reinforced with wide iron bands. Having turned the key in the lock, he unsnapped the hasps and laid back the lid. Inside, stored in oiled and waxed bundles, was the story of Joscelin's life as a mercenary, a knight, and lord of a great marcher castle. An old Dane ax of the kind that King Stephen had favored came first to Brunin's hand. There were a few minor rust pits and he set it to one side for cleaning and reoiling. A waxed hide unrolled to reveal several hunting knives and an English seax. The hilt needed attention, but since Brunin had never seen Joscelin carry the weapon, he assumed that it was kept as a memento rather than being functional. Another ax came to hand, some spearheads and arrow points, a mace and a morning-star flail. Brunin grimaced at the latter. He had trained in its use…or tried to, but it was a fickle weapon, as likely to wrap itself around. the head of its wielder as strike an enemy. Mastered, however, and as demonstrated by Joscelin, it was a fearsome thing to use, capable of splintering bone with a single blow. He wrapped the leather grip around his wrist, grasped the handle, and experimentally swung the ball and chain.

"My mother said you'd be playing. She knows you too well."

He spun around to find Hawise standing behind him, laughter in her eyes.

"Playing?" he repeated and looked affronted. "You don't 'play' with one of these." He put it in her hand.

"What were you doing then?"

"Practicing. The moves aren't subtle with a flail, but they have to be controlled, otherwise you'll do more damage to yourself than your opponent."

She swung the chain, winced at the jerk of the ball against her wrist, and, hastily handing it back, came to inspect the rest of the contents of the chest. He glanced over his shoulder but there was no sign of a maid. Hawise was here without a chaperone, and it was by her mother's consent. Sybilla was putting a lot of trust in him and her daughter.

"Is there a reason for you seeking me out?"

She slanted him a look through her lashes. "Who said that I

had sought you out? Perhaps I wanted to look inside my father's weapons chest."

"Perhaps." He laid the flail to one side and gestured. "Most of it is clean of rust. Your father wanted me to check after the winter damp." He was pleased at the conversational way that the words emerged—as if her presence was not raising the fine hair along his forearms. The contents of the chest had been interesting a moment ago, but now all he could think about was the way the fabric of her gown was drawn tight to her waist by the side lacings and how the arrangement emphasized the curve of her breasts.

Thus far Brunin had managed to keep his hands to himself, but there had been moments when the temptation had almost proved too much. Their courtship, if such it could be called, was taking place under the sympathetic but watchful eye of Sybilla, and the less sympathetic but equally watchful scrutiny of her father. Hawise was his daughter, his child, and while he accepted that she was old enough to wed and bed, he was uncomfortable with the notion of her taking the steps that led to those events. Sybilla would say, "Let them be alone awhile," and Joscelin would agree, but his notion of "awhile" was somewhat narrower than his wife's. Even when they were unchaperoned, as now, and Joscelin was absent, Brunin felt that he should be looking over his shoulder. The need to be on guard was a constant, anxious counter-balance to his ardor.

Hawise knelt before the chest, gathering her skirts to one side so they would not be in the way. One foot peeped from beneath the hem, revealing a laced goatskin shoe and a narrow ankle clad in silk hose. Brunin swallowed at the sight and heat flooded into his groin.

"I remember this sword!" she cried, removing the one that Brunin was supposed to oil and check for sharpness. "When I was a little girl my father used to wear it all the time. It came from Brittany with my great-grandfather." She laid her hand to the hilt and drew the weapon from the scabbard. The blade was still mirror bright, but then Brunin knew that it was checked twice a year, even if Joscelin possessed newer swords.

"Do you remember when we used to fight with wooden swords?" she asked.

"Only too well." He grimaced and rubbed his arm. "You might not have been skilled, but you were lethal."

She poked out her tongue at him and, rising to her feet, faced him with the blade. Then, slowly, she sheathed it. Probably she had not intended the gesture to be suggestive, or erotic, but it was, and Brunin's breath came so short that it was almost like being punched.

Hawise too seemed to realize what she had done, for she hastily replaced the weapon in the coffer. He saw the ripple of her throat as she swallowed. "I came to tell you that my mother has given us the high chamber in the north-west tower for our own...after we are wed," she added. "And she has promised us a bed and furnishings."

"That is generous of her," Brunin heard himself say. The words sounded stilted to him, as if he were speaking at a formal gathering and not to Hawise personally. The word "bed" leaped out at him.

"I...We are going to sweep it out later today and sort out which hangings to put up on the walls. Do you have a preference?"

He shrugged. "None. Whatever you wish."

She looked at him. "Is your head hurting?"

"No...well, only a little. Why do you ask?"

"Because you're frowning, as if you are troubled."

Brunin decided that riding out with Joscelin would have been much less dangerous than staying here. "Hawise, I..."

"What?"

He came to her and set his hands at her waist. The feel of her body warmth through the taut cloth, the scent of her, was too much. "This," he said and angled his head to kiss her. Her lips were full and soft and, after the briefest hesitation, they parted beneath his own. She raised her hand and set her palm to the side of his face, then down to his throat and around the back of his head, where her fingers tightened in the hair at his nape. The feelings created by her touch were exquisite. She leaned into the kiss and pressed herself against him and Brunin swallowed a moan. Raw lust warred with moral responsibility. Your lord's daughter, he told himself with the rational part of his mind. Your future wife: you have the right, said the part that was burning to be quenched. She must have been torn both ways too, for after a moment, she broke the kiss and drew back, breathing hard. Her eyes were hazy and she licked her lips as if savoring the taste of the kiss.

"Jesu," she said and gave a husky laugh that almost caused him to break into a sweat. "If this is a foretaste of what is to come, then there will be naught left of me on my wedding morning save a pile of ashes."

He laughed too, attempting to diminish the hungry tension. They were both sensible. Opportunities for dalliance like this were rare and never lasted long. They could have made clandestine assignations, of course, but they both knew what was at stake and what was expected of them. She would come to her wedding most properly a virgin and there would be proof on the sheet in the morning. For there not to be would be a source of shame and a blight to the start of their married life. A woman who yielded was not to be trusted. A man who took advantage and caused the shame was dishonorable. "Those who play with fire..." he jested weakly and, closing the lid of the weapons chest, sat down upon it. In the corner of his eye, her father's hauberk gleamed, reminding him of its owner's presence. The heavy pulsing at his groin subsided to a slower, duller ache. It seemed a long, long time until midsummer.

Hawise tilted her head to one side. Her cheeks were pink, but the mistiness was leaving her eyes. "I have never asked you," she said, "but how many women have you bedded?"

Brunin was taken aback. "What sort of question is that?" He folded his arms, half smiling, half defensive.

"A curious one? Since we are to be wed, I want to know such things about you."

"Why?" He began to feel uneasy. "Surely a marriage is a beginning. We do not need to drag our past behind us."

The flush in her cheeks deepened and spread to her brow. "But we are shaped by what has happened in the past. That's why my mother wanted me and Sibbi to have some say in our marriages—because she didn't. That is why your father sent you to us at Ludlow, rather than keeping you at Whittington, and why mine hesitated before he committed himself."

"Did you hesitate too?"

"Of course. It was the most important decision of my life."

Her frankness made him smile. "I am glad you decided in my favor."

"And you?" she demanded. "What did you say?"

"You want the honest truth?"

"You know I do. What are you going to say? Never look a gift horse in the mouth?"

"No, but that is what my father said when my grandmother remarked that it was a pity you had to have red hair and a Breton mercenary for a father."

Hawise drew herself up.

The smile became a chuckle. "Hold your indignation. Those were my grandmother's words, not mine. Out of her hearing, my father said that your family were probably thinking it a pity that the blood of the Conqueror should flow through the veins of an objectionable old crone."

Hawise was diverted into a splutter, but not for long. "And what did you say?"

He sobered. "I couldn't believe my good fortune. I knew it was a possibility, but I had never dared to hope. There are many families your father could have chosen. And to know that you had been given a say in the matter and not refused..." He fell silent, pondering what to say without exposing too much of himself. "It was a great honor and responsibility," he said at last. "I swear you will never regret your choice." There were no words of love. He would not have known how to speak them, or even be familiar with the emotion. He knew lust; he knew the warmth of friendship and affection. Sometimes she exasperated him beyond bearing, and sometimes he ached with the need for her presence. But he was no troubadour, and his feelings were conflicting. He knew that emotions could be both enemy and friend and he was wary.

"I will hold you to your oath," she said with a smile and a tilt of her head. "But you still haven't told me the number of women you have bedded."

He looked exasperated and amused. "I do not see that it matters...unless you think I need the experience."

She blushed. "No...but it is natural for women to wonder."

"Is it?" His eyes shone with a salacious masculine gleam. "Is that what you talk about together when the men are out warring or hunting?"

"Sometimes." Hawise folded her arms and made a face at him. "But not in the same fashion as you men do. You all laugh and brag about your conquests to each other and are not thought the worse for your deeds or boasting. But if a woman does that, she is branded a slut and a whore. If I do not come to my marriage bed a virgin, then I am shamed. If you do not, then it is a matter of no consequence...save that some will laugh at you for not having the knowledge and pity me your lack of experience."

He shrugged. "Some men brag of their conquests in the same way that some women will browbeat others by talking of their clothes and possessions," he said. "It is a means of making themselves appear more important and powerful than they are." He gave her a rueful smile. "I am sorry if you are vexed, but my experience is my business alone. All I will say is that you can rest easy that no woman in Ludlow is going to look at you askance and say she had me first."

The subject matter had put a high color in her cheeks. "I am glad for that, even if Marion tries to tell me otherwise."

He looked indignant. "That was no more than a kiss."

"Not to hear Marion speak."

Brunin exhaled hard. "You were there. You saw what happened. And I have never laughed or bragged about it. There is only Marion who keeps it alive and out of pique. As soon as your parents settle a husband on her, she'll forget she ever wanted to be my bride."

"Mayhap, but it doesn't help that the last offer my father made to that knight of Bishop Gilbert's was turned down. Marion's been brooding like a thundercloud ever since."

"I—" He closed his mouth and looked toward the stairs as they heard the sound of footfalls. Moments later, Annora poked her head around the door and said that Sybilla wanted Hawise. Then she waited to escort her. The maid's shrewd gaze went to the closed weapons chest and Brunin seated upon it and calculated the distance between the couple.

He was tempted to make the sarcastic observation that they still had all of their clothes on, but decided that it wasn't worth the aggravation, and besides, Annora was only doing her duty. Murmuring that he would speak with Hawise later and repeating that he had no preference as to the hangings in their prospective chamber, he returned to his task.

Once he had checked and oiled the weapons, secured the chest, and returned the key to Sybilla, he went to inspect Jester. Three days of rest seemed to have cured the leg strain and when he rode the horse around the bailey at a bareback trot, there was no sign of the injury. Satisfied, he returned the gelding to the stables and gave him a thorough grooming. It was a pleasure to do so, for, despite his comical ugliness, Jester's glossy copper-bay coat put many a more elegant mount to shame. By the time he had finished working on his mount, Jester's hide was shining like a mirror, Brunin's arm was aching, and so was his head. Overcome by a nauseous lassitude caused by the dregs of his concussion, he lay down in the empty stall next to Jester's. The groom had cleaned it out and refurbished it with a pile of thick, fragrant hay, redolent with the scents of the meadow from which it had been cut. Rather than seek out his pallet, which would have meant toiling up a set of narrow tower stairs, Brunin lay down in the horse bedding and closed his eyes.

# 21

MARION SAT IN THE WINDOW SEAT AND LOOKED OUT through the open shutters on the late spring afternoon. She had just caught sight of Lord Joscelin's troop returning from their day's business in relaxed formation. Within the body of the room, the maids were industriously sweeping the floors and dusting cobwebs from the plastered walls. The room in this tower was generally used as a guest chamber, but Brunin and Hawise were to take it for their own after they were wed.

Marion had watched Hawise return with Annora, had seen that the former was flushed and smiling and had known bitter envy. She comforted herself with the notion that Brunin was only doing his duty, that his family was forcing him into this marriage and that he still secretly yearned for her. She envisioned Hawise dying in childbirth nine months from the marriage and herself taking Hawise's place. She would be a good stepmother to the baby Hawise had borne and she would produce a string of healthy sons for Brunin.

"Red and green," said Hawise, hands on hips, gaze studying the walls. The plaster was limewashed and already painted with a frieze of leafy green scrolls, punctuated by deep red flowers.

Marion sniffed. She would have chosen blue to enhance her eyes and because it was more expensive. Different too. There was plenty of red and green in Sybilla's apartments.

"Marion, what do you think of red and green?"

She gave an enthusiastic nod and smiled. It wasn't her fault that Hawise had no taste and she had no intention of helping her with suggestions. When the time came, Marion would have her blue and her gold and everyone would marvel.

"The bed can go here," Hawise said, planning in her imagination. "With hangings along that wall, and coffers over there."

Marion turned from the window and wrapped her forefinger around one silky fair braid. Behind her, among the trees on the other side of the river, steel caught the flash of the sun.

Sybilla was considering with Hawise. Looking at them standing side by side, Marion was consumed by misery. She ought to be the one making this room into a home, not Hawise. Cecily looked miserable too, but then all this must be a reminder of what she had lost. Even if she hadn't been wildly in love with Roger of Hereford, she had once had her own apartments to rule over.

"My stomach hurts," Marion said abruptly. "I'm going to lie down."

Immediately Sybilla was all concern. "You should have said, sweetheart. Shall I make a tisane for you?"

Marion shook her head. "I suppose it's no more than my flux coming on, and you are too busy here." She could not prevent a note of bitterness edging into her voice. The fact that Sybilla called her "sweetheart" only made it worse.

"I am not too busy to care for the needs of my family," Sybilla said, giving Marion a severe look which warned her not to play the martyr. "If you are truly in pain, then all of this can wait."

Yes I am, Marion thought, and you have no notion of how deep.

Hawise stood by the window arch to view the room from a different angle and decide where the candle prickets should go. She turned to consider the light flowing through the open shutters and her gaze lingered on the view from the tower window. The river shone with the reflected green of the spring trees. A pair of swans preened near the bridge, made four by their images in the water.

Above the riverbank, the woods climbed the slope to Whitcliffe. It was a tranquil scene, one to lift the heart, especially with her father riding homeward, his troop encircled in a small halo of dust. Above the river, within the woods, something twinkled as brightly as the light on the water. Hawise narrowed her eyes and realized with a jolt that it was armor. But it wasn't her father and his troop. They were on the road and clearly visible.

The sound she made brought her mother, Marion, and Cecily to the window, crowding beside her. Sybilla whitened and stifled a cry against the back of her hand. Hawise watched in horror as her father's troop was set upon by an armed conroi, their shields and banners proclaiming them as de Lacy men. They were too far away for Ludlow's archers to do much, and even a skilled marksman would have been hard pressed to separate the sudden melee of troops. It was like watching a cauldron boil and spill over.

"God on the Cross, he will be killed!" Sybilla gasped, swaying on her feet. Her first husband had been slaughtered in an ambush, but, hard as it had been to bear, she had not witnessed him being massacred before her eyes.

Hawise saw de Lacy's banner waver and then topple as his standard-bearer was run through by a lance. The wyvern banner rippled boldly on its shaft, but, moments later, it too dipped and vanished as the fighting intensified. It sailed upright again as another knight took it up, but so too did de Lacy's banner. Sybilla, usually so composed and calm, uttered a soft moan and collapsed in a faint. Uttering a cry of concern, Cecily dropped to her knees at her mother's side.

"They're not going to win through," Marion said. There was a strange look in her eyes: shock and terror and horrified delight. She clenched her knuckles on the stone sill, her posture stiff and intent.

Hawise swallowed. There had to be something they could do: send out the castle guards; rouse the town. Her father was forcing his way toward the bridge, carving a path by sheer skill and strength of arms. She could see his wyvern shield clearly now and follow the rise and fall of his arm. Then de Lacy himself placed his mount in her father's way and the two men exchanged a fierce volley of blows. More of de Lacy's followers surged forward, reinforcing their lord, and her father had to yield ground, fighting desperately now.

The chamber door opened and Brunin wandered in, yawning and stretching, his tunic burred with stalks of hay and his hair sticking up in untidy spikes. He had slept longer and more deeply than he had anticipated, but had woken feeling refreshed and relaxed, his head truly clear for the first time in days. He had decided that it might be diplomatic to go to the north-west tower and see what the women were doing. While he had no deep interest in the appearance of the room, he knew women set great store by such things and it would be diplomatic to make the right kind of noises. Crossing from the stables to the tower, he thought he heard a shout at the gates, but the guards often called to each other and his mind was preoccupied with thoughts of Hawise, so he paid it little heed. The thick stone blotted out all other sounds as he climbed the stairs to the top chamber, and thus he was unprepared for the sight that met his eyes: Sybilla on the floor; a crying Cecily crouched over her, patting her face and hands; Marion leaning at the window; a wild-eyed Hawise turning between the latter and her mother. His first thought was that Sybilla had suffered a seizure.

"What's happened? Is your mother—?"

"It's not my mother," Hawise cried. "My father's being attacked by Gilbert de Lacy."

"What?" Brunin strode to the window. Grudgingly Marion yielded him space. What he saw paralyzed him. His breath clotted in his chest and a great surge of shock emptied him of all ordinary sensation. The battle beyond the bridge on the far bank of the river was desperate and it was obvious that Joscelin was going to be brought down.

"Do something!" Hawise struck his arm such a blow that he staggered and what air remained in his lungs was forced out on a harsh gasp. He inhaled, but it was like breathing through wool. The enormity of what was happening rendered him immobile, the transition from a state of passive awakening to horrified awareness was too rapid and intense to deal with.

She struck him again, her own reaction taking a different form. "He's going to be killed before our eyes, while you just stand there like a lump of wood!"

He stared at her.

"It's true what they all say; you are a coward," she spat. "You don't have the courage when it comes to the sticking point! You said you'd never give me cause to regret my choice and already you are proven a liar!"

Her words cut through the numbness and for a moment everything was exposed to the air in full, blinding pain.

"I will go myself and may you be damned!" She flung away from him toward the door.

The pain burst in a red mist that flooded him with its heat and gave him back the use of his limbs. Striding after her, he seized her arm in a bruising grip, swung her around, and shoved her roughly back toward Sybilla. She staggered and almost fell, her eyes blazing with tears.

"Prepare yourselves to tend the wounded," he snarled and, turning his back on her, strode from the room.

He was dimly aware of descending the tower, of going to the weapons chest and lifting out the ax that he had earlier oiled and sharpened. Of donning Joscelin's spare gambeson and hauberk. The latter was loose across his shoulders and long on the body, but there wasn't time to care about such things. Jamming the morning-star flail through his belt, he grabbed the ax and descended to the bailey.

There was no one to command the guards on the walls, for Joscelin's constable and marshal were both fighting for their lives in the melee, as were most of his knights. Brunin had been well and truly flung into the heart of the fire; the command and the consequences were his. No more pulling back, no drawing the blows. This was as real as the excoriating words Hawise had flung in his face.

The act of donning armor had cleared the red mist from his brain but it was as if a stranger issued terse orders to the soldiers and sent forth messengers to the town. The grooms had hastily saddled Jester; even as they brought him from his stall, Brunin was already reaching to the stirrup and swinging astride.

He nodded the command to open the postern that led out to the bridge and rode Jester out at the head of four knights, two serjeants, and a dozen footsoldiers. A tocsin was ringing in the town and the burgesses were pouring from their dwellings, armed with spears and staves, pitchforks, clubs, and axes.

Brunin increased the pace from a trot to a canter, from a canter to a controlled gallop. Jester's shoes rang on the bridge timbers. Brunin gave him his head and leaned forward. While he had been making ready, his heart had been thundering in spate, but now the flow was slow and hard. He knew precisely when to touch the reins, when to turn the horse, when to raise the ax. All of it, training, instinct, and raw, bright rage, fused into one powerful motion as he spurred the gelding into the heart of the melee and, in a smooth, controlled movement, brought the ax down upon the helm of one of the knights pressing Joscelin. A blaze of satisfaction burned through him at the scream, at the sight of blood, at the crumpling, falling body. An image of Hawise's scorn-filled face shimmered before his eyes and he struck again. Hard, sure, strong. He would show them again and again and again what he was made of and why they should fear to awaken a sleeping dragon.

Joscelin was fighting on foot, the ground beneath him slippery with the blood pumping from the throat of his fallen, dying mount. Brunin parried a blow aimed at Joscelin and flipped the attacker's sword out of his hand. The knight yelled in pain at the pressure on his tendons and retreated. A second blow from Brunin hit the shield edge and splintered the wood. The knight's horse plunged sideways, fouling de Lacy who was trying frantically to reach Joscelin. Cursing, de Lacy tried to rein aside, but his destrier stumbled in a coney hole and pitched the Baron over its mane. De Lacy landed hard, his sword flying from his grip. Ernalt de Lysle spurred forward to protect him and the downward blow of Brunin's ax was met upon the blade of a sword. Sparks glanced from the strike of steel on steel and slivers of metal flew from the weapons. Brunin disengaged and struck again, but by now de Lysle's shield was in position. The ax thudded into the linden planking and wedged there. De Lysle wrenched, and Brunin was forced to relinquish his hold, but as he did so his hand was already grasping the flail, and he brought it around and down. The spiked ball struck de Lysle across the back of the wrist and, with a scream, the knight dropped the sword and snatched his hand away. Blood webbed between his fingers and it was clear that he had lost their use. He tried to protect himself with his shield, but it was wrenched away by one of the Ludlow townsmen, who toppled him from his horse with a blow from his mason's mallet. De Lysle hit the ground hard, slamming both breath and wits from his body.

"Don't kill him!" Brunin commanded the townsman. "Take his weapons and bind him. Even if his soul's worthless, his ransom won't be."

"Do I get a share, sir?"

Brunin flashed a savage grin. "I'll see you recompensed," he said and turned back to the battle in time to see Joscelin standing over the fallen Gilbert de Lacy, his sword at his throat.

"Yield or die. It is all the same to me whether I take you prisoner or kill you here." Joscelin's breath sawed in his throat and a red trickle ran down his neck from a nicked earlobe.

De Lacy's gaze flickered, assessing the situation, and he raised one hand in surrender. "I yield." He gagged on the words as if they were poison.

Joscelin snapped his fingers. Two footsoldiers hauled de Lacy roughly to his feet. The Baron's throat corded with the effort of suppressing a scream and the knowledge that his enemy had suffered battle injuries brought a grim smile to Joscelin's lips. It wouldn't worry him if de Lacy died from his wounds. Seeing their lord captured and Joscelin's cause bolstered by the troops from the castle and the men of the town, who continued to pour across the bridge, those of de Lacy's men who were capable fled the field.

Brunin looked at the ax he had retrieved from the battleground. The steel-blue edge wore a clotted border of other men's blood. He would have to clean it again, he thought absently, otherwise the rust would take hold with a vengeance. The dead and the injured of both factions strewed the field. Three of the dead knights were his work, and de Lysle could easily have been a fourth. Brunin had fought with the detachment that came of being pushed over the edge, but he had kept his awareness, and now feeling was returning in increments. He could smell the blood and the hot stink of horse entrails, hear the groans of the wounded, and see beyond the victory of rescue to the red carnage. He began to tremble and had to make a conscious effort to stiffen his spine. There were things he could not afford to confront just now; things that had to be thrust to the back of his mind and shut away.

Swallowing his gorge, he turned from the bloody field and, leaving de Lysle to the townsman and a serjeant, caught the reins of the knight's sweating stallion. Clicking his tongue to the beast, he led it across to Joscelin.

"You need a horse, my lord."

Joscelin stared up at him. One of his eye-whites was blotted with red, either from a wound or the tremendous effort he had expended to keep himself alive. His knuckles were skinned and his sword made the blood on Brunin's ax blade look naught but a smear.

"You saved my life, boy," he said in a hoarse voice. "And that is the last time I am ever going to call you that. You have more than earned your manhood and the right to stand among my knights." Seizing the horse's reins he swung into the saddle. Brunin saw him wince and suspected that the move was not as easy as Joscelin had made it look, but there was the matter of pride, the need to display strength in front of the vanquished Gilbert de Lacy. "You are welcome into my family. I say now, for all to hear, that I am proud to call you son."

Heat burned Brunin's face at the compliment, but there was as much pain as pleasure in his response. At the back of his mind, clamoring to escape from the place where he had locked them, were Hawise's words. She had accused him of cowardice, had flayed him with her tongue. He had only to recall the blazing contempt in her eyes to feel nausea surge in his belly.

The men of Ludlow crossed the bridge and re-entered the keep, battered, bloody, but triumphant. Brunin watched the serjeants remove de Lacy and de Lysle to the Pendover tower where there was a chamber with a heavy oak door and secure bolts. Sybilla came running out onto the sward and threw herself upon Joscelin, weeping, frantic, feverishly examining his injuries. Joscelin was somewhat taken aback by the reception from his usually pragmatic wife, but after a moment took her face in his hands and kissed her full on the lips, all sweaty and battle-mired as he was.

"I thought I was going to see you killed in front of my eyes!" she sobbed. "I couldn't bear it! Not after Payne. Not after so many years!"

Murmuring platitudes to his wife, Joscelin turned toward the domestic quarters. He would deal with his prisoners when he had dealt with his own injuries.

Brunin looked briefly for Hawise, but there was no sign of her and he was glad that she had not come flying out to greet him. He knew that he ought to follow Joscelin and Sybilla to their chamber. He knew that Joscelin would be generous with his praise and Sybilla, given her current state, all over him with gratitude, but he didn't want that. And he didn't want to see Hawise.

Dismounting from Jester, he led him away to the stables, shrugging off the congratulations, the back-slapping and camaraderie offered by the other men. They wanted him to be one of their number, but for the moment he could not cope with their loud-mouthed enthusiasm and their desire to talk about every move and blow of the victory snatched from defeat.

"Sir, shall I take him?" asked a stable boy, his manner both nervous and excited. It would only take a word from Brunin, an encouraging glance, to unleash the lad's tongue.

"No, I'll deal with him myself. Tend to the others. Let me be." Brunin spoke in short sentences, the most he could manage. The energy of the battle was still churning inside him and was not going to subside in a moment.

The boy opened his mouth. Brunin drew a deep breath. "Go," he said with ragged control. "Don't argue."

Alert to danger, the lad tugged his forelock and ran off. Brunin pressed his head against Jester's flank. His headache had returned and he thought his skull was going to explode.

"Brunin?"

He turned his face sideways along Jester's warm flank to look at Hawise and thought that she had a deal less sense than the groom's youngest apprentice.

Her voice was nervous and uncertain. "I…My father said you saved his life, and I saw what you did on the field."

"And I suppose that seeing is believing," he snarled softly. He held out his hands, palms down, showing her the dark blood rimming his fingernails and staining his knuckles. "Is this the kind of courage that you want from me? Is this proof enough of being 'blooded'?"

She stared and he saw her swallow. He hoped that she felt as sick as he did.

"I…I should never have said what I did." She wrung her hands as if washing them. "All I could think of was that my father was going to die."

"And that I was a 'coward who was going to do nothing,'" he said contemptuously, not in the least mollified by her admission that she was in the wrong. That she had thought the words was enough, whether she had spoken them or not.

She reddened. "I…It was the way you walked into the chamber as if naught was wrong. And then you just stood there."

"I wasn't allowed a moment to lose my wits and gather them again," he said furiously. "Damned in the space of a breath. Not much faith for a marriage, is it?"

Her eyes darkened; her chin came up. "I came to apologize, not to be railed at."

"Well, perhaps I don't feel much like forgiving you," he said out of the pain thundering through his skull and was both gratified and assailed by remorse to see the way she recoiled. "You knew the words that would cut deepest," he added, "and you used them." He turned back to the horse, his fingers working jerkily to loosen the girth, his mouth set in a tight line. Sensing the violent tensions in the air, the gelding flinched and sidled. "I know where I stand, and it's at naught. You might as well be my grandmother."

Her voice rose and cracked. "You are twisting everything awry!"

"Am I?" He glared at her. "Just leave me alone. I don't want you." It was a lie. A swollen, aching lie. He had never wanted and despised anything so much in his life.

She stepped up to him, whether to cajole or remonstrate further he neither knew nor cared, for he was done with reason. Seizing her around the waist, he dragged her against the hard rivets of her father's hauberk and kissed her. Not the sensual, tactile embrace of earlier, but one wild with need and lust, with anger and the remnants of battle frenzy. He held her tight, sealing her mouth with his, imprinting her with every pent-up emotion contained inside him. For a moment she stood frozen within his grip, too shocked to do anything but bear the brunt of the storm; and then she began to fight, pushing at him, kicking him in the shins, and finally clawing his face with her nails.

He noticed little of the pain, for his body was still keyed up from the combat, but the fact that she had scratched him at all, that she was fighting him, brought him to a precipice. To subdue her in rape, or let her go. The choice between manhood and cowardice. Ernalt de Lysle had had no qualms, he remembered.

He tore his mouth from hers and shoved her away. "Go," he gasped. "Get out of here before I do harm to you and my honor beyond hope of repair!"

Her eyes were huge with shock; her breath sobbed into her deprived lungs.

Shaking, Brunin turned back to his horse and set his hands to the saddle. He clenched his fingers against the wood and leather, willing her to have the sense to flee while she still could. One more push was all it would take. He was already over the edge and finding little purchase to maintain his grip on sanity.

"Just go!" he almost sobbed.

He heard her breathing and it was like the sound of his own inside a helm during battle, and then there was a deeper, harsher breath, the rustle of her gown on straw, and she was gone.

Brunin slumped against Jester's flank. His legs were as weak as string and suddenly Joscelin's spare hauberk was a leaden weight that threatened to bring him down. Bending over, he shrugged and struggled out of the garment with trembling hands. The mail slithered onto the stable floor in a jingling thud. The gambeson followed and the air was suddenly pungent with the stink of released sweat. Brunin swallowed a retch. He was becoming aware of the pain of strained muscles. Few blows had landed on his body, but the effort of wielding the Dane ax had taken its toll. He raised his hand to rub his face and encountered two stinging stripes of pain where Hawise had clawed him in her panic. He felt a fresh wave of hostility and then of despair.

Cutting off his thoughts, he saw grimly to the remainder of Jester's harness, rubbed the gelding down, and fetched water and fodder. The hay dust made him sneeze and clung in a seedy film to his skin. He needed a bath, but had no intention of returning to the domestic quarters. That moment would have to come, but he couldn't face it yet. Hawise was right. He was a coward. And with that thought, he was back on the treadmill like a doomed ox.

Cursing, he left Jester to his hay and his water and abandoned the stables, but still he did not return to the domestic chamber. Joscelin would want to speak to him, but not immediately, not while the women were tending his hurts and making a fuss of the fact that he was still alive.

Head down he made purposefully for the alehouse by the castle gates. As well as ale there was dark wine from Gascony and the lands of the Rhine. There were women too, who would judge him only by his ability to pay in silver and give him the release he needed.

❖❖❖

Hawise hid in her mother's garden until the fit of weeping had run its course. She was shivering with shock and fear from the encounter in the stables and, with the added ingredient of remorse in the brew, was in a complete turmoil. She was deeply ashamed of the words she had cast at Brunin when he had wandered into the chamber, unknowing, unsuspecting, still as sleepy as a half-awakened cat. They were words that should never have been uttered and God alone knew the damage she had wrought. Something vital between her and Brunin had been broken; she had tried to mend it, but it had all gone terrifyingly wrong. She thought that he did not know how to mend it either. When he had grabbed her, he had been no different to Ernalt de Lysle at Shrewsbury Fair. She shuddered and had to wipe her forefinger knuckle beneath her eyes to remove a fresh welling of tears. It was only two months until she and Brunin were to wed…God help them both. They couldn't marry like this, and yet it was expected of them—their duty. Her mother was always saying that there was no such word as "cannot." But there were many others in its place and they filled Hawise with dread. "Duty" and "obligation," "loveless," "forsaken," "despised."

❖❖❖

Joscelin's wounds were several, but superficial. The reflexes that had served him as a young mercenary had slowed but a little with age, and the slight edge he lacked had been more than compensated for by the weight of experience. He had made the right decisions when turning ax and blade and mace. He knew that in the morning he would be as stiff as a rusty sword blade, that muscles which were fluid now would not be so accommodating once they had cooled.

He bore with Sybilla's fussing, allowing her to bind and bathe while he recovered his equilibrium. The act of tending him appeared to have restored her balance too, for she had ceased to tremble and some of her color had returned. Around them, in the bower, the other women were succoring the wounded. The dead had been removed to the chapel.

"What will you do with my cousin?" Sybilla asked. Her voice had recovered its usual low pitch, but it was breathless, as if she were struggling with tears or deep anger. She handed the bowl of bloody water to her maid and bade her dispose of it.

"I do not know yet," he answered cautiously.

"I would set his head on a spear and proclaim it from the bridge."

"I had thought about it."

"There is nothing to think about."

Definitely anger, he decided, as he saw the darkness in her eyes. He knew how she felt, but his own fury had been channeled into battle and he was too tired to add fuel to the fire and let it burn up. "If I give him the just deserts you suggest, then I risk dire consequences to myself. Gilbert de Lacy may have acted like a common criminal, but he has more influence than a petty outlaw."

"Surely you do not mean to let him go?"

When Joscelin had first contracted to wed Sybilla, well-meaning friends had warned him that he would need every filament of his iron will, that Sybilla Talbot was a headstrong, stubborn shrew who would run rings around him if he yielded but an inch. But Joscelin had preferred to find a balance between the clenched fist and the open hand, and they had dealt well enough together. Sometimes it was diverting to watch her running those rings, to let her have her way—but not on this occasion. "No," he said. "I do not mean to let him go…or at least not without a considerable amount of compensation." He pushed to his feet and felt searing pain from his cuts, duller ones from his bruises.

"You think he will pay a ransom?"

"He will have no choice…or his family will not." He took her hand. "It is a bridge to be crossed later, when both of us are not thinking through a fog—yes?"

She conceded a short nod, but her mouth remained tight. He looked around the chamber. "Where's Brunin?"

Sybilla looked too and shook her head. "I don't know."

"Hawise is not here either." Joscelin frowned. Given the swamp of emotions engendered by the violence of battle, he had an idea where his daughter would be and that it was dangerous.

Sybilla squeezed his hand. "There are worse things in the world," she said, "and neither of them are fools."

Joscelin grimaced. "Aye, you're right," he sighed. "I owe the lad my life and more." A look of wonderment crossed his face. "I have never seen anyone so young and untried fight like he did…as if he were possessed."

Sybilla's expression became pensive. "If I did not already love him before, I would love Brunin now for saving your life…but I worry that his act was rash."

"Certainly it was rash," Joscelin replied, "but not the worst I have seen in my years of soldiering."

"My first husband took foolish risks in battle when the fighting madness was upon him. In his youth, he had good fortune and the swiftness to stay alive, but one day his youth and his luck deserted him. I fear for Hawise if she is to wed such a one."

Joscelin shook his head. "Brunin's was not the battle madness that remembers nothing," he said softly. "Whatever had hold of him, it was cold. I saw his eyes and he was in full command of his wits. I—" He looked toward the door as his youngest daughter entered the room. Her face was flushed and her eyes puffy as if she had been weeping. Stalks of straw clung to the woolen hem of her gown. There was no sign of Brunin.

Full of paternal turmoil, Joscelin went to her. Brunin might just have saved his life, but if he had damaged one hair of his daughter's head...

"What is wrong, sweetheart? Where is Brunin?"

Hawise gave him a watery look. "In the stables," she said with dimpling chin.

"Has he harmed you?"

"No." Pushing vigorously past her father, Hawise went to help one of the maids with the wounded men.

Joscelin started to follow her, intent on asking some hard questions, but Sybilla caught his arm. "No," she said. "Leave her to me. If it is a matter of the heart, she will talk more easily to another woman...and women have more understanding of each other than a man will ever do." She smiled to take the sting from her words. "If you ask her now, you will only go blundering like a drunk across a flowerbed. You have less delicate interrogations to conduct, have you not?"

Joscelin cleared his throat. "Yes," he said, "you are right." With a final anxious look in his daughter's direction, he beckoned to a couple of knights. "If you see Brunin before I do, then send him to me. I need to speak with him."

❖ ❖ ❖

Joscelin squared his shoulders, raised his head, and gestured to the guards. They unbolted the stout oak door and went before him into the chamber where Gilbert de Lacy and Ernalt de Lysle had been thrown. Both men were still in their battle sweat, their wounds untended, and with not so much as the succor of a cup of water between them. They had been standing by the window arch like a pair of hounds on a wet day, but now they turned to face him, trepidation in their faces.

"You are wondering if I am here to make an end of you." Joscelin sauntered into the middle of the room. "Well, so am I." Heavy with embroidery and seed pearls, his woolen tunic swished as he walked. He had deliberately chosen his best garments, laden his fingers with rings, and pinned his gold cloak clasp at his shoulder. He was still lord of Ludlow and was going to take great pleasure in rubbing Gilbert de Lacy's nose in the fact.

"If you were going to kill me, you would have given the command on the battlefield." De Lacy's voice was hoarse and Joscelin knew that thirst must be burning his throat. "You know that I am a far greater danger to you dead than alive."

Joscelin breathed out hard. "And just now perhaps I would rather have the greater satisfaction of seeing your corpse than dealing with your living flesh."

De Lacy opened his arms and bared his breast. The movement caused pain to flicker across his face, from which Joscelin surmised that he probably had broken ribs. "Then do it," he said.

"But then I tell myself that easy satisfaction is no substitute for lasting gain. It's like the difference between futtering a whore and lying with the woman of your heart."

"So it is your earnest desire to keep me alive?"

Joscelin's smile was arid. "It is my earnest desire to make you pay for the privilege...and for the privilege of leaving Ludlow." His eyes flicked to the wheat-haired knight at de Lacy's side. The young man was swaying where he stood. He had a bloody wound to his right wrist that needed stitching and, judging by the swollen discoloration of his hand, several small broken bones. His eyes were hazy, the lids flickering as he strove to remain aware.

"Bring water," Joscelin commanded a hovering attendant. "And ask Lady Sybilla to send her women when they have finished tending our own wounded. There has been enough blood spilled this day."

"I would have killed you if I had reached you," de Lacy said, giving him a look filled with equal measures of bafflement, loathing, and respect.

"But you did not. My future son-by-marriage made certain of that. Cut me down and you will find able deputies standing behind me."

"The FitzWarin brat is a mere boy!" de Lacy scoffed.

"It was no 'mere boy' who led those men out of Ludlow and struck down your knights," Joscelin retorted with an edge to his voice. "He has fully come into his manhood, and you ignore both him and Hugh de Plugenet at your peril." He raised his hands, palm outward. "Peace. I will not bandy words with you. I know what you think of me and I could live up to your worst expectations by casting you into my dungeon in shackles. However, since I know what I think of myself, I will give you the courtesy of this chamber and tending and clean raiment while you are my prisoners." He lowered his hands and wrapped them either side of his belt buckle. "My lady wife believes that I should set your head on a spike on the bridge. For the moment, it's an image I cherish in my imagination. Let us hope that your relatives think you worth the ransom. Since you are such a preux chevalier, I dare ask no less than a hundred marks lest I smirch your high reputation."

De Lacy choked. "A hundred marks! By Our Lady's veil, you are naught but a thief!"

"No, Lord Gilbert, I am a common mercenary," Joscelin retorted. "And as such I know the worth of everything down to the last coin—including honor."

De Lysle's eyes rolled up in their sockets and he collapsed like a corpse slashed down from a gibbet. Joscelin left the room, his stride hard, his breathing heavy. The women arriving to tend the prisoners squeezed into a corner of the stairs to let him past. Joscelin flicked them a look and saw that Sybilla had set Marion in charge of them.

"De Lacy's companion needs stitches in his arm," he said brusquely. "Do what you must and then leave."

"Yes, my lord." Marion inclined her head over the pile of linen bandages she carried in her arms.

With a grunt of acknowledgment, Joscelin continued on his way, intent now on finding Brunin.

❖❖❖

The stables were empty of all save grooms and stable boys. Jester had been rubbed down, fed, and watered. Joscelin slapped his rump and asked a hovering lad if he had seen Brunin.

"Gone to the alehouse, my lord," the boy replied, pointing toward the bailey. "He and the lady Hawise...they had a quarrel."

"About what?" Joscelin asked, remembering Hawise's distressed and disheveled appearance when she entered the bower.

"I do not know, my lord. I could not hear all of it. She was trying to make amends for something, but he wouldn't let her, and then I heard the sound of a struggle."

Joscelin narrowed his eyes. "And then?" The snarl in his voice made the youth gulp.

"And then Master Brunin told her to go before he smirched his honor and hers...and she did. I saw her run across the yard. Master Brunin stayed awhile with his horse; I heard him cursing. And then he went off toward the alehouse."

Joscelin made a face, for he knew what it was like for a young man after short, sharp battle when the blood was still afire. The slightest spark could ignite dry tinder. Likely a lover's quarrel had turned into a near conflagration. Brunin had done well to control all that tension and Hawise had probably learned a valuable lesson. Sybilla would draw the details out of her. He would indeed only be a drunk blundering across a flowerbed. The thought of a blundering drunk led him to ponder. Brunin might have proved that he could fight like a demon when it came to the sticking point, but there was more to command than ability on a battlefield.

Turning on his heel, Joscelin left the stables and headed for the alehouse. He did not know what he was going to find, but he hoped he did not have to be too harsh, for he understood all too well.

As he drew near, there was a scuffle in the shadows and an

embracing couple hastily drew apart. One of the ale wenches hastened past him, her dark hair straggling around her shoulders and
her unlaced chemise exposing the swell of her breasts. Eyes averted,
she curtseyed to Joscelin on the run and made herself scarce.

"My lord, you are seeking me?" Brunin followed her into the
light. His hair was wet, probably from a dunking in a water butt,
and his eyes were dark and wide like a night creature's.

"Are you sober?"

Brunin fenced the question. "I am not drunk, my lord."

"I am pleased to hear it. A man needs release after battle, but
not until all of his duties have been discharged."

"You have duties for me, my lord?"

He saw the vigilance in the lad's eyes and silently commended
it. He was holding himself together well given that he had just
been interrupted with a whore and had probably consumed more
ale than he was willing to admit. Both voice and legs were steady,
but it took more than one cup to taint the breath like that. Likely
the unrequited lust was paining him too.

"Not so much duties as new responsibilities," he replied.

Beyond the alehouse torches, a woman laughed throatily and
they both glanced toward the sound. Joscelin saw the two scabbed-
over stripes on Brunin's cheek. They had not been there as they
rode back from battle.

"You and my daughter were overheard quarrelling."

Brunin's expression closed. "It is between her and me," he said.

Joscelin nodded brusquely. "I will not interfere, except to say
that you should not let the heat of battle cloud your judgment."

"No, sire."

The young man's tone was as expressionless as his marked face.
"Women are a law unto themselves," Joscelin said wryly. "You
might think you are the master, but a woman always knows who
is mistress."

"You said you had responsibilities for me, sir."

Joscelin sighed. Brunin was clearly on his pride, and who could blame him. "Yes," he said. "On the morrow I will make it official, but tonight I want to say that you have earned your spurs. In my eyes, you are no longer my squire, but a knight full-fledged." He gave Brunin a hefty clap on the shoulder.

Brunin stared at him. "I did nothing, sire." His breathing was as harsh as tearing silk. Whatever else he had managed to shrug off, Joscelin's words had pierced his defenses.

Joscelin snorted. "I do not call what you did, nothing. You turned the battle around; you saved my life. Because of you, Gilbert de Lacy is my prisoner. The outcome could have been very different."

Brunin frowned. "I don't deserve the honor, my lord."

"Let me be the judge of that."

The young man glanced over his shoulder. "Just now I..."

Joscelin's lips twitched with amusement. "Yes, I know what you were doing and likely why. But leave the whores and the drink to the soldiers."

"Yes, sire." Brunin cleared his throat and looked down at his boots.

"Come with me." Joscelin took his arm and drew him across the bailey toward the chapel. The stained glass was lit from within and, as they drew closer, the soft sound of chanting could be discerned like a back thread running behind the bolder sounds from the alehouse.

The heavy door was open and Joscelin slipped inside. It was not a large chapel. Indeed, Joscelin had plans to enlarge it, but for now it served. Tonight it was a mortuary for the men of Ludlow killed in the skirmish. Washed and tended by the castle's women, the bodies had been laid out before the altar and candles lit at the four corners of each makeshift bier. The smells of incense and spring greenery were not sufficient to mask the stench of death.

"Tonight," said Joscelin softly, "I will kneel in vigil to honor these men, and tomorrow, in grief, I will bury them. I will speak to their wives, to their children, their mothers, and promise that they will not starve…except for love and the want of a familiar face coming home through the door on a warm summer's evening or a fire-lit winter night." He looked keenly at Brunin to see if he was absorbing the lesson and saw that his eyes were glittering in the candle-haloed darkness. "That," he said, "is the nature and burden of responsibility. Hold your head up and shoulder it as best you may."

# 22

*MARION STARED AT THE YOUNG KNIGHT WHOM DE LACY* and one of the guards had just laid on the bed. Through the blood and bruises of battle, she recognized Ernalt de Lysle, with whom she and Hawise had once flirted at the Shrewsbury Fair, and the sight sent a surge of shock through her. His complexion was waxen, his eye sockets tinged with blue, but through the wreckage wrought by battle his features were still clear and fine and his hair shone like ripe wheat. She pushed back his sleeve, studied the damage to his wrist, and recoiled.

"He is worth nothing to you if he dies," de Lacy said in a grating voice. "His family will pay naught for a corpse."

Marion swallowed her gorge. "He is not going to die, my lord," she said, raising her chin at him. She set about cleaning and stitching the injury. Sibbi had always been the best at this kind of task, but Sybilla had trained them all, and Marion was competent. She had been prepared to sulk at being delegated the task of caring for the prisoners' injuries, but the sight of Ernalt de Lysle had infused her mind with images from a troubadour's tales. She was the gentle, merciful maiden, bestowing charity and care upon the wounded, handsome knight.

De Lysle's lids flickered open as she tended to him and his eyes were as she remembered them: colored like the sky but as clear as glass. She was not about to let them grow hazy with fever and death. She would save his life and he would be eternally grateful to her.

❖❖❖

Sybilla sat down on the rope-frame bed and set one arm around Hawise's shoulders. "It does not take great wisdom to see that you and Brunin have quarrelled," she said. "I do not know the reason, but bear in mind that all of us have been out of our wits today."

"I insulted his courage," Hawise whispered, looking down at her hands. "He will never forgive me that."

"You insulted his courage?" Sybilla gazed at her in surprise. "I doubt that very much."

"I did. I called him a coward." Hawise sniffed. "I was beside myself when Papa was being attacked. I didn't mean the words, but I said them. I tried to apologize but he wouldn't listen. Instead he—" She broke off and hugged herself.

"Did he hurt you?"

"No...Well, not much and only because he was holding me too tightly. He didn't hit me."

"So you were embracing?"

Hawise swallowed and shook her head. "It was not an embrace. I scratched his face and he bid me go before he harmed me against his honor."

"Ah," said Sybilla, a wealth of experience and knowing in the word. "Wounding a man's pride is never wise. Best to let his blood cool and then speak to him again."

"But what if he spurns me?"

"He won't."

Hawise raised brimming gray eyes. "How do you know?"

Sybilla's smile was wry "Your father and I often had similar quarrels when we were first wed—not on the same subject, but for the same reasons. Either he or I would say something that hurt the other and it would end in a blazing argument...but you are grown and we still share the same bed." Tenderly she brushed a stray wisp of Hawise's hair away from her face. "It will be all right; you will see."

Hawise sniffed and wiped her face with her fingertips. "I do not know what to say to him."

"The words will come to you when they must. But perhaps you could do something too...Make a peace offering."

A considering look entered Hawise's eyes. Whenever her parents argued, which was seldom these days, her mother would make amends on her part by sewing Joscelin a garment. She had even heard him jest that all he had to do when he wanted a new tunic was to pick a quarrel. She also knew that there were several rings and brooches in her mother's jewel casket that stood as apologies for short temper and lack of consideration. But a tunic or shirt was hardly a gift that fitted the crux of the argument. "I will make him a banner," she said. "I know that we have some spare yellow silk in one of the coffers."

Sybilla nodded with approval. "Well thought of," she said. "A man's banner is one of the deepest symbols of his pride. If you stitch one for Brunin, it will be a token of your faith in him."

Hawise rose to her feet. "I will begin it now," she said, feeling as if a burden had been lifted from her shoulders. Dusk had fallen; there were still other duties to perform, but she could at least find the fabric and the embroidery silks.

Later that night, bearing a lighted candle, she went with her mother to the chapel to pray for the dead. Brunin was there with her father. He glanced at her once, but in the darkness and candle shadow she could see nothing in his eyes or expression. He was guarding himself as much as he was guarding the bodies. Hawise had to content herself with the thought that she would prove her pride in him by sewing the banner and that matters would be different in the light of a new morning.

However, the light of a new morning brought not reconciliation but a messenger from Whittington. The man had ridden through the night to reach Ludlow; as Brunin emerged from the church, stiff from his vigil, his eyes gritty with exhaustion, he was greeted with the news that his father was gravely ill with a high fever and he was summoned to his bedside as fast as he could ride. There was no time to sleep, only to break his fast, pack his saddlebag, and ride out.

Brunin's headache had returned during the night and now it pounded against the walls of his skull like a huge black rock. His stomach rebelled at the dish of wheat frumenty that Sybilla urged on him.

"You have a long ride," she said. "You cannot do it without sustenance."

Almost retching, Brunin forced the porridge down.

"Your father said it was nothing, he refused to rest, and he grew worse," the messenger told him. "Now he's raving out of his wits and they brought the priest to him yester sunset just as I was setting out."

Brunin pushed his bowl away, the bottom third still filled with the boiled wheat, knowing he could not stomach another mouthful. "Is anyone else sick?"

"No, sir. Your lady mother has been unwell, but then—" He broke off and attended to his food.

"But then what? Tell me!"

"But then she's with child again, sir, and suffering with sickness as women do."

Brunin thrust to his feet and immediately felt as if someone had shot a crossbow bolt through his skull. He paused for a moment, closed his eyes, and summoned his strength. The thought of his father dying made him feel as if a vast, dark chasm were opening beneath his feet, and deep within it, darker than the darkness of loss, was the knowledge that as the heir he would have to take the FitzWarin barony into his hands and rule it.

He barely made it outside the hall before he was violently ill. The spasms ripped through him like the strokes of a lash, dragging him inside out, flaying him raw.

"Best to get it over with now," Joscelin said, and he felt the solid brace of the older man's hand on his shoulder. "I won't ask if you are fit to ride; I can see you are not, but sometimes a man has to push his will beyond his limits."

Slowly Brunin straightened. His stomach felt as if there were a fist inside it, tightening, clenching, drawing every part of his being downward.

"You have the strength," Joscelin said compassionately and, taking Brunin's right hand, placed a pair of spurs in it. "I was saving these for your knighting," he went on, "but yesterday you earned the right to wear them and call yourself a knight."

The words brought a sudden pressure to the back of Brunin's eyes. He looked down at the spurs through a glitter of moisture, and then up at Joscelin. The gray gaze was knowing and filled with concern; the mouth held its natural curve so that it looked as if Joscelin were smiling, even though he wasn't.

"Put them on," Joscelin said gently. "And you had better take my old sword from the weapons chest. The roads are not infested with outlaws as they were in King Stephen's time, but there are still dangers out there, not least from the Welsh."

"Not least," Brunin agreed shakily as he managed to rally. Stooping, he fastened the spurs to his heels. When he rose again, Joscelin clasped him to his breast. "Godspeed," he said.

Brunin returned the embrace, clinging for a moment to Joscelin's solid bulk, then pushed himself away and headed for the tower to fetch the sword. When he arrived, Hawise was there before him, her father's spare sword-belt in her hands. Brunin swallowed. He was not going to be sick again.

"Let me buckle it on for you," she said.

"I can manage. I've done it often enough as a squire," he answered gracelessly, without meeting her eyes, and held out his hands for the belt.

"Then let me be your squire now."

He said nothing but allowed her to kneel and pass the belt

around his waist, to fasten the ties with nimble fingers. His own would have fumbled at the task this morning and, although her presence was unwanted, he realized she was doing him a favor. While she worked, he stared blankly at the wall.

"I want to mend what happened yesterday," she said in a low voice as she brought the scabbard and laced it to the swordbelt. "But I cannot do it alone."

His head was thundering, making thought and understanding impossible. "What do you want me to do?"

"Forget everything that was said. Put it behind us."

Brunin grimaced as a particularly vicious bolt of pain stabbed through his skull. Rising from her knees, she faced him. "I don't want us to part in bad blood." She raised her hand to touch his scratched face. "I am sorry."

Brunin shook his head, then wished he hadn't. "My wits are so bludgeoned that I forget my own name just now," he said. Raising his hand to cover hers, he gave it a brief squeeze. "Pray for my father," he said, "and for me."

As a way of mending the breach between them, it was a feeble rope, but it was a rope nonetheless and Hawise grasped it with both hands. "Of course I will," she whispered. "God speed your journey." Standing on tiptoe, she kissed his other cheek, not quite venturing his lips. Nor did he offer them, for his mind, such as existed beyond the thundercloud in his skull , was occupied with thoughts of his journey and what awaited him at the other end.

❖❖❖

Marion entered the prisoners' chamber with two maids in tow and a serving boy bearing a breakfast of frumenty and ale for de Lacy and his knight. Outside, Brunin was preparing to leave for Whittington and his stricken father, but Marion had more important things to do than bid him farewell.

Despite spending a sleepless night, she had dressed carefully in a gown of blue linen and braided her hair with silk ribbons of the same speedwell hue. She had cleaned her teeth with a hazel twig and chewed cardamom seeds to perfume her breath. She walked with small, light steps so that her footfalls barely sounded on the rush-strewn floor.

Marion curtseyed demurely to Gilbert de Lacy who was standing by the window, staring out across the river. Bidding the serving lad leave the food dishes on the single coffer in the room, she went to de Lysle's bedside.

He was warm to the touch and his face and throat gleamed with sweat. Marion bade one of the women bring her a bowl of tepid water and a cloth. She asked him how he was faring, her voice demure and sweet.

His eyelids flickered and Marion admired the heavy, dark-gold lashes. Although he had a low fever, his eyes were lucid and they met hers with recognition. "I have felt better, demoiselle," he said and submitted his wrist to her examination.

The flesh surrounding her stitches was puffy, red, and hot to the touch, but there was neither smell nor sign of the inflammation spreading further up the arm, for which she was greatly relieved and said so.

He grunted. "I suppose I must be grateful for small mercies." His tone was petulant, but Marion forgave him, for he looked so vulnerable—like a little boy clad in the bones of a grown man.

He took the bowl of frumenty she offered him, but, although he was clumsy, refused her offer to feed him. "Why should you care if I starve or not?" he asked brusquely. "You seem tender of my welfare, yet I am an enemy."

Marion lowered her lashes. "You are not my enemy, sir," she murmured. "I remember you kindly from the fair at Shrewsbury where your lord and Sir Joscelin made a truce. I know that it is broken now, but I was bidden to attend to your needs, while you are kept here, and…" Her voice dropped to a whisper. "…and I find no hardship in doing so."

Ernalt exchanged glances with Gilbert, who had turned from the window and was gazing intently at Marion like a hawk watching small movements in a wheat field. The Baron made a terse, circumspect gesture.

"Indeed," de Lysle replied a trifle more courteously, "it is no hardship in turn to be tended by so fair a guardian—although a cage is still a cage."

"I can do nothing about that," Marion said defensively.

"Mayhap not. Besides'—he gestured to his injured arm—"a bird with a damaged wing cannot fly far. Better the cage…for the nonce at least." He ate the frumenty to the last scrap and, thanking her, handed back the bowl. It was no coincidence on his part that their fingers touched. The contact brought a flush of scarlet to Marion's cheeks.

The rushes on the floor crackled behind her. Flustered, Marion turned to Gilbert de Lacy who stood watching her, a horn of ale in his hand. His face was marked blue and yellow with bruises and the intensity of his stare frightened her. "Has Lord Joscelin said anything to you about us?"

"No, my lord. Indeed, he would not."

"And what of Lady Sybilla?" Gilbert demanded harshly. "Surely she speaks to her women?"

Marion shook her head and rose to her feet. The melting feelings engendered by Ernalt de Lysle's proximity vanished like wind-blown smoke. "Not of you, my lord," she said, remembering that Sybilla had told her not to talk to de Lacy. *He will try and worm knowledge out of you to no good purpose,* she had warned, her mouth drawn tight. *Do not give him the smallest opportunity for he will seize it with both hands.*

The guards, who had been standing inside the door, made a show of bracing their weapons. De Lacy eyed them, gave a contemptuous snort, and walked back to the window.

Marion went to the door. On the threshold she paused and looked over her shoulder at Ernalt de Lysle. Meeting her glance, he inclined his head and laid his hand across his heart, fingers and palm flat. Marion uttered a small gasp and fled.

When the door had been bolted behind the guards and the men were alone, de Lacy turned around.

"With a little coaxing, she will peck corn out of your hand like a tame pullet," he said.

Ernalt studied his wrist. The stitched wound had been left open to the air to let it dry. It was sore and tight and throbbed in time to the beat of his heart. "You want me to coax her?" He was not averse to the notion. She was as pretty as a spring morning and as full of promise. He smiled at his lord. "You certainly seemed to frighten her off."

De Lacy snorted. "I'm the ogre. She has been reared on Sybilla's tales of my perfidy and savagery, but you are different. You follow me because you have given me your knightly oath and your loyalty is proof of your worth." Here he raised an ironic brow and Ernalt responded with a smile in a similar vein. "You are young and handsome and it was obvious from the way she was looking at you that she's ripe for the plucking." De Lacy folded his arms. "I may have turned a blind eye to it, but I know perfectly well that it's a task you're good at."

"What, 'plucking'?" Ernalt's smile became a grin.

"In a manner of speaking. Seducing young women away from the safety of the maternal coop and into the briars." De Lacy bent him a stare that was half jesting, half severe. "And yes, I want you to coax her. She may be of great value to us."

"In what way?"

De Lacy hooked up a footstool with the side of his boot and sat down. "If you are patient with her, you can find out about the movements of the people in this place. How many soldiers does de Dinan keep on active duty at any time? What are their routines…what are de Dinan's routines? Cozen her into telling you."

"That should not be difficult," Ernalt said. "From what I remember, she is jealous of Lady Sybilla's daughters and craves flattery and attention the way a plant craves water."

De Lacy gave a decisive nod. "Then I will keep out of your way when she makes her next visit and leave you to bait the trap. If you are good at your work, it may be that she will give us more than just information."

Ernalt raised his brows. "Help us escape, you mean? Do you think that she has such a capacity?"

De Lacy rose and returned to the window. Bracing his arms on the stone surround, he stared out. "I think that she has, but she needs careful handling."

Ernalt clenched the fist of his damaged arm to feel the needles of pain in the stitched wound. "Subtle as the spices in a blanc-mange," he smiled.

De Lacy gave a grunt that might have been amusement, but Ernalt could not tell, for his lord was still staring outward. "I would never have guessed from his early showing that the FitzWarin boy would have shaped up to become so fine a warrior," de Lacy commented after a moment. "He will bear watching."

"I could have taken him," Ernalt said. "My horse was at the wrong angle, that's all. If he'd been fighting beside de Dinan, he'd have been cut down in the first charge."

"Perhaps," de Lacy said, "but whatever tactics he employed, they worked and he fought with competence."

Ernalt fell silent. De Lacy might be speaking the truth, but he didn't particularly want to agree with him.

# 23

THE SUN WAS STRIKING NOONTIDE AS BRUNIN RODE INTO Whittington on a lathered, blowing Jester. He was too cold to feel its warmth on his spine, too preoccupied to notice the green of the trees or the watery glint of the marsh surrounding the keep. The attendant took Jester's bridle and led the horse away to the stables. Splashed with mud from his hard ride, hair wind-blown, Brunin strode toward the keep. Joscelin's sword banged at his side and he clutched the scabbard to hold it steady. Servants and soldiers watched his progress, but he didn't see them, for his mind was on a single goal.

Avoiding the great hall, he mounted the outer stairs to the private quarters and, setting his hand to the lion's head ring, heaved open the door.

His mother's women stared at him with open mouths and shock-widened eyes. A small child, black of hair and eye like himself, let out a wail and was picked up by Heulwen, the Welsh nurse. Her hands patted; her voice soothed. *"Tawelwch nawr, tawelwch nawr, cariad bychan."*

Her voice resounded inside Brunin's head, which felt like a cavern that was alternately echoing with nothing and overstuffed with wet fleece. He hesitated on the threshold, forcing himself to take measured breaths instead of gasping as if he had run all the way from Ludlow on his own legs. The women were not weeping and, until he had burst into the room, had been going about their daily tasks; therefore his father yet lived and was not about to expire on the moment. Lit prayer candles stood in all the niches though. Clenching his fists, he went to the second door, which partitioned the bedchamber from the day room, and pushed it open.

The sweet, fetid stench of sweat and sickness made him reel and take an involuntary backstep. For a moment he almost continued retreating, but, with a determined effort, he controlled himself and, breathing shallowly through his nose, approached the bed.

His father was propped upright and supported by numerous cushions and bolsters. His unlaced shirt exposed a glistening mixture of herbs and grease, which had been spread across his chest to ease his breathing. Brunin was shocked at the sunken cheekbones, the hollow eyes with lids like scraps of shrivelled leather, the fever-blistered lips. Sweat beaded his father's scalp, glistening through the receding hazel-brown hair. Seated either side of him like mourners at a tomb were Mellette and Eve. The family chaplain was present too, and Brunin's brothers. A deathbed.

Brunin dug his short fingernails into his palms and joined the tableau. "Is he...?"

Mellette glared at him. Her eyes were red-rimmed and inflamed, but without tears. "You took your sweet time." Her voice was a haggard croak. "Fortunately he still lives."

It was an unfair accusation, for Brunin could not have arrived any quicker unless he had wings, but he did not argue, merely flicked her a look.

His mother's eyes were brimming. She moved to one side, making room for him at the head of the bed.

Brunin leaned over his father. The heat emanating from him was like a brazier and the smell of the herbs so pungent that it was almost visible. His father's breath bubbled in his chest and emerged through his open mouth in a hoarse crackle.

"Father...sir?" Brunin leaned over and gently touched his shoulder. "It is Brunin. I have come from Ludlow."

There was no response, save perhaps a quickening of the chest and the rattle of deeper-drawn air.

"He won't hear you," Mellette said. "And even if by some miracle he does, you won't get any sense out of him. The fever's put him out of his wits."

"What hope is there?"

"The hope of prayer, my son," said the chaplain.

"Hah! It hasn't done much good so far," Mellette snapped. "My son at death's door, his wife carrying badly, a murrain among the sheep, the Welsh all over the border like rats in a granary, and no one to put a stop to it." Her gaze flashed to Brunin, sharp as broken glass.

The chaplain looked uncomfortable. Brunin tried again. "My lord father, there has been a battle at Ludlow. Lord Joscelin has taken Gilbert de Lacy prisoner and demanded a ransom of his family."

FitzWarin moved his head and groaned softly. His eyelids strained as if trying to ungum one edge from the other.

"I have been knighted on the field of battle," Brunin added, addressing his words to his father, but intending them for Mellette, who was eyeing him narrowly. "I will tell you more later, but, in the meantime, I promise to hold our lands together while you recover."

"Even if you have been knighted, that does not grant you manhood," Mellette said with a jaundiced look at the scabbard hanging by his left hip.

Eve spoke up from the other side of the bed. "It has to be enough. What other choice do we have? And do not say Ralf. He is younger than Brunin and less experienced...nor has he had the benefit of Brunin's training."

"Be careful with your assumptions," Mellette snapped. "You know naught of my mind."

"More than you think, madam," Eve replied, trembling with the effort of holding her ground and answering back.

"Must I die to the sound of bickering too?" FitzWarin's voice was a rusty wheeze, pursued by a bout of severe coughing. Eve hastily set a wine cup to his lips.

"Drink, my lord," she said in a panicky voice.

He shoved her hand aside, and the wine spilled down the front of her dress in a bloody stain. For a moment he struggled to breathe through the phlegm clogging his lungs; finally he won through.

"How can I drink, woman, when I can't even breathe?" he gasped and slumped back against the bolsters. But his purple color slowly eased to red and his gaze wandered with an effort to Brunin. "I cannot separate dream from truth," he said hoarsely. "Did you say there was a battle at Ludlow?"

"Yes, sir." Brunin told his father what had happened, but sparsely, putting no meat on the bones. "And then your messenger arrived."

FitzWarin winced. "Blame the women for that. I am not yet at death's door. And Joscelin has given you your knighthood."

"Yes, sir."

"Then you must have acquitted yourself well." He licked his swollen lips and gestured to his wife, demanding the wine that moments ago he had flung aside. Eve refilled the cup from the flagon and tilted the rim toward her husband's lips. He took several swallows and suffered Eve to dab away the trickle that ran from the side of his mouth. "Joscelin would not give such an accolade lightly." He reached to take Brunin's hand. "I put Whittington in your care until I am better."

"Yes, sir." Brunin felt the heat of his father's blood pulse against his own flesh, swift as a river in spate, and knew that now he himself must either sink or swim.

❖ ❖ ❖

"I'm glad you're home," Richard said, as Brunin entered the old bedchamber that he had once shared with his brothers.

"You are?" Brunin looked warily at his second brother. Two servants had assembled a rope bed and were busy stuffing a mattress with clean straw. Brunin slung his baggage roll down at the side of it and wondered when he was going to find time to sleep. "I suppose absence has made the heart grow fonder then."

Richard shrugged. "Ralf thinks that all he has to do is shout to make people obey and respect him."

Brunin gave a sour grin. "He hasn't changed much then. Where is he?"

"Gone to Oswestry." Richard rubbed the back of his neck and looked uncomfortable. "He's got a girl there."

Brunin arched one eyebrow. "He's gone to see a girl when our father is so sick that he has a priest at his bedside?"

"He says he's gone to gather news. The Welsh raids have been growing more bold and there's talk of the King going to war against them."

Brunin wandered the length of the room, looking at the embroidered hangings. Since his last visit, his mother had completed a scene of summertime and added a border of stylized wild strawberries. He paused by his youngest brother's bed. William had been an infant when Brunin had gone for training to Joscelin. Now he was eleven years old and the practice sword and shield on his rumpled coverlet were badges of approaching manhood. Brunin picked up the sword and swung it, rotating the hilt at speed, swishing the air. He had watched soldiers perform such tricks when he himself was a boy and had been awed. He smiled ruefully at the memory.

Richard watched him. "Is it true that Lord Joscelin made you a knight?"

Brunin sighed and cast the wooden sword back onto Thomas's bed. "Yes, it's true," he said, "but not in a moment. It took nine years, and I'm still not sure that he was right."

❖❖❖

Ralf arrived as dusk was falling. The distance between Whittington and Oswestry meant that he had had time to sober up a little and was able to dismount unaided from his horse—which had not been the case when struggling into the saddle outside the alehouse. He knew he should have remained at home, but he had been unable to bear the stench of sickness and the oppressive atmosphere. His mother hunched like an old woman, but clutching a belly ripe with yet another child, her eyes full of haunted despair. His grandmother purse-lipped and angry. Everyone looking to him to make it right. It was what he had always claimed to want; he had even muttered that the FitzWarin barony was his lost birthright. But for the inconvenience of his milksop older brother, he would have been the heir. Now that the prospect was imminent, however, he was terrified, and since he dared not admit that terror, even to himself, he had run away to the alehouse and the arms of wool merchant's daughter Sian ferch Madoc. She didn't care who he was. She was small and well endowed, maternal and welcoming. He wanted to make her his mistress, but he knew his grandmother would not countenance her presence at Whittington. The only way he could see her was to ride to Oswestry.

"Your brother is here, sir," said the groom as he took Ralf's horse.

"Which one?" Ralf took a lurching backstep, then managed to steady himself.

"Master Brunin."

Bitterness and relief flooded his throat. The scapegoat had arrived. There was no longer any need to worry who would take the blame.

"And my father?"

"Word is that there is no change, sir."

"See to the horse." Ralf wove unsteadily toward the hall. Before he entered, he doubled up against the lime-washed wall and heaved up the last quart of ale he had drunk. Wiping his sleeve across his mouth, his nose and eyes streaming, he lurched toward the door, but before he could make an entrance, his elbow was seized and he was pushed down onto the stone bench by the door.

"Our grandmother will crucify you if she sees you in that state," Brunin hissed.

Ralf squinted up at him. In the soft spring gloaming, Brunin's eyes and pupils had merged into one dark circle like a hunting cat's. He was wearing a dust-stained tunic; there was a sword at his hip with a plain grip and hilt, and spurs glinted at his heels. He looked seasoned and dangerous.

"Why should you care? Thought you'd be glad to see her nail me up."

Brunin smiled sourly. "I would not be glad to see her do that to any of us. Besides, with our father so ill, we need all to be of one mind, not squabbling and divided."

Ralf sleeved his face and stared up at his brother. Something had changed, but his brain was too fuddled to decide what.

Brunin sat down on the bench beside him and threw back his head. "You have never liked me, and in truth I have responded in kind," he said with closed eyes. "But if we don't mend our differences now, we never will."

Ralf snorted as if with contempt, but he could think of nothing contemptuous to say. He wanted to grasp the olive branch being held out, but he did not know how to without seeming weak. The fact that he had ridden in drunk, and discovered Brunin on the territory that had long been their battleground, had set him at a further disadvantage. "Where did you get that sword?" he demanded with a gesture.

Brunin used his left hand to draw the blade straight up and out of the scabbard. "It is Lord Joscelin's old one. He said to take it for protection on the road." He handed it across.

Ralf set his fingers around the tightly bound buckskin grip and tested the heft. He held the hilt flat on his palm and checked the balance, then thumbed an edge that was as bright and thin as a sliver of new moon. A little oversharpened with wear perhaps, but still a good weapon. "If it is his old one," he said, enunciating the words carefully, "then he must have fought with it when he was a mercenary."

Brunin's eyes opened and narrowed. "Yes. What of it?"

"Nothing...It must have carried him through many trials."

"You once said that you would rather be trained at the hands of an earl than at those of a common mercenary."

"Much good it did me." Ralf handed the sword back to his brother. "I didn't envy you when Joscelin de Dinan took you to train, but you had the last laugh, didn't you?"

"I'm not laughing," Brunin said quietly. His eyes glittered in the darkness as he looked at Ralf. "What news did you gain in Oswestry…assuming you did more than go there just to put distance between Whittington and yourself and avail yourself of some female comfort."

"Hah, you're well informed," Ralf said sourly. "Enough to know nothing."

"Then tell me."

Ralf's stomach rolled queasily and he thought he might be sick again. "King Henry's going to war against the Welsh," he said. "The news is all over the town like the stink of blood on a slaughter day. There's a summons to muster in Northampton at midsummer."

Brunin's glance sharpened. "You are sure?"

"I'm drunk, not deaf," Ralf said belligerently. "The messenger'll be here by the morrow and you'll hear for yourself. Henry's set to rein in Owain Gwynedd before any more of our territory goes down his throat."

Brunin swore under his breath. Frowning, he began to count on his fingers. "We owe the service of at least six knights," he said, "or the value of such, and God knows how much silver's in the coffers. I'll check on the morrow and have the scribe draft letters to our vassals."

Ralf wiped his hand beneath his nose and sniffed loudly. "Sian says she does not know if her father will stay in Oswestry or retreat over the border. The rumor is that Iorwerth Goch and the heirs of Rhys Sais are gathering followers to join Owain Gwynedd's troop."

Brunin said nothing, but Ralf could tell he was thinking hard. "Sian is your woman," he said at length.

Ralf shrugged. "I suppose you could call her that." He cleared his throat and looked at the ground. "She's got red hair," he mumbled, and suddenly had to stagger away to be sick again.

Brunin watched, feeling sorry for him, and irritated, but behind that irritation was a thawing of hostility. Perhaps he owed this Sian more than he knew. Ralf tottered back to the bench and put his head in his hands. His fair hair flopped forward over his fingers. "Our grandmother would explode like a barrel of pitch if I brought Sian to Whittington," he groaned. "I can't marry her, and I can't keep her under this roof...but I can't afford to keep her anywhere else."

Brunin gave a wry smile. "It's a long traipse to Oswestry... or Wales."

Ralf thrust out his lower lip. "I won't give her up."

Brunin made a gesture with his spread hands to indicate that he acknowledged the dilemma but had no solutions. He did not ask if Ralf's opinion of red-haired women had changed. That much was obvious. He thought of Hawise. Of the storms of the previous couple of days. He was not sure that they had weathered them yet. He remembered little of their farewell; only that she had said she was sorry, her eyes wounded with imminent tears. He grimaced. If Henry was going to take on the Welsh and he had to ride with the English force, then there would be no wedding in June. A blessing or a curse, he could not decide; nor, given his current difficulties, did he very much care.

"I need sleep," he said and, stretching like a cat, rose to his feet. "And you do too, but first you had better dunk your head in the water butt. Then we'll go and see how our father fares."

A shudder ran through Ralf as he gained his feet. "I hate the sick room," he said in a low voice. "I hate the stench and the way our mother and grandmother sit there like two mourners at a bier."

"How do you think our father feels?" Brunin answered, his voice harsh to cover his guilt. He had felt exactly the same as Ralf on walking into the bedchamber. "Do not let your own self-pity overcome your compassion or your duty."

"Hah, you're turning into a priest again," Ralf snapped, and lurched off in the direction of the water butt.

❖❖❖

Marion inclined her head to the guard and waited while he opened the door to the prisoners' chamber. They had been here a week now and had settled into a routine. Their care had continued to fall to Marion, for Sybilla refused to go near them, as did Hawise, and that suited Marion very well indeed for it meant she had Ernalt to herself.

As she entered the room, her stomach darted with anticipation. She directed the maids accompanying her to lay the food they were bearing on the coffer and then told them to make de Lacy's bed. De Lacy himself was sitting by the window, staring out as he always did. He seldom acknowledged the presence of the women and kept his distance—for which Marion was glad, for he made her nervous. So did Ernalt, but for entirely different and much more delightful reasons.

"How is your arm today, sir?" she asked softly.

"Much improved, demoiselle, owing to your diligence and care." His voice was vibrant and pitched low, so that it struck her somewhere between midriff and loins, and spread in delicious rings of sensation. He rolled back tunic and shirt to expose the wound. It was drying nicely and would soon be ready to have the stitches removed.

Marion sat on the edge of his bed and took the pot of honey salve from her basket of nostrums. She was acutely aware of his gaze as she removed the stopper from the jar, scooped a dollop onto her forefinger, and anointed his exposed arm.

"So gentle," he murmured. "I will miss your touch when my wound no longer needs attention."

She blushed and looked quickly over her shoulder, but the women were busy with their bedmaking.

"They are not listening," Ernalt said. "But I wish you could stay. It is so lonely confined to this chamber and my lord is not the best of company."

"Lady Sybilla would never allow it," Marion whispered, studying him from beneath her lids.

"Just to play a game of chess or merels. Would she truly be so cold as to deny such a request?"

"I...don't know."

"Then will you ask her?"

Marion gnawed her lip. "She has no cause to love you or your lord."

"She is right to be cautious. But is loyalty to one's lord so bad a thing? It was my duty to follow him and do his bidding. To refuse would have been dishonorable." He gave her a warm smile. "Although captivity does have its compensations."

Marion started to withdraw from his wrist, but he captured her hand in his. "I do not want to lose my wits to boredom. My heart I have already lost, and the lady looks at me as if she does not know what she has taken."

Marion gasped and snatched her fingers away. "You must not talk like that!"

"What is wrong with the truth?"

The other women had finished making de Lacy's bed and were turning back into the room. Cheeks flaming, Marion rose from Ernalt's bedside.

"Ask her," he said again. "By your mercy, demoiselle."

Marion stood aside and he rose while the women saw to his covers.

"What if she refuses? What then?" she said in an agitated whisper.

"Then I must accept and respect her judgment. But I trust your good sense to make her see sense too," Ernalt said smoothly.

❖❖❖

"Knowing Henry, he'll want money as well as men," Joscelin sighed to Sybilla, "but I expect some of the service can be commuted to coin." Husband and wife were in the private chamber, talking over the royal summons to the assembly at Northampton where the forthcoming campaign against the Welsh was to be organized.

"Will you go with him into Wales?" Sybilla's voice was deliberately neutral, and, because of that, Joscelin recognized her anxiety.

"That depends on what he asks. If he desires my sword, then I am honor bound to give it to him."

"I am proud of such honor, but I fear it too."

He ran his hand down her arm in a gesture of comfort and understanding. "You would fear more without it, love."

Sybilla sighed. "I suppose I would," she capitulated. "The wedding will have to be postponed." She glanced toward the window embrasure where Hawise was busy at her embroidery. Yellow silk spilled over her lap and her lips were pressed firmly together in concentration. "Unless you want it to go forward in the midst of preparations for war."

Joscelin shook his head. "That would be overloading an already piled trencher, both for them and for us. Besides, the lady Mellette will expect a wedding of great splendor and ceremony, and neither her family nor ours will have the time for that until the autumn at least…perhaps longer if FitzWarin does not recover from his illness."

Behind them came the soft sound of a throat being cleared and they turned to look at Marion who was twisting her clasped hands together at waist-level.

Joscelin raised his brows. "Child?"

"I was wondering if I could take a chess set to our hostages," she said hesitantly. "It would be an act of charity."

"Charity!" Joscelin snorted. "Do you not think I gave them enough charity when I spared their lives?"

"Yes, my lord." She looked at the floor and bit her lip.

"Did either of them ask you to do this?" Sybilla asked suspiciously.

"Sir Gilbert spends all his time looking out of the window," she said breathlessly. "Sir Ernalt says that he will lose his wits to boredom. I thought that—" She broke off.

"Sir Ernalt is also very handsome," Sybilla said with a knowing look. "Perhaps you have lost your wits to his appearance."

"No, my lady." Marion reddened. "He is indeed fair to look upon, but he is our prisoner and, because of his lord, our enemy. I thought it no great sin to give him a chess set. If I was wrong, forgive me."

Sybilla opened her mouth, but Joscelin pre-empted her with a wave of his hand. "I do not suppose that Ludlow will fall for the giving of a simple chess set," he said. "You have my permission."

"Thank you, my lord." Marion did her best not to skip away, but her delight was still obvious.

"Was that wise?" murmured Sybilla.

Joscelin gave her a sour smile. "It was certainly charitable," he said. "Oh, let her have her way. All to the good if it gives her more experience as a chatelaine and hones her maturity."

Sybilla looked skeptical but said nothing.

Hawise glanced up from her sewing to watch Marion take a chessboard and box of pieces from one of the coffers. Marion gave her a blinding smile but no explanation, and in a moment was gone from the chamber.

Now that she had raised her head from her needlework, Hawise paused to rest her eyes.

"You are progressing well with the banner," Sybilla said, joining her.

Hawise sighed. "But I do not know if it will be ready for June." She smoothed the silk beneath her fingers. A half-embroidered wolf in crimson and black snarled across the bright background. Crimson and black lozenges decorated the borders too. "Perhaps he is more like a cat," she said with a smile, "but no man would go into battle with a cat blazoned on his banner."

Sybilla smiled at the words, but in a preoccupied way. "My love, your wedding day is set for midsummer..."

"Yes, Mama." Hawise knew what Sybilla was going to say. She

had heard the rumors in the hall. "You are going to tell me that I have longer than I thought to stitch this banner."

Her mother nodded. "Yes, child. The King has called a council for midsummer, and from there his barons will muster and ride into Wales...and that probably includes your father and Brunin."

Hawise studied her sewing. "What if we were to wed despite the muster?"

"There would be very little time." Sybilla looked dubious. "Perhaps it would be wiser to delay the marriage. You and Brunin will have enough to deal with, without the adjustments being husband and wife will demand of you."

"I know that, but I have had time to think while I have been stitching Brunin's standard. We have been betrothed for over a year and I have known him for more than half my life." She swallowed, for she had not often challenged her mother's opinion. "I think that it will be easier if we are wed. I want..." She bit her lip. "I want to have the same as you and Papa have—to be able to talk and touch freely, knowing that a chaperone's eyes are not watching our every move. I want to have Brunin to myself without guilt or fear. When all eyes are upon us, we are like mummers. We act our part, without being our true selves."

"I thought after the argument you and Brunin had that you would desire more time before the wedding."

"No, Mama. Perhaps that was one of the difficulties. If we could just have—" She broke off and picked up her needle. It was something to do and gave her an excuse to drop her gaze from her mother's searching one. "It would have made a difference," she said in a firmer voice. "If my father goes away to war, you and he will have your chance to say a proper farewell. But Brunin and I will not." She made a slow, neat stitch, forcing herself to concentrate.

"Yes, I see," said Sybilla slowly. "And I understand. You have grown up, haven't you? I will speak with your father, and Brunin's family will have to have their say...and Brunin too."

Hawise watched her fingers take another stitch. Brunin most of all. She would not dwell on the thought that he might prefer a postponement.

"You do know that being wed will not put an end to arguments," Sybilla warned ruefully. "Indeed, it may even provoke them."

"Yes, Mama, I know." Hawise answered with a smile. "I have watched you and Papa, but at least you have a chance to resolve them away from other eyes."

"So be it." Sybilla rose to her feet. "You are certain about this?"

Hawise nodded. "I have had a long time to ponder while sewing this," she said, a mischievous curve to her lips. "Perhaps men should embroider and think instead of taking up the sword to solve their disputes."

Sybilla laughed. "That would be beyond their capabilities. Solid heads are for butting down walls, not embroidery!"

Hawise laughed too. Her mother left, but it took a while before Hawise resumed her sewing, for her hands were trembling and she did not want to spoil the neat, intricate work. She had set the cart rolling. Now she had to hope that any obstacles on the road ahead were navigable.

# 24

FITZWARIN STOOD BY THE WINDOW IN HIS CHAMBER AND watched the patrol ride in, Brunin at its head, Warin and Richard behind. He noted the disciplined order of the men and the way that everyone, even his brothers, deferred to Brunin. He noted too the way he held the shield tight in to his body, and the easy but alert posture in the saddle. And then he thought back to a day in Shrewsbury almost ten years ago and knew just how much he owed Joscelin de Dinan. Of course, the lad had always had it in him, but not every hand could have drawn it out.

He inhaled deeply and, at the peak of the breath, felt the air catch and scrape in his tender chest. He started to cough, and had to brace his arm on the window embrasure as the spasm ripped through him.

"Told you, you shouldn't be out of your bed," declared Mellette sourly. "But then no one listens to me." She pointed a peremptory finger at an attendant, who hastened to serve FitzWarin with a cup of watered wine.

"I'll have a long enough lie-down in the grave without practicing now," FitzWarin retorted. He cast a jaundiced look toward the bed from which, a fortnight ago, he had thought he would never rise. No one else had either. He was still as wobbly as a spring lamb, but each day a little more of his strength returned, and he was able to expand his boundaries further. Before the day was out, he was determined to mount his horse and at least ride around the yard. He needed to be recovered enough to attend the Welsh muster, and before that to ride to Ludlow.

"I don't understand de Dinan's sudden haste," Mellette said. She was clutching the parchment that the messenger from Ludlow had delivered an hour ago. She could not read, but she had had the scribe repeat the words several times over and had committed them to memory. "Midsummer or Michaelmas, what does it matter when the pair are wed?"

"I know not, but there will be good reason."

"Hmph." She gave herself a shake like a hen ruffling its feathers. "Perhaps he's got the girl with child."

FitzWarin's lips twitched. "If that had happened, that parchment you are holding would be smoking in your hand. What's more, we would not be worrying about the threat from the Welsh. We'd have the garrison of Ludlow washing against our walls by now."

"Don't be foolish," Mellette snapped. "De Dinan's soft in the head but his wits are not entirely mashed." She came to the window and narrowed her eyes at the dismounting patrol. "I suppose you are going to agree to de Dinan's wishes?"

"I have no cause to refuse. And if Brunin has, I am sure he will tell me."

They watched Brunin stride from the yard. He removed his helm as he walked and pushed down his arming cap so that his black hair stood up in tousled spikes. The shadow of a beard clung to his jawline and outlined his mouth. He had borrowed FitzWarin's hauberk and the rivets shone in the sun.

"He has become a man," FitzWarin said. "You should think on that in your dealings with him."

Her lips compressed. "He looks like his grandfather," she said. It was more of a complaint than an observation and FitzWarin clenched his teeth. It might be worth founding a nunnery just to send her there and have peace.

"Indeed, if he is like him, then I will be glad," he retorted, turning from the window.

❖❖❖

Brunin made his report to his father. Their borders were clear and the villagers reported no raids, but there was an atmosphere. "It is nothing I can lay my hand upon, save to say that it is like the still before a storm, or a hard snowfall," he said. "But it could be as much about the Welsh waiting to see what King Henry brings to them as preparing to assault our borders...I do not know, and that is the truth." He rested his hand lightly upon the hilt of his sword as he spoke, the gesture instinctive. FitzWarin looked at the smooth skin, as yet unscarred by war and the grind of living, although already there were one or two marks of experience. His throat ached at the thought of all the promise contained in the young man standing before him...and all the ways that such promise could fail.

"Then we must stay vigilant and wait it out. Come summer I should have the strength to attend the muster." He flexed his forearm as he spoke and smiled at Brunin. "You will need a hauberk of your own if you are to accompany me...and a sword."

Brunin returned the smile. Then his eyes flickered to his grandmother and the expression died to neutrality.

Mellette folded her arms. "Joscelin de Dinan's sent his messenger again," she said irritably. "Says that he wants you to marry his girl before the June muster rides out." She clucked her tongue. "Means a deal of scrambling to be prepared in time. In my day we didn't do things in such unmannerly haste."

Brunin looked from his grandmother back to his father. The hall was filling with the men arriving from the patrol and taking their places at the dining trestle. Ralf and Richard came to join the family group.

"Did Lord Joscelin say why?" Brunin asked, frowning deeply.

FitzWarin shook his head. "Not in so many words. Only that he wanted to have such matters sorted lest the war prove difficult."

"But a betrothal is as binding as a marriage."

"Indeed, but it carries less obligation," his father said. "You will be his son-in-law rather than his daughter's betrothed. Not only will the ties be more binding, but there is also the hope that, should matters turn ill during the campaign and you or Joscelin be killed, you will leave an heir to Ludlow in your wife's womb."

Brunin's face remained expressionless but FitzWarin noted his son's heightened color. "Lord Joscelin said nothing of the matter when I rode out," he replied in a somewhat constricted voice.

"Well, other concerns were to the fore. Now we have a breathing space to consider and act as we think best. Joscelin writes that his daughter is eager for the match." FitzWarin's look was shrewd. "I see no reason for you not to be as eager as the girl. Perhaps the wedding will not be as great as one with more planning, but that is more of a woman's concern." He flicked his gaze to Mellette, who looked as if she might choke on bile. "If Sybilla and Hawise are content to have it this way, then I see no reason why our womenfolk should object. Indeed, with your mother in her condition, it can only be to the good."

"Yes, sir," Brunin said stiffly.

"Why the clenched jaw?" FitzWarin demanded. "If you have objections, spit them out now."

"Perhaps he does not relish the idea of duties beyond those he already has," Mellette mocked. "Or perhaps the girl does not appeal to him."

Brunin's flush darkened and FitzWarin grinned. "There'll be no worry on that score. He'd have to be made of stone not to appreciate her. He'll get over the shock soon enough."

"Yes, but will she?" Ralf retorted, giving Brunin a playful punch to the arm.

"She will have no choice." Mellette sent a withering glance toward her second grandson, then scowled at FitzWarin. "At least they are to be married by the Bishop of Hereford; that counts for something. I suppose we had best make preparations. I won't have Sybilla Talbot and Joscelin de Dinan lording it over us, not when

Brunin is the Conqueror's great-great-grandson." Head high, stick thumping the floor, she stalked in the direction of the women's quarters, there doubtless to turf out chests and nag her daughter-in-law. The men exchanged rueful glances, which became grins, and then soft laughter, although Brunin's had something of a forced edge.

❖❖❖

A pile of linen in her arms, Marion waited while the guard unbolted the prisoners' door. He and his companion had been deeply engrossed in a game of merels and he barely glanced at her as as she entered the room. Pulling the door shut, he slid the bolt back across and returned to the board.

Ernalt was waiting; the moment the bar slid home, he took the linen from her, placed it on his bed, and drew her into his arms. "I thought you were not coming," he whispered, his mouth close to hers.

"It was difficult to escape the women. They watch me closely. I said I would not be above a few minutes. I cannot stay." She spoke in short, whispered rushes. A swift glance showed her that Gilbert de Lacy was kneeling before a small prie-dieu, his hands clasped in prayer and his eyes tightly shut. Whenever she and the women of the household paid their visits, he kept himself aloof, never speaking, not even acknowledging their presence. She knew that he wanted to become a Templar knight, a fighting monk, and that their chosen path was chastity, but even so, it seemed strange to her that he should behave as if she and the other women did not exist.

Ernalt, on the other hand…Oh, Ernalt. Her breath came short and her loins melted as he cupped the side of her face with his palm. "I wish you could," he muttered. "You do not know what these visits mean to me."

"And me," Marion confessed with an excited little giggle.

"Listen, I am not just a hearth knight; I have lands of my own, and when Lord Gilbert goes to the Holy Land, his son will need my craft and loyalty. I want...I want to make you my wife...if you will have me." He lifted her hand to his lips and kissed her fingertips.

Marion's stomach wallowed with a mixture of fear and longing. "I would need Lord Joscelin's consent for that," she said, "and he would never give it."

"Perhaps not now...but when a truce is made." He increased the pressure of his palm against her cheek, forcing her to look at him. "The word of Joscelin de Dinan is not everything. You are a grown woman and free to wed as you choose."

Marion gave a soft gasp. They were words she wanted to be true, but she knew that they were without substance. "No, I am not free."

"You are only as caged as you wish to be." He leaned in closer and touched his lips to hers; it was the gentlest brush of skin on skin, before he drew back. She shivered at the contact and closed her eyes.

"I promise you that when I am free, I will marry you," Ernalt whispered. "You will be Lady de Lysle and your own mistress. No one will command you to do anything, for you will be the one giving the commands."

"I would have to obey you though," she whispered, feeling drunk on his closeness, on the scent of him and the warmth emanating from his skin.

"Would that be such a hardship?" The hand that had been at her cheek trailed over her throat and lightly down her body. She shuddered as the caress skimmed the peak of her breast.

"No." Her voice was no more than the pressure of her breath. "You know it would not."

He touched and stroked her, strengthening the spell. "But first I have to be free."

"When the ransom is paid you will be."

"But my lord will be greatly impoverished. If we could escape..."

Marion's eyes widened.

"You could help us," he said, still stroking. "I want to be able to give you everything when you are my wife. Why should your guardian have it?"

"I...I have to go." But she could not move for he had hemmed her in against the wall and the only way forward was into his arms. His hands continued their soft magic and he held her gaze with his own. When she tried to look down and away, he forced her head up.

"It wouldn't have to be much, love. No one would have to know."

"Then how...?"

"Bring us more sheets and towels. If you are asked, say that my lord has asked for them."

"Sheets and towels?" Marion was nonplussed.

"And tablecloths...anything that can be tied together."

Her eyes flew to the window as she realized what he intended. "No! You will be killed!"

"We'll be killed anyway, because Lord Gilbert has no intention of paying the ransom and when de Dinan runs out of patience he will hang us both. You don't want to be responsible for that, do you?"

Marion swallowed and mutely shook her head. The image he had conjured was too terrible to contemplate.

"Do it for me." He pulled a ring from his middle finger and slipped it onto hers. "Take this as a pledge of my faith; see, it has my seal on it. I swear on my honor that I will make you mine."

Marion felt as if she were being swept headlong down a river in spate. She could see the banks on either side, but was too far away to grab them. "I cannot," she whimpered tearfully. "You ask too much of me!"

"Would you have us fester here until we are brought out onto the battlements in chains and hanged?"

"Don't..." She pressed her hands to her ears.

Gently but firmly he grasped her wrists and pulled them down.

"Do what you must," he said softly, "but, for our sakes, make the right choice."

He let her go then, and Marion fled. Knowing that the guards were waiting outside, she had to conceal her agitation until she was out of their sight and hearing. Leaning against the hard stone newel post, precariously balanced on the tower's wedge stairs, she closed her eyes and listened to the sick pounding of her heart.

"I can't, I can't," she muttered to herself like a sinning nun desperately telling her prayer beads. But instead of the prayer beads she had a gold ring bearing the seal of a knight on horseback, sword raised. It was loose on her finger and she turned it around and around. Supposing Lord Joscelin chose to send out a warning to Gilbert's family by executing his knight? Everyone said that Lord Joscelin was soft-hearted, but she knew he must be capable of ruthlessness too. He would not have survived and prospered during the war between Stephen and Matilda otherwise. Could she afford to take the risk? Ernalt said that he loved her; he had given her his ring and promised to make her his wife. It was more than she had ever been offered before.

Marion wiped her eyes on her sleeve and tried to control her trembling. She could not return to the bower in this state, and the women would be looking for her by now. She was still unsure if she would do as Ernalt asked, but her resolve was stiffening by the moment. Removing the ring, she slid it onto the cord around her neck that held her crucifix. Then she tucked it down beneath her shift so that it lay between her small breasts and bumped with each erratic beat of her heart.

❖❖❖

"Don't worry, she will do it," Ernalt said as he tore up the linen Marion had brought, making strips to be braided into a rope. "She just needs time to settle the notion in her head."

De Lacy made a sound in his throat. "The lass strikes me as being as steady in her wits as a two-legged milking stool." He came to help tear up the linen. "If she doesn't bring us more, this rope will be too short. In fact," he added grimly, "just about enough to hang the pair of us."

"Marion will bring it," Ernalt said confidently. "She was frightened, but she was eating out of my hand—which is just what we want." He grinned at his lord. "What's more, we'll have a good distraction. Hawise de Dinan is to wed the FitzWarin heir within the month. They'll be too occupied with the nuptials to pay attention to us." Ernalt smiled. "You see, Marion tells me things."

De Lacy grunted. "Let us hope that she doesn't balk when it comes to the moment."

"She won't," Ernalt said with conviction. "I promise you that."

# Man and Woman

## 25

"Do you not think Marion seems strange of late?" Sibbi asked. She had arrived two days ago in anticipation of Hawise's wedding and the young women were talking together in the bridal chamber.

Hawise looked surprised at first, and then thoughtful. "Perhaps it is because you have been away from Ludlow and dwelling with your husband's kin," she said. "I suppose she does not chatter like she used to, but then we are no longer close like we were as children." She grimaced. "I don't think she's ever forgiven me or our parents for my betrothal to Brunin."

"It must be hard for her to watch you marry him then," Sibbi remarked with her usual sympathy for those in difficult circumstances.

"She hasn't said anything." Hawise's tone was defensive for Sibbi's gentle concern had filled her with guilt. Perhaps she should try to be kinder and take more notice of Marion, but then Marion herself had made no effort to bridge the troubled waters between them. Indeed, now Hawise thought about it, Marion spent very little time in the bower these days. She wasn't just quiet, she wasn't there. "I'll speak to her," she said reluctantly.

Their mother entered the chamber, a frown set between her eyes and her lips drawn in a tight purse. "Ridiculous," she snapped, hands on hips. "Sheets and tablecloths do not walk out of the coffers of their own accord."

The maid at her side was wringing her hands and declaring with loud distress that she could not explain their absence from the locked linen chests. "They were there yester eve when I looked, my lady. I swear on my life they were!"

"Then either someone is a thief, or they have been mislaid by one who has no more wit than a headless chicken!" Sybilla snapped, and lifted and let fall her hands in an exasperated gesture. "Jesu, I do not have the time for this now; our guests are almost here. Take a couple of the serjeants and go into the town. Ask the mercers for a dozen yards of bleached linen. I'll sort this out later."

"Yes, my lady." Relieved to have escaped so lightly, the maid ran.

Sybilla breathed out hard, looking decidedly harassed. "The FitzWarins are almost here," she told her daughters. "Their outriders have just arrived." Summoning another maid to attend her, she hastily stripped her gown and donned a fresh one of rose-colored linen.

Hawise swallowed and involuntarily set her hand to her throat and then her veil. Her hair was confined in a net beneath so that it couldn't straggle anywhere and rend propriety, and she was wearing a sober charcoal-gray wool enriched with silver embroidery.

"You look fit to greet a queen," Sibbi said soothingly, and hugged Hawise.

"A queen perhaps, but not the lady Mellette," Hawise said ruefully.

"It's not the lady Mellette whom you should be bothering about," Sibbi said, gentle mischief sparkling in her eyes. "I can remember the days when you didn't care what anyone thought of you. You would greet visitors from the top of a store-shed roof with a rip in your gown and a smudge on your nose."

That had the desired effect. Hawise thrust out her chin and drew herself erect. "I do not care now," she said loftily, "but I am old enough to know that some folk judge not only yourself by appearances, but all your kin too. I won't give the lady Mellette cause to open her mouth."

"She does not need cause, that one," Sybilla said as she twitched the folds of her gown into place, then raised her arms while the maid wrapped a braid belt around her waist. "But it is only for a few days and I suppose we can manage. It's annoying about the linen though." She clucked her tongue. "I should have kept a closer eye on the women. They all swear they are innocent, but someone must know what has happened to the things."

"What's missing, Mama?" Sibbi asked.

"The napery for some of the lower tables. Sheets that would have covered at least two guest beds. Towels that should accompany the fingerbowls."

Sibbi and Hawise shook their heads, as baffled as their mother. Marion, who would have been consulted too, was nowhere to be seen, but since the castle was like a beehive at the height of summer, her absence wasn't sufficiently out of place to remark upon.

The women went down to the bailey to await their guests. Hawise felt queasy and took herself to task for being foolish. She knew Brunin; she had met his family before. The standard courtesies ought to come as naturally as breathing, but just now breathing was difficult. It was as if a tight band were constricting her from throat to midriff. She was wishing that the wedding had been postponed to Michaelmas as her parents had originally suggested.

"Courage, daughter," her father said, arriving by her side and squeezing her shoulder beneath his broad, warm hand. Joscelin was clad in his court robe of purple wool and wearing his sword. He had dampened his hair and the comb marks lay through it like a layer of feathers, complementing the hard jut of his features. He looked every inch the stern warlord and Hawise was moved to feel pride and awe.

As the guards shouted from the walls and horns blared to greet the entry of the FitzWarin party through Ludlow's gates, Marion joined the welcoming group. Her cheeks were flushed and her breathing was, if anything, swifter than Hawise's.

"Where have you been?" Sybilla demanded with a frown.

"One of the pantry men asked me about bread for the chamber

cupboard, and then someone else wanted to know about candles," she panted, smoothing her hands down her blue gown. "I'm not late."

"No one said that you were, child," Sybilla said, returning her attention to the fore and thus missing the narrowing of Marion's eyes.

"I'm not a child," she muttered under her breath, pressing her right hand to her breast where a close observer could have discerned a small lump beneath the blue woolen fabric.

As the riders approached, Hawise noticed a horse-drawn litter in their midst. At first she thought that it must be for Mellette, but then she saw the old woman riding with her menfolk, her spine as straight as an ash lance, the angles of her face made harsh by the bleached linen wimple supporting and framing her jawline. Brunin rode at his father's side. Jester's comical face was adorned with new harness, enamelled red and gold discs decorating the buckles and jingling at the browband. He had a fine saddle cloth of red and gold too, and these were the colors that Brunin wore, his tunic the deep hue of vein-blood and hemmed with dark yellow embroidery. His complexion was already summer-brown and with his raven hair and dark eyes he had an exotic look like one of the Syrian silk traders she had seen at Shrewsbury Fair. His gaze engaged with hers and for a moment the surroundings blurred and she was locked into the hot, brown stare. And then her father was stepping forward to greet FitzWarin and his sons, and her mother to welcome Mellette, and Hawise was able to disengage and look elsewhere.

The curtains to the litter parted and Brunin's mother was helped out by two attendants. Hawise went forward to greet her, and was shaken out of her own anxieties by the sight of Eve FitzWarin's pallid, almost gray complexion. "Welcome to Ludlow, my lady." Hawise curtseyed to her future mother-in-law, managing to hide her shock at Eve's appearance

"Thank you, daughter. It will be easy to call you that." A tired smile curved Eve's lips, but didn't light her eyes, which remained quenched and dull. She extended her hand and Hawise noticed how swollen her fingers were and how cruelly her gold rings bit into the flesh.

"Will you come within and rest?" Hawise took the proffered hand, which was clammy and hot and made her want to recoil.

Eve laid her other palm to her belly. "Thank you," she said. "I have had better experiences of carrying my children and in truth I am weary."

There was no opportunity for Hawise to see Brunin alone. The women retired to the domestic chambers to discuss the forthcoming marriage and indulge in gossip; the men formed a similar group in the hall. The maid returned from the town with new linen to replace the missing napery and Sybilla set her women to hemming with haste.

"When I was married, my father held a grand tournament," Mellette boasted to the gathered women. "Knights came from miles around to compete and there was feasting for a week. In those days we knew how to celebrate."

"Indeed, my lady," Sybilla said politely. "Then I hope you will not be disappointed with lesser celebrations here. Our preparations by necessity are to join King Henry's muster, although perhaps we can entertain you with some feats of arms on the sward. Besides, you would not want to sit in a draught for too long and Lady Eve's condition is delicate. Another cup of wine?"

"I am no wilting flower," Mellette retorted. "I have the iron of the Conqueror in my blood."

Hawise watched the battle of words and wits between her mother and Brunin's grandmother and felt a little sick when she thought that soon this fight would be hers. Her tongue was quick, but she was no good at subterfuge. Rather than responding with a soothing murmur as Sybilla had just done, Hawise would have replied that iron was wont to go rusty. The thought provoked a nervous giggle and she had to smother it against the back of her hand as Mellette's eyes narrowed.

"Yes, my girl," she said, lips curling back from the stumps of her teeth. "The iron of the Conqueror. Your sons will share the same ancestors as the King."

Ancestors that included a common Falaise tanner, a madman, and a washerwoman, but that wasn't safe or polite to say either. She swallowed hard, but the laughter continued to bubble inside her.

Mellette took a taste of the wine in her refilled cup and fastidiously dabbed her upper lip. "I hope your daughter knows how to conduct herself on the morrow."

"She has been well instructed," Sybilla answered frostily. "I am sure that neither she nor your grandson will disgrace themselves."

"And what of the night duty? Have you instructed her in that too? Does she know what to expect?"

"She knows," Sybilla replied, tight-lipped.

"You think me an interfering old woman." Mellette gave a sour smile. "But I was asking for the girl's sake. No one told me anything. They put me in bed with a stranger and instructed me to do my duty and obey his will." She looked at Hawise. "It was rape by any other name, like being stabbed with a blade, and there was enough blood to make me think that he had indeed mortally injured me. She should know what to expect."

Eve made a small sound and pressed the back of her hand to her mouth. With a gasp she excused herself to the garderobe in the corner and the sound of her retching echoed back into the room.

Sybilla looked furious. "Your experience has no bearing on my daughter's. You are vindictive to frighten her."

"Better to know than to harbor fond dreams," Mellette said harshly.

"I am not frightened." Unable to silence her voice any longer and emboldened by her mother's loss of patience, Hawise spoke out. "Brunin will not hurt me."

"There speaks the voice of experience." Mellette's voice dripped with sarcasm. "What do I know of men with all my years, eh?"

Hawise sprang to her feet. "Naught but malice and envy and hatred! You don't see the sunlight because you never look up!"

"Hah, and thus I don't tread in dung!" There was a glitter in Mellette's eyes that was almost relish. "You have a lot to learn, my girl."

"Then I will learn it with Brunin, and I will rejoice." She turned to her mother who was watching her with a mixture of dismay and approval. "May I have your leave to retire, Mama?"

"I think you had better," Sybilla said in a neutral tone. "Before manners deteriorate further." She did not say whose manners.

Head high, Hawise turned from the venomous crone, deliberately omitting to curtsey, and swept into the small chamber that would be hers for the last time that night. "Bitch," she muttered and fought scalding tears of rage. She suspected that inducing such emotions in others was half Mellette's pleasure. She enjoyed watching her victims lose their tempers while retaining her own. Probably it gave her a sense of superiority and power and a purpose in the world.

When her breathing had calmed and she felt less like hurling a table at the old woman, she tiptoed softly from the room and onto the landing, intent on making her escape. Eve FitzWarin was sitting on the stone window-bench, looking out across the bailey, clearly having made a small escape of her own. She was breathing deeply of the fresh air flowing through the narrow channel of the window and her gaze was fixed upon the summer green of the trees beyond the castle walls.

Hawise halted. She could not just walk past and pretend not to have seen her. This was Brunin's mother; imminently to be her own mother-in-law. "My lady?"

Eve turned from the window and studied Hawise with her sad, smudged eyes. "I hope you were not upset by Lady Mellette's words."

Hawise frowned while she pondered whether to speak the truth or a path-smoothing platitude. "I think that she intended them to upset, my lady," she answered after a moment. "And not just myself."

Eve gave her the pale semblance of a smile. "I am not car-rying this babe well," she said, laying her hand upon her belly. "The sickness comes suddenly and as it will with no regard for propriety."

It was an excuse, not the truth, Hawise thought. "I am told that I have no regard for propriety either," she murmured.

Eve's smile developed a wry twist. "All to the good," she answered softly. "I have never had the backbone to hold my own with her." She glanced toward the door, not needing to say which "her" she meant. "She chose me for her son because I was dutiful and biddable and she knew that I would not take her place in the bower. Now she is growing old...and so am I. It is time that there was a new challenge...new blood. From what I have seen, you will take up the battle that I could not fight."

"It doesn't have to be a battle," Hawise said, but with a note of uncertainty in her voice.

Eve looked bleak. "It already is, and one you have to win...unless you want to follow in my footsteps. I would wish such a fate on no woman."

Hawise swallowed, feeling out of her depth. "Your husband, my lady. Could he not..."

"My husband is no Joscelin de Dinan," Eve replied bitterly. "He does what he sees as his duty toward me, but he has no more notion of what women want than a pig has of flight. Nor, if the truth be known, does he want to become embroiled in 'women's business.' As long as I am there to place a cup of wine in his hands and warm his bed, he cares not. In my turn I am no Sybilla Talbot to stand my ground, but you..." She looked Hawise up and down. "You are different."

"So is Brunin."

Eve nodded. "Yes, he is," she said. "Lady Mellette is right. He is much like his grandfather." Her gaze grew soft and sad. "I have often wondered how Warin de Metz would have fared with a less abrasive wife."

"She brought him the land and the prestige," Hawise said.

"As you are bringing Brunin one half of Ludlow. I pray that you can both set everything to rights. Whatever Mellette says or does, I want you to know that you are most welcome within our household, and I am pleased to call you daughter."

"And I am glad to call you mother," Hawise answered gracefully.

Eve shook her head and gave a knowing laugh. "No, you are not. The best you can do is adapt and tolerate."

Before Hawise could decide how to respond, there were footsteps on the stairs and Marion arrived, breathless and pink from the steep climb. She stopped short when she saw Hawise and Eve, then came on, pausing to curtsey to the latter.

"Where have you been?" Hawise asked.

"That's my own business." Marion tossed her head. "I'm not always asking you where you have been, am I?" She swept into the main chamber and Hawise winced.

"Matters are difficult between us," she told Eve. "Marion used to be sweet on Brunin and it has stung her pride that I am to marry him."

Eve looked thoughtfully at the space through which Marion had just passed. "I remember her from a visit your household made to Whittington," she said. "She tried very hard to impress Lady Mellette, which indeed she did, but..."

"But Lady Mellette wanted Ludlow to add to the FitzWarin gains," Hawise finished the sentence. "I know my worth in her eyes."

"It is the value you set on yourself that matters." Suddenly Eve's voice dragged with tiredness. "I think I will go and lie down awhile."

"You can use my bed if you don't want to go back into the main chamber," Hawise offered.

Eve gave her a grateful look. "Bless you, daughter," she said.

# 26

SINCE HIS ARRIVAL ON THE EVE OF THEIR WEDDING, BRUNIN had seen little of Hawise. After a brief greeting in the courtyard, surrounded by family and retainers, she had retired with the women and he had been drawn into the hall with the men to discuss not so much his imminent nuptials as the forthcoming Welsh campaign. At the formal dinner, later in the day, bride and groom had again been separated, he sitting with his family, she with hers, as for the last time she took her formal place as a daughter of her father's household. In future, that place would be as a FitzWarin wife. There had been little opportunity for conversation, let alone whispered words; no occasion to don even a semblance of the familiarity that they had once shared. After their recent confrontation, he was not even sure that it was possible.

Now it was the morning of their marriage day and there was no time left to find out. Brunin wondered if Hawise felt as apprehensive as he did. He had no intention of sharing his anxieties with any of the grinning men circling the chamber like friendly but dominant dogs of the same pack. Their teasing and advice were all part of the ritual and he had perforce to endure them. He had done his own share of teasing and prank-playing in the past. Only let this day and night be over, he thought. Only let everyone depart and the celebration end. Except that after celebration came separation and war.

"You'll outdo the bride," his father grinned, looking him up and down. Brunin's tunic was fashioned of plum-colored Flemish twill, thickly embroidered with thread of gold at cuff and hem and throat. His belt and shoes were stamped with gilding, and his scabbard leather polished until it gleamed like Jester's hide.

"I hope not." Brunin looked around at the men. They were all eager for the festivities, for a chance to make merry before they rode out to join Henry's muster. For some it might be a final chance; there was an air of urgency, and a need to seize the moment. Since he might be one of those who did not return, Brunin could feel the weight of expectation pressing down on him. "Perhaps my grandmother will though, in that purple."

FitzWarin stifled a guffaw and glanced toward the hearth where Mellette was ordering servants about from the comfort of a curule chair. Her walking stick jabbed; her tongue assaulted. She was wearing a silk gown, somewhat outdated for it belonged to her youth, but the hue was a deep royal purple, expensive beyond belief and seldom seen outside the households of the highest magnates in the land.

FitzWarin clasped Brunin's shoulder. "It is you who carries the pride of our family, and I am glad that you do." His tone was bluff, for he was ill at ease with compliments and emotion.

The door opened and a man robed in the dark habit of a Benedictine monk approached them. "His Lordship the Bishop desires to know if you are ready to come to church," he said.

"Is the bride ready?" FitzWarin asked.

The monk inclined his head. "So I understand, sire."

Brunin felt his throat tighten. "Then so am I," he said in a constricted voice, and went to the door. In stately procession the FitzWarin family crossed the sward to the castle's chapel. Servants, retainers, and well-wishers crowded around the outside of the building craning necks, pointing, exclaiming. Parents lifted small children onto shoulders; older children ran for the fistful of silver pennies that FitzWarin flung into the heart of the throng.

Inside the chapel, the Bishop of Hereford was waiting for them, his cope so encrusted with embroidery and gilding that it was almost as stiff as the covers of a psalter. His gaze flicked over Mellette's purple gown, but his expression remained diplomatically neutral. When he suggested that she might like to be seated on one of the benches lining the walls, she declined, declaring that she intended to stand and witness the marriage at close quarters.

Brunin looked toward the chapel's far door, willing the bridal party to arrive. His palms were slick with cold sweat, his heart in his throat. Mellette gave an impatient mutter. Then the door opened and a blaze of summer light poured into the room. For an instant Brunin's eyes were dazzled by the brightness. When he could see again, Hawise was walking toward him and it was an image he was to carry with him for the rest of his life.

The gown of saffron silk clung to her figure then flowed from the hips, the fabric shining like a river at sunset. As she walked, her hand upon her father's arm, the strap ends on her brocade belt flashed with gold. Her hair shimmered to her waist, citrine highlights from the gown glinting upon the garnet-dark waves. Her brow was crowned with a garland of pale dogroses and early gillyflowers, and she carried a second garland in her free hand. She walked stiffly and her complexion was pale, but that pallor only emphasized the deep water-gray of her eyes and the fine coppery arches of her brows. He felt as if he were standing in the midst of one of the romance lays that the troubadours sang in the halls on feast days. In a moment he was going to wake up on his pallet and find that he was still a squire; that there was harness to clean and horses to groom; that his knighthood was an illusion and so was the young woman who had come to stand at his side with downcast lashes and breathing swifter than his own. Against his expectations the moment continued, the colors bright and intense, the sounds too. He could hear every shuffle of foot, every intake of air, every rustle of cloth; was aware, with a feeling that was so intense it was almost pain, of Hawise at his side, her arm still upon Joscelin's…and of Joscelin himself, taut-jawed with suppressed emotion.

The Bishop demanded to know of the families if mutual consent had been given to the match and, satisfied, asked the same of the couple. For a moment Brunin's voice stuck in his throat, but he forced it past the tightness, and it emerged clear and strong. Hawise raised her head and gave her own similar assent, looking directly at Brunin. From somewhere behind his right shoulder, Mellette clicked her tongue, obviously seeing this as more evidence of unseemly boldness. Suddenly his lips twitched. So did Hawise's, before she hastily lowered her gaze.

Fortunately the urge to lapse into a display of even less seemly mirth was overridden by the need to remember and perform the rituals of the marriage ceremony, but the shared humor had served to dissipate some of the tension. If Brunin's hands were not quite steady as he slipped the ring on Hawise's finger and gave her the gold pieces that were a symbol of his ability to provide for her, nevertheless he did not fumble. Hawise then knelt to him in token of her willingness to submit to his will, her head bowed, her silk dress a pool of gold on the chapel floor. Mellette muttered something about hoping it was more than just show.

Brunin raised Hawise to her feet and bestowed on her the kiss of peace. Her skin was cold, her breathing swift, but he felt her cheek lift in a smile beneath his lips. The Bishop folded his stole around their joined hands and blessed the bride and groom before conducting a wedding mass and a sermon concerning the duties that married couples owed to each other and their families.

Then they were walking side by side from the chapel, to the cheers of the crowd, the throwing of barley grains and a storm of rose petals. It was done. Man and wife. For better or worse.

Brunin ducked as his youngest brother William flung a fistful of barley from close range and the grains stung his skin like small hailstones. Grabbing Hawise's hand, he flouted all propriety by running with her toward the safety of the great hall. Laughing, she hastily snatched up the trailing hem of her dress and ran with him, exposing a scandalous amount of ankle in the process.

Joscelin chuckled and shook his head, his eyes full of laughter and sadness. His youngest daughter would always be his youngest daughter, but today he had given her into the keeping of another, and it was the start of a change that would take her further into womanhood and further away from him. Sybilla was both smiling and exasperated. The FitzWarin family stared with various expressions of astonishment, disapproval, envy, and badly disguised amusement. This marriage was going to change their lives too.

❖ ❖ ❖

Since the men were soon to ride to King Henry's summons at Northampton, the wedding feast was not as elaborate as it would usually have been, but still there were numerous courses and plentiful wine. There were fish from the river beyond the castle, and eels from the Severn. Pigeons in wine sauce, coneys glazed with honey, chicken pies, platters of roasted songbirds, eggs colored with saffron. White curd tarts flavored with rosewater, junkets, delicate almond pastries, and spicy gingerbread.

Hawise nibbled, but could not find the appetite to appreciate the food. Despite the beauty of her gown and the display put on in her honor, she thought that other people's weddings were infinitely more enjoyable.

"Not hungry?" Brunin asked.

Hawise shook her head.

"Neither am I...although doubtless I'll be starving on the morrow..."

She stared at him with widening eyes.

"I didn't mean because of...that," he said hastily. "I meant when all this...this..." He waved his hand at the crowd of diners. "...performance is over."

"I was thinking the same myself." She crumbled a piece of bread, gazing at the new gold ring gleaming on her middle finger, and frowned.

"What's wrong?"

"I was thinking that within a few days I must watch you and my father ride off to war, and that it is going to be very hard."

He gave her a puzzled look. "No harder than it has ever been."

"Yes it will." She turned the ring on her finger for a moment as if doing so was a key to unlocking what she wanted to say. "I wasn't married to you before. I wasn't allowed to think of you as 'mine.' Now that you are, I have more to lose."

"Is that how you think of me now—as yours?"

She thought she saw a glimmer of interest in his eyes, as if the notion was new to him and pleasing. Perhaps there was even a hint of smugness. "How else should I think of you? I had my duties laid out for me in the chapel this morning."

The smugness vanished. "Duties, yes," he said, "and responsibilities, but those are cold words when measured against 'mine' and 'yours.'"

"Yes, they are," she said. "And even colder when compared to love and faith." She looked at him steadily. "I would rather do my duty out of love for you than obligation, because then it becomes not a duty at all." Then she laughed and reached to the large, silver-gilt goblet they were sharing. A loving cup and, of all the ironies, a gift from Mellette FitzWarin along with sundry other items of silver plate. "I have drunk too much already," she said after she had taken a sip of the potent brew, spiced with cinnamon and black pepper. "What will your grandmother think of a bride who is gilded on her wedding night?"

Brunin looked rueful as she passed the cup to him. "I don't think it much matters whether you're sober or flat drunk." He took a mouthful and swallowed. "It is my ability to take your maidenhead that matters. We'll be judged and either damned or commended by the state of the sheets on the morrow." He glanced toward his grandmother. "Drink if you want." He returned the cup to her. "I doubt she was sober on her own wedding night."

"She was," Hawise said and made a face. "Or certainly aware enough to have the event burned into her memory."

"She told you about it?"

"Yes. In her usual way."

The look he narrowed at Mellette before he lowered his gaze and schooled his expression to neutrality was annihilating. "Our wedding night doesn't have to be hers."

"God forbid," Hawise said, and could not prevent a shudder. Involuntarily she glanced toward the open shutters where she could tell from the light that the sun was going down.

The musicians had been playing softly throughout the meal, but now they were preparing to strike up livelier tunes so that the guests could dance off some of the food and drink they had consumed. Brunin turned away to his left and, a moment later, hauled little Emmeline onto his lap. The child's cheeks were as scarlet as holly berries and her eyes as bright black as those of a little dormouse. Her silky raven hair had been braided with red ribbons, but it was beginning to wisp free from the bindings and tangle around her face. Hawise wondered if her own firstborn child would be as dark as Brunin and his sister, or fair and robust like the rest of the FitzWarins and her de Dinan and Talbot blood-line. Perhaps she would know in nine months' time. The thought sent a jolt through her stomach and loins.

Emmeline giggled at Hawise, exposing perfect small teeth and pink gums and wriggled to go down again. "Dance," she said in a peremptory little voice, tugging on Brunin's hand. "Come and dance."

"She is like my grandmother," Brunin chuckled wryly. "She thinks her word is the law."

Bride and groom rose to lead the dance at their wedding, and were accompanied by a determined, dark-eyed little girl who glued herself to them for the first and second measure, before finally being lured away by Sibbi and Hugh. The third dance was for Hawise and Brunin, a figure of eight and crossing of hands and bodies. Right side, left side, right again. Outer hip to outer hip and return. Fingers meshed, eyes linked, feet moving to the time and tune of the music, the tabor beating the rhythm like a hard, swift heartbeat.

❖ ❖ ❖

In the Pendover tower, Gilbert de Lacy secured one end of the rope around the coffer under the window splay. "Ready?" he asked, baring a grin.

Ernalt looked out and then down. It was a long drop to the rock-strewn grass at the base of the tower. He nodded stiffly, not relishing the coming moments, but filled with exhilaration at the thought of escaping under de Dinan's nose. They had spent the day smearing the paler sections of their makeshift rope with ashes and soot from their fire and Ernalt had taken pleasure in smirching the carefully worked embroidery on some of the pieces, imagining that it was the toil of that bitch of a daughter and her mother.

Earlier that day Marion had brought them food, wine, and, from somewhere, a couple of dark cloaks and hoods, smuggled in beneath her own outdoor mantle. She had provided two knives as well, good and sharp.

"You will return for me...you swear?" she had said, her eyes filled with a wide, wild pleading.

Other women had used similar words to Ernalt before. Depending how cruel he was feeling, he would either promise or leave them in no doubt, but the outcome was always the same; he never went back. This time, however, the stakes had changed. "I swear," he had said and, framing her face between his palms, had kissed her mouth. "Only wait for my sign."

Now he fastened the dark cloak at his shoulder and drew up the hood. The last stroke of the compline bell tolled and faded into the sounds of laughter and music wafting through the open shutters in the great hall.

"They will all be singing a different tune on the morrow," de Lacy said with a short laugh as he tossed the rope out of the window. Squeezing himself out of the narrow opening, he took a firm grip on the braided twists of linen and towel. He had removed his rings to stop them snagging on the fabric and threaded them around his neck. "Pray that the material is strong and our twining good," he said to Ernalt. "Otherwise I will greet you in the next world."

Ernalt gave a tense nod and watched the rope go taut as Gilbert trusted his full weight to the lengths of knotted sheet and towel, and let himself down the wall. Peering out, Ernalt watched the dark shape swing out and down, out and down. He wiped his damp palms on his tunic and swallowed. His heart was pounding as if it would break from his chest. His turn in a moment…if the rope held, if no one saw them and raised the alarm. Pray God that they were all too busy celebrating.

De Lacy was in his middle years but still strong and athletic. He soon reached the base of the wall and gave the rope a sharp tug. Crossing himself, Ernalt climbed onto the ledge and squeezed himself through the opening. He knew that the rope would be strained from the weight already put on it, and tried not to let his imagination follow that path. Concentrate on the task in hand. One hand over the other; pay out the rope; push and leap, push and leap. The stone was gritty against the flat soles of his boots, the rope burned against his palms, and he could feel the tight tug of strain upon his recently healed wrist. He waited for the alarm cry that would sound the knell on their escape, but there was nothing…only the distant *mélange* of music and laughter from the hall and the occasional voice raised in drunken bonhomie. One more push and settle, one last jump, and he landed in the long grass at the base of the tower. De Lacy was waiting for him in the shadows and together, moving with the low stealth of cats, they scrambled along the bottom of the wall toward the river.

❖❖❖

Brunin was being boisterously disrobed in preparation for the bedding ceremony as in similar wise Hawise was being prepared in the bridal chamber above this one. He bore the rough tugging and bawdy remarks with an outward display of aplomb. If he could not have privacy without, then he would have it within.

"Yes," slurred a drunken Ralf, "I've often wondered whether he'd got the balls to see matters through, but it's all right, he's got both of them!"

Brunin briefly faced his brother. "Satisfied?"

"Not as much as your bride had better be!"

Joscelin loudly cleared his throat and handed Brunin a cloak to cover his nakedness. "I hope you are more sober than your brothers," his new father-in-law muttered angrily.

Brunin fastened the clasp with steady fingers. "I have shared three cups of wine with Hawise all evening," he said, not adding that the bridal goblet was twice the size of a usual measure and that Hawise had probably swallowed the lion's share. He couldn't afford the oblivion of drink.

Joscelin was still frowning. "I…" He rubbed the back of his neck, his complexion turning a rich shade of plum. "Have a care with her," he said. "I do not want to see her tears on the morrow."

"Neither do I…sir." Brunin wondered if Joscelin realized the weight he was adding to the burden.

Joscelin gave a curt nod. "I'm trusting you with my daughter…"

"My wife," Brunin replied to make a point and saw Joscelin gather his emotions together like a harvester tying a shock of wheat in the wind.

"Aye, you have the right of it…your wife." Joscelin gripped his shoulder. "If I don't trust you with her now, then it's too late for both of us." Removing his hand, he stepped back. Brunin could still feel the imprint of the square, strong fingers, hard as a mail glove, reminding him. But if Hawise didn't trust him, what then?

"Hah, no need to look so grim, lad," his father said, and his own hand came down hard on Brunin's shoulder, obliterating the feel of Joscelin's grip. "It's your wedding night, not your wake."

"He hopes!" Ralf guffawed, and received a hefty bear cuff from FitzWarin.

"Your turn will come, whelp, and if you conduct yourself half so well, then you will count yourself fortunate!"

That silenced his second son like a splash from a pail of cold water and Ralf fell back among the other well-wishers, his expression suddenly miserable. Brunin raised a brow at him. Sooner or later their father would have to know about Sian.

The more sober men of the wedding party were entrusted with bearing the torches to light the way to the bridal chamber, and Brunin was half led, half jostled up the tower stairs to the great wooden door amidst bawdy jests about knocking with a stout staff before entering.

❖ ❖ ❖

"They're on their way," said Sibbi, who had posted herself near the door to listen out and give warning.

Hawise caught her breath. Her stomach was a queasy hollow. She hoped she wouldn't disgrace herself by being sick...although if she managed to vomit over Mellette FitzWarin, that might be some consolation. As the women had undressed her, Brunin's grandmother had studied her with the uncompromising, critical eyes of a horse-coper at Shrewsbury Fair perusing a nag of doubtful pedigree.

"Good hips for breeding," Mellette had said, "just as long as she proves more fecund than her Talbot side."

"That is in the hands of God," Sybilla had replied, lips pursed in anger.

"Indeed, my lady. We'll all be praying hard for a fertile furrow to be ploughed this night."

Hawise had had to compress her own lips very tightly. It was obvious that the old besom was trying to provoke a reaction and the best defense was not to give her one.

Sybilla had fastened Hawise's cloak around her shoulders and arranged her tresses over it in a gleaming, fiery skein.

"You have beautiful hair," Eve FitzWarin said softly.

"Let us hope that the color doesn't carry forward into the children," Mellette said, continuing to be outrageous.

"There has always been red hair in the de Dinan bloodline," Sybilla said icily. "I pray that it does. Marion, stop hiding in the corner and pass me the comb...Saints, girl, you're as green as a new cheese!"

Marion swallowed. "Too much wine," she said. Her breathing was rapid and the frightened expression on her face, together with her shaking hands, might have led a newcomer to believe that she was the anxious bride rather than Hawise.

The sight of her distress momentarily distracted Hawise from her own anxieties. She assumed that Marion was upset because she was seeing her dream of wedding Brunin being shattered before her eyes.

"You don't have to stay, Marion," she said gently. "I understand." She was pleased with the way her own voice sounded: mature and modulated like her mother's.

"No," Marion spat like a cornered cat. "You don't even begin to understand, and you never will!" She thrust the comb into Sybilla's hand, ran to the door, wrenched it open, and fled. An instant later the women heard the sound of bawdy welcome as Marion encountered the male wedding party on its way up the stairs.

"I'd have that girl soundly whipped if I were you," Mellette said, folding her arms beneath her bosom.

"But you are not me, and I will deal with Marion as I see fit...with respect, my lady," Sybilla answered, and used the comb to stroke and smooth Hawise's hair in a gesture of affectionate reassurance.

Mellette made a "hmph" sound but held her peace, allowing her expression to speak for her.

"Courage," Sybilla whispered to Hawise. "It will soon be over. Your father and I will make sure that the guests do not linger beyond what has to be done."

Hawise nodded and steeled herself as the groom's party surged into the room, voices and laughter loud with drink. Two of Brunin's younger brothers were jesting to each other about Marion, whom they had obviously enjoyed pressing up against on the stairs as she tried to squeeze past. In the midst of all the guffaws and shouting, Brunin, by contrast, was as still as stone. Perhaps his complexion was a little heightened, and the pupils of his eyes were so wide that his eyes seemed black, but otherwise he appeared to be as impassive as a lump of storm-battered granite. Hawise felt as if she were made of small grains of sand, disintegrating against the surge.

Bishop Gilbert entered the room on the heels of the revelers. Raising his arms, ivory crozier in hand, he roared for silence with a voice of carrying power. Mostly it was obeyed, with only the odd titter and belch challenging its authority.

The Bishop beckoned Brunin and Hawise forward to stand before him. "We are gathered to witness that there is no bodily flaw in bride or groom that will cause the marriage to be null and void." He gestured and Sybilla gently unfastened the pin and pulled Hawise's cloak from her shoulders. Hawise suppressed the instinct to cover her breasts and pubic mound with her hands. Only let it be over, and quickly, she prayed. Sybilla gathered up her sheaf of hair and held it away from her body so that every part of Hawise was exposed to the stare of the wedding guests...and her new husband.

"I am satisfied," he said in a low voice.

"Not yet he isn't!" someone shouted before his exuberance was muffled by a more responsible companion.

Cool fabric slid against Hawise's skin and with deep relief she thrust her head and arms through the openings in an exquisitely embroidered linen chemise.

Now it was Brunin's turn and Hawise had to raise her head and look upon him as his father removed the cloak. He stood quietly, the rise and fall of his chest measured and controlled, his own gaze fixed beyond hers at a point somewhere on the wall. Her eyes hastily skimmed over him as a matter of form, but she absorbed nothing. Even had his nakedness revealed horned hooves and a tail, she would not have noticed at this moment. "I too am satisfied," she croaked, ignoring the splutter from the impromptu jester at the room's far end. Brunin was similarly reclothed in an embroidered nightshirt and the couple brought to the bed. Sybilla and Eve drew back the covers to reveal the smooth bleached linen sheet covering the mattress and the guests were asked to witness the proof that any blood spilled on it could not have come from earlier artifice. Bishop Gilbert sprinkled the sheet liberally with holy water and blessed the bed. The women led Hawise around to the left side and placed her in the bed. Then the men, with a deal more manhandling and bawdy talk, threw Brunin in with his bride.

"Go on, lad. She'll be a better ride than that nag of yours!"

"Hah, he's got to mount her first and then try to stay on!"

"You know what they say about red-haired women...mayhap she'll ride him!"

Comments bantered back and forth, becoming bawdier by the moment. Finally Joscelin had had enough and bellowed the word with sufficient resonance to sound against the rafters. "There is meat and drink aplenty in the hall for those who have not taken their fill. Time to give the bride and groom some peace...and before I hear cries that peace is the last thing they will have tonight, remember that Hawise is my daughter, my youngest child, and Brunin is Lord FitzWarin's heir. As I said...enough!" Spreading his arms, he began to usher everyone out.

"Well said, my lord," Mellette declared and for once there was a gleam of approval in her eyes. "Bedding ceremonies always turn into unseemly circuses." With a curt nod, she left the room, accompanied by Eve and FitzWarin.

Sybilla kissed Hawise on the cheek, and then Brunin. "May you both find joy," she said with a warm smile.

"Thank you, Mama." Hawise wished that she could leave the

room with her mother, wished that it was someone else's wedding night and that she was no more than a casual onlooker. Her father was at the door. He looked once over his shoulder and tried to smile. Sybilla came to him, took his arm, kissed his cheek too, and drew him from the chamber.

The moment that the latch dropped, Brunin leaped from the bed and shot the bolt across the door.

"I trust neither my brothers, nor some of the knights," he said. "I cannot prevent them from listening at the latch, but I can stop them from bursting in."

"You think they would do that?" Hawise left the bed too, putting off the inevitable.

"I know they would," Brunin said with a wry laugh. "Especially with the drink inside them. A bride and groom are always fair game for sport on their wedding night and I've done my share of teasing."

"Ah yes, the packhorse bells tied to the mattress when Hugh and Sibbi were wed. Sibbi told me it took them an hour to unstring them all."

He shrugged. "By which time they were at ease with each other. It was a good ploy." He got down on his hands and knees to examine the underside of their mattress, but no one, it seemed, had been prepared to be as inventive, or to risk the ire of the bride's father. Rising to his feet, he faced her and dusted off his palms. "There is one rule that I am going to make inviolate after the display of that sheet on the morrow."

"What?" Hawise folded her arms defensively over her breasts, but quickly unfolded them again. She would not show him how tense she was.

"That this room is ours. That anything we say or do beyond this threshold belongs to us alone...be it talking, or gaming, or quarrelling, or lying together. We will have the antechamber for guests and visitors and official business, but that doorway is where it all stops."

"You have no complaint from me on that score," Hawise said fervently. She glanced toward the bed and the waiting, pristine undersheet.

He pushed his hands through his hair and sat down on his clothing coffer. "I've been thinking about that damned bed all day," he said.

"You have?" Her voice emerged as a tight croak.

"It's been hard not to with all the reminders."

Hawise saw that he was frowning. He had apparently borne the preliminaries better than she had, but appearances could be deceptive—especially in his case. Going to her own coffer, she knelt and threw back the lid. "Do you remember the day when you were cleaning my father's weapons and I came to you?"

"Yes, I remember." He gave her a cautious look. "Which part of that day are you asking me to recall?"

"All of it."

"Why?"

"Because of everything that happened. If there had been a bed in that chamber, we might have used it. It was very sweet between us...wasn't it?"

"Yes, it was." His expression remained guarded. Hawise desperately hoped that what she was about to do would bring down the barrier. She had to see beyond it.

"Then Gilbert de Lacy attacked and I accused you of cowardice when nothing could be further from the truth." It was hard to hold his gaze, but she forced herself to do so. "I would throw my words into a void of forgetting, but since we both have good memories, it cannot be done."

A thin smile broke through his wariness. "It is only the good memories I would foster."

She returned his smile with a strained one of her own. "Liar," she said.

"I did not say the unpleasant memories would go away, but that I would foster the good ones—or try to anyway." The curve of his lips deepened. "For example, I will try to forget that my new wife just called me a liar."

Hawise hesitated. Once she had known him well enough to seize a cushion and throw it at his head, but that was before the day of which they had just spoken…before his father's illness and their joining as man and wife. She had wished for a chamber where they could be alone. Now she had that wish and, like a little girl holding her first distaff and spindle, was unsure how to begin turning a morass of fleece into smooth-running yarn. She mentally shook herself. Unsure, yes. But that did not mean entirely without notion, and the latter was the reason for being on her knees at this open coffer.

"I have other names that I wish to call you instead, if you will let me," she said.

He arched one eyebrow but the smile remained and her instinct told her that he was diverted. "Such as?"

Hawise licked her lips. Here was the part where she set the spindle spinning, drew out the fleece, and hoped that she had sufficient dexterity to make a thread fine enough to weave the pattern of their lives without clumping or breaking. Reaching inside the chest she withdrew a linen bag, and from it removed a roll of yellow silk. "Such as honorable and brave and fierce. I thought of those words when I was making this for you." She handed him the wrapped banner, feeling suddenly shy and at the same time filled with bright anticipation. "I didn't want to give you this in front of everyone else. It is my personal gift to you."

He was no longer smiling as he reached and took it from her. Carefully he unfurled it and then stared at the black wolf snarling on the yellow background, bordered by chevrons of scarlet and black.

"I heard that your grandfather carried a similar banner," she added.

She saw him swallow. "The black wolf was his, yes."

"And now it is yours." She closed the coffer and rose to her feet. "Do you like it?"

"I do not think 'like' is the right word." He traced the outline of the embroidered beast with the spread fingertips of his right hand. "It must have taken you weeks to do this."

Hawise gave a shaken laugh. "It did, and although you do not see it, that beast has taken its share of my blood, but I begrudge it not. First and last it was and is a labor of love…and perhaps a penance too." She raised her head. "When you ride out with our fathers to King Henry's muster, I will be proud to see that banner flying with theirs."

Brunin rose from the coffer and spread the silk over it. For a long time he continued to look upon the banner, and then he turned to her and took her hands in his. "Perhaps I have some words for you too," he said.

Hawise's heart began to pound. "Such as?" She tried to make her voice light, echoing his question of a moment since, but it was edged with a tremor.

"Such as wife, helpmate, friend."

She took one of her hands out of his and with great daring reached to his face. "Husband," she murmured.

He kissed her, his free hand moving through her hair, meshing it through his fingers until he reached the tips then drawing back and repeating the move; and all the time his mouth moved softly on hers in small, nipping kisses like minnows against her fingers in warm summer shallows.

She answered the touch of his lips with kisses of her own, her loose hand dropping to his shoulder and cupping the curve, feeling the warmth and weight of muscle beneath the thin linen chemise. Beyond the anxiety at stepping into the unknown, something greedy and needful stirred. Her fingers tightened on his shoulder and she leaned into the kisses, offering her lips, wanting more.

Brunin drew Hawise to the bed and lay down with her. The mattress was well stuffed with goose down so that it was both firm and yielding to the touch, almost echoing the properties of flesh. He faced her, one hand still in her hair. He loved the warmth of it near her scalp, and the cool heaviness at the ends…and those ends led his fingers down over the tip of her right breast and finished at her waist, again and again until her breath shuddered in her throat and she thrust into the caress and he felt the hard bud of her nipple through the linen chemise. It was heady to hear her response and it encouraged him to lean over her, stroke her hair away from her face and kiss her more thoroughly while he unfastened the throat lace of her chemise. It was but loosely tied and the knot came free to his stealthy tug.

He nibbled the angle of her jaw, the soft skin of her neck and throat, perfumed with spices and rose oil, and then the flesh exposed by the unfastened chemise. He cupped her breast and ran his thumb over the erect nipple, and she arched toward him, her fingers tightening at the nape of his neck, her breathing short and swift against his ear and temple. The way she answered his touch sent a jolt of sensation from gut to loins. He followed the line of the chemise, tugging downward, exposing the upper curve of her breasts. The candlelight gleamed on her skin, tinting it with gold, and beneath his fingertips he felt her shiver into gooseflesh. Her teeth found his earlobe and nipped. Her tongue flickered against the angle of his jaw and again the jolt shot through him like distant lightning. His own breathing quickened and his palm sprang with sweat as he slid his fingers beneath the fine linen and curled them over her breast. She made a sound in her throat. So did he. The feel of her and the sight of his hand moving on what yesterday had been forbidden territory and was now his to possess fed his arousal. The lightning flickered, still on the horizon, but constant now, without respite.

His mouth followed his hand. When his lips closed on her nipple, Hawise cried out and her nails dug into the back of his neck. Her body arched and she curved one leg toward him. He clasped her ankle in his hand and stroked upward beneath the chemise, exploring calf and knee and finally outer thigh. Hawise set her arms around him, her hands at his shoulders, and he moved over and on top of her.

She gasped as his weight came down and he immediately lifted himself on his arms.

"I'm sorry, did I—"

"No, you didn't hurt me." She gave a short little breath and for a moment they stared at each other. Her legs were parted. He was between them and the only barriers separating his flesh from hers were two thin layers of linen. He lay upon her, his hips pressed within the bowl of her pelvis, and all the blood in his body seemed as if it were pulsing in his groin and against the hardness of her pubic bone.

"Jesu," she whispered and uttered a small, broken laugh, but there was no humor in it, just the hesitancy of fear and the tension of hunger. "Do not stop now, else one or other of us will not have the courage."

Brunin suddenly spluttered and some of the gathering pressure released. He dipped his head to her breast and muffled a laugh against her skin.

"What is it, what have I said?" She tugged on his hair, giggling herself, rubbing upon him at first by accident of laughter and then with a deliberation engendered by pleasure and instinct.

"I hope you are not accusing me of cowardice again." He had meant to say the words with a grin, but her action was making it very difficult and his words emerged with hoarse constriction.

"I didn't mean…" Overly sensitive to the words, she started to apologize, but he gripped her hand.

"I know you didn't."

"So then it must be me who lacks courage," she whispered.

"You missay us both." Sitting up, he pulled his nightshirt over his head. Having cast it aside, he pushed hers up above her hips and over her breasts, his hands following the contours of her flesh. She had to lift her body to help him free the chemise where it was trapped beneath her and between their bodies, and it was an erotic dance that pressed skin upon skin, each imprinting the other with a light dew of sweat.

Free of the linen, she was like a snake that has just shed its skin, bright and sinuous in his arms. "Being afraid does not mean lacking courage," he whispered against her mouth before he kissed her again. "Without one you cannot have the other." He trailed his hand down to her pubic mound and explored. First she tensed, and then she gave a small whimper. This time he didn't stop to question, for the sound was accompanied by an upward thrust of her hips that encouraged him to pursue his investigation. He watched her response and learned. He touched and learned yet more. Her legs parted. The skin of her inner thighs was soft against the back of his hand and she shivered and made little sounds that raised the hair on his nape and made him ache to the bone. She was as moist as honey on a hot summer day, and it was more than he could finally bear.

She cried out when he entered her, then swallowed the sound against his shoulder. He didn't ask if he had hurt her, for he knew that he had, but when he made to withdraw, her nails dug into him.

"No," she gasped against his ear. "Go on!"

"I..."

Her mouth slanted across his cheek and down. She found his lips and kissed him hard and long, shutting off protest, urging him, for if there was pain, there was also pleasure.

The feel of her wrapped around him, inside and out, made Brunin groan against the seal of her lips. He was going to come undone, to shatter into a million fragments. He lay on her, fighting the dissolution, scarcely daring to move while the kiss went on and on. Finally, gasping for breath, he took his mouth from hers and raised up on his braced elbows to look down at her. Her eyes were dark-pupilled and wild, her lips swollen. She looked wanton and beautiful and it was not his loins that shattered into myriad pieces but his heart. He gazed down the length of their bodies, at her parted thighs and himself between them, possessed and in possession.

"Hawise." He sighed her name and lowered his mouth to resume the kiss. She welcomed him with binding arms and eager lips. Her lips pushed downward, deepening the contact, giving unspoken consent. He answered her with a measured thrust and then another, and his body began to tremble, every muscle taut. He needed respite, but there was none, only the heat of the kiss and her flesh clinging smoothly to his like an oiled scabbard sheathing a sword. Sweat dampened his spine and her fingers traced the center line to his buttocks and then she spread her palms and moved with his rhythm. He broke the kiss and buried his head against her throat. Her body rose against his and he felt her pulse hammering against his clenched jaw, faster than a galloping horse. Her breath whined through her teeth. And then it stopped and her nails dug into his buttocks. Her lips parted in a silent cry. He lunged and the world contracted to a single point and then exploded in exquisite sunbursts of raw sensation.

Slowly his senses spiraled back into his body. Breathing hard, he raised his head.

"Hawise?"

Her eyes flickered open and focused on him. For a moment she stared solemnly, and then she smiled and reached a languid hand to his face.

"I did not hurt you too much?" he said anxiously.

"No…" She gave a small laugh. "Well, not beyond bearing and the pleasure outweighed what there was." She followed the contours of his face with an exploratory forefinger. When she reached his lips, he took her hand and kissed it, then rolled over, bringing her with him.

Hawise ran her hand over his torso in a lazy, exploratory way, sensual now rather than lustful. "Your grandmother tried to frighten me with tales of her own deflowering," she murmured. "I feel sorry for her."

"You won't in the morning," Brunin replied and yawned. In the aftermath of his release, a delicious lassitude was seeping through his body. His limbs felt loose, as if his bones had melted and his eyelids were almost too heavy to hold up.

"Meaning?" She licked him with the tip of her tongue.

"Meaning that she will be first in the room and leader of the ceremony to inspect the sheet," he mumbled.

Hawise had forgotten about that. She pushed away from him and threw back the covers on a wave of cold air. The linen was creased but still as pristine as new snow. "There's no blood," she said in a dismayed voice as she stared at the clean sheet.

"What?" Brunin had been preparing to fall asleep. Now, washed in cold air and roused by the worry in her tone, he leaned up on one elbow and studied the sheet. A glance at her and down at himself revealed red smudges on her inner thighs and a glisten of blood along his softening manhood. "That's easily solved." He rolled over, lay face down in the warm space she had just vacated, and rocked back and forth a couple of times. "Sit there," he said, moving to one side and pointing to the faint red smears he had left on the linen. Biting her lip, Hawise straddled the center of the bed and looked at the resulting daub.

"I thought there would be more than this," she said.

Brunin gave her a sidelong grin. "I suppose that depends on how good a lover the man is."

She made a face at him. "You are cocksure."

"If I wasn't before, I am now," he retorted, and ducked as she hurled a bolster in his direction. Grabbing it, he threw it back at her and then launched himself. She squealed as he landed half on top of her. They pummelled and rolled in the bed until they were breathless with laughter, until her eyes were bright and soft and he was hard again. And this time he was not so tentative when he entered her, and she was bold enough to wrap her legs around him and return his thrusts, for even if she was sore, she craved the pleasure too, and the power of being the pleasure-giver.

When they were finished, Brunin murmured, "Now look at the sheet."

She lifted her head and saw that the first, sparse smears had been lost in an embroidery of blotches and scrawls that covered the bed from one side to the other and almost top to bottom, so boisterously had they wrestled.

"My grandmother will be beside herself," he murmured sleepily. "And I am going to have some explaining to do to your father before he kills me...if you don't kill me first. Come here." He set his arm to her waist, drew the covers around them, and closed his eyes. "Your hair smells of spice," he mumbled, and in moments was asleep.

Sore but content, Hawise lay next to her husband in her marriage bed and smiled.

❖ ❖ ❖

Kneeling by her own pallet, Marion bowed her head and pleaded to God to let Ernalt survive the climb down the wall and make good his escape. She prayed that he would remember his promise and return for her, and she prayed for the strength to endure on her own part. Beneath her entreaty was the bowel-loosening terror that God would not listen, and that she would never see Ernalt again. She could endure anything but that...anything.

# 27

*H*AWISE OPENED HER EYES. THE NIGHT CANDLE HAD LONG since gone out and the bed curtains were closed, engulfing her in total darkness. She could hear the sound of breathing, steady and slow in sleep, and feel the weight of Brunin's forearm across her body. She sensed that he was lying on his stomach, his hipbone pressed to hers, his breath against her shoulder.

Their slumber had been disturbed several times by revelers arriving to thump on the door and offer drunken, salacious advice.

"Ignore them and they'll go away," Brunin had muttered, pulling the bolster over his head.

He was right, but it had taken a while for the night to quiet down around them.

There was a deep ache in the small of her back and a sharper pain between her legs; but it was bearable discomfort and when she thought about the alchemy of their lovemaking, it brought a flush of heat to those parts. She could face Mellette FitzWarin with equanimity this morning for she had gained knowledge that Brunin's grandmother had never possessed, and through that knowledge came power—and not only for herself. She reached out and touched her husband's hair. He murmured in his sleep, his hand tightening at her waist.

Hawise was aware of more sounds in the antechamber and realized that this was what must have woken her. She nudged

Brunin and he came awake at once, sitting up and parting the bed curtains in a single motion. A few rays of morning light glimmered through cracks in the closed shutters, turning the room beyond the cocoon of the bed curtains to a twilit gray.

There was a loud knock on the bedchamber door and Sybilla spoke. "Brunin, Hawise, it is full morning. Unless you are going to spend the day abed, will you unbar the door?"

There was a strange note in her mother's voice, Hawise thought, as if she were trying to sound normal and not succeeding.

"Staying abed sounds a fine idea," Brunin murmured to Hawise as he groped about on the coverlet for his nightshirt, "but I doubt we'd get any peace…one way or another."

He fumbled into the garment. Then he slipped his hand beneath her hair, laid his palm on the back of her neck, and gave her a strong, swift kiss.

Treading barefoot across the rushes, he went to the door and unbolted it. Bright sunlight puddled the floor of the antechamber from the unshuttered windows and that light now flowed into the bedchamber, picking out the reds and greens in the wall hangings and sparkling on dust motes. At a gesture from Sybilla, a maid went to the shutters and threw them wide, banishing the gray to the full gold of morning.

Brunin bowed to his mother-in-law and grandmother, to Sibbi and Cecily, and eyed the retinue of maids in their wake. He had expected a larger party of witnesses and could only assume that folk had imbibed too deeply and while nursing their sore heads and nausea in the hall were waiting for the wedding sheet to come down to them.

"You both slept well?" Sybilla asked.

"Yes, my lady." It was the required answer, if not exactly the true one, given the periodic interruption of revelers banging on the door and bawling lewd advice and the number of times he had woken to feel Hawise sharing his space when he was accustomed to lie alone on a straw pallet. Then there had been the occasion he had risen to use the piss-pot and spent a long time gazing upon the silk banner she had sewn for him until the night candle guttered and went out.

Hawise emerged from the bed curtains. She had donned her shift and she came to stand at his side, her hair curling about her face in eldritch tangles. The maids bustled, setting down a ewer of steaming water, a jug of wine, and a loaf of bread. A warm, yeasty aroma filled the air.

"You are well?" Sybilla asked, studying her intently.

"Yes, Mama...well indeed," Hawise replied, blushing. Mellette compressed her lips and stumped straight to the bed curtains, drawing them wide and pulling back the covers. For some time she stood and stared, then looked over her shoulder.

"Lady Sybilla, will you bear witness?"

Her face expressionless, Sybilla went to the bed, glanced, and turned away. "I am satisfied," she said. "Let the sheet be taken to the hall and displayed to all witnesses." Returning to the couple, she raised a brow at them. "You know that comments are going to be made," she warned.

Brunin shrugged. "Comments are of no consequence," he said. "What happens between my wife and myself behind those bed curtains is our business. They have their bloody sheet. Let them read into it what they will."

"I can read naught but success," Sybilla murmured, "otherwise my daughter would not be wearing her smile so easily, or standing so close at your side."

Brunin inclined his head and said nothing.

Mellette moved away from the bed and if her gaze on Brunin was cold, the one she bestowed on Hawise contained a mixture of wariness and respect. "You're made of sterner fiber than I thought," she said. "God willing, you'll deliver a son from this sowing." Her tone suggested that only a male child would come from what had obviously been a frenetic coupling.

Hawise had to bite back a smile "God willing," she repeated

and looked at Brunin, her eyes dancing on his blank expression. His lips twitched and straightened.

"I am sorry to shorten your wedding morn," Sybilla said briskly as two maids set about stripping the sheet and a couple of others hovered, waiting the instruction to attend to Hawise's toilet, "but I have grave news. Brunin, Joscelin wants you in the hall as soon as you are dressed."

He was immediately alert. "Why, what has happened?"

"Last night Gilbert de Lacy and his companion escaped from the Pendover tower."

"Escaped?" Brunin's brows rose in astonishment. "How? They were in the highest room."

"Down a rope fashioned from my missing napery," Sybilla said grimly. "Joscelin's preparing to ride out and see if he can intercept them, but I fear they are long gone, either to Ewyas or Wigmore."

Brunin turned. Attendants were waiting to help him dress—not in the wedding finery of yesterday, but in serviceable garments for the hunt. He didn't bother to wash. He could do that when he returned; whether they found de Lacy or not, there was going to be some hard riding ahead. He donned his clothes in short order, topped his tunic with a leather gambeson, and, swordbelt in hand, made for the door. On the threshold he paused, turned around, and retraced his steps to Hawise.

"I'd rather have stayed in bed," he said.

"So would I. Have a care."

He kissed her with softness and strength, and although he meant it for both of them, it was also intended as a sign to his grandmother and his mother-in-law.

Hawise watched him stride across the antechamber, the sword in his hand, his carriage balanced and lithe. A pang started in her midriff and arrowed to her loins. She could feel herself stretching, going with him. She had lain with him and a part of her was in him even as a part of him stayed with her, both in the mind and body.

"You will want to bathe," Sybilla said and at a gesture the maids stripped Hawise of her chemise. Hawise was aware of her mother's scrutiny and knew that she was seeking for bruises or evidence of harsh treatment.

"You wished us joy," Hawise said, "and we found it. As to the sheet…well, you have seen blood on a small wound. If you remain still, it swiftly dries and makes little mark, but were you to wipe it on a towel, the stains would look more and worse than they are." She glanced at Mellette who was listening with narrowed eyes. "We had a wild fight with a bolster the second time," she said, and giggled. "I won."

Mellette turned away with a grumpy sound. "It's a woman's duty to submit to her husband."

"I did, my lady, most thoroughly I did." Sybilla's doubtful expression softened into a smile, albeit a preoccupied one.

"But I still won."

Mellette was staring at the silk banner laid out on Brunin's coffer and for once she was silent.

❖❖❖

Sir William de Sutton, who had been in charge of the garrison the previous night, spread his hands in a bewildered gesture. "Never thought they'd go down the wall, my lord. Drop's so steep only a madman would risk his neck." He rubbed the back of his own and looked anxiously at Joscelin's set expression.

"And no one saw anything?" Brunin asked. He was holding Jester's reins by the cheekstrap and waiting to mount up. His father, three of his brothers, and a contingent of Ludlow's guards were preparing to ride out and scour the area. Joscelin's slot-hounds, usually used to trail deer and boar in the broad green forests, were tugging on the kennel-keeper's leash, eager to be away. Brunin suspected it was going to be a wasted effort. Too much time had elapsed and there were many landholders not far from Ludlow who might give their fealty to Joscelin, but were not unsympathetic to de Lacy's claim. It was quite likely that they would lend the fugitives mounts to be on their way.

"No, sir," de Sutton said. "I released as many of the men from duty as I could with it being the wedding celebrations and all." He gave Joscelin an anxious look. "They'd darkened their rope with soot. Wasn't found until the guard went to slop out their piss-pots this morn and discovered the room empty."

"Someone is a traitor," Joscelin said grimly. "They must have had help from within, and when I find out who it was, I will string them from the battlements by their entrails." He gestured the men to mount up and the guards unbarred the postern gate. The hounds had been given a scent of the bedstraw from the prisoners' mattresses and, as soon as they were through the doorway, began to bell. Across the river they plunged and up toward tree-clad Whitcliffe. But it was as Brunin had thought and as Joscelin had known in his heart: their quarry was long gone and it was too dangerous to follow the tugging hounds and ride beneath Wigmore's walls.

"Sybilla was right. I should have parted Gilbert de Lacy's head from his body and spiked it on the bridge," Joscelin muttered as they returned empty-handed to Ludlow.

"It is easy to be wise after the event," said FitzWarin. "But you must find out how they escaped."

"It must have been either a maid or a bribed servant," Brunin said. "I doubt any of the garrison would know where to begin looking if asked to fetch a sheet or a tablecloth."

"Whoever it is, they will wish that they were dead when I have done with them…and then perhaps I will grant that wish," Joscelin snarled.

❖❖❖

"I didn't. I swear I didn't!" Marion sobbed hysterically. "I would never do such a thing. Why do you accuse me?"

Sybilla had brought her into the side chamber where the girls had slept as children and drawn the curtain firmly across. "Marion, you were the last to visit Gilbert de Lacy and Ernalt de Lysle—and on your own when you should have had at least one of the maids with you. What am I to think?"

"I have done nothing," Marion gulped. "I brought them wine and honey cakes because everyone was celebrating, that's all."

"The guards say they have granted you admittance unchaperoned on several occasions...for which they will be punished." Sybilla folded her arms and frowned at Marion in bafflement. "What am I to do with you? You must have known that you were treading on dangerous ground by going to see those men alone. You must have known it was wrong."

"I felt sorry for them..."

"No shepherd should ever feel sorry for wolves," Sybilla snapped. "You saw what happened beneath our very walls. If not for Brunin and the garrison, Lord Joscelin would be dead."

Marion continued to sniff and sob. "No," she denied, shaking her head from side to side. "I didn't...No!"

Sybilla was torn between the maternal urge to comfort the girl and rage at the betrayal. She had spoken of wolves and shepherds and was wondering in which camp Marion belonged. Biting the hand that had fed and nurtured her for all these years was the act of a wild thing, not one of the fold, but Sybilla could not divorce the two. Perhaps Marion could not either. The girl's wits had always been the most fragile part of her being. She thought of the two men who had escaped from the tower. Gilbert de Lacy would not exert the kind of influence that would draw a young girl to the chamber alone. But the other one possessed the angelic face of temptation and Marion was ever in search of romantic attention from the opposite sex.

"You gave them the sheets and towels to make a rope, didn't you?" Sybilla demanded sternly. "Do not lie to me." She grasped Marion's shoulder and shook it. "Answer me, you foolish girl!"

Marion shook her head. "I did not know they were going to make a rope," she wept.

"No? What did you think they were going to do with the tablecloths? Conduct a banquet?" Sybilla's tone dripped scorn.

"Ernalt said his lord used them when he prayed. He said that it was some ritual used by Templar knights."

"And you believed him?" Sybilla's voice rose in pitch.

Marion wept harder, her tears making dark blots on her gown. "Lord Gilbert said he would never pay the ransom and that if they did not escape, Lord Joscelin would hang them both."

"So you committed the sin knowingly."

"I didn't want you to hang Ernalt!" Marion coughed and began to retch. "Please don't hate me, please!" She threw herself upon Sybilla.

The urge to fling Marion away and see her sprawl on the floor was almost overpowering but, with a tremendous effort of will, Sybilla curbed it. "I am furious with you," she said in a voice rigid with control, "and very disappointed, but I do not hate you. You know what you have done, and that it changes everything. I do not doubt that Ernalt de Lysle was a most persuasive young man, but, if so, you were more than willing to be persuaded."

Marion raised her head, leaving a snail trail of tears and mucus on Sybilla's fine woolen gown. "What will happen to me?"

Sybilla extricated herself from Marion's grip. "I do not know," she said flatly. "It will be for Lord Joscelin to decide."

Marion stared up at her through swollen eyes, her mouth a square wail. "No, oh please, no!"

"You should have thought of the consequences," Sybilla said grimly. "You will stay in here and reflect on the enormity of what you have done. I am not prohibiting you from the main chamber, but, given the circumstances, I doubt you will want to share company with the other women and our guests."

When Sybilla had gone, Marion lay down on the bed, her body racked by tremors. She was gripped by emotions that tore away her fragile carapace and attacked all the soft and vulnerable places deep inside. Sybilla might not hate her, but she hated herself, and she was angry at Joscelin and Sybilla, at Hawise and Brunin for driving her to these extremes. It was their fault as much as hers and they too should be seared by the guilt that was rending her asunder.

Ernalt...Her drowning mind clung to the thought of him as if to a spar on a deep, cold sea. He would return for her. He would lean down and raise her up and make her whole again. She clung to that thought. Whatever happened, she would hold on tight and wait for him.

❖ ❖ ❖

"Christ on the Cross, I will whip her bloody!" Joscelin snarled, his eyes the hue of a stormy sea—dark gray and quenched of light.

Sybilla, who had waited her moment and told him when they were alone in their chamber, hastened to stand between him and their door as he strode toward it. She had seen him enraged before when a younger, more volatile man, and knew how to deal with the situation -or thought she knew. Taking a bull by the horns always had its dangers. "I thought of doing that myself when I first confronted her," she said, "but there is no point." She raised her hands, palm outward. "It will not bring de Lacy back."

"Mayhap not, but the girl needs teaching a lesson she will not forget and it will be my pleasure to give her that lesson." His movements jerky with the force of his rage, he started to unlatch his belt.

"No." Sybilla stepped forward and laid her palms against his breast. "Her wits are half lost already. Beating her will only make her worse, and it will mar your own nature."

"Then perhaps it needs marring for I have certainly been too soft." He pressed forward against her restraint, but not hard enough to make her fall back.

"I know you could do it," Sybilla said. "There is that in you which makes you capable...but do you want to unleash it? What would you become?"

Joscelin's hands left the belt and Sybilla realized with an inward slump of relief that she had control of the situation. "Even if she is missing a wit or two, this cannot go unpunished," he growled. "Gilbert de Lacy is loose; the ransom is lost." The lines bracketing his nose and mouth deepened. "This was no blind folly. Her eyes were open. It was more than foolishness."

"Yes, but seeing the world in a different, skewed way. You are right, it cannot go unpunished, but a beating will do nothing save scatter a few more of her wits."

"Then what?" It was a rhetorical question. Joscelin turned away to prowl the room. She watched him. He still had the heavy, leonine grace that had attracted her even at the outset of their relationship when she was not sure if he was her enemy or not. "I cannot betroth her. Even were I to find a suitable man or one willing to take the risk, I would not want to feel responsible for the aftermath. After this, though, I do not want to keep her at Ludlow…or even look at her." He walked back to his wife, his face set with revulsion. "I may not be the kind to beat women, but I fear that if I have to be in the same room as her, I might think of the harm she has wrought and find that spark." He dug his hands through his hair, leaving deep channels in the gray-salted auburn. "Ach, I don't know. I've to ride to the King's muster by the end of the week and I've too much to do. Leave it for now; just keep her from my sight. I'll decide what to do when I return…but like as not it will be a nunnery."

Sybilla did not argue, for she was of the same mind herself, but a part of her remembered Marion as the tiny, parentless waif tucked inside Joscelin's cloak and wanted to weep.

❖❖❖

The shutters were open to admit the first light of morning into the bedchamber. Parting the bed curtains, Hawise heard the drip of rain amidst the draggled birdsong and, gazing over at the window arch, saw that the narrow lancet of sky was dull gray. It was a day to dally beneath the covers and rise late; a day to play chess or merels in the hall, to sit with embroidery near the warmth of a brazier, a cup of wine to hand. What it was not, was a day for travel.

Brunin murmured in his sleep and reached for her. She let the curtain drop and curled herself around him, trying to shut out the crowing of the midden roosters. Brunin must have heard them too, for he muffled a curse against her throat. His body was warm and loose with slumber and she adapted herself to its contours. He rolled on top of her and she opened her thighs, welcoming, still sleepy herself. They had retired late last night for there had been much to do, and once abed they had not slept at first. The awareness of parting from a delight so recently discovered had left them greedy and wanting. Even drained and replete, an edge of hunger remained: a sensation in the gut like distant lightning. She rose to meet and match him, taking and giving a farewell present of pleasure and comfort. At the least it would be weeks before they could share themselves with each other again.

There were noises in the antechamber. Discreet coughs, shuffling, the murmured conversation of servants just that morsel too loud to be natural.

"It's raining," Hawise sighed as she pushed Brunin's hair off his brow and absorbed the thundering of his heart against her body. "We could keep the curtains closed and stay abed all day."

"You think they would let us?"

Her lips twitched mischievously. "The bolt's across the door. They'd have to fetch an ax to break in."

He ran his hands over her body and withdrew from her with a kiss. "I would not put such a thing past my grandmother." Leaving the bed, he padded across the rushes to the window and, screwing up his face, gazed out at the weather. "The armor will be as red as blood with rust by the time we reach Wales."

Hawise shivered. "Don't say that."

"What?"

"Red as blood."

He returned to the bed and, sitting on its edge, stroked her night-tangled hair. "It will be all right," he said gently. "None of us are inexperienced and Henry is a good general. We'll be home before the swallows fly."

He had said the same things last night, and so had she. There was no point in traveling the same rut. She just wished that he had not used those words about his armor. Nor did his comment about the flying of swallows comfort her, for it held a mournful ring.

"I wish I was riding with you."

"So do I," he said with a smile. "A few days ago it seemed strange to share a bed. Now my camp pallet will seem empty with only myself for company."

Hawise bit her tongue on the remark that there were always women in the army's tail who would solace a man for a coin. Such words would only reveal her own insecurity and to no good purpose.

"And my bed the same," she murmured. A pensive look crossed her face. She was to leave with her in-laws and travel to their marcher holdings: to their keep at Alberbury and then to Whittington to await Brunin's return from the Welsh campaign. After that the plan was that she and Brunin would go on a progress of the other FitzWarin manors scattered throughout the country, in order that the new bride might be fêted before returning to Ludlow, hopefully before the winter. However, there would be no traveling for her party today. They were not bound by the same time constraint as the men, and she could not see Mellette and Eve FitzWarin being eager to set out in a deluge, especially as Eve's health was so fragile. "Still," she said bestirring herself to help him dress, "the reunion will be that much sweeter for absence." She kissed his throat, tasting salt on the tip of her tongue.

He returned her kiss, but she could see that although she was still held in his thoughts, they were already divided. And suddenly she knew and understood what her mother was feeling on those occasions when she would stop for a moment in the bower, a piece of Joscelin's clothing in her hand, and look toward the window.

# 28

"THE WELSH WON'T KNOW WHAT HAS HIT THEM," RALF gloated. His blue eyes gleamed and he touched the hilt of his sword. He had recently been knighted and was itching to draw steel.

Brunin leaned to adjust his foot in the stirrup and glanced behind at the column of men. The lowering sky was reflected in the ranks of hauberk-clad warriors, marching out from the walled city of Chester in their gleaming mail like so many silver-scaled codfish pouring from the throat of a net. The clop of hooves and tramp of marching feet filled the morning with the sound of an army going to war: two thousand knights, attended by squires and grooms and footsoldiers, and a large contingent of archers, some of them Ludlow and Whittington men. The baggage wains rumbled along at the back, laden with barrels of salt pork and flour, with wine and cheese, with fodder for the horses and tents for the soldiers.

"Owain Gwynedd is no fool. It would not do to underestimate him," Brunin replied. Although his words were cautious, he thought that the array looked magnificent, especially the banners, his black wolf snarling out beside Joscelin's wyvern and his father's own wolf's-head standard.

"What is Owain Gwynedd going to do against our might?" Ralf scoffed. "Our footsoldiers are better armed than the wealthiest of his men. The Welsh will never stand against us; Rhuddlan will be ours within the week."

Brunin thought that such optimism might well be true, but the Welsh were unpredictable. They might not stand against a force like this one, might melt away into their mountain strongholds like mist before sun, but they were cunning in other ways. Being marcher born and bred, Ralf must know it too, but perhaps, like everyone else, he preferred to think on their bright armor rather than the rag-tag Welsh hiding in the woods with their bows and slings, waiting to pick off stragglers and spook the baggage ponies.

Once out of Chester, Henry divided his army, sending the bulk of the men and the baggage along the coast road to Rhuddlan. He himself chose to cut through the Welsh forests with his lighter troops and a seasoning of fully armed knights with the intention of flanking the town. He had employed Welsh guides and was filled with the complete confidence of a man whose every enterprise had thus far flourished. Joscelin was commanded to travel with the slower-moving baggage section, but the FitzWarins were with Henry's lighter contingent.

"God speed you," Joscelin saluted as he prepared to ride on. A grin flashed across his face. "I hope it doesn't rain or you'll all be as draggled as drowned rats."

"And you won't?" FitzWarin asked with a raised brow.

"Not with a baggage wain to shelter in, and no trees to send drips down the back of my neck."

"Hah, but we'll reach Rhuddlan long before you."

The banter served to relieve tension. Just before he rode off, Joscelin turned to Brunin. "Have a care to that banner," he said with a nod at the black wolf. "My daughter put a deal of time and effort into making it and I would not see it or its owner brought down."

"Neither would I," Brunin held out his hand. "I will see you in Rhuddlan...Father."

Joscelin snorted, for the appellation was still so new that it sounded strange, especially when Brunin's own father was at his side. He clasped the young man's hand and forearm, nodded in farewell, and reined his destrier to join the baggage line.

❖❖❖

Alberbury Castle was a small but stout affair of stone and timber, standing close to the Shrewsbury road and hard on the Welsh border. The FitzWarins held it from the Corbet family who were tenants-in-chief. Although it was not their main estate, was much smaller than Ludlow and very close to the threat from Wales, Hawise loved it from the moment she set eyes upon it. Perhaps it was the sense of intimacy. It was as if the place had opened wide to embrace her and then held her fast like a swaddled infant in maternal arms.

"Too small," Mellette disparaged it with a sniff, "and too buried. And I don't like doing homage to the Corbets for this place...hucksters and thieves, the lot of them."

Hawise kept diplomatically silent. Eve looked weary and her expression betrayed that she had heard this complaint ad nauseam.

"We'll stay long enough to have the horses shod and give that lazy farrier something to do. Make our presence known. Then we'll move on to Whittington."

Eve grimaced and rubbed the small of her back. "I was hoping to stay a little longer."

"Are you not well, my lady?" Hawise asked with concern. Gaunt hollows shadowed Eve's delicate cheekbones and she moved as if it were not a baby in her womb, but a burdensome lead weight.

"Just tired." Eve forced a smile. "I need to rest."

"You can do that at Whittington," Mellette said curtly. "All the children have been born there. I'll not have you birthing the babe here under a Corbet's rule."

"There are still four months to my confinement," Eve protested. "Spending one of them here will make no difference."

Mellette's lips tightened with stubborn determination. "Even so, the men will expect to find us at Whittington."

"If they are not all summer in the saddle," Eve answered with a hint of petulance.

"Can't see why it should bother you if they are...although it might bother the bride." Mellette looked Hawise up and down as if expecting her to grow a belly on the spot. "Unless of course she has news for us."

"Whether I had news or not, I would still miss my husband," Hawise said. "I would like to stay here awhile and become acquainted first." She managed not to place her hand on her belly. Her flux was not due for another week at least and she was not going to play Mellette's game.

Eve cast her a grateful look, but Mellette remained intractable. "Latrines'll be full long before a month's up," she said as if that were the end of the matter and walked away before anyone could argue.

Eve made a face. "She always has to have the last word," she whispered.

Hawise narrowed her eyes. "That is all they are," she said. "Words. The only power she has is that of fear. You see it in cats. They puff up and yowl and hiss before a dog, but if it came to a fight, the dog would win."

Eve looked both alarmed and diverted. "You are not going to fight her, are you?"

Hawise laughed ruefully and shook her head. "Not unless I must. I will grant her space and respect if she grants the same to me."

❖ ❖ ❖

The weather was close, threatening rain, but as warm as a sweaty armpit. Beneath successive layers of ring mail, padded undertunic, tunic, and shirt, Brunin felt like a vegetable in a boiling pottage pot. The Welsh forest hemmed the sides of the road in swathes of impenetrable green and without sunlight it was like riding through a tunnel into the otherworld. The humid weight of the air bore down on King Henry's troops. Small black flies bedeviled the horses, so that even placid Jester was driven to stamp and jib with irritation.

The Welsh guides led them along scantily used pack-pony tracks that sometimes degenerated into little more than sheep trails. The sky darkened and so did the tree canopy until green almost turned to black. Brunin felt as if small trickles of sweat were creeping down his spine, but knew it was impossible, for the padding of his tunic absorbed all the moisture that sprang from his body. Jester's bright bay shoulders and flanks had darkened to a liver hue and salty streaks rubbed along his bridle line. The gelding sidled, his mulish ears flickering, and Brunin leaned forward to tug them—as much to reassure himself as his mount.

"Christ," Ralf muttered at Brunin's side. "How much closer can the trees grow before the path disappears?" He glanced around, the whites of his eyes gleaming, and shrugged his shoulders inside his new hauberk. "It is as if there are ants crawling down my spine."

"You feel it too?" Until recently Brunin would not have credited his brother with that much sensitivity, but matters had changed. Ralf had softened, Brunin had developed a tougher shell, and of late they had been able to meet in the middle.

"It's like being the hunted instead of the hunter," Ralf went on. "I like to know what's around the next corner, not be led along like a blind beggar." He reached to the tokens hanging around his neck: a medallion of St. Christopher and a Lorraine cross on a leather cord. He pressed both to his lips. "Give me open ground any day."

"Give us all open ground any day," Brunin replied grimly, trying to relax his tense muscles. He thought of Hawise and the tender farewell she had given him, and his mouth softened into an unconscious half-smile of remembering. God grant that this Welsh campaign ended swiftly so that he could ride to Whittington and join her. The few days of companionship since their wedding had unleashed a dammed-up hunger within him that went far beyond the superficial lust of a bridegroom for the pleasures of the bedchamber. He needed Hawise for the sustenance of his soul as much as his body needed food and drink. It was the banner that had released the flood…that and the unreserved way she had given herself to him. Even now, when he had yielded much into her keeping, he was not sure that he could ever match her generosity of spirit.

"Drink?" Ralf pulled his water costrel over his head and handed it across to him. Brunin took a long swallow and turned to toss the stone bottle to Richard who was riding in their wake with several FitzWarin knights.

Ahead of them there was a sudden yell and the standards shuddered and clacked together. A horse reared, another one screamed, and a ripple ran down the line. Richard dropped the costrel and it smashed on the ground, splattering its contents afar. A sharp piece jabbed his horse on the fetlock and it plunged into Jester and Ralf's stallion.

"Ware arms!" the roar went up. "Ambush!"

Swearing, Brunin swung his shield down onto his left arm and drew his sword. Ralf's gray stallion was plunging and snapping, making it difficult for Ralf to draw from his scabbard. And then the Welsh were upon them: a yelling, bare-legged horde who wore little or no armor and were armed with knives, light spears, and swords, and who struck faster than summer lightning. They ran in, slashed the destriers' hamstrings or ripped guts and saddle girths, then went for the rider of the stricken mount.

Brunin turned Jester with his thighs and struck at the sheepskin-clad Welshman who had been about to thrust a knife into the gelding's haunch. He felt the edge of his sword connect with the softness of flesh, grate on bone, and chop through. The warrior fell and Ralf's stallion trampled him underfoot. Panicking at the feel of the writhing body beneath its hooves, the destrier back-danced, crushing the warrior's rib cage. As the man died, Brunin felt the battle calmness surround him in its crystal bubble. He could see clearly, hear sharply, move with the swiftness of the wind, but that swiftness still seemed slow to his eyes. Every sense was attuned to the fight. He was a hawk on the wing, a lion on the hunt, a bright-scaled pike in the battle's flow. He heard his father shouting, saw his horse go down, spurting blood. Brunin spurred Jester forward and brought down the Welshman who had been about to finish FitzWarin. He used his shield to beat off another assault, backed around, and struck. His father was on his feet by now, sword in hand, shield guarding his left side.

"Take him!" Brunin started to dismount from Jester but his father waved him back into the saddle.

"No! To your left!"

Brunin pivoted, his arm instinctively raised. The Welsh spear stuck in the shield instead of his body and FitzWarin strode forward to engage the warrior. The fighting closed over their heads. Richard lost his horse to a Welsh gutting blade and had to fight on foot beside his father. Jester sustained a cut to the hindquarters, and Brunin a blow to his hand that numbed his fingers and crawled his sword grip with blood.

A bleeding horse burst past them, its rider spurring hell for leather. "The King is down!" he bellowed. "Save yourselves! The King is down!" Knights and serjeants fled in his wake, expressions bleached with terror. Brunin felt the panic spreading through the ranks like forks of underground lightning. Fear squeezed his own gut, but his choice was made. With his father and brother horseless, he couldn't flee. Ramming his wolf standard in the ground beside his father's, he prepared to defend it hard and bitterly.

Through the milling battle, he heard another cry. "*A moi! A moi! Le Roi Henri! Le Roi Henri!*" A trampled banner wavered aloft, the lions of England smirched but still snarling on their spear, and beside it the silks of de Clare of Pembroke. The fighting redoubled around the banner in a concentrated ball of men, and then it unraveled into vicious individual combats. Brunin spurred forward and a Welsh footsoldier flew from Jester's right shoulder. The shield on the left defended Brunin from a spear thrust and gave him the time to reach over and bring down his challenger with the full side of his sword.

The royal standard retreated on the path, drawing back toward the FitzWarin wolves, and Brunin recognized the King: he had lost his helm and no one else had hair of so fierce a red. Blood was trickling from Henry's temple and his complexion was stark white, rendered green in the hollows by the grudging light from the trees. Blood glistened on his mail too but there was far too much to be his own. Henry snarled a command at one of his knights and the man raised a hunting horn to his lips and sounded the retreat. The Welsh were dispersing, for although they had inflicted serious damage on their quarry, the impetus of their ambush was spent and the Normans had regrouped. Any more gains would cost more blood than most were prepared to spill. However, there was such a thing as harrying, and although the Welsh had pulled back to the forest, now they sent arrows whistling from cover to thud among the horses and knights. Brunin reached down and took his father up pillion on Jester's back. He plucked the banners from the ground and heeled the gelding in the flanks. To one side he was aware of Ralf hauling Richard onto his own stallion and kicking hard.

"Sons of whores!" FitzWarin gasped in Brunin's ear as Jester settled into his deceptively ground-eating lope.

Brunin had neither the breath nor attention to answer. At any moment he was expecting an arrow to come whirring out of the trees and bring the horse down. It was not until they had traveled another mile that he dared to slow a blowing Jester to a walk and sit up in the saddle. His hands were slippery on the reins with blood and sweat. He could feel moisture crawling down his face and hoped it was the latter. The earlier barrier of calm indifference was fading and he was beginning to feel dizzy and sick. He swallowed a retch and fixed his gaze on his banner, striving to draw from it the sustenance he needed. There was a long way to go and they were literally not out of the woods yet. His father was coughing. Brunin turned to look at him in concern, but FitzWarin waved his hand in negation. "I'm all right. Took a blow to the ribs when I lost the horse…You?" He pointed at the blood webbing Brunin's hand.

"It's not serious." Brunin turned to check his brothers, but both Richard and Ralf were unharmed beyond minor cuts and bruises.

Harried all the way, Henry's badly mauled party finally rejoined the main troop on the safer coast road. Brunin went in search of a chirugeon to stitch the cut on his hand and endured the stab of a needle with the aid of a flagon of strong, honey-sweetened wine.

"You were lucky," the chirugeon said. "A pinch deeper or to one side and you'd have lost the use of these two fingers." He clucked his tongue and bent over his handiwork.

Enduring the tug of the thread, Brunin thought of Hawise sewing his banner, imagined the prick of the needle working thread through silk. As if catching the drift of his thoughts, the chirugeon made a jest about being a good embroiderer.

"You'll have a scar, but a neat one…like forked lightning," he said. "There. Done." The man nodded with satisfaction and, having smeared the wound with a speckled green salve, moved on to his next patient.

Brunin rose and walked slowly toward the place where his father and Joscelin had pitched their tents. His stomach wallowed as if he were on the deck of a ship and he wondered why he was fighting it. Better over and done with. And then he saw his father striding toward him, Ralf and Richard behind, and knew from the look on their faces that something was terribly wrong, and that weakness would have to wait.

❖ ❖ ❖

Finally, at Mellette's nagging insistence, the women set out for Whittington. Hawise had learned the hard way that the old lady never gave up. If she could not obtain her way on the first attempt, she would conduct a siege campaign, bombarding, undermining, stiffly bargaining; using every trick at her disposal until the opposition was frazzled into a state of guilty exhaustion.

Surrounded by sheepskins and cushions to protect her from the jolting of the cart as it rumbled along the road, Eve sat in the baggage wain with little Emmeline. Hawise would have preferred to ride, but since that meant keeping company with Mellette, who refused to countenance the wain, she was enduring the buffeting with Eve.

"I will be glad when this child is born," her mother-in-law sighed as she placed a cushion in the small of her back.

Hawise was holding the ends of several colored woolen strands while Emmeline pulled them taut and wove them into a length of braid. She looked away from the child and anxiously at Eve. "We should not have left Alberbury."

Eve closed her eyes and leaned her head back. "No. Mellette is right. If I had stayed any longer, I would not have had the strength for this journey. I am so tired all the time, and it gets no better." She laid her hand across her belly. "At least for the moment the child is quiet. Last night I thought it was going to kick its way out of my body."

Hawise could think of no answer to the remark. What did she know of carrying and bearing a child? Anything she said would be a mere platitude, spoken from ignorance. Nor, with the arrival of her flux four days ago, did she have a door to that particular world. That was another reason she didn't want to ride with Mellette. The older woman had been making her disappointment known in no uncertain terms. She had got with child in the first month after her marriage. So had Eve. She hoped that Hawise was going to prove more fecund than Sybilla.

Eve slept as the cart wound its way along the Shrewsbury road toward Whittington. Emmeline finished her braiding and Hawise had then to dress the little girl's hair with the handiwork. The length of "ribbon" was uneven and lumpy, but the bright red and yellow colors of the wool glowed out against Emmeline's raven-black hair.

"Now I'll make one for you," Emmeline announced. They chose the colors—green and white—and Hawise told her a story about knights and giants and a woman under an enchantment.

"And then the giant said..." Hawise paused and tilted her head, listening.

"What did the giant say?" Emmeline prompted, nudging her. When Hawise did not respond, the little girl raised her voice. "What did the giant s—"

"Hush." Hawise listened harder. The cart shuddered to a halt and Eve awoke with the soft cry of a dreamer disturbed.

Going to the baggage cart entrance, Hawise peered out. A troop of riders had surrounded the cart and in the boil of dust, she saw several shields that she recognized, including the one belonging to Guy L'Estrange, constable of Whittington. "Stay," she commanded Emmeline, and climbed out of the cart.

As she approached the men, she saw the wounds, the bandages, the damaged shields and injured horses. Her immediate thought was for Brunin even though she knew he was with the King. Mellette made a strange sound; not a wail—it was too deep and harsh for that—but it came from the soul and it raised the hair on Hawise's forearms. She watched in horror as the elderly woman began a slow but inevitable slide from her saddle. One of the cart attendants, who had been holding the lead horse, darted to catch her and he eased her to the ground where she lay unmoving, white as death.

Hawise hurried to bend over Mellette's still form. "What has happened?" she demanded of Guy L'Estrange.

"Madam, you should go no farther on this road but turn back to Alberbury with all haste." L'Estrange's face was composed of grim angles. There was a scabbed-over cut at the side of his mouth and, as he spoke, it broke and trickled fresh blood. "Iorwerth Goch has raided over the border with the men of Powys and seized Whittington."

Against her fingers, Hawise felt the pulse beating in Mellette's throat. Still alive then. "Seized Whittington?" She looked up at the knight. The words were in her mouth, but they tasted of nothing.

"And garrisoned it with their own. There were too many of them…We were outnumbered…overrun…They came so swiftly that we did not know what had hit us." He clamped his jaw and she saw a shudder ripple through him.

Hawise stood up and gestured the attendant to bear Mellette back to the baggage wain. She was aware that they were all looking at her, aware too that she still held a child's tangle of woolen strands between her fingers.

"Have you sent a messenger to Lord FitzWarin?" she asked.

"Yes, my lady, as soon as it happened."

She nodded. "Then, as you say, we must turn back and consider what is to be done. I will tell Lady Eve and see that Lady Mellette is made comfortable." She beckoned to one of her own escort and bade him ride ahead to Alberbury so that the keep would be ready to receive the group, including wounded. A worrying thought occurred to her. "Is there a danger to Alberbury?"

"There may be, my lady, although perhaps not yet, since it is that much closer to Shrewsbury."

She nodded again and returned to the wain, feeling suddenly that speed was of the essence. The news had snatched all sense of security and she had to prevent herself from looking skittishly at the woods beyond the road, almost expecting to see the gleam of a Welsh spear.

By the time she climbed into the wain, Mellette had revived from her faint and was sitting bolt upright against the cushions, her lined face as gray as old pastry and her eyes glassy. Emmeline was gazing at her grandmother with frightened fascination.

"What's happened?" Eve asked. Her glance flickered to Mellette. "She hasn't spoken a word." Anxiety filled her voice. "What are the Whittington men doing here?"

Outside someone yelled an order and the cart began to back and turn on the road with much rumbling and jolting.

"We're returning to Alberbury," Hawise said. "The Welsh have overrun Whittington."

Eve's stare widened. "Oh, dear Jesu!" She took Emmeline in her arms. "Another day and we would have been there!"

The thought gave Hawise a momentary qualm, but she thrust it away. "I suspect they deliberately struck with only the constable in residence. It makes for easier pickings and fewer complications…not that I think our presence would have deterred them," she added.

Eve shook her head, looking stunned. "I do not believe it," she said. "My husband…my husband will…" She swallowed and pressed her sleeve to her lips. "Holy Mary, I am not well."

The wain shuddered as the driver brought it around. One of the horses must have shied, for the cart gave a violent lurch and the women were flung against one another like apples in a half-full barrel. Emmeline began to wail. Hawise had almost fallen on Mellette and, as she struggled upright, she saw the older woman's eyes fixed on her with gimlet intensity. "We will regain Whittington," Mellette said through stiff lips. Her hand fastened around Hawise's wrist like a hawk's talons fastening on a perch. "It is ours; we will regain it."

Hawise swallowed and looked down at the mottled fingers hooped with gold rings. She could feel the nails imprinting her flesh, and the bite of a bevel where one of the rings had twisted around. She felt revulsion and anger, fear and pity. From under the sparse lashes, a single tear rolled and was lost in the deep creases of the old woman's face. Mellette glared, daring Hawise to remark on the detail.

Hawise broke the vicious grasp and would have made her escape to her mare's saddle and the company of the soldiers, but Eve uttered a gasp that made her spin around. Her mother-in-law was ashen, her pupils so dilated that they almost obliterated the soft hazel irises. Her hands clutched her belly.

"My lady?" Hawise looked at her in concern.

Eve's gaze was that of a terrified trapped animal. "I am in travail," she whispered. "God help me."

# 29

THEY REACHED ALBERBURY IN TIME FOR THE BABY TO BE BORN
there and for the priest to be fetched from the village. The
child was another girl and died within minutes of being baptized.
Eve lived long enough to hold her daughter and make confession.
Hawise had never seen so much blood. The smell of it clogged
the bedchamber. The bright color, the sticky slipperiness filled her
with pity and horror...and fear. She knew that women died in
childbirth. Her awareness had been compounded by the years of
growing up with Marion, but until now, the pictures that Marion
had painted, vivid though they were, had been related at a distance
once removed. Now she understood...and wished that she were
still ignorant.

Dazed, she stumbled from the bedchamber and, leaning against
the wall, took several deep breaths of air scented with no more
than the mustiness of stone. All she wanted to do was go and hide
in a corner with her eyes closed and her hands over her ears and
pretend it had not happened, but that was impossible. The care of
Alberbury and its occupants belonged to her now, and she had to
decide whether to relinquish that power to Mellette as Eve had
done, or take control and responsibility into her own hands.

"Holy Mary," she whispered, and swallowed the knot of panic
in her throat. Now, suddenly, she better comprehended her
husband and the effect of the burdens and expectations loaded

upon him. Taking another slow breath, she pushed away from the support of the wall.

Emmeline was playing in the hall with two daughters of a garrison soldier. Three little girls pretending to be grown up: one nursing her rag doll while Emmeline made a bed for it and the third carrying a basket over her arm and haggling with an imaginary trader. Hawise was poignantly and painfully reminded of herself and Sibbi and Marion. It was as long ago as forever and as immediate as now.

Emmeline looked up and her dark eyes widened. "Has Mama had the baby?" she asked.

Hawise swallowed. "Come with me." She held out her hand and could have wept at the trusting way that Emmeline took it and skipped beside her to the door. In a moment she was going to shatter all that trust and joy.

Outside the sun was dipping toward the horizon, although it would not be dark for several hours. A couple of grooms leaned against an outhouse door in casual conversation. Hens scratched in the dust. Soldiers paced the battlements and looked toward the Welsh border. The sight of the men on full alert was both a comfort and a worry.

Hawise drew Emmeline to a bench placed against the sun-warmed wall and sat down with her. Was this how her mother had dealt with Marion when she first came to Ludlow? "Sweetheart," she said, and then stopped. The words had to be said and there was no way of making them less devastating.

Emmeline swung her feet and looked at the tips of her shoes poking out beneath the hem of her dress.

"You know your mama was not well."

Emmeline sucked her underlip and nodded. "Because of the baby."

"Yes…"

"But now she's had it, she'll be better." She gave Hawise a look enormous with trust and the need for reassurance.

Mary Mother, Hawise thought, and set her arm around the

child's narrow shoulders. "Your mama was more poorly than we knew and the baby was born too soon to live."

Emmeline gazed at her, the peat-pool eyes solemn and deep, the contours of her face soft with an infancy that Hawise was aware of stealing.

"I am sorry, sweeting, but your mama and your baby sister have died and their souls have gone to God in his heaven."

The stare continued for what seemed like an eternity, wide and merciless, and then slowly, with equal lack of clemency, Emmeline's eyes filled with tears. Hawise gasped and clutched the child fiercely to her body. "I'm sorry, I'm so sorry." Her own eyes burned and overflowed.

For a time Emmeline wept hard, but she was not inconsolable. Her mother had been a large part of her life, but there were many other women in her world too: maids, Heulwen the nurse, her grandmother, and lately Hawise and the women of the de Dinan household. Once she had weathered the initial storm, she sat up and, sniffing and hiccupping, studied Hawise through tear-drenched lashes.

"When can I see them?"

"Later," Hawise said, thinking of the gory battleground she had left behind. She wiped the heels of her hands beneath her own eyes.

"When later?"

"Soon...as soon as they have been prepared for the church."

After a long cuddle, they returned to the hall. The news had clearly spread for Emmeline's two companions had abandoned their game and been taken away by their mother. Hawise delivered Emmeline into Heulwen's arms, and returned to the bedchamber.

The maids had stripped and disposed of the bloody bedsheets. A fresh mattress case had been fetched and stuffed with new, fragrant bracken and straw. The midwife had recently finished washing Eve's body, and now she and her assistant were robing her in a clean chemise, lifting her up, laying her down. Eve's limbs were loose and tensionless, her flesh pale and doughy. A granite-faced Mellette handed the women Eve's dress of red-gold silk.

"Her wedding gown," she told Hawise. "Must only be the third or fourth time since her marriage that it has been out of the coffer."

Hawise watched in tear-stung, silent pity as the women went about their task. The laces had to be let out to their widest to accommodate Eve's waistline and the bright color was a terrible contrast to the waxen hue of death.

Hawise had to swallow before she was able to speak. "We should send word to Lord FitzWarin."

Mellette shook her head. "No point. Once they hear about Whittington, they will come here...they will know soon enough." She pursed her lips. "There is naught to be done about this"—she gestured to the bed—"but at least our other loss can be rectified."

"Is that all you care about, madam? Whittington?" Hawise flashed her an appalled look. "Do you not feel the pity and grief of Lady Eve's death?"

Mellette's jaw tightened until her tendons strained in her wrinkled throat. "She was a good wife to my son, but mourning the dead will not bring them back. I cannot afford my menfolk to be distracted by their grief if we are to regain what is ours."

"I hardly think you will stop them grieving," Hawise said curtly.

"No, but I will not give them an atmosphere in which to wallow— and neither will you." Mellette's voice was as harsh as a quern stone.

Fetching a comb, Hawise combed and smoothed Eve's hair. The dull gold was stranded here and there with the first gray but, whatever privations her body had suffered during pregnancy, her tresses had remained as thick and lustrous as a harvest wheatfield. Hawise wound the braids with silk ribbons and arranged them upon Eve's lifeless bosom. The midwife leaned over and placed the swaddled infant in its mother's arms. The baby resembled a child's tiny doll with perfect features. Even the eyelids, dainty and pink as tellin shells, were lined with downy lashes. Hawise swallowed the ache in her throat, and then she wondered why she was holding back her tears and let them flow, uncaring of Mellette's censorious stare.

❖❖❖

The FitzWarin men rode into Alberbury in the midst of a drenching summer downpour. The sky was bruised with clouds and thunder rumbled in the distance—fittingly from the direction of Wales. The men were soaked through their cloaks and hauberks, through gambesons and tunics to the skin. As they turned off the Shrewsbury road and approached the castle, Brunin's gut clenched. Against the stormy sky and the brooding green of the trees, the stone and timber structure of the walls stood out in sharp relief. Torches burned in some of the window arches, although many were shuttered against the weather. He fixed his eyes on the beckoning golden eyes like a starving man given a distant sight of bread.

They had sent armed scouts ahead to announce their imminent arrival, but Brunin knew that until he rode through the castle entrance and heard the gates close at his back, the fear would haunt him—as it haunted every man in the troop—that Alberbury too might no longer be a stronghold and a sanctuary to the FitzWarin family. His father rode at the head of the men, his head carried high and his face carved in sharp angles and hollows. He looked exhausted but the set of his mouth was resolute and harsh, shunning all offers of comfort.

They had ridden hard from Wales, and on their journey had fought skirmishes with scouts from Owain Gwynedd's army and a troop of Iorwerth Goch's Welsh retainers. Many of the FitzWarin men had sustained fresh injuries on top of those they had taken fighting for Henry in the forests beyond Basingwerk. The horses were stumbling with exhaustion and their riders were in little better case: red-eyed, incoherent, chilled beyond bone to the very marrow of the soul. Once, Brunin thought he had felt the brush of a cold hand across his hair and a moistness on his face, not of rain but of lips. He had woken from a saddle doze with a grunt of alarm and been eyed strangely by the serjeant riding at his side.

The King had given the FitzWarins permission to leave his campaign, but he had spared them no troops and no aid beyond sympathetic words and a wave of dismissal. Owain Gwynedd was the initial threat. Iorwerth Goch could wait. Joscelin had perforce to remain with the King, but he had given FitzWarin a knight and three serjeants. They had proved their worth during the skirmishes, but it would take a concerted effort to winkle the Welsh out of Whittington. Brunin wondered grimly what sort of account Guy L'Estrange was going to give of events that would leave him with an iota of credibility.

Soldiers paced the wall walks and there was a double guard on the gates that swung open to admit them. Brunin drew rein in the bailey and slid from Jester's steaming, soaked back. The grooms hastened out from the stables to take the horses. Glancing around as the gelding was led away to a rub down and a hay-filled stall, Brunin saw Hawise hesitating in the entrance to the keep and felt a thread of energy flash through his weary body. Raising her gown above her ankles, she ran across the bailey toward him, shoes splashing in the mire, auburn braids leaping beneath her veil.

"Brunin, Brunin…Brunin!" She reached him and flung her arms around his neck. He raised his hands and embraced her hard, drinking in the scent of her, the comfort of her presence and the way she made him feel whole by the very way she had run to him. He turned his head, found her lips, and kissed her, his mouth cold, hers warm and yielding. After a moment she broke away, but he followed her, still seeking with his lips for the security of hers but finding only her cheek and the taste of salt. Belatedly he realized that she was weeping, and not with joy.

"Hawise?"

The rain tipped down. The front of her dress bore a long wet stain from his hauberk. She pressed her sleeve across her eyes and raised her chin. "We heard about Whittington," she said in a wobbling voice, "but I am afraid there is more bad news."

"More?" Involuntarily he swung to look at the gates, his hand going to his sword hilt.

"No, not of battle." She took his arm and he felt her steel herself. "Your...your mother is dead. The baby came too soon and we could not stop the bleeding."

The words fell on him like rain and slowly soaked inward. "When?" he heard himself ask through stiff lips.

"Two days since. We have been looking for you." She tugged at him. "They have been laid in the chapel."

He followed her to the hall where she furnished him with a cup of sweetened wine laced with ginger and pepper. He watched her go to his father and embrace him too. FitzWarin received the gesture with no more reaction than a statue, his expression one of stone. Water streamed from his garments and soaked into the floor rushes. He took the wine she offered him, drank it in one gulp, thrust the cup back into her hands, and, blank-eyed, strode toward the chapel.

Brunin wanted no more than to retire to a darkened chamber and lie down with his arm across his eyes. To sleep, to draw Hawise close and bathe his wounds in her healing warmth. What he wanted would have to wait. Duties and responsibilities would not go away just because he turned his back on them.

Hawise had taken up the role of chatelaine, making sure that the soldiers all had wine, that the kitchens were organized to provide bread and pottage, that blankets and sleeping space were available, and that there was aid for the wounded. A young lad helped Brunin out of his wet equipment. Hawise arrived with a dry chemise and tunic for him, but only on her way elsewhere.

"Where is my grandmother?" he asked. He felt like a poled ox, staggering, numb, but still on his feet.

"In the chapel, keeping vigil. She pretends that she is unmoved, but that is not true." Hawise looked around the hall. The stink of wet cloth and unwashed bodies was beginning to create an almost visible fug. "In truth I am glad, for I would rather do this on my own than have to keep looking over my shoulder." For the first time she noticed his bandaged hand. "You are wounded?"

He heard the sharpness of anxiety in her tone and forced a smile of reassurance. "It's been attended to," he said, "although if you could..."

She helped him don the clean chemise and dry tunic. The faint smell of spices from the clothing coffer clung amid the folds and he inhaled the sustaining scent. Hawise, Sybilla, Ludlow. He knew that he needed to go to the chapel too, but it could wait. The dead, however dear they might be, had an eternity of waiting before them, and a few moments more would not matter. "Where," he asked, "is Guy L'Estrange?"

❖ ❖ ❖

"My father will be wondering why you are still alive." Brunin's tone was neutral.

Guy L'Estrange looked at the floor rushes. "I am wondering that myself," he said wearily, his face gray with despair.

They were in the small retiring room behind the dais, which was partitioned off from the hall and contained space for a coffer, a bench, and two chairs. It was cozier than the hall in winter and offered a modicum of privacy on the lower floor of the keep.

Brunin wrapped his hands around his belt. "How did Iorwerth Goch come to seize Whittington?"

L'Estrange grimaced. "He brought his full host against us at dusk. We were preparing to close the gates and they came up out of the woods at us before we knew what was happening...We would have had time, but they had brought two fodder carts through the entrance and overturned them so that we could not close the gates. We were tricked—easily tricked." His mouth twisted in self-anger at the last word. "As soon as I saw what had happened, I rallied the soldiers, but it was too late. There were Welsh soldiers in the cart and they held on long enough for their main force to arrive. Goch's captain offered surrender or death to every man, woman, and child in the place. That was my only choice. For myself I would have chosen to die, but not the women, not the children. I do not ask your forgiveness, or your father's—how could you give it? All I ask is for the opportunity to live long enough to redeem myself and take revenge."

"For that you will have to consult God and my father," Brunin said.

L'Estrange rubbed his palms over his face. "I still do not understand how it happened. One moment there was nothing, the next we were overrun."

Brunin knew that he should be angry beyond reckoning, but for the moment his emotions were numb. Besides, he had experience of Welshmen who attacked out of nowhere and created bloody mayhem. If a king were susceptible, then a constable could fail too, even an experienced one. "The Welsh are good at watching and waiting their moment," he said. "They have to be since they have fewer resources."

"I should have sent out more patrols…"

"Yes, you should," Brunin said flatly. "But 'should have' is no use to either of us." He breathed out hard. "What concerns us immediately is that Iorwerth Goch is over the border in full strength too."

L'Estrange nodded. "He won't attack Alberbury though. The Welsh seldom use siege tactics; they don't have the resources. If they can't win by sudden assault, they melt away into their forests and hills."

Brunin tightened his grip around his belt. "I need no lessons in the ways of the Welsh," he said curtly.

"No," said L'Estrange in a low voice, and dropped his gaze.

Brunin reined back the spark of anger that had flickered through his numbness. It was his father's place to deal with L'Estrange, and he knew the danger of trampling upon a pride that was almost battered to extinction.

"I am blaming you no more than you blame yourself," he said, "and that is blame enough." He moved to the curtain across the entrance. "We'll talk later, and doubtless my father will speak to you when he has finished in the chapel. We have to decide what is to be done, not waste the time in recrimination."

A subdued L'Estrange followed him back out into the hall. "I am sorry for the loss of the lady Eve," he muttered. "She will be sorely missed."

Brunin paused and gazed out across the hall, busy with men, filled with the smell of their damp garments, woodsmoke, and root pottage. "Yes," he said softly, "she will." He looked around at L'Estrange. "You always take for granted what you have until it is gone. And then you realize how much value it truly held in your life."

❖ ❖ ❖

The chapel was a small timber building adjoining the keep. Built as a convenience for the lord and the garrison, it was a sparse, military affair. There were a few embroidered hangings on the walls and the altar boasted candlesticks of silver gilt, donated by Mellette's father at her marriage. FitzWarin knelt in prayer before the bier of his wife and child. Outside he could hear the rain thudding down and smell the wet air through a half-open shutter. The candles surrounding the corpse fluttered, but at least none went out. He could not believe that he was kneeling here, keeping vigil for his wife. A month ago she had been ripening with child as they stood together at their son's marriage and watched the uniting of the lines of FitzWarin and de Dinan, and, with it, the promise of half of Ludlow for their grandchildren. Now it was all so much dross.

The breeze from the window stirred the wisps of fair hair at her brow that had been too short to braid. Her skin was white and cold, unlike the living, pliant warmth that had occupied his bed for twenty years. Now there would be an empty space. Even if he filled it with another woman, it would not be the same…ever. He looked at the shine of the silk wedding gown and remembered standing in the church porch to make his vows. He had been astonished at her beauty, and frightened too. How was he going to live with a creature so perfect and ethereal? He had no sisters and no knowledge of women. She would surely break in his hands. And yet he had been the envy of every man at the wedding, young and old. If only they had known. If only he had known…and now it was too late.

There was a step behind him and Mellette laid her hand on his shoulder. "Come away," she said. "You can return later if you must. There are other matters that need your attention."

He rose and turned, pushing her hand aside. "There were always other matters that needed my attention," he said bitterly. "Never her."

Mellette looked at him as if she thought he had lost his wits. "She had enough of your attention to give you seven living children."

"And an eighth that killed her."

Mellette gave him a severe look. "Childbearing is always a fight between life and death," she said harshly. "Women face it as men face war. It is their lot and their duty. Eve knew it well and shirked none of it."

FitzWarin turned from his mother. The cold air from the window was like breath against his cheek. "I never saw her smile," he said.

His mother's expression grew impatient. "Weep and grow maudlin and have done. The dead are the least of your duties."

FitzWarin felt anger rising through the dark morass of his shock and grief. "Do not prate to me of duty." He clenched his fists. There was pleasure and revulsion in imagining them striking the old woman. "If you knew yours, your tongue would be behind your teeth. My father was remiss in his, not to silence you with a scold's bridle."

"How dare y—"

"Get out!" he roared and the sound echoed around the chamber, rending the living, crying out to the dead.

Mellette stared at his balled fists. "You shame yourself," she said and stalked out.

FitzWarin closed his eyes and fell to his knees. The silence after she had gone was blessed and just enough to pull him back from the edge of madness. He buried his face in his hands and wept.

# 30

SEPTEMBER SUNSHINE FLOODED THE WALLS OF LUDLOW IN
rich golden light. Hawise was enjoying the benediction of
this end of summer warmth after the dire weather of the last six
weeks. She was also enjoying her moment of respite at Ludlow.
Brunin and his father had ridden to rejoin the King. There was
talk of peace with the Welsh, but the terms had yet to be agreed
and there was no guarantee that Owain Gwynedd would agree
to what Henry wanted. There was also no guarantee that the
FitzWarin would have Whittington restored to them.

Mellette had remained at Alberbury, but Hawise had returned
to Ludlow where she could await Brunin in warmth and companionship, rather than dwell in Mellette's cold, dowager world. She
had brought Emmeline with her. There were many youngsters at
Ludlow with whom the child could play, and the less restrictive
atmosphere would help her recover from the loss of her mother.

"You have had a difficult beginning to your married life,"
Sybilla commented as the women walked the dogs along the
riverbank below the castle.

Hawise laughed bleakly. "I have had no married life. Brunin
and I shared a bed for a week at Ludlow. At Alberbury we had
to sleep in the hall, wrapped in our cloaks with Emmeline burrowed between us. There was no space for privacy of any kind
and everyone was in shock and mourning for the loss of Lady

Eve…and of Whittington." She grimaced at her mother. "Lady Mellette stamped around being vile to everyone and it was left to me to order the household so that it didn't descend into chaos. Brunin's father…" She shook her head and watched two of the dogs splash into the river shallows after a moorhen. The indignant bird ran across the water and took off in a panic of dark wings. Emmeline giggled and pointed.

"He took it hard," Sybilla said with a knowing nod.

"He was like a sleepwalker." Hawise bit her lip. "His eyes were open, but they were only seeing what was in his mind and the rest of us might as well not have existed. Brunin has had to take up the slack."

"Then God have pity on Lord Fulke, and be praised you were both ready for the responsibility."

Hawise gave a rueful smile. "Prepared," she said, "not ready." She looked at her mother. "I don't regret it though."

"Then you are ready," Sybilla said sagely.

They walked on, their path bordered by a second blooming of cow parsley and tall ox-eye daisies. The dogs shook themselves all over Emmeline, making her squeal, but in the next moment, child and hounds were running along the path, filled with exuberance.

Hawise's half-sister Cecily joined them from the castle, a light cloak pinned at her shoulders. She was wearing a fine linen veil that exposed her throat and the glossy shine of her braids. Somewhere between spring and autumn a smile had returned to her face. She was being courted by Walter de Mayenne and negotiations had been entered into. Both sides were eager for the match to be made binding.

"I asked Marion if she wanted to come too, but she said not," Cecily said as she fell into step with her mother and Hawise.

Sybilla sighed and gave a small shake of her head. "I do not know what to do with the girl," she said. "The more I reach out, the more she withdraws from me, and yet I hate to see her trapped in a corner like a frightened wild thing."

"She said she was busy with her sewing." Cecily raised an eloquent eyebrow.

"Marion would sew from dawn until dusk if we let her," Sybilla explained to Hawise. "She only leaves her needle to eat and sleep. Sometimes Cecily can persuade her to come for a walk but of late she has shunned even that. I make her run errands for me and do other tasks, but the moment her hands are free, she is back at her stitchery...or else washing her hands."

"She makes clothes," Cecily said. "Men's clothing mostly: shirts and braies and hose."

"For whom?" Hawise asked, although she already had an inkling of the reply.

"Whatever imaginary lover dwells in her mind, although I suspect he wears the face of Gilbert de Lacy's knight. I put what she makes in a coffer. Such garments are always useful for guests and alms-giving days."

Hawise brushed her hand over the seed-heavy grasses at the side of the footpath and felt chagrin. Once, for a brief span and almost to her downfall, her own dreams had worn the face of Ernalt de Lysle. "What is to become of her?"

Sybilla looked troubled. "Your father said before he left to join the King that he intended to arrange her a place in a nunnery. Certainly she is not fit to be wed, and after what happened, your father will not contemplate keeping her in our household. It is a sorry mess," she sighed. "I often wonder what I could have done differently when she was a child to change things."

"The damage was already done when she came to us, Mama," Cecily said, giving her a hug.

"But I feel that I have failed in not undoing it...Ah, no more, I do not wish to think on it." Sybilla waved her hand and quickened her pace to show that the matter was closed.

Later, as the maids latched the shutters upon the dusk and lit the candles in the bower, Hawise sat down at Marion's side. Marion had placed her tapestry frame so that it caught the best of the candlelight from the wall sconce. She had abandoned the delicate sewing of earlier and was now working in couch stitch and woolen thread on a strip of linen.

"Do you want some help?" Hawise asked.

Marion shook her head. "No," she replied in a pale, flat voice. "It's mine. I don't want anyone else to touch it."

"What's it for?" Hawise tilted her head. The picture was in its infancy but appeared to depict a castle or similar building and a woman standing in the doorway. Outlined to the right was a man on a horse.

"To hang on the wall, of course." Marion flicked her a contemptuous look as if she thought Hawise was a lack-wit.

"In here?"

The contemptuous look hardened. "It might be." Marion bent her head to her task.

Hawise watched Marion manipulate the needle. Her finger ends were rough where she had pricked herself, despite the use of a thimble. "You cannot hide in this forever. No matter how many pictures you sew, there is still a world beyond the window."

"A world, or a nunnery?" Marion sneered. The needle jabbed in and out.

"What else did you expect?" Hawise thought of her own labor on Brunin's yellow silk banner. A labor of love. Marion's looked like desperation. "It's Ernalt de Lysle, isn't it?" she asked. "You're making them for him."

"You know nothing," Marion snapped and turned her shoulder so that she was facing away from Hawise, shutting her out.

"It makes it seem real that you have to sew for him, like a wife or a sweetheart."

"It is real." Marion reached for the shears and snipped the thread. "I told you, you know nothing." Raising her head she looked toward the end window where a maid was pulling the last set of shutters closed.

❖ ❖ ❖

A week later, Joscelin and Brunin returned to Ludlow from the royal court.

"What happened?" Hawise asked her husband when, for the first time since the week of their wedding, she had him to herself. He had dismissed the squire who would otherwise have helped him unarm and she had sent away her maids and a male attendant once they had finished filling the wooden bathtub. Steam rose in misty swirls from its surface scented with astringent thyme and juniper.

Brunin had come directly from the stable yard and he stank of hard riding. He pushed his hands through his hair which was flattened and greasy from wearing an arming cap and coif. "What didn't," he said.

Hawise was burning with curiosity but she damped it down and fetched him wine and griddle cakes. They would be dining in the great hall with everyone else but the meal was still a couple of hours away and she could tell he needed sustenance.

Brunin drank the first cup of wine fast, began a second more slowly, and set about demolishing the griddle cakes with the efficiency of the ravenous.

"Henry and Owain Gwynedd have agreed to a peace," he said, as he finished his fourth. "Owain's pulled back from Rhuddlan and sworn homage to Henry and Henry's withdrawn from his campaign. The Welsh might have tweaked the lion's tail but they cannot withstand a concerted assault, and Henry doesn't want to keep an army in the field through the autumn and winter. It suits all sides."

"And Whittington?"

Brunin drained his second cup. "Whittington," he said heavily, as if speaking the word were a burden. He unlatched his swordbelt and threw it across the coffer, not in anger, she thought, but in weariness and resignation. "Whittington is lost—for the moment."

"Henry would not aid you?"

Brunin snorted. "You would not believe the hoops of fire we

have had to jump through like tumblers' dogs." He stooped so that she could pull the hauberk over his head. While she laid it across the coffer with his swordbelt, he stripped the rest of his garments and stepped into the tub. She heard him gasp.

"Too hot?"

"Perfect," he said, closing his eyes. "It's one of the things I've dreamed about…when my dreams haven't been nightmares."

Hawise stooped to his discarded clothes. There was a tear in his shirt that would need mending once it was washed. With a restraint that came from effort rather than instinct, she did not badger him, but left him to speak in his own time.

Finally he cupped his hands in the water, swilled his face, and looked at her through spiked, black lashes. "The King didn't want to begin another dispute with the Welsh that would cause further unrest along the Marches. He gave Whittington to Roger and Jonas de Powys who claim it as theirs, and enfeoffed my father with a manor in Gloucestershire instead." His voice was expressionless.

Hawise stared at him. "He cannot do that!"

"He can, because he is the King. It is the same dispute that vexes your father and Gilbert de Lacy, save on a smaller scale. There are two claims and Henry has ruled that, for the moment, the de Powys brothers should hold Whittington."

"But that's not fair!" Hawise cried.

"So we told Henry—and in words more forceful than that." He swilled his face again and pressed the water away with his hands.

"And what did he say?"

"That playing Solomon is always difficult…that there are hundreds of such disputes waiting to be resolved after the wars of the last fifty years. He finds the de Powys brothers useful and, since they have their feet in both camps and are fluent Welsh speakers, he's prepared to be sympathetic to their claim. Iorwerth Goch will yield the castle to them and, in the meantime, Henry compensates us with one of his own manors."

"And that is it? You lose Whittington forever?" Hawise knelt by the tub and began scrubbing his back with the washcloth, putting all the vigor of her indignation into the action.

"No," Brunin said, and with a hiss half turned and took the cloth and soap dish away from her before she flayed him alive. "There is still room to appeal through the courts and get the lands restored, but for the moment possession is nine-tenths of the law." He shook his head as she made to protest. "We were overrun by the Welsh. We were looking the other way when we should have been attending to our walls. Henry has given Whittington to the other claimants as a salutary lesson and because it suits him to have men of Welsh blood but English loyalties holding the keep."

"But you were looking the other way because he had summoned you to his Welsh campaign."

He shrugged. "It makes no difference. We still had a garrison at Whittington and the responsibility was ours."

"And if possession is nine-tenths of the law, will you get it back?"

He was silent for a time, and Hawise was beginning to wonder whether to ask again or leave it alone when he finally drew breath to reply. "Yes," he said softly. "We will get it back, however long it takes. The name of FitzWarin will not be forgotten at Whittington." His jaw tightened and Hawise saw the lines of strain in his throat and across his shoulders. If he did not already have a headache, he was going to suffer a blinding one soon.

She took the cloth back from him and, this time, she was careful and her hands were very gentle, and after a while he relaxed, and then he grew tense again for different reasons, and for a while the matter of Whittington was of less importance than the dance of touch.

❖ ❖ ❖

From the corner of her eye, Marion watched Brunin catch Hawise around the waist, pull her to him, and nuzzle her throat. Hawise laughed and gave him a bright look through her lashes and a nudge with her hip before slipping from the embrace to place a freshly laundered chemise in one of the traveling coffers.

They couldn't keep their hands off each other, Marion thought sourly. Even if they were married, it was scandalous. There was a burning feeling inside her that she identified as jealousy—and fear that she would never have what they had. They were preparing to visit several FitzWarin manors, returning by way of the estates of Hawise's dowry, and Marion was glad that they were leaving. Their laughter seemed to linger in the corners of the keep and even when she thrust her fingers in her ears she could still hear it inside her head. At night, lying on her pallet, she knew that in the next tower they were in bed together. Her mind felt the sweat of their bodies as they slid against each other, heard the sounds of pleasure they made, and was burned by the reflected heat of their lust. All night it kept her awake, like a fire licking in small cat-tongues along the pathways of her blood. Her loins were heavy and ached with dull need. Her thoughts were feverish, and the name of Ernalt de Lysle was on her lips as she counted her prayer beads through restless fingers and spoke his name like an invocation. She conjured his image and imagined him in the bed beside her. He would tell her how beautiful she was. He would stroke and caress her and in her turn she would wind her fingers in his golden hair and draw him down and they would become one.

Every night she would fall asleep to this vision of light and awaken in pitch darkness to nightmares of blood. Sometimes it was a wedding sheet, smeared with the red proof of her defloration; sometimes many sheets, twisted into a long rope like an umbilical cord dangling out of a moonlit turret window, the knotted end drip-dripping into the grass…and sometimes she would dream that Ernalt had thrust a knife into her belly and she would waken with a scream, clutching her stomach, and for an instant she would think she saw him lying beside her, drenched in blood, blue eyes staring into eternity.

Joscelin and Sybilla were leaving Ludlow too; a visit to their other manors was long overdue. Marion was supposed to be accompanying them but she had no intention of doing so. She knew Joscelin had plans to put her in a convent along the way and she was never going to let them imprison her thus.

Hawise left the coffer and went into the outer chamber to speak to her mother. Marion heard the women talking and the sound of light laughter. She felt excluded and miserable. Brunin sauntered across to the window, braced his arm on the splay, and looked out, his other hand resting lightly at his belt. She looked at the scar running from the base of his fingers toward his wrist. It was still new enough to be pinkish red and showed the marks where the stitches had lain. Marion thought of them touching Hawise's body and shied away from where that led. But not swiftly enough, for he turned his head and looked at her with his knowing, sable gaze.

She thrust out her lower lip. "Everyone blames me, but it wasn't my fault."

"It was your choice though...and if Lord Joscelin decides to support you in a nunnery rather than beneath his own roof, then that is his choice too." He faced her. "After all, you are not happy here, are you?"

She looked down at her hands. "I wanted to marry you once," she said. "But I'm glad I didn't, and I am happier than you know."

His expression grew wry. "That is for certain." For a moment he hesitated as if he were going to say more, but then with a slight shake of his head he left her and she heard him go into the other chamber and speak to Hawise, his voice losing its wariness and developing a softer timbre. For an instant she had a vision of herself, Brunin, and Hawise as children, playing in the bailey. The memory of her own laughter haunted her. She had been happy then, but that memory was little more than a faded echo.

Out in the bailey the dinner horn sounded. Marion wasn't hungry, but she followed everyone else to the great hall. Let them be lulled by her passivity. She had to be cunning.

The smell of bread, onions, and meat as she entered the hall almost made her retch. Near the end of the hall were two trestles set out for travelers and minor guests. Seated at one of the benches was a man dressed in the sober garments of a merchant and, as she passed, he raised his eyes to her. She was surprised and affronted that a man of his class should bandy looks instead of lowering his gaze…until he deliberately touched his cloak clasp. Her gaze widened upon Ernalt's brooch and her breath locked in her throat. Somehow she managed to keep on walking, somehow she succeeded in taking her own place at the high trestle in a manner that did not cause remark. But she could not prevent her hands from shaking as she broke the bread and sprinkled salt into her portion of lamb stew. Her partner for the duration of the meal was Lord Joscelin's squire. Fortunately he had the ravenous appetite of a developing adolescent and although he attended to her, his courtesy was a matter of form and he was more interested in the food than watching her. Now and again she looked furtively toward the foot of the hall to check that the traveler was still there. He was eating with gusto and talking to his companions as if he had never looked at her or shown her Ernalt's brooch. Biding his time, she thought, as she must bide hers.

When the meal was finished, Marion murmured an excuse about taking a walk to aid a queasy digestion, insisted that she would be all right, and went outside. She strolled the bailey paths, trying to look nonchalant, although her heart was thundering and she had to keep rubbing her hands because they were wet with perspiration. A chill wind was blowing across from Whitcliffe, and she wished she had brought her cloak, for her armpits were icy.

He caught up with her near one of the bailey store sheds and, with a swift glance around, drew her into the lee of the timber wall.

"Mistress Marion." His eyes were of a brown almost as dark as Brunin's. His hair, by contrast, was the yellow-gray of old fleece. He wore no sword, but a large dagger was slung from his belt and the solid weight of his garments spoke of prosperity.

She looked around fearfully. "You have a message for me?"

He opened his hand and held out the brooch. "Sir Ernalt sends you this as a token and bids you to tell him a time when it will be safe for him to come for you."

Taking the brooch, she closed her own fingers over it, feeling the residual warmth of his hand and the hardness of the gold. Ernalt had kept his word. He had not forgotten. Her joy made her feel almost as sick as her misery had done before. "My lord and lady are leaving to visit their lands in Devon," she said in a trembling voice, "and they want me to accompany them."

"When?"

"Soon. Two days' time, I think." She searched his face and anxiety rippled through her. "They want to put me in a nunnery."

His eyes narrowed. "Two days…"

Marion gave him an eager look. "You could bring me to him."

"No, mistress, that was not my instruction and, besides, it would be too dangerous."

"No more dangerous than him coming to me," she said with a puzzled frown. "Indeed, less so."

He looked at her hand, clasped over the brooch. "By that token you know that Sir Ernalt loves you beyond measure, but you must also know that he is ambitious. He wants you to be the lady of a great castle. He wants to see you gowned in silk and to treat you like a queen."

Marion smiled with pleasure at the words, and then her eyes widened as the deeper meaning reached her. "Ludlow…" she said. "He wants Ludlow."

"Only so that he can secure your future. Gilbert de Lacy's wife would be the Lady of course, but you would be mistress of the chamber and her deputy. You would have rooms of your own and Sir Ernalt would be the constable." His voice grew soft and persuasive. "With Joscelin de Dinan and his family absent, the castle will be easier to take and there will be no bloodshed. But we need someone inside to help us."

She started to shake her head.

"You aided Lord Gilbert and Sir Ernalt to escape. If you do

not help them now, then your only reward for loyalty will be incarceration in a nunnery. If you do your part, then you will gain gratitude and respect beyond measure…and have your love for the rest of your days. Your loyalty is to him, is it not?"

Put like that, the truth was indisputable. Marion swallowed. "What must I do?"

When he had gone, Marion hastened back to the bower. She did not have to pretend to be ill, for her stomach was churning with anxiety and she was sick several times. No one questioned her when she went to lie down on her pallet. Lady Sybilla brought her a cold cloth for her forehead and, after a few gentle words, mercifully let her be. She stared at the painted ceiling. Her choice was made; her path set. A nunnery and a lifetime of prayer and repentance, or Ernalt and Ludlow. No choice at all.

# 31

A HUNDRED YEARS AGO, THE MANOR OF ALVESTON HAD belonged to King Harold of England. It was the same size as Alberbury but, since it was sufficiently distant from Wales and had never been a source of dispute during the long and destructive civil war, lacked a castle. Although a tranquil place, it was not quite a backwater. The land was fertile and the village of Tockington with its prosperous mill was also part of the grant.

"An insult," Mellette had muttered as she stalked around the manor, finding fault with everything. "If the King thinks we are going to be satisfied with this poky rat-hole, he is sadly mistaken. Did we fight for his cause all those years to be thus rewarded?" She had pointed out woodworm holes in a bench seat and stirred a disgusted toe in the ancient floor rushes, raising a cloud of chaff and small flies.

Hawise had put such failings down to bad stewardship. The manor was no palace, nor even a castle, but beneath the neglect it had a pleasant aspect. But, of course, it wasn't Whittington and she could see why Mellette's dignity was incensed.

"It is not an insult," FitzWarin had grated, his voice made harsh by more than just irritation. His cough had returned with the onset of the damper autumn weather and, despite doses of horehound tisane and wearing a token of St. Anthony around his neck, was proving persistent. "It is a sop to keep us quiet while the dust settles. We take it through the courts and we sue for Whittington's return."

"Hah, and who should have the last say but the King?" Mellette snapped, not in the least appeased.

"Henry will do right by us," FitzWarin had replied, setting his jaw grimly—whether at the subject matter or in endurance of Mellette's carping was unclear.

"And this...this worm-eaten hovel is an example of his justice?"

Wincing at the memory of the argument, one of many, Hawise glanced at Brunin. They had gone riding in the autumn gold, partly to explore the new lands and partly to escape from Mellette's oppressive presence. The old lady had always been shrewish and hard to please but recently her querulous behavior had become unbearable. Hawise was relieved that she and Brunin would soon be leaving the FitzWarin household and joining her parents at their manor of Hartland in Devon. She could hold her own with Brunin's family, but having to do so every waking moment was wearing. Brunin had said little, but Hawise knew him well enough to recognize the reticence of endurance...and something else that reminded her of the silent, dark-eyed boy who had first arrived in Ludlow, wary and vulnerable as a cornered wild thing. The presence of his grandmother was like a shadow over him, and recently the size of that shadow had been growing as Mellette's behavior deteriorated.

They followed deer trails through the woodland between the village and the river. There was little breeze, but unfelt movements of air sent leaves twirling groundward in silent feathers of mottled green and gold.

"It is strange," Brunin said, gazing around.

"What is?" Hawise smiled.

"This. To ride through the woods with only you for company and enjoy the peace of the day. Usually when I go riding in a forest, it is among armed men and our hands are never further than an inch from our swords."

"But you cannot give up the habit of watching and listening, can you?" She looked around too, trying to imagine what it would be like to face sudden ambush. The notion made her shiver.

"No." His smile remained but his eyes were somber and she saw the way he glanced at the healed scar on his right hand.

"Are you pleased that the King has given this land to your family?"

"Providing it is a sweetener and not a permanent replacement for Whittington, yes," he said, adding with a rueful grin, "It is your family too now."

"I know that, but I am still growing accustomed to the notion."

"Not comfortable, is it?" He clucked his tongue to Jester and turned along a trail branching away from the main one.

Hawise thought of several different answers, all diplomatic, and abandoned them. Between her and Brunin there would be honesty. "No," she said, "but I can bear it."

He made an ambiguous sound that might have been amusement or just wry acknowledgment of her words.

"I know the strength of the FitzWarin will and I am honored to be a part of it."

He gave her a glance filled with sardonic humor. "Then I must cherish your pride and honor, and not ask about happiness."

"That is for Ludlow," she said. "In which you are promised a half-share. I may now be a FitzWarin wife, but, by the same law, you are now a de Dinan son. God willing, when I bear our children, they will have the pride of both heritages."

"God help them, you mean," he said with a grin, then he sobered and glanced at Hawise who had laid her hand against her belly. She saw his look and hastily took the reins again.

"It is too early to tell," she said brusquely. "Far too early." Her flux was late, but by less than five days. Her bleeds were usually regular; she could generally time herself by the phases of the moon, but a late or missed flux did not necessarily mean a pregnancy. Mellette had been watching the laundry baskets like a cat at a mouse hole, waiting for signs of the monthly bleed, her eyes growing brighter and narrower with each morning that passed.

Brunin said nothing and spoke instead to the horse, slapping its neck, the gesture intended to smooth away the momentary awkwardness between himself and Hawise.

They came to a small, unoccupied shelter in the forest: the occasional dwelling of a swineherd or a woodsman. There was kindling and neatly cut wood stacked nearby, and the remnants of a fire in which were scattered the small bones of a hare. Brunin and Hawise did not linger, merely marked the place and continued through the trees until they thinned out on the edge of the village.

A sound came to their ears and the sensation of a regular thump, thump, thump beating up through the ground. Hawise tilted her head to listen. "Music," she said with a brightening of curiosity in her expression. The smell of roasting pork wafted on the cool autumn air and someone laughed loudly, the sound saturated in ale. "It's not a saint's day that I recall."

Hawise and Brunin left the trees and rode into the village. Smoke was rising from several outdoor cooking fires over which cauldrons simmered and it seemed that the entire population of Tockington was outdoors. Indeed, more than the entire population, Hawise thought as she counted the number of houses and matched them to the amount of people. Either that or the village was a most fertile community. A large firepit had been dug in the garth of one of the more prosperous dwellings and a hog and a sheep were roasting on two spits suspended over the flames. Nearby two women were serving bread and ale from a trestle piled with loaves and earthenware jugs. Children shrieked and darted, playing chase among the adults, some of whom were talking in groups and drinking ale from fat pottery cups while others danced in rings to the vigorous music. At the center of one of the rings stood a young couple: the man wearing a dark green tunic, the woman a lavender-colored dress. Both had garlands of leaves and berries in their hair, and the girl's brown tresses hung to her waist.

"It's a wedding," Hawise said, her eyes lighting up. She nudged her mare with her heels. "What an auspicious time to introduce ourselves." She looked at Brunin, her eyes sparkling. "Do you have some silver in your pouch?"

He laughed. "My father warned me that taking a wife would be like cutting holes in my purse."

She gave him a lofty look. "If you would rather not give a bride-gift, that is your choice, but they've seen us so it's too late to sneak back into the trees."

"I'll be glad to give a bride-gift," he retorted. "Providing there is recompense."

"What sort of recompense?"

He smiled at her through narrowed lids. "Something in keeping," he murmured and turned his attention to the village reeve and the seniors of Tockington who were approaching their horses.

❖ ❖ ❖

Marion stood on the wall walk of the Pendover tower. The night was dark and overcast with the occasional stutter of rain blown from the mouth of a gusting wind. Unconsciously she played with Ernalt's ring. Tonight its cord hung outside her gown. She would have worn it on her wedding finger, but it was too large. Her cloak was pinned with his golden brooch too.

Joscelin and Sybilla had left without her, for she had been deemed unfit to travel. She had feigned some of her malaise, but excitement and worry had genuinely upset her stomach and she had given a convincing portrayal of being too sick to go on a journey. The convent, however, still loomed large in Lord Joscelin's plans for her. She had overheard him saying to Sybilla that he would deal with the matter as soon as they returned.

Marion took a few paces along the wall walk. There was no sign of the guard but she could hear the scrape of his boots moving away from her as he marched between the towers. She leaned over the battlements, listening so hard that she felt as if her ears were about to bleed with the effort. Three times the messenger had come from Ernalt and three times she had given him information: about guard positions, about numbers, about the senior officers left in the keep. She had measured the distance between these battlements and the ground. This was her last chance to withdraw from the bargain she had made.

She thought she heard a whistle and her heart began to thump. Leaning over, she peered down between the merlons, but could see nothing. The whistle came again, louder this time. Biting her lip, she took the ball of twine she had brought from her chamber and, after a single hesitation, wrapped the end twice across her knuckles and cast the ball over the wall. She felt it running loose and then the sudden tug as it was caught at the foot of the wall. Further rapid movements rippled up the string, tightening the bands around her hand. Two fierce tugs told her that the task below was completed and she began pulling in the thick twine, fist over fist. It seemed to take an eternity and although she knew that the guard would not return yet, she was terrified that she would be caught.

Blessedly the twine's load finally came into sight: a ladder fashioned from plaited leather strips. It was light and insubstantial, but strong enough for men to scale. Marion dragged the ladder onto the wall walk and secured it in one of the crenel slots. Then she unfastened and balled up the twine and threw it down again as a signal that all was ready.

The flimsy ladder wobbled as the man below set his weight to it. Marion's eyes darted to the fastenings. What if they weren't secure enough and he fell to his death? Eyes wide with fear, she watched the ties stretch and yield as he climbed, but the knots held and after what seemed an age but she realized could have been no more than a couple of minutes, fingers grasped the stonework and Ernalt hauled himself over the edge and gained the wall walk. He was panting hard, for he had made the climb in his mail shirt. His sword hung from a baldric at his back.

"Well done, my love," he said with a fierce laugh. His arm went around her and his mouth came down on hers in a hard kiss that stole her breath and made her shiver. "Well done indeed!" He half turned to give three swift jerks on the ladder and then kissed her again, his hand running possessively over her body as it might run over the flank of a favorite hound.

Her face blazed with joy at his praise. "You are pleased then?"

"Beyond measure. You have not forgotten the rest, love?" He cast his gaze along the wall walk.

"No, the chamber door is open and the women are abed."

He nodded. "Go and join them," he said. "Keep out of the way and wait for me to fetch you."

Marion nodded. "What are you going to—"

He set his hand across her lips. "Best that you do not ask too many questions, sweetheart. What the eye does not see, the heart does not grieve over—or so they tell me. Go quickly now...my lady." He kissed her again.

Marion sped back to the women's chambers on a surge of emotion so mixed and powerful that she was almost beyond coherence when one of the senior maids, Dame Aude, demanded to know where she had been.

"T-taking some air," Marion stammered, cheeks burning. "There is no rule against it."

Dame Aude looked disapproving. "No, but the night air harbors evil humors, and you were too ill to make the journey with my lord and lady."

"I have come to no harm and I am back now," Marion replied with lowered eyes and meek voice. She turned toward her alcove, but she could feel the older woman's eyes boring into her spine.

"When Lady Sybilla returns, it will be my duty to report everything to her," Dame Aude said reprovingly.

"I will remember your diligence," Marion replied and had to bite her tongue on the triumphant remark that Lady Sybilla was never going to return and that very soon Aude was going to have to answer to "Lady Marion."

Once in the safety of her own small chamber, she sat on her bed and occupied her time winding a length of thread around the ring that Ernalt had given her, narrowing the diameter until it fitted her wedding finger snugly. Soon. Soon she would be a bride and a great lady.

❖ ❖ ❖

Ernalt's men, who had been hiding near the river, climbed the leather ladder one by one. Their breathing was loud in the silence of the night and their weapons made small clinking noises as they footed each rung. As the soldiers reached the battlements, Ernalt directed them into the top room of the tower where the women were sleeping. Several screams floated up the stairwell and then abruptly ceased, causing Ernalt to give a soft chuckle. A good slap could be instrumental, although he hoped Marion hadn't been one of the screamers. He intended to make her do so for different reasons soon enough.

As the last men struggled over the merlon and reached the wall walk, Ernalt heard the sound of the guard returning. The man was tunelessly whistling to himself, a lantern in one hand and a spear balanced on his shoulder. As the light fell on the soldiers, his eyes widened in alarm. He had time for one shout before Ernalt's knife took him in the throat and he fell to the wall-walk boards, his blood spraying the crenellations like red rain.

Leaving the body to its death throes, Ernalt led the others down into the tower. A swift glance at the women's chamber showed him a closed door and a soldier standing guard outside it. "No trouble, my lord," he said with a smile. "One old crone came at us with her distaff, but we dealt with her."

"Remember what I told you," Ernalt warned, wagging a fore-finger. "No harm is to come to Marion de la Bruere."

"Yes, sir."

Ernalt gave a terse nod and moved on. There was still much to do before Ludlow was theirs.

Ernalt's men crept along the walkway leading from the Pendover tower and behind the chapel. Another guard was silenced and dispatched. In the tower near the gate, the off-duty men were playing dice and supping wine. They knew nothing until the intruders emerged like shadows darker than the darkness and set upon them.

Throughout the castle it was the same. Each tower was invaded and its occupants, if they were male and of fighting age, put to the sword. The women other than those in the bower were herded into one of the barns in the bailey and guards set over them. Reddened blade in hand, Ernalt ran to the postern gate by the river entrance. Here, a few of the garrison were putting up a fight, but they were outnumbered and too stunned to be efficient. It did not take long to overpower and kill them, even those who cried for mercy.

As the last man fell, Ernalt gestured two of his soldiers to unbar the gate and open it for Gilbert de Lacy's men, waiting in the woods over Whitcliffe.

❖❖❖

In the bower, Marion stared at the body of Dame Aude. As de Lacy's soldiers had burst in, Aude had begun screaming at the full pitch of her lungs. A mailed serjeant had moved to silence her and the foolish old woman had attacked him with her distaff, brandishing it as if it were a spear. The soldier had ducked in surprise at the assault, and then he had laughed, straightened, and struck Aude a blow to the side of the head that had felled her like a Martinmas sow. Her heels had drummed on the rushes; blood had run from her nose and her right ear. The soldier had bellowed at the others to stay where they were and not cause any trouble.

"And do not think I'd stay my hand for any of you!" he had snarled. "You'll not be harmed if you stay put. Try anything and you'll realize how easy her death was. You'll be dealt with by my lord Gilbert when he has the time for you." With a final glare of warning at the women, he had stalked out, banging the door hard shut behind him.

Jehane, a maid who was Dame Aude's particular friend, knelt by Aude's body. "She's dead," she said in an appalled whisper.

Marion rubbed her hands together. They were slick with cold sweat. Ernalt's gold ring shone on her heart finger, giving her courage. "She shouldn't have challenged them," she said in a quavering voice.

Jehane gave her a hard look and fetched a blanket to cover Aude's body.

A young black-haired maid had opened the shutters and was peering out. "God save us!" she cried and made the sign of the Cross on her breast.

Marion hastened to the window and, pushing the girl aside, stared at the shadowy men weaving among the buildings. They were not being as circumspect now, for some carried torches. The sound of steel striking steel hit the night and she saw a shiver of white sparks in the bailey as a garrison serjeant fought for his life and lost it. "Gilbert de Lacy has come for Ludlow," she said in an expressionless voice.

"What? How could that happen?" Jehane demanded.

Marion did not answer. From the direction of the castle gates a tremendous cheer rolled through the night. Moments later the bailey was ablaze with scores of torches. Someone had set a store shed on fire and flames leaped skyward. Billows of thick gray smoke churned toward the shutters. Screams, shouts and pleas for mercy sparked in the choking gray coils. Marion slammed the shutters fast and went to sit on a bench away from the other women. Ernalt had come to claim her, that was all that mattered.

It seemed that she sat there for a long, long time, rocking gently back and forth, rubbing the bright ring he had given her, waiting for him. The candles burned down but after what had happened to Aude, no one was brave enough to venture out and fetch new ones, or visit the well to replenish flagons and ewers. Nor did anyone sleep. The other maids knelt around Aude's body to keep vigil and pray, even though they had but two candles between them. Listening to their chant, Marion muttered a prayer of her own, but it was not for Aude's soul.

Shortly before dawn, Marion heard voices outside the chamber, muffled by the thick oak. Moments later the door opened and Ernalt entered bearing a torch.

"Come," he said to her and held out his hand.

She had intended to go to him with dignity and grace, but his extended fingers were a lifeline and as she passed Aude's body she broke into a run. He gripped her hand in his and pulled her to his side, away from the torch. The resinous flame illuminated a smear of blood on his face and a long, beaded scratch near his eye corner.

His mouth curled with dark humor as he studied the women. "Ladies, the castle is now in the possession of its rightful lord, Gilbert de Lacy. His banner flies from the battlements and his men garrison the walls. Those who owe service and allegiance to Sybilla Talbot have leave to depart at dawn. Those who wish to remain and serve Lord Gilbert and his lady may do so."

The women stared at him in horrified silence. Someone whimpered and stifled the sound against the back of a wrist. Then Dame Jehane summoned sufficient boldness to speak. "What of this lady? She should have a decent burial and the coward who murdered her should be brought to account…or have you no shame?"

"The burial she shall have," Ernalt said, "and you need not fear that she will be lonely in her grave. You would do well to guard your tongue lest you join her. You are not dealing with a softsword like de Dinan anymore."

She whitened and looked down, her courage spent, and he left the room, pulling Marion with him. "If you have a fancy to any of them, take your pick," he told the guard, "but don't tell Lord Gilbert I said so. You know the kind of notions he entertains. The black-haired one looks as if she'll give you a wild ride and the one in the green dress has a mouth on her that you might want to use."

The soldier smacked his lips and grinned.

"Where are we going?" Marion demanded as he led her down the winding stair. She hadn't liked that exchange with the guard about the other women.

"To our chamber, where else?" He brought her out into the bailey. The smell of smoke was much stronger here and several of the timber utility buildings were on fire. Her past life was in flames.

"Why?" she demanded, feeling sick with guilt and fear and remorse. Through their linked arms, she felt Ernalt shrug.

"It's a cleansing fire," he said. "Those sheds were rotten anyway and there was nothing of value inside them. The men like to see fire...helps them to burn out their wildness."

Marion shuddered. To her the fire wasn't cleansing. She could feel its heat branding the stain of her treachery into her soul. Hell could be no worse.

He led her across the grassy area beside the well, a common gossiping place for the women. Her eyes were drawn to the rows of corpses and the dark torchlit puddles of blood on the grass. The youth who chopped the wood for the kitchens stared sightlessly at her, a jagged wound gaping in his throat. Beside him lay Rhys, the half-Welsh soldier who had carried her on his shoulders when she was a small child and given her honeycomb and told her stories. The top of his head was black and jellied. Hot fluid rose in her throat and she had to stop to retch.

"It is the nature of warfare," Ernalt said impatiently. "Think yourself fortunate that you're on the victorious side. If you don't like it, don't look."

An orange glow filled the sky and within the smoke there was a choking stench. "You've fired the town!" she cried in horror. Her mouth tasted sour and her throat was stinging.

"I told you, the men need it to cleanse themselves, especially the mercenaries, and those burghers need teaching a lesson. The rightful master of Ludlow has returned and he'll not brook supporters of de Dinan in either town or castle." His tone grew impatient. "As I said, think yourself fortunate, sweetheart. You're with the conquerors."

The way he said "sweetheart" sent a flash of terror through her, for he sounded like a common soldier talking to his whore, but she had no time to brood on the matter, for he was drawing her up the stairs by the hard grip of his hand, opening a door and ushering her inside the chamber that belonged to Brunin and Hawise. When she hung back on the threshold, he pulled her inside, and shut the door with a well-aimed kick. Someone had lit candles in the wall niches and on the pricket by the bed.

"Lord Gilbert has taken de Dinan's chamber for his own, but this one is almost as fine," he said. "We'll be merry here for what's left of the night and you can stay here on the morrow…Indeed, it might be for the best." He gestured toward a flagon and cups standing on a coffer. "Pour wine, will you?"

Marion did as he bid, although her throat was so tight that she knew she would be unable to swallow. When she turned with the cups, he was seated on the bed, watching her through heavy lids. He held out his hand for the wine and she saw that his fingernails were darkly rimmed with blood—like those of the butchers in Ludlow's shambles. Except that the shambles probably didn't exist anymore and the blood was not that of an ox or sheep.

He saw the direction of her stare and smiled. "A warrior's ointment," he said, "but if it displeases you I'll wash it off. I've known women who like to be tupped by a man hot and fresh off the battlefield…but you're not one of them, eh?" He reached for her and she evaded him with a small gasp. Her wine slopped over the rim of her cup and splashed her gown with red.

"Or perhaps you like to play games?" His eyes narrowed lustfully.

"I don't want to play any g-games," Marion said, her voice tight with panic. "You said I would be your true love and chatelaine of Ludlow."

"And you are." He spread his hands. "I came for you, did I not? We have a finely appointed chamber to ourselves. Have I ill-treated you?"

Her hands were shaking. "N-no, but you are not the same as you were."

"Neither are you, sweeting." He went to another flagon

standing on the coffer and tilted water from its lip into a bronze bowl. "I will wash my hands until they are as lily white as your own," he said. "Blood doesn't always show up though, does it?"

"There's some on your face too..." she said unsteadily and tried not to think of what he meant.

"Then wipe it off for me." He splashed his face with a handful of water and tilted his head toward her. "Any lady would do that for her love. Use your sleeve," he said.

Feeling nauseated, she raised her arm and dabbed his cheek with her cuff. He caught her wrist and pulled her against him. "Come," he muttered. "I will teach you a game you'll like."

"I—no—I..."

"How do you know until you've tried it?"

"But we are not wed. It would be a sin!" Fear flooded her limbs. The glance she cast toward the door gave her away for he swung her around so that he was between it and her.

He laughed. "You are worried about sinning after what you have done?"

"I...I did it for you."

"Then you will not balk at whatever else I ask."

"But we should be pledged." She looked up into his face. There was no softness in his expression. His grip on her was tight, almost but not quite painful. The bed loomed in her side vision.

He unpinned her veil and let it drop to the floor. "Sweeting, I would take you before a priest this very night, but they are all too busy ministering to the dead and the dying. I know this is important to you, but those in extremity must come first. It will not matter for a night and a day."

"Then surely it is worth waiting until we have made our vows before witnesses." She quivered in his embrace. When a man removed a woman's head covering, it signified his right as a husband, but she also knew that it was a symbol of a woman stripped of her respectability.

He gave a sigh in which there was irritation. "I'm not a patient man, sweetheart. Strike while the iron is hot is what I say…and my iron's hotter than the heart of a forge. I'll quench it now and pay in the morning."

Those were not the words Marion wanted to hear. Where was the gentleness? Where was the worship and the gratitude? "No," she said in a trembling voice, but her protest was smothered as his mouth came down on hers and it was indeed as hot as a brand. His angled cheek sealed off her nose and she couldn't breathe. His tongue roved her mouth. Suffocating, she beat at him with clenched fists until he pulled back and she was able to take a great gulp of air, her eyes wide with shock and springing with tears.

"Frightened?" He unlatched his belt and let it slide to the floor. "There's no need to be. If you scream it'll be with pleasure." He gestured. "Take off your gown. It would be a pity to ruin it."

"I am virgin still," she said in a shaking voice.

"I'll make allowances. After tonight it won't be an obstacle."

"I…I don't want to. I want to see Lord Gilbert."

"Too late." He shrugged out of his hauberk. "If you go out of that door, what do you think will happen to you? The men are still half wild and, like it or not, you're a spoil of war. Whatever your claim to high birth, when all is said and done you are a maid of the chamber and fair game to be passed from soldier to soldier. You need my protection." He stood straight, his hair ruffled from the removal of the mail shirt. "You have my ring, you have my brooch; soon you'll have my seed. Those are pledges enough. It's too late to have second thoughts about becoming a nun."

Marion began to sob. Ernalt tugged off his tunic and the smell of his battle sweat reeked in the air. He unlaced her gown, his fingers hard and deft, and dragged the garment over her head. Her chemise followed, leaving her naked to his stare, save for her hose and shoes. His eyes raked her from head to toe, but lingered at the juncture of her thighs. "As fair as your hair," he said. "I have a fancy to be a coney in your cornfield."

He laid her down on the bed, his breathing suddenly rapid

and harsh. Marion's sobs were locked in her chest as his weight fastened her down and his mouth seized her breath. The roughness of his hose and braies scratched her thighs. Her jaw was strained by the grinding strength of his. She had wished for this, had dreamed of it with need, fascination, and fear for as long as she could remember, and now that the moment was at hand, the need had turned to rejection and the fear was terror.

Ernalt braced himself on one hand and reached down between them, fumbling at his braies. She knew what he was doing. She had glimpsed grooms in the stables taking a piss, had observed drunken couplings at Shrewsbury Fair. She also had a distant recollection of seeing her parents, of being frightened of the strange, pained sounds they made. The memory assaulted her now, for Ernalt was making some of the same sounds as her father, and her own stifled whimpers were just like her mother's.

She felt a hot nudge against her thigh and then higher, against the soft, secret part of her: the womb passage that bled each month except when a woman was with child, when all the blood was stored up and came in one disastrous, carmine rush. Ernalt forced his way inside her and the pain was excruciating…This must be what it was like to give birth, save in reverse. Instead of pushing a child out, she was being riven by a monster forcing its way in.

The pain was so sharp that it took her voice and all that emerged was a hoarse crow. Ernalt cursed, withdrew, moistened himself with saliva and thrust again. Marion stared at the roof as he had his way. At first each heave of his buttocks caused such rending agony that she thought she would split asunder, but after a while her bruised flesh grew numb and it was only at the crest of each thrust that she felt a twisting pain in the small of her spine. Was this love? Was this what the troubadours sang about in their lyrics? It was a deception…or perhaps a deserved punishment for her betrayal.

His movements grew jerky and swift and he sought her lips,

grinding his mouth down on hers, filling her voiceless throat with his groan as he spilled himself in her.

When he withdrew, he looked down at himself. "You were right," he said. "You were a virgin."

She closed her eyes, frightened to look in case there was an ocean of blood. Brunin and Hawise's wedding sheet had been no reassurance. There was a seeping heat between her thighs and she was too terrified to move.

"Don't worry. You'll grow to like it."

She felt his weight sag the mattress beside her and heard him yawn. "I can't sleep for long; my lord will want to see me soon enough. A couple of hours will have to suffice." He yawned again. "Don't think about leaving. You're mine now, and you'd not get far."

Within seconds he was asleep, his breathing stertorous and rough. Marion placed her hand over her belly. The ache in her back was deep and grinding and she feared that she was mortally wounded. How could she flee when she hardly dared to move? Besides, his earlier warning had made it clear what would happen to her if she did leave his protection. Slowly, gingerly, she sat up and looked at the sheet. What she saw almost caused her to faint. Blood streaked her thighs and pooled on the sheet, although there was less than at the time of her flux. There were smears on the linen where he had wiped himself. For a long time she could do nothing but stare and shake, but finally the trembling eased and she stumbled from the bed. With cold, clumsy fingers she struggled into her chemise and gown. It took a long time for she was trembling violently and it was hard to see through her tears. Her veil she left on the floor. There was no point in putting it on. Veils were for respectable women and she was a whore.

❖❖❖

Brunin and Hawise joined the wedding celebrations, eating their fill of roast mutton and batter pudding cooked in the drippings from the roasts, and followed by fruits stewed in honey. Hawise gave the bride the silver fillets from her own braids and, beneath his wife's amused, knowing gaze, Brunin presented the groom with the coins he had had in his pouch. The villagers' estimation of their new overlords rose when Brunin proved that he could converse in simple English, and Hawise abetted him. The guests, being young newlyweds themselves, also went a long way to securing the people's seal of approval. When Hawise and Brunin joined in the dance of the handfasting carole and knew the movements, it brought shouts and claps of approval.

"That was good fortune," Brunin said as he and Hawise rode homeward, leaving the villagers to continue their celebration. "They were able to see us as more than just demanding landlords." He laughed. "My grandmother would have a seizure if she could see us. Consorting with peasants only leads to the rot of natural order, she says."

"But you count it worth the silver in your pouch?" she asked with a mischievous smile.

"As much as you count it worth your hair ornaments."

Hawise fingered the bare end of her braid. "I am sure that my husband will buy me some more."

He snorted. "With what? Besides, I have yet to claim recompense for you making me hand over a bride-gift in the first place."

She gave him a sultry look through her lashes and said nothing.

As they rode through the woods, Brunin became aware that Jester's pace had grown uneven. The horse was well rested and Brunin had not stretched him beyond a trot. Since they were near the hut in the forest, he rode up to it, drew rein, and dismounted.

"What's wrong?" Hawise slipped from her mare's saddle and looked anxiously at him.

"Nothing, I hope." Brunin ran his hand down Jester's foreleg and picked up the hoof. "A stone." He reached to his belt knife and, straddling the gelding's foreleg, dug out the offending chip of flint. "It's probably bruised the frog, but no lasting damage."

Hawise had tethered her mare to a stump standing near the woodpile. "I wonder if this has ever been a trysting place," she murmured. Leaning against the doorpost, she gave him another look from beneath her lids.

His groin was suddenly as hot and heavy as a lead ingot. He sheathed his knife, tethered Jester beside the mare, and, setting his hand to Hawise's waist, drew her inside the hut. "It is now," he said. It smelled of must and fungus, of earth and old smoke, and it was exciting because it was so different from the formality of a bed in the keep.

He unfastened his cloak and laid it over a pile of old bracken in the corner. "My grandmother would have a second seizure if she knew," he grinned.

"A good thing then that she's ignorant," Hawise murmured, her hand busy between them, stroking him to a pitch where he thought he would burst. He brought her down with him onto the bed of cloak and bracken. "And that I know when to keep my mouth open...and when to shut it..."

It was too hot to last more than a few moments, but the intensity was so blinding that he felt as if the marrow had been sucked from his bones. Hawise lay beneath him and, running her fingers through his hair, took satisfaction beyond her own from the pleasure she had given him. He was never more hers than when she had him to herself, like this. They dozed awhile, rolled together in the fur-lined warmth of his cloak, and woke to kiss and touch lightly, both of them stretching out the moment yet knowing that soon it must end. Even so, it was almost dusk before they continued homeward and the setting sun on the tree trunks burned the late afternoon with the colors of fire. The world had a weird, mysterious light, as if they had suddenly crossed into the land of faery.

"You have a leaf in your hair," Hawise said languorously.

He smiled and, teasing it out, scattered it from his fingers. "Oak," he said and refrained from remarking that her wimple was a touch disordered and the ends of her braids looked like foxtails. He rather liked the dishabille and he didn't want her to fuss.

By the time they came in sight of Alveston's palisade, the sun had set, the sky was turquoise and cold, and the moon was rising. Smoke drifted from the manor house louvres and torchlight shone in the auxiliary dwellings. They had barely started on the path to the main gate when one of the guards detached himself from his duty post and ran toward them.

"Now we'll have to pay for dallying so long," Brunin said out of the side of his mouth. "What's the betting they've been about to send out a search party."

"Sir, my lady." The guard drew level with their mounts and the expression on his face banished all levity from Brunin's. This was no matter of greeting tardy strays. His immediate thought was that something had happened to his father, or that his grandmother had succumbed to the seizure about which they had been jesting.

"What is it, man? *Speak!*"

The soldier took a deep breath. His eyes flickered between Brunin and Hawise as if unsure where to settle. "It's Ludlow, sir. Gilbert de Lacy's taken the castle and fired the town."

# 32

*S*YBILLA STARED AT THE ROW OF STITCHES. SHE COULD NOT remember sewing them, but the evidence of her eyes was testament to her industry. She was like Marion, mindlessly seaming garments as if the lines of thread held the meaning of life. She wondered if Marion was dead. She also wondered if the girl had had any part in Ludlow's overthrow. Reports were scattered and unclear. All that was known for certain was that Gilbert de Lacy had taken both town and castle in a single night of blood and fire.

"I was a young bride when I came to Ludlow," Sybilla told Sibbi and Hawise who had arrived with their husbands at Joscelin's call to arms. She gazed out of the window. From the high chamber at their manor of Stanton, where they had moved from Hartland, she could see the sheep grazing the harvested fields and watch an autumn wind tossing the trees. "It had a wooden palisade then and the towers were only half built, but I was still bursting with pride that such a place should be mine."

"Mama…" At a loss for words, Hawise touched her arm. Everyone was still reeling from the news of Ludlow's loss. Reality was like a blurred piece of window glass, thick and distorted.

"There were times when the war came so close that I thought we would lose everything, but we held on and I thought we had survived." She gave a tremulous sigh. "Now I am old, and what pride I had..." She broke off and with a shake of her head picked up her needle, but her eyes were too full to sew.

"We'll win it back," Hawise said fiercely. "Papa has sent an appeal to the King and our vassals are rallying daily to our banner."

Sybilla nodded. "Yes," she said, her voice tight with the effort of controlling tears, "we'll win it back, but when I think of the struggle when I thought that struggling was over, I feel very tired." She turned as Joscelin entered the room and immediately pushed her lips into the semblance of a smile. It was one thing to unburden herself to her daughters who, as women, were fellow conspirators, another to expose her weaknesses to her husband, who needed her strength.

His tread was heavy as he crossed to the flagon and poured himself a cup of wine. The years that usually sat so lightly on him were now a visible weight. He too, she thought, was growing old and tired. It was a terrifying thought.

"There is news," he said and took a deep drink.

And not good, she could tell. Abandoning her needlework, she went to him. "Tell me."

He looked into the depths of his cup. "Several of our vassals have renounced their oath to me and chosen to declare for de Lacy."

She winced and asked him for names. When he gave them, she was disappointed but not surprised. Even during the settled times there had been opposition to their tenure of Ludlow. Her claim was on the distaff side and his was through marriage to her. Nor had they produced sons to follow them, only sons-in-law, and not every man was keen to follow a FitzWarin or a Plugenet. "They do not matter," she said. "William de Criquetot and Walter Devereux were always weak reeds. We have other, loyal men to call upon."

He conceded the point with a shrug and another cup of wine. "We'll be ready to march on Ludlow by the morrow," he said. "The less time de Lacy has to become entrenched, the better. FitzWarin has a troop waiting at Alberbury, and he's called in support from all of his vassals."

She could feel him going through tallies in his head, collating, thinking, planning. Once such crises had been challenges to meet or cunningly circumnavigate. Once. When they were younger. Sybilla drew herself up. Maudlin self-pity would solve nothing and she would not add to Joscelin's burden by weeping. "I will write again to the King," she said. "And Bishop Gilbert will add his words to mine. Henry must act on this matter."

"And who knows which way Henry will jump," Joscelin said bleakly.

❖❖❖

In the cramped side chamber allotted to himself and Hawise, Brunin was examining the rings in his hauberk for split or damaged links. His hands were black from the iron and grease, and his gaze intent on his task. Hawise wondered if it were a little like her mother's sewing: a mindless repetitive action that served to pacify frayed and querulous energy. Her own habit was pacing, a trait that she had inherited from her father. The thought of him made her lengthen her stride until she came up short against the chamber wall.

"It has hit my father hard that men who have sworn him fealty have renounced their allegiance and given it to de Lacy," she said.

He looked up from his inspection. "There have always been pockets of sympathy within the ranks of his vassals for Gilbert de Lacy. They would rather have the direct line rule them than a woman with a Breton husband."

Flushed with indignation, Hawise turned from the wall to face him. "But Gilbert de Lacy's line has not ruled here for more than fifty years!"

"That makes no difference in some men's eyes," Brunin said. "Whittington was given to my grandparents on their marriage by the Earl of Derby, long before your mother came into possession of Ludlow, but the span of years has not prevented Roger and Jonas de Powys from taking it...and King Henry from upholding their claim."

Hawise sat down beside him. "I thought I understood how you and your family felt when Whittington was lost," she said, "but I didn't have an inkling...until now."

"And how does it feel to be the landless wife of an impoverished knight?"

She drew herself erect. "We're neither landless nor impoverished."

"But considerably less well off than we were." He rippled the mail through his fingers to inspect the next section. "Our forefathers possessed only their swords and their wits—or mine did. But it's a heavy price to pay in pride." His tone was neutral, his face blank, which told her that he was affected more deeply than he was willing to admit.

"You will always have that." Her glance fell on the furled black wolf banner.

He followed the direction of her gaze. "Yes," he said somberly. "That can't be taken."

For a while there was silence as he continued to work his way through the hauberk. Hawise rose, began pacing, stopped herself, and folded her arms before she was tempted to chew her fingernails. On the morrow he would ride with her father and FitzWarin to Ludlow. Having seen him in battle, she was afraid for him.

Her flux had begun on the night that they received the news about Ludlow. Either naturally late or a bleed brought on by the shock of the tidings, no one could say, but all she knew was that she was not pregnant. They had tonight to conceive a child, and then he would be gone to war. For a moment she considered pushing the hauberk aside and falling upon him in broad daylight. However, there was no more than a curtain across the chamber doorway—and they might be interrupted by anyone, including her father and Emmeline.

Brunin shifted the mail again, searched, and then looked up at her. "Your father heard news other than the defection of his vassals," he said. "Has he told you about Marion?"

"He has said nothing. What of her?" Her stomach turned over. "Has something happened to her? Is she dead?"

"To him she is," Brunin said grimly. "It seems that she let a rope down from the Pendover tower wall and allowed de Lacy's men to tie a ladder to it. She kept watch while they did it…" He paused and looked down at the dark iron rivets and she knew that he was holding back.

"What else? *Tell me!*" she demanded.

His mouth twisted. "You will not like to hear this. Ernalt de Lysle has taken our chamber for his own and installed Marion there as his whore."

The cold feeling increased. The notion of Ernalt de Lysle and Marion sporting in her marriage bed was so vile that Hawise almost retched.

"I thought about saying nothing," Brunin admitted. "But if we regain Ludlow, you would see and hear for yourself."

"I will burn the bed and the sheets and scrub the walls with lye," she spat vehemently and returned to her pacing, but the room was not large enough to contain her turmoil. She felt as if she had been violated and was certain what she would do to Marion if she ever came within strangling range.

Brunin set the hauberk aside, wiped his hands on a linen rag, and halted her wild stride by taking her in his arms. She gripped his sleeves, digging in her fingers as if seeking a handhold on reason.

"God help me, I want to see both of them dead!" She pressed her forehead against his breast, tears spilling. "How can it have come to this?"

She felt his palms against her spine, firm, strong, steadying. "When I first came to Ludlow, Marion greeted me as if I were a prince, not some dubious changeling with a common mercenary for a grandsire. To have that sort of adoration was balm on the raw places…" He shook his head. "And now new places are raw."

Hawise lifted her head from his breast and saw the revulsion, anger, and sadness in his face. If only for a moment, and with her, the neutrality was gone, and she was glad of it, for it made her feel less unworthy.

"Why did she do it?" she asked. "How could she?"

"For love," he said. "Or for love denied."

"Love!"

"You saw how she sought it: like a drunkard craving wine." There was an odd note to his voice. "I know because it could have been me."

Hawise's throat tightened. "That's not true."

"I held back; she ran forward. That's the only difference. Pretending you don't need, or admitting you do: which is the more honest?"

She frowned. "But if I were your father's enemy and I asked you to put a ladder over the castle wall in the dead of night, would you do it?"

"No, I wouldn't."

"Not even for love?"

"No, because duty and loyalty would hold me in check. Marion has a conflict of duty with your family. She thinks that they have abandoned her...that they do not love her as Ernalt de Lysle loves her."

"And for certain he does not!" Hawise said abruptly. "He loves himself and the notion of glory and—"

"You do not need to tell me about the true nature of Ernalt de Lysle," Brunin growled. "But he has the gilded charm to make women fall for him, and a plausible tongue."

Hawise blushed and dropped her eyelids. That was all too true. There but for the grace of God...

"Marion was ripe to fall into his hand." A look of reluctant compassion crossed Brunin's face. "Despite what she has done, I cannot help but pity her."

"We should have watched her more closely," Hawise said, not certain that she could find pity in her own heart at the moment.

"Hindsight is a hard taskmaster. None of us realized how desperate she was."

"What will happen to her when we retake Ludlow?"

Brunin pulled her closely against his body. "That will be for your father to say, and I am glad I am not him." He brushed a loose strand of hair away from her face and his expression was bleak. "Whatever he decides, he will still be more merciful to her than Ernalt de Lysle."

# 33

$\mathcal{M}$ ARION OPENED HER EYES. SHE WAS ALONE IN THE BED, BUT the feather mattress still bore the indentation of Ernalt's body and when she touched the sheet it was warm. Leaning up on her elbow, she winced at the morning through her tangled hair. Her mouth was dry and tasted foul and a blinding headache pounded her skull like an internal fist. She had no recollection of the previous night...or only as far as the second flagon of wine. Matters had grown hazy then, before blurring into oblivion. The fact that she was naked and that there were red suck marks on her breasts and finger-shaped bruises on her thighs revealed what the night had held.

"You're awake then," Ernalt grunted. "Christ, I've seen better-looking harridans." He moved into her line of vision, already dressed in shirt, hose, and braies.

"Why don't you bed with one of them then?"

"I've thought about it, sweetheart." He plucked his tunic off the coffer and tugged it over his head. "But then you'd have to find somewhere else to sleep and I doubt you'd like the company half so well as mine."

Marion sat up. Her stomach was rolling like a barrel in a flood. She was too queasy to retort. Besides, she had learned that a wrong answer would result in a slap. Never to the face, of course. He didn't want her appearing in the hall with black eyes or a split lip.

That kind of abuse was for the common men. More to the point, Gilbert de Lacy would have frowned on such uncouth behavior.

"Get yourself cleaned up." Latching his belt, Ernalt advanced to the bed and patted her cheek, his fingers hard enough to sting, although not leave a mark. "Your face is your fortune—that, and the sweetest, tightest scabbard in which I've ever sheathed my sword. Remember that, and you'll do well."

"But you love me...don't you?" she pleaded. If he loved her, everything would be all right.

"Yes," he said. "Of course I love you."

His tone was impatient but at least he had said the words. She wanted to ask him about their betrothal, but she didn't want to provoke his anger. He had assured her that they would kneel before a priest, but he desired her to have a proper wedding with a grand feast and many guests. Marion desired that too, but sooner rather than later. She needed to be his wife, not his whore.

Leaving the bed, she realized she was still drunk, for the world tipped and reeled and when she took a step she almost fell. She had a raging thirst that she knew could only be cured by more wine. Last night's flagon was still on the coffer, but contained naught save sticky dregs. Attendants would provide Ernalt with a flagon if he commanded, but it was different for her. She might have given de Lacy's men a way into the castle, but that did not mean they viewed her as a heroine for the deed. Many of them saw it as just another example of the duplicity of women. When she walked through the castle it was as if she did not exist. The soldiers avoided meeting her gaze and stood aside when she passed, as if even the air surrounding her were tainted. Lord Gilbert's servants ignored her when possible. Those of Lord Joscelin's who remained in Ludlow shunned her with hatred in their eyes. If she wanted wine, she would have to fetch her own and run the gauntlet of all those unspoken words.

She tottered into the latrine and sat down on the wooden seat. Her head throbbed and the smell of the waste shaft almost sent her delicate stomach over the edge. "Jesu," she moaned softly. She could hear Ernalt moving about in the main chamber. He was whistling to himself, which meant that he was currently as satisfied with his life as she was wretched in hers.

As she was leaving the latrine, the sound of a hunting horn wound through the open shutters. Ernalt ceased whistling and turned toward the sound with pricked ears.

"What is it? What's wr—"

He made a peremptory gesture. "Be quiet."

She held her breath and the horn came again, three sharp blasts from the direction of the gates.

Ernalt swore. He strode to the door, heaved it open, and bellowed for an attendant.

She stared at him with widening eyes. "What's happening? Tell me!"

"How should I know? It's the alarm horn." He was already unfastening his belt and lifting his gambeson off the clothing pole. "Likely Joscelin de Dinan has come for a second fight beneath the walls. If he has, he'll die." Striding to the door, he flung it open and bellowed for a squire.

Marion set her hand to her breast as her heart began to pound. If Joscelin retook Ludlow, she was doomed. If he failed, then she had the chance of a life…but what kind? She was already reeling beneath the weight of her conscience. If she had to look upon Joscelin's body…or Brunin's…Uttering a small cry, she fled back into the latrine and hung over the fetid hole, retching.

❖❖❖

"I told you, there is nothing wrong with me," FitzWarin growled. "Christ's wounds, can't a man cough and spit without being fussed over like an old woman! I'll let you know when I'm ready for the grave. In the meantime, you can stop scowling like that and pass my gambeson."

Brunin didn't stop scowling, but did as his father asked. They were camped in the remnants of a hill fort that had been occupied by outlaws for a time during the wars between Stephen and Matilda. Autumn mist floated knee-deep over the land and there was a dampness in the air that was aggravating his father's weakened chest. Not that FitzWarin would admit to such weakness. As far as he was concerned, a cough that made him sound as if his lungs were full of rusty nails was a minor inconvenience.

"You are stubborn," Brunin said.

"Hah, since when has that been a failing of the FitzWarins? You'll need every ounce of your own before we've finished if we're to have Ludlow and Whittington restored. Neither are going to be handed to you on a trencher." FitzWarin's lips thinned. "I will do what I must, as will you."

In silence Brunin helped him don his armor. He had not realized how thin his father had become, but now, standing close, pulling padding over unfleshed shoulders, tugging the mail shirt over the gambeson, he felt as if he were dressing an old man, and not the proud, muscular warrior who had filled his childhood with a mingling of fear and admiration. The best years had gone, Brunin thought. The world was autumnal and looking toward winter. It was not the frame of mind with which to approach the task in hand. He set his jaw and with brisk efficiency finished performing the duties of a squire. Better not to think at all except on a purely practical level.

FitzWarin nodded brusque thanks and a brief, intense look passed between father and son, saying much that would never be openly acknowledged. "Fasten up your ventail," FitzWarin said gruffly. "You don't want to take a spear in the throat. I intend to have six sons remaining at the end of this day."

"Who is fussing now?" Brunin asked with a smile, moving to buckle his throat protector.

"Don't be insolent," FitzWarin said, but his lips twitched.

Joscelin was waiting for them outside the tent, fully armed. The steam from his cup of hot ale rose into the cold air. A red sun was lipping the horizon to the east and the soldiers were finishing their dawn meals of bread and bacon. A groom brought up his destrier, a hot-blooded sorrel, twitchy with oat-feeding, its hooves dancing a drumbeat in the moist grass.

FitzWarin eyed the beast dubiously. "You hear of old men trying to recapture their youth with disreputable women and wild horses," he said.

Joscelin gave a fierce grin and finished the hot ale in several large gulps. "And how you envy them," he retorted. "Do you know any disreputable women?"

"Plenty, but none that I'd pass on to you." FitzWarin turned aside to cough and spit.

"Selfish bastard." Joscelin went to the sorrel and slapped its glossy neck. "I intend taking every advantage I can get," he said. "And a young, spirited stallion is one of them. I'm experienced enough to control him. It's the wild young men who need the steadier horses...isn't that so, Brunin?"

"Yes, sire," Brunin said neutrally as their own attendants arrived with his father's bay and Jester, the latter sloping along in his usual world-weary fashion.

"It will be like old times," Joscelin said, his tone overhearty. "Do you remember when we rode together for the Empress Matilda and none could stand against us?"

FitzWarin grunted. "Yes, I remember. There is no need to jolly along these old bones. They know the tune of their own accord." Turning to his destrier, FitzWarin set his foot in the stirrup and swung astride with the ease of a lifelong horseman. "And I can still dance the steps as fast as any man living, and faster than those I've killed." He reined his stallion about. "Come, let us ride and recoup these lands of yours, for our grandchildren."

Brunin mounted Jester and fell in behind his father and Joscelin. He unfurled the wolf banner and watched it catch and float in the morning breeze before handing it to a serjeant. Ralf rode up to join him on his gray, his handsome face wearing a morose expression. As they passed the baggage lines, his gaze swept to a woman standing outside one of the tents. Her face was pale and her eyes red, but she was not weeping. Brunin glanced too.

"I know I should not have brought her," Ralf said quickly, "but her father disowned her when he heard that she had taken up with a Sais, and I could not have sent her alone to Alberbury...not with our grandmother there."

Brunin stemmed the retort that Ralf should know better than to bring his leman to a battle-camp. As his brother said, what else was he supposed to do? "Lady Sybilla will need more women for her chamber," he murmured, "and Hawise would gladly take her under her wing. She is short of companions."

Ralf's fair complexion reddened. "I am not looking for charity," he muttered.

"And I wouldn't offer it," Brunin retorted. "I do it not from charity, but because I know she would suit."

"She is Welsh..."

Brunin shrugged. "What of it? So is Emmeline's nurse. So's Madoc the groom."

"I thought after what had happened to Whittington..."

Brunin shook his head at his brother. "Ralf, you're an ass," he said, "and I almost love you."

Ralf gave him an offended look. "There's no need to be insulting."

The road to a battle wasn't particularly a place for mirth, but Brunin threw back his head and laughed.

❖❖❖

In Ludlow's great hall, the women were preparing to receive and treat the wounded. Marion ran a strip of linen bandage through her fingers. The fabric was soft and yellowed with age and had once been a swaddling band. She knew that the other women were looking at her. Their eyes pricked her like needles. Most of them were de Lacy's camp followers, but a few Ludlow women had remained. No one actually said "whore" but she knew what they were thinking. She wanted to shout into their scornful faces that Ernalt was going to marry her as soon as Joscelin de

Dinan had been defeated—that she would make them pay for their contempt.

"Swaddling bands eh?" One of the women pointed to the linen in Marion's hands. "Best keep some back, wench, you'll likely be needing them."

Marion looked haughtily down her nose. Griselde was a knight's wife, but as common as tripe despite her rank. She had protruding teeth and a way of sucking saliva through them that made Marion feel sick.

"Still," Griselde said with a gesture of her large, mannish hands, "if you give your knight a big belly, that might tempt him to the altar."

"He wants us to have a great wedding," Marion deigned to reply. "We are waiting until Lord Gilbert has Ludlow for certain."

The woman snorted. "If he were as smitten as you seem to think, he'd have had you before a priest on the first night. Instead, he merely had you, didn't he, my love?" She laughed at her own humor.

Marion flushed with rage. "You'll regret saying that."

The woman's eyes brightened with scorn. "No, wench, the regret will be yours. You're not the first to be taken in by comely looks and false words and you'll not be the last—especially where that knave is concerned."

"That's not true!" Marion cried. "You are jealous because you've got a face like a horse and no man will look at you."

Griselde chuckled at the insult. "Yes," she said. "I may have a face like a horse, but it's the ride that matters, not the looks of the animal. Most men would jump at the chance to straddle a winsome filly like you, but for the long distances they return to the plodding mares with the comfortable saddles and big, childbearing backsides." She slapped her own hefty rump. "I've known Ernalt de Lysle since he was a brat setting fire to cats' tails and practicing archery on the yard hens. There's one of the village girls has a daughter she claims is his, but he won't acknowledge it. And one of Lady Amabel's maids had to be sent to a nunnery."

Marion's hands were shaking. "Did he give either of them a gold ring?" she demanded in a seething voice. "Did he give either of them a brooch?"

"No, only shortened girdles...but then they didn't have access to a castle."

"Griselde, that's enough; let her be," said one of the other women.

Griselde shrugged. "She needs to hear some home truths." She looked at Marion. "Good luck to you, girl. Whether he marries you or not, you'll need it."

Marion wiped her hands on the swaddling band and tossed it aside. Griselde was just jealous and lying to upset her. Ernalt meant it; he was going to marry her. She would not think about her flux. It was due and would arrive at any day. She recognized the signs from the soreness of her breasts and the bloated feeling in her stomach. She was not with child; she knew she wasn't.

From outside there came a sudden flurry of yelled commands and a stench of fatty smoke gusted through the open shutters of the hall windows. A maidservant screamed in fear and several of the women exchanged nervous glances.

"It has begun." Griselde scowled around at the others. "Why are you all looking like frightened mice? This is what sorts the true garrison wives from the limp ninnies."

Marion glared at Griselde, hating her. Once she was wed to Ernalt and in a position of authority at Ludlow, she would have the sow thrown out.

The stench grew stronger and the first casualty was carried in, an arrow sunk deep in his shoulder.

"Bastards have fired the gates with brushwood and pig fat," he gasped through bared teeth. "They're going to break through!"

Marion ran from the hall, uncaring whether the others thought her a "limp ninny" or not. The vision of the men of Ludlow bursting into the keep and wreaking their vengeance filled her with terror. They wouldn't stay their hands for the sake of her womanhood; nor would Ernalt be spared. She thought of the killing that had gone on when, with her help, Ernalt and de Lacy had stolen into the castle—the shrouded corpses lining the wall by the well—and her stomach rebelled. She clung to the wall near the kitchens, retching. Each breath she drew between spasms was filled with the reek of burning. Her ears were assaulted by the clash of hard battle: shouts of command; the excited rage of battle cries; the screams of wounded men and horses. She straightened and swallowed, trying to stem the convulsing of her stomach. Thrusting her fingers in her ears to dull the sounds of battle, she ran for the safety of the chamber she knew she should never have left. Once within, she bolted the door and pushed a heavy coffer in front of it. The effort bruised her thighs and set deep furrow marks in the palms of her hands but she did not notice. All she cared about was shutting out the world so that it couldn't reach her. When her barricade was done, she crawled to the far side of the bed where the shadows were darkest and curled against the wall in a fetal huddle, a bolster over her head.

❖❖❖

On seeing Joscelin's approach, Gilbert de Lacy had sent soldiers to the attack—Welsh and Irish mercenaries, Brunin had judged by some of their outmoded apparel and the preponderance of facial hair and bare legs.

Joscelin had brought up siege machines—rams and perriers and ladders—and also a cart containing barrels of soft, white lard and a pile of rancid, fatty hams. Even in the autumnal cold, the smell was stomach-turning. It had been difficult, dangerous work piling dry furze and barrels of fat against the tightly closed gatehouse doors while arrows whined overhead and de Lacy's men made constant, destructive sorties. Despite the efforts of Joscelin's own archers to keep the men on the battlements pinned down, several de Dinan men were struck. But, finally, the kindling was in place and blazing torches were hurled into the noxious pile to set it alight and burn through an opening to the bailey. Out of arrow range, Joscelin's serjeants waited with the iron-shod battering ram. On the wall the defenders frantically tried to hurl cauldrons of water down on the gates, but were vulnerable to Joscelin's bowmen. Such water as struck the spot hissed away to steam and caused the black smoke to boil up as if from the mouth of hell, driving back attacker and defender alike.

When the smoke was on the cusp of dying down, Joscelin sent in the ram to pound the burning timbers. The sound of the great iron head hammering on the oak was like grounded thunder and the head of the ram itself grew as hot as a sword blade on a smith's anvil. The solid boom reverberated through Brunin's body. Jester's ears flickered and he sidled. Brunin drew his sword and licked his lips. When the gates gave, the fighting would begin in earnest.

"I never thought when I saw those gates hung that I would be the one assaulting them," Joscelin said as he swung into the saddle and adjusted the wyvern shield on his left arm.

FitzWarin rode up on his other side. "Why should you?" His voice was raw and cracked with coughing. "It was treachery from within that caused this, and at a time when you might reasonably be thinking of a peaceful old age."

Joscelin gave a bitter laugh. "The only peace I've known has been snatched out of the hands of war like a starving dog seizing bread from a campfire and wolfing it down. I had more time for peace during Stephen and Matilda's dispute than I have had since Henry assumed the throne."

From within the heart of the fire came a splintering crack as the gate timbers gave beneath the battering head of the ram. They could hear the defenders yelling as they tried frantically to shore up the imminent breach. Again and again the ram struck at the weakening timbers and suddenly a jagged hole opened up. Soon there was a gap large enough for a horse and rider to charge through. Brunin drew on the reins, thrust his shoulder behind the shield, drew his sword, and spurred Jester into the mouth of hell. Reeking black smoke filled his lungs and stung his eyes. Someone came at him from the right side and he cut hard with the sword, feeling the edge connect and bite. His opponent screamed and went down, but another immediately took his place.

De Lacy's men swarmed to defend the broached entrance. A near-spent arrow lodged in Brunin's mail, another whizzed past his helm. The archer was brought down by one of the de Dinan bowmen. He saw his father and Ralf battling with several knights and spurred Jester to their aid, but before he could reach them, his rein was seized by a serjeant. Brunin hacked downward, aiming for his opponent's collar bone, and was rewarded by a grunt of pain, but the soldier held on and wrenched Brunin from the saddle. Jester skittered sideways, reins trailing. Brunin landed hard and felt white pain surge through his shield shoulder. The serjeant leaned over him, dagger in hand. Brunin kicked out and punched with his sword hand. The serjeant reeled and Brunin grabbed his dropped sword, scrambled to his feet, and attacked. His shield arm was numb, and he knew that he had only one swift chance if he were going to live. Dagger in one hand, sword in the other, the serjeant had no shield either. Brunin aimed for his legs as the most vulnerable part of his body, for they were unprotected. Twice the serjeant parried the blows. The third time, Brunin cut him down, but received a dagger slash that partially opened the healing scar from Wales.

Brunin staggered over to Jester and caught the trailing reins in his bloody right hand. Clenching his teeth, he set his foot in the stirrup and gained the saddle. Two serjeants came at him and he reined out of their way, knowing that if they managed to position themselves one either side, he was finished. He dug his heels into Jester's flanks and urged the gelding out of the fray. The air was cloudy with powdered lime that had been thrown by both attackers and defenders, burning the throat, flaying the eyes. He spurred Jester through the flaming gateway and cantered to where Joscelin's chirugeon had set up his post. The chirugeon was bending over FitzWarin, who was sitting on the ground, his chest harshly rattling as he fought to breathe. Brunin's vision contracted down to that single sight. He thrust his feet from the stirrups and leaped from the horse. Pain tore through his shoulder, but he scarcely noticed it. Ralf had removed his helm and was kneeling at their father's side, pale fingers of lime streaking his cheeks. As Brunin crouched beside him, Ralf raised streaming, anguished eyes.

"A lime jar exploded against the brow-band of his helm," he said, "and he breathed in the powder...He's been coughing ever since."

"I have tried to make him swallow milk," the chirugeon said, "but I fear to small avail."

Brunin stared at his father's scarlet, almost purple complexion, the blue lips, the struggle for air. "Where's the priest?" he demanded, glaring around.

Despite his desperate condition, the last word galvanized FitzWarin to his feet. "No!" he choked. "Not...dead...yet...Tell you...when...I want a priest..." Raising the chirugeon's horn of milk to his lips, he spluttered the potion down in an astonishing testament to the strength of will over the body's frailty.

❖ ❖ ❖

Encroaching nightfall streaked the sky with bands of gray-purple. From Ludlow the sound of horns blaring the retreat was sweet to the ears of the exhausted attackers, for it was de Lacy who was sounding them, but, with darkness imminent, Joscelin could not pursue the assault and the gains he had made had cost his men dear in life and limb. He too was forced to pull back and consolidate. He positioned soldiers in the taken gatehouse, fully aware that on the morrow the fight would begin again to take the core of the castle.

FitzWarin's breathing had eased somewhat, but remained a ragged, bubbling wheeze, and it was obvious that he could neither fight on, nor command men. The chirugeon had clucked his tongue over Brunin's hand and restitched the wound, washing it in mead and then smearing it with beaten egg white before applying a bandage. The shoulder he had shrugged over. It wasn't broken, but there was sufficient damage for it to be unwise to bear a shield for a week at least.

Brunin was sitting outside their temporary shelter, eating bread he didn't really want in order to keep up his strength, when Joscelin came to see him. Wine—which he did want—was rationed. No one could afford to be drunk tonight. He nodded over his shoulder into the tent where FitzWarin was resting, propped up against blankets and bolsters to aid his breathing. "He is awake if you want to speak to him," he said. "I do not think that he dares to sleep lest he does not wake again." He took a fast mouthful of the wine, remembered that he was moderating himself, and let it go down his throat in small swallows.

Joscelin gave him a direct look, his flint-gray eyes filled with sadness. "I am sorry," he said.

Brunin glanced toward the walls of Ludlow. The stench from the burned-out gates overlaid the comforting smoke of their watchfires. "So am I."

A vast ocean of meaning was contained in the six words they had exchanged, most of it too dark and painful to articulate.

"How's the shoulder?"

Brunin began to shrug and stopped. "Better than the hand," he said, then looked inquiringly at Joscelin.

"I am unscathed." Joscelin tried to laugh, but the sound fell far short. "The devil's luck, so my enemies have always said. Who knows, perhaps they're right." He ducked into the tent. Brunin took another slow swallow of wine and bent his head. The heat from the campfire throbbed through his hand. He thought of Hawise with a longing that was almost desperation.

❖ ❖ ❖

Joscelin sat down on the low campstool at FitzWarin's bedside. As always such furniture appeared to have been made for a smaller frame than his: his knees were up around his elbows. FitzWarin was propped up on blankets and bolsters which had been padded around the backrest of his shield. His breathing was labored and his eyes were closed.

Slowly he lifted his lids. "It's you," he said in a voice that was like the harsh scrape of besom twigs across a clay floor. The faintest of smiles curved his blue-tinged lips. "I thought for a moment that fool boy had gone and fetched the priest."

"No, it's me. And that 'fool boy' as you call him has proven his mettle time and again today." Joscelin returned the smile. "Perhaps we are the fools."

FitzWarin snorted. "My seed gave him life; you raised him. What chance does he have?"

Joscelin chuckled reluctantly, acknowledging the sally. "More than us," he said. "He is married to Hawise, and she is her mother's daughter without a doubt." Then he sobered. They both knew that the banter was a cover for deeper, unspoken emotions.

"And he receives half of Ludlow...whatever's left of it."

"Gates and towers can be rebuilt." Joscelin gave a shrug, as if it did not matter...but it did.

FitzWarin's gaze followed a late-season moth as it fluttered around the tent, creating fuzzy shadows on the linen sides. "But first they have to be retaken."

Joscelin shot out his fist and caught the moth just before it blundered into the candle flame and singed its wings. "Yes," he said. "First they have to be retaken." He moved from the stool to cast the insect out into the night air. Doubtless its second chance at life would be wasted in the greater conflagration of someone's campfire, but he had given it that grace. Returning to his seat, he leaned toward FitzWarin, his hands clasped. "You cannot stay here," he said.

"I know that. I am going home to Alberbury on the morrow—nearest I can die to Whittington." His smile was a travesty.

There was no point wasting time in denials. "Take Brunin with you," Joscelin said. "He should not fight anyway, when he cannot hold a shield or properly grip a sword."

FitzWarin stared at him, his eyes still fierce blue within the death-smudged sockets and filled with knowing. He pushed himself upright against the cushions and Joscelin saw him swallowing and struggling not to cough. "I have said I do not need a priest, but that will soon change." Spasms racked through him. Joscelin reached to the jug on the floor, poured a cupful of watered wine, and held it to FitzWarin's livid lips. More dribbled down FitzWarin's chin than he actually swallowed, but the coughing abated sufficiently for him to draw breath.

"All I can hope is that Brunin is ready. It will be a heavy burden I lay on him."

"He is ready," Joscelin said, his voice tight with suppressed emotion.

"Do you remember that day at Shrewsbury when I asked you to take him?"

Joscelin gave a pained smile. "I remember it well." Facing Gilbert de Lacy at the weapon booths. If he knew then what was going to happen, he would have made a fight of it and damn the consequences.

"I wasn't sure then that he would ever be ready. Some say he is like my father…and indeed to look upon Brunin in the shadows is like seeing his ghost. But he's not like my father at all. He's like me."

"No," Joscelin contradicted. "He is like himself. And he stands in nobody's shadow."

FitzWarin nodded. "I knew from the first why I asked you to foster him," he said hoarsely, "and you have not disappointed."

"Neither has he," Joscelin said, swallowing a tightness in his throat.

For a long time he sat with his friend. They said little more. FitzWarin had neither the strength nor the breath for conversation and Joscelin could think of nothing to say. Yet the silence had import for it was a leave-taking. Sitting for the last time with FitzWarin, Joscelin felt as if he were saying farewell to his own vitality.

# 34

W IND-BUFFETED AND WET, HAWISE RODE TOWARD ALBERBURY
in response to a summons from her husband. His father
was dying and Brunin needed her. The messenger had arrived at
Stanton yesterday and, as well as the summons, had brought the
news that her father had taken the gates and the gatehouse towers
at Ludlow, but that de Lacy still held the rest of the castle. Her
father needed more men, thus Sybilla was out seeking and buying
the support that Joscelin needed.

Dusk would soon be upon the small traveling party, which
consisted of Hawise and four men-at-arms. She had not brought a
maid, for none of them could ride as well as she and would have
slowed her down. Her domestic household was following with
little Emmeline at a pace dictated by the speed of the baggage cart.

Puddles filled the ruts in the road and the sky was a chill gray,
darkening over the Welsh hills. Hawise hunched into her cloak.
She was cold, hungry, and bone-tired but knew that journey's end
was not going to bring her succor. A dying man, an anguished
husband, a cantankerous old lady. She had to face those hurdles
whatever. Worrying about them would make no difference, unless
it diminished her ability to cope.

Lights flickered through the gathering murk and it was with
equal feelings of relief and dread that she rode into the village of
Alberbury. There were few folk about. Having shut up her hens

for the night, a woman was hastening back inside her cot, arms huddled beneath her mantle. A man was ushering two pigs up a rutted track toward the shelter at the side of his house and his wife watched him from the door as she whisked batter in a bowl with a bunch of twigs, two children peeping either side of her skirts. Hawise glanced and for a moment was wistful, wondering how it would be to change places with that woman. To have her man enter the house and bar the door against the weather and to sit cooking batter cakes over the fire with everyone safe, warm, and within reach. She gave herself a mental shake. Doubtless the woman sometimes thought of how it would be to live as a fine lady with servants to do the cooking, a feather mattress to sleep upon, and no worries about where the next meal was coming from or how the rent was to be paid.

They turned down the road to the castle and the curtain wall rose out of the dusk. The heavy wooden gates were barred and one of Hawise's escorts had to bang heavily on them with the side of his fist.

"Open in the name of the lady Hawise FitzWarin!"

The sound of the draw bar grating out of its socket filled the rain-drenched air, followed by the squeak of hinges. "We had not looked for you until the morrow, my lady," the surprised guard apologized as he made haste to admit the bedraggled party.

"We rode hard," Hawise answered curtly. "Does Lord FitzWarin yet live?"

"Aye, my lady."

She nodded and knew that she could have answered her own question, for the church bells were silent and, had he died, they would have been tolling a knell.

A second guard had gone running to announce their arrival. On the heels of the grooms and a lad bearing a torch, Brunin came striding through the deluge. The pale bandage on his right hand stood out in the gloom and, when he reached her, she saw from his blank expression that things were bad indeed.

For a moment they embraced in the cold strike of the rain. Then, without speaking, he took her hand in his good one and brought her into the keep. A fire burned in the central hearth and a cauldron of pottage simmered gently over the flames. A neatly dressed young woman was tending the mixture and keeping an eye on a griddle laden with flat cakes.

"I came as swiftly as I could ride." Hawise extended her hands to the warmth of the fire and felt the first thawing sting in her fingertips. She had not realized how chilled she was.

He gave an empty smile. "It seemed forever. I have been counting the moments since the messenger rode out... You cannot know..." He clamped his jaw and turned his gaze toward the flames.

"But I do," she said softly and wrapped her arm around his. He sighed and she felt some of the rigidity leave his body.

"The priest is with my father now," he said. "I've sent messengers out to my brothers other than Ralf and Richard, but I doubt they will be in time. He breathed in powdered lime at Ludlow. It would greatly harm a man sound of wind, and to one in my father's condition..." He shook his head. "The wonder is that he has lasted this long."

She looked anxiously at his hand. "You took hurts yourself."

"Nothing that will not mend," he said impatiently. There was another brief silence while he flexed his fingers within the bandages. "My grandmother has retired to the women's chambers," he said. "I sent someone to tell her that you'd arrived, but I do not know if she will come down, or wait for you to go to her."

Hawise glanced involuntarily toward the stairs and hoped that she was not going to see Lady Mellette descending them. "She would have been here by now had she chosen to greet me," she replied, "and I am sure she can wait a few moments while I talk with my husband and warm myself." It came to her that they stood on the cusp of change. Brunin was about to become lord of Alberbury and all the other FitzWarin lands. She would be their lady, and she was no Eve FitzWarin to bow her head and do Mellette's bidding, meek as a sheep. Brunin's grandmother must know that her power was waning...and perhaps fear it too. But would she make a fight of it, relinquish grudgingly, or just let go? And how would Brunin deal with her when she had been the cause of so much wretchedness in his life?

"My lady, would you like some pottage?" The young woman who had been tending the cooking pot brought Hawise a deep wooden bowl filled with the hot soup and a spoon with which to eat it. Her accent bore the strong lilt of Wales. She had green eyes flecked with glints of reddish brown and strong auburn brows. "It's leek and barley, my nain's recipe."

Hawise thanked her with a smile and wondered who she was. Not a servant to speak so familiarly, but not of Hawise's own rank to be stirring a cooking pot in the main room. There were two silver rings on her wedding finger and the brooch at the throat of her gown was silver too and set with amber and garnets.

"I have not seen you at Alberbury before," Hawise said diplomatically.

The girl blushed and looked quickly at Brunin, and then over her shoulder as if expecting to be rescued. "I am but recently arrived, my lady. My name is Sian ferch Madoc and I am...I am..."

"And she is hoping that you will find a place for her among your women," Brunin interrupted. "I should have introduced you, but as you can tell my mind is so full that some details have gone wandering. You should know that she is under Ralf's protection...and that she is welcome."

Sian was blushing harder now. A mistress then, Hawise thought, and wondered how that sat with Lady Mellette. Perhaps that was another reason why the elderly lady was not in the hall. But then William the Conqueror had been the product of a liaison between the Duke of Normandy and a girl from the town's merchant quarter and Earl Robert of Gloucester had come from similar circumstances too.

"If she makes pottage like this, she is more than welcome," Hawise said with a smile.

"I knew you would see it in those terms," Brunin said, and she saw the gratitude and relief in his eyes...and also in Sian's. Hawise realized how much power she did indeed have the potential to wield. A smile or a frown, agreement or disapproval was all it took to alter lives and atmospheres.

❖ ❖ ❖

In the dark hour before dawn, Brunin's father died, bequeathing to his eldest son the FitzWarin lands and the fight to regain Whittington.

Brunin crossed himself and stood by the bedside, illuminated in the flicker of a dozen beeswax candles. Their faint honey scent was mingled with the tainted deathbed aroma of struggle and sweat, and with the colder, sharper scent of the rain-drenched night where one of the superstitious maids had opened a window to let the dead man's soul depart instead of lingering with the body. The sound of the priest's soft chanting filled the room, no longer a counterpoint to the harsh rattle from the man on the bed, but a single purity.

Brunin felt unutterably tired. It was as if all the burdens had passed to him like a black cloak, pocketed with stones. Hawise stood quietly beside him, her head bowed over her clasped hands. At his other side Ralf and Richard shuffled their feet, their fair heads gleaming in the candlelight. His grandmother stood at the head of the bed, her body and features carved in stone.

Brunin cleared his throat. "Let the women wash and prepare my father for chapel, and then we will keep vigil. When that is done, I will take the oaths of my vassals and see that news is sent to the King."

One by one the mourners and witnesses left the room until there remained only Brunin and Hawise and his grandmother. Brunin knew he should leave too, but his feet refused to move. While he stood here, he could almost imagine that his father was only sleeping, that he would open his eyes and mutter something querulous about the nagging of a "fool boy." While he stood here, he did not have to deal with everything that awaited him.

Mellette turned to him. "Why do you linger?" she said, as if she could reach inside him and see all the seething doubts. "The dead don't arise until judgment day."

For a moment he was a small child again, caught in transgression and fixed by her knife-edge stare. Even here, even now, she had the ability and the desire to wound. He drew himself up, shouldering the cloak and its weighted burden. "Perhaps the dead are more fortunate than we know," he said and went from the room.

With set jaw and clenched fists, Mellette watched him leave.

Hawise narrowed her eyes. With quiet authority she directed the women to heating water for washing, to lighting more candles, to finding herbs and oils. She poured wine and brought it to Mellette. "My lady, you must bend before you shatter and destroy everyone else into the bargain," she said.

"What do you know?" Mellette snapped.

"That our lives would be easier if you could find it within you to show some gentleness toward the living—no matter our unworthiness."

Mellette opened her mouth.

Hawise gave her the goblet. "I am now lady of Alberbury," she said firmly. "Brunin's wife. To whom do you think he will listen? What do you think he will do with you?"

"You are insolent!"

"No, my lady, I am practical." Facing Mellette, Hawise was acutely aware of the flickering candles in the niches around the bed, of the women making preparations for the tending of the dead man, of the body itself, still warm and malleable. Her heart was pounding, her mouth was dry, but she stood her ground. "I will have no battlefields in this house. You have a right to respect, my lady, but so do I, and so does my husband."

Mellette gave her a scornful stare. "Respect does not come of right. It has to be earned."

"So it does, my lady." Hawise inclined her head to Mellette and turned to the task in hand.

The old woman frowned and for a long moment remained where she was, standing like a lone tree when all the forest around it had been chopped down. Then she rallied. A shudder rippled through her body and she uprooted herself to go and join the women by the bed. Hawise quietly yielded her the senior place, for Mellette was FitzWarin's mother and she had the right.

❖ ❖ ❖

Brunin set his foot in the stirrup and swung into the saddle. The rain had stopped but the ground underfoot was boggy and the air was as misty as witch's breath.

"Have a care," Hawise said as she handed him his shield. "I have knelt in too many vigils of late."

Brunin threaded his arm through the hand-holds. His shoulder twinged, but the ache was not too bad. His sword hand was protected by a hawking gauntlet stitched with mail rivets. "So have I," he said and almost managed a smile. "I hope to be summoning you to good news within a few days."

"I hope so too." She forced a smile in return. She would not send him back to her father with tears and wailing. There had been enough sorrow to fill a cauldron already. FitzWarin had been laid to rest in Alberbury's church beside his wife; the funeral had been a muted affair. Brunin had taken oaths of fealty from those vassals close enough to attend the burial. Those left at Ludlow would give their allegiance when he arrived back at Joscelin's camp. The rest had been summoned to ride from their villages and manors to give their oaths at the Christmas feast.

Beside Hawise, a wan-faced Sian watched Ralf swing to horse. Mellette stood with her head up and her shoulders back. There was no sign of the walking stick that she used around the castle's rooms. Hawise wondered at the terrible burden of the old woman's pride: how much it had cost and was still costing her and those who had to live with her.

❖❖❖

Brunin patted Jester's neck and stared without speaking at Ludlow. The gates had gone, except for some charred remnants, and the timbers of much of the gatehouse tower had burned too. That particular damage must have been sustained during his absence. Most of the bailey buildings were blackened ruins and the timberwork on the middle tower of the inner bailey was scorched. Joscelin had a grip on the superficial structures, but the heart of Ludlow remained in de Lacy's keeping. So much loss for so little gain.

"Has there been word from King Henry?" Brunin asked at length.

Joscelin looked gloomy. "Not yet, but then he has larger fish to fry than this. I sent a second messenger yesterday morning, but whether he will have more luck than the first…" He let the words trail away, then sighed. "I've faced more difficult challenges and if de Lacy can wait fifty years to take his chance, then what is a couple of months?" He laid his hand on Brunin's shoulder in a gesture that sought reassurance as much as giving it.

"Nothing," Brunin said with a smile that did not reach his eyes. "A couple of months is nothing."

They were setting up one of the trebuchets to hurl stones and rubble from the ruined gatehouse tower when one of their scouts came galloping among them. "Banners, sir!" he cried. "There are men on the Wigmore road!"

"Whose?" Joscelin ceased leaning against one of the support struts, his brow creased with anxiety.

Brunin ducked under the trebuchet arm and stood at Joscelin's side. "Surely not Mortimer."

"No, sir, not that I could tell. Welshmen I'd say…at least fifty and well armed. About half a mile's distance."

"Flag of truce?" Joscelin demanded, not wasting words.

"No, sir."

"Then we assume they're not riding to assist us." Joscelin began barking orders.

"Could be the King's men," Brunin said as he strode with Joscelin toward the horse lines.

"The King's men would come under a banner of leopards, and my scout wouldn't mistake them for Welsh," Joscelin said grimly. "I suspect that word has got out and, as always, the kites are circling to see what they can plunder."

Within the heart of Ludlow, a horn sounded. Joscelin and Brunin listened to the notes, looked at each other, and, cursing, began to run. Whoever was advancing on Ludlow, the defenders viewed them as allies.

❖❖❖

"That's it, we have them!" Ernalt de Lysle cried. A messenger had arrived breathless from the wall walk with the news that a troop of Welsh mercenaries led by Roger and Jonas de Powys of Whittington were almost at the castle gates. "Now we'll show the bastards who owns Ludlow." He strode across the chamber, seized Marion in his arms, and gave her a kiss that flattened her bruised lips against her teeth. "Look for a blood-red sky tonight, sweetheart!"

"Why...I...I don't understand."

"Have you been deaf these last days?" he demanded, releasing her so abruptly that she almost fell down. "Lord Gilbert sent for aid and the de Powys brothers have answered!" He barked a laugh. "That'll salt their tails."

She rubbed her arms and gazed at him in perplexity. "Whose tails?"

"De Dinan's and FitzWarin's."

"Oh." She continued to look blank.

He made an impatient sound. "The de Powys brothers hold Whittington," he said. "Their bloodline held it when the FitzWarins were no more than common castle guards in Lorraine, and they've long been the allies of Mortimer and de Lacy."

When he had gone, Marion went to the window with the wine flagon and her sewing. She had eschewed the hall and the company of the other women whom she had decided were all coarse sluts. She would not besmirch herself by stooping to their level.

The gown she was making was cut from a bolt of fabric looted from Sybilla's coffer: blue wool brocade purchased at last Shrewsbury Fair which had cost Joscelin the earth. Marion had felt no qualms about taking the cloth. If she hadn't, someone else would, and it was perfect for a wedding gown. She threaded a length of blue silk yarn through the eye of the needle and began to sew as if her life depended on it. At first her stitches were exquisite, but as she drank her way down the flagon, and the sounds of battle began to echo off the battered walls, they grew increasingly erratic and ungainly.

❖❖❖

The night was cold and black; rain spattering in the wind. Brunin stood outside the palisade of Caynham's hill defenses and stared, wishing he could see through the darkness and know how far away the enemy was. The fine hairs on his forearms were standing upright and there was a prickling sensation down the middle of his spine.

"No point in looking now," Joscelin said. "Come and eat. They won't attack until morning."

Brunin took a deep breath. The air smelled of autumn and the year's ending. He passed through a gap in the rotting wooden palisade and followed Joscelin to one of the watch fires. He wasn't hungry, but he accepted the bowl of watery stew from the soldier who handed it to him. At least it was hot, although it would take more than soup to warm his bones. The extra men brought by the de Powys brothers had tipped the teetering balance in de Lacy's favor and, amid fierce and brutal fighting, Joscelin had been driven back…and back…and back. Everything gained had been lost. The enemy had pursued them as far as the camp at Caynham, but nightfall had caused them to draw off in order to tend their wounded and regroup.

"They won't need siege engines," Brunin said bleakly. "They can ride three abreast through some of the gaps in those palings."

"Yes, but they have still got to come uphill at us and it may

be that we can break out southward and lose them in the forest."
Joscelin looked at Brunin. "It's not over yet. Never think that."

Brunin drank from the bowl of stew, tasting the layer of mutton
grease floating on the surface. "But there has to be an end to it,"
he said. "Someone has to call enough."

Joscelin's eyelids tensed. "Do you want to do that? Do you
want to walk into their camp with a flag of truce tied to your
horse's tail and cry that you quit?"

Brunin flushed beneath the scorn in Joscelin's voice. "You
know I would not do that," he said, "any more than de Lacy
would yield to us, but there has to be a middle way."

Joscelin chewed on his thumbnail. "Like the middle way for
Whittington?" he said harshly. "A long wrangle through courts
of law with proofs demanded for the right to every single blade
of grass and pile of dung, and in the meantime some piddling fief
tossed from Henry's hand like a man throwing a used chicken
bone to a dog at the end of a meal?"

"You do not need to remind me of the choice my family was
forced to make," Brunin said. The neutrality of his voice was a
warning. "If there had been a viable alternative, my father would
have taken it. As it is, we still have hope." He did not add that,
after tonight, that hope might be lost. Joscelin knew it too. The
stew had congealed as it cooled and he tipped the remnants out
on the ground.

"I did not mean to smirch your pride," Joscelin said.

"I know that," Brunin answered. "You spoke out of your own."

"Always goes before a fall," Joscelin said wearily.

❖ ❖ ❖

The sun rose above the skyline in a red ball of fire. Joscelin sat his
sorrel destrier, his shield on his left arm, his lance in his right. "If
we can fight our way out of this, we'll ride for Stanton," he said.
"De Lacy will not pursue us that far out of his territory." He gave
Brunin a hard stare. "Get yourself free. I want no heroic sacrifices.
Understood?"

Brunin responded with a grim salute. He had made his confession to Joscelin's chaplain. He had had a scribe pen a message that was to be sent to Hawise in the event of his death; Joscelin had done the same for Sybilla: clearing life's ground, scouring it down to a bare courtyard.

"Good." Joscelin nodded stiffly and turned his mount side-on to the sun.

❖❖❖

"They're leaving, my lord," said Ernalt de Lysle in an urgent tone.

"I have eyes to see that for myself," de Lacy growled. He gathered his stallion's reins. "There is time enough to strike. Too soon and those old battlements will hamper us." He glanced toward the rising sun. "FitzWarin is yours if you want him."

Anticipation gleamed in Ernalt's eyes. "It will be a pleasure, my lord."

"No," said Gilbert, shaking his head. "It will be a hard fight." He turned to look around at the waiting men. "Probably the hardest fight of your lives. This," he said grimly, "is where it ends."

❖❖❖

Brunin struck with his sword and parried with his shield. The movements were instinctive, the fruit of years of training. His precision was cold, his mind as clear as ice. Nearby, Ralf was bellowing and laying about him like a wild bull and wasting far too much energy in rage. As Brunin dealt with his opponent and moved on to tackle the next, he looked for Joscelin and saw him hard pressed but holding his own. Perhaps…just perhaps, they might be able to win free. The hope flitted through his mind and was dashed as a blade caught the rising light and descended. Joscelin's parry was weak and Brunin saw him flinch as the cutting force of the sword was turned on his mail, but not the bruising impact. His young chestnut stallion reared and plunged. Joscelin lost his stirrup and, before he could regain it, was pitched over his mount's neck.

Brunin whipped Jester around and spurred him across the melee, roaring the de Dinan name as a rallying cry. Joscelin struggled up from his fall, scattering men with his shield, making them fear the danger of his sword, but he was injured and bruised and the sorrel had bolted. Before Brunin could reach him, Joscelin was assaulted again, his shield wrested from his left arm, his sword smashed out of his hand, and he was forced to his knees on the bloody ground.

Brunin forgot everything that Joscelin had said about heroic sacrifices and rode straight for the thick of the fray. Men fell away before him, either leaping from the path of the reaper or being cut down, but he neither saw their faces nor heard their screams.

"Christ, Brunin, no!" Joscelin roared and was struck back-handed across the mouth by a soldier wearing a mailed glove. His head snapped back and blood welled into the cuts made by the iron rivets. Brunin slammed aside the serjeant blocking his path, determined to reach Joscelin, and in so doing paid less attention than he should to the assault from his left.

"Brunin!" Joscelin's voice was a full, bloody bellow of warning and despair. Ralf was shouting too. Brunin twisted to meet the blow but he was too late and his damaged shoulder not strong enough. The lance head struck against the side of his shield, slatted inward, and plunged through mail, gambeson, and flesh. The lance shaft was flawed and with a splintering crack the ash stave snapped off, leaving Ernalt de Lysle clutching a jagged haft. The blow rocked Brunin back against his cantle and jarred his spine. He could feel himself falling and tightened his thighs. There was no pain, only a flowering numbness that spread from the head of the lance and flowed through his body. Blood darkened around the point of entry. Joscelin was staring in wide and grieving horror. The gelding plunged, hindquarters straining, and the jolt sent the first spark of pain through Brunin's body.

De Lysle cast aside the spear and drew his sword, but was blocked for an instant by the blundering of one of his own men.

"Go!" Joscelin roared to Brunin. "In God's name, ride!" The last word was lost on a grunt as his captor belted him again, knocking him to the ground.

Ralf reached Brunin and, seizing Jester's rein, yanked the horse around. "Do as he says!" he cried, whacking Jester's rump with the flat of his sword. The gelding flinched and lunged into a gallop. Brunin reeled in the saddle and almost toppled from it, but the years of discipline and training paid their debt and through a vision of black stars he hung on as they disengaged from the unequal melee and raced for the safety of the nearby woods.

Jester could gallop forever; his pace was not swift, but it was smooth and his stamina was heroic. De Lysle spurred after Brunin and Ralf with a handful of mercenaries from the Welsh contingent. At first Brunin thought that he and Ralf were going to be captured, but their small head start gave them the lead they needed to stay in front and while the other horses tired, Jester continued his one-paced lope. Ralf began to lag behind, but their pursuers had slowed too, their battle-sweated mounts unable to maintain their speed. Arrows whined over their heads in a parting salvo. Ralf cursed as one thrummed into the high back of his saddle and cracked the wood. He spurred his flagging stallion and it found a final burst of speed to reach the safety of the trees.

The forest embraced them. Brunin was not sure whether it was Jester's breathing he could hear, or his own, harsh and guttural. The pain was harder now, a deep, welling throb. He glanced down at the wound. There was blood, but it was oozing sluggishly, not pouring out. That might all change if the lance head was removed; he had seen men expire in a fountaining gush from doing just that. But to leave it in situ was certain death too.

"Brunin?" Ralf rode up alongside, his ruddy complexion blanched of its usual high color. He snapped off the arrow thrusting up from his saddle and cast it aside with a look of revulsion.

Sweat crawled down Brunin's spine and his vision blurred at the edges. "We must keep moving...they won't give up the pursuit until they are certain they won't catch us." He swallowed. His men would be fleeing the battle, making their escape as best they could. "Gather the others, such as you can find," he panted. "Bring us together."

Ralf looked appalled "I cannot leave you!"

"I am all right...Do it."

Frowning hard and obviously debating with his judgment, Ralf reined away. Brunin hung his head and clung on hard, willing himself not to fall, forcing himself through the hot beat of the pain. He had seen men speared in the guts before, had heard them too. Most died within hours of the event...but some lingered. A few lived to tell the tale...but they were always the ones in whom the iron had pierced no vital place. At least he wasn't screaming yet, but he knew it would come.

❖❖❖

Hawise watched Emmeline and the steward's daughter whipping their wooden tops in Alberbury's bailey. She had recently finished speaking to the steward about how many of the castle's pigs they were going to keep and how many were to be slaughtered for salting down and eating through the winter months. The swine, sublimely unaware of their fate, were being herded out of the castle gates and turned toward the nearby woods to fatten on the seasonal glut of beech mast, acorns, and roots.

"I used to have a top when I was a child," she said with a reminiscent smile. "Indeed, I think it might still be tucked away in one of my coffers."

She called Emmeline over, and the child ran to her, brown eyes sparkling, raven hair caught back in a red ribbon. "Let me have a turn," Hawise demanded, laughing. Taking the braided leather whip from the little girl, she set the painted wooden top spinning with a deft flick, and then chased it across the courtyard. The wind swirled her skirts and blew her veil away from her face. The steward smiled at the winsome sight she made and Emmeline and her friend giggled.

"I can see that you were skilled, madam," the steward said as Hawise whipped the top back to her starting point.

"Indeed I was!" she declared with breathless delight. "I used to compete with my husband, and I would beat him quite often...although he was always better at juggling than I was. My father said that we should have been tumblers' children." She stooped to return the top to Emmeline and discovered that Mellette had emerged from the hall. Leaning hard on her stick, she was advancing determinedly toward Hawise and the steward.

"My lady, you should not trouble yourself," Hawise said, starting toward her, but Mellette waved her away with a sour look.

"When I see my grandson's wife running around the yard like a hoyden when she should be discussing affairs of business, then it is my duty to trouble myself," she snapped.

Hawise swallowed her irritation. She would win this battle as she had won the others, but to have to keep fighting them was wearisome. "I have dealt with the matter of the swine, madam," she said firmly. "And it is indeed yourself you are troubling—and needlessly." Hawise proceeded to give Mellette a detailed résumé of the points she had discussed with the steward. When Mellette disagreed crabbily with the number of hams to be salted, Hawise listened and murmured that she would consider her views. She did not raise her voice, but it was firm and confident.

"You have no notion—" Mellette began, but Hawise raised her hand.

"I have heeded Master Steward's advice and heard yours. It is for me to decide," she said with certainty.

"You are too headstrong for your own good."

The steward shifted uncomfortably and Hawise felt sorry for him, caught as he was between two women like a grain between grindstones. "Did no one ever say the same of you, my lady?" she asked and then she smiled and shook her head. "I do not suppose that they ever dared."

Something that was almost, but not quite, wintry humor sparked in the old woman's eyes. "Only my husband," she said, "and my father when I told him what I thought of the marriage he had made for me. I…" She fell silent and looked toward the gates as a shout came from one of the guards on lookout duty. The girls stopped playing with their tops and for a moment time seemed to cease its advance and petrify all of them in the moment.

The spell was broken by the sound of the draw bar shooting back and the gates opening. Uncaring that it was another exhibition of hoydenish behavior, Hawise gathered her skirts and ran toward the gatehouse. Mellette followed, leaning heavily on the stick. When the steward offered her his arm, she gestured him away.

Two horsemen rode through the entrance; others followed behind. Ralf's helm was hanging on its strap from his saddle pommel. His gray stallion's hide was marked by many superficial wounds. Ralf was riding him very close to Jester. The gelding was sweat-caked and he too bore injuries. Brunin rode with hanging head and hands gripping the saddle tree with white-knuckled concentration.

"Brunin?" Hawise ran to his saddle, fear tearing her heart.

He raised his lids, the motion slow as if they bore the heavy weight of death pennies. His eyes were fogged with pain, the pupils wide and dark. Hawise knew the look; she had seen it often enough in the injured men she and her mother had tended down the years.

"He's sore wounded," Ralf said in a stricken voice. "He's taken a lance in the belly."

The words hit Hawise like a mighty slap and for a moment she stopped breathing and her mother's advice echoed inside her skull. *The best you can do for a man pierced in the gut is to give him a triple dose of poppy in wine and pray that he goes to sleep and does not wake up. If he does, dose him again and pray harder.* "No," Hawise said unsteadily. "No…" And then she clenched her teeth and closed her mouth so that nothing else could emerge.

"Ralf, I will thrash you for terrifying my wife," Brunin croaked. "Only let me dismount and I'll do well enough." He smiled at Hawise but it was a travesty.

He sounded like FitzWarin, Hawise thought, insisting even as death approached that everyone was making too much fuss.

Richard had dismounted to take Jester's bridle. Brunin leaned hard on the pommel and with a tremendous effort lifted himself out of the saddle and to the ground. Ralf caught him and Brunin leaned against the horse, sweat beading his brow. He was hunched over and Hawise could not see the wound; she didn't know if he was concealing it from her, or whether it just hurt less to stand thus.

"Can you walk?" she asked. "Or should I have your brothers carry you?"

"I think that…" he said, enunciating each word clearly, "for the moment, walking is beyond me." His knees buckled and he sagged against Ralf, who caught and bore him up, his expression terrified.

❖ ❖ ❖

Hawise's hands were shaking. She washed them in the bowl of hot water that Sian had brought to the bedchamber and splashed her face. She could not afford weakness now. Everyone was looking to her. The nearest chirugeon was in Shrewsbury, and by the time he was fetched, it would be too late. Perhaps it was already.

Closing her eyes she summoned her courage. She was the daughter of warriors and her mother was renowned for her fortitude and wisdom. "I am capable," she said fiercely to herself. "There is no one else." She came to the bed. Brunin had revived and was looking at her with pain-dark eyes.

"It was Ernalt de Lysle," he said as she knelt at the bedside and gestured Sian and Ralf to stand around him. In a moment they would need to remove the hauberk and gambeson. "I had my eyes on your father…I didn't see de Lysle until it was too late."

Hawise had not asked about her father. She knew that the news was bad, but didn't want to hear it, not now. One thing at a time. "Don't speak," she said. "Not for your sake, but for mine. Later will do."

"You think there is going to be a 'later'?"

"You are not going to die on me," Hawise said, and somehow

her voice was hard and steady. "What would that say to your grandmother about my abilities as a healer and nurse, and yours as your family's heir? I am going to fight for you, and if you do not fight with me…then I call you coward, and this time I will not take it back."

Behind her, Mellette hissed through her teeth as she heard the words. Brunin reached out and grasped Hawise's hand in his. "I'll fight," he said. "Plant my banner at the foot of the bed and cry no quarter. There is too much unfinished business to let it fall."

It was a slow and awkward task, removing his outer garments. Hawise did not want to dose him with poppy in wine until she had seen the extent of his injury. There was a potion called dwale, compounded of different, deadly herbs, mixed in quantities that would stun rather than kill, but they had to be administered with a severe purge so that the body voided them before they could paralyze completely. Given the area and nature of Brunin's wound, she dared not administer that either. All she could do for him was numb his senses with strong mead, but she didn't want him drunk out of his mind.

After the armor came tunic and shirt. Hawise untied the string of his braies and pulled those down too. His skin was smooth and golden, the faintest down of black hair feathering from navel to the crisper curls surrounding his genitals. The left side, above one hip, was marred by an ugly wound and the flesh around it wore a spectacular flush of bruised discoloration, all shades of sloe and plum and raspberry. The core of the injury was black with congealed blood, surrounding the stump of the ash lance. The head of the lance was embedded deep in the flesh. With trepidation Hawise sniffed the wound and was relieved to find there was no taint.

"Perchance I can ease the lance head back with greased quills over the barbs," she said, beckoning Mellette forward for her opinion. Whatever their differences, shutting her out when her experience might be of use would be foolish. "I don't think it has pierced any vital point."

Mellette came and she too sniffed. "You are right," she said. "By God's mercy the head hasn't pierced the gut or kidney, but there is still great danger. You could push it all the way through, but there is no telling whether that would cause more or less damage than pulling it back."

"Have you ever done this before?"

Mellette pursed her lips. "Once." she said. "He died three days later. It is in your hands." She turned away. "Whatever you decide, you should poultice the wound with honey and lard."

Hawise swallowed. The old woman was punishing her for that earlier dismissal…or perhaps detaching herself from impending tragedy. Absconding the battlefield at the first skirmish instead of facing the full, bloody fight.

Hawise looked around at Ralf and Sian. "I will need more hot water," she said, "and honey and lard as Lady Mellette said. Also goose quills. One of the scribes is bound to have some."

❖❖❖

It was over. Hawise toweled blood from her hands and stared down at her husband. He was quiet now. The only sound in the room was Ralf's muffled sobbing and the counterpoint of Sian's comforting murmurs. Hawise would weep later; for the moment she was numb, all feeling banished to a sealed chamber at the back of her mind. She could not have functioned otherwise. Wordlessly she pointed to the pitcher of mead and a maid hastened to pour. Taking the cup, Hawise went to the window arch and inhaled the brisk autumn air, filling her lungs with its freshness, ridding them of the taint of blood and pain.

She heard a heavy tread behind her and Ralf's hand came down on her shoulder; it was broad, thickset, quite unlike Brunin's. "I do not know how you did it," his voice was rough with emotion.

"Neither do I." Hawise took another breath of clean air and faced him. "But you played your part. Without your strength and your presence, he would have struggled more."

A look of grim remorse crossed Ralf's blunt features. "I used to envy him," he said. "I used to wish that I was the firstborn. When we were boys I even hated him and wished he was dead—especially after he took up a position with your father. It should have been me…" He looked over his shoulder at the still form on the bed. "It should still have been me," he said, his voice almost breaking. "I should have taken that wound, not him."

"No." Hawise shook her head. "You are speaking out of your guilt. He would not see it that way, and neither should you. You do not wish him dead now—"

"Christ's blood, of course I do not!" He cast another anguished look toward the bed where Brunin lay as still as an effigy.

"Well then." He was afraid, she thought, afraid that the responsibility for the FitzWarin lands might end up being his. "Do not dwell on such thoughts. Doubtless, in your childhood, he thought similar things about you." Leaving Ralf, she returned to the bedside. Brunin's breathing was shallow but regular. His hand twitched on the coverlet.

She had succeeded in easing both stump and lance head from his flesh without causing too much additional damage. She had washed the injury in wine vinegar and poulticed it as Mellette recommended with honey and lard, and she had given him white poppy and valerian to make him sleep. There was nothing else to be done for him now, except keep vigil and pray that he did not succumb to the wound fever or the stiffening sickness, both grave threats given the size and depth of the injury.

While still capable of speech, Brunin had related the bare bones of the disaster that had befallen them at Ludlow. At best her father was de Lacy's prisoner; at worst he was dead. If the former and held in the castle where he had been master, he was probably wishing his life over indeed. She would not think about that. Push it away; deal with it later. The next thing to do was send a messenger to her mother and sisters, although they probably knew by now…and another to the King, demanding that he intervene. Busy, she must keep herself busy and not give her imagination a foothold. She sent an attendant to summon Alberbury's scribe.

Ralf muttered something about checking the guards on the wall walk and gate and left the room at a near-run, almost colliding with his grandmother. The elderly woman limped to the bed and, leaning on her stick, studied her grandson.

"I give you credit for your mettle," she said. "I doubt many young women of your age could have done what you have done."

"When you are thrown into a river, you have no choice but to swim or drown." Going to the other side of the bed, Hawise took Brunin's hand. His eyes remained closed, but his breathing caught and his fingers tightened around hers. "I used to wonder why my mother was so fierce about making us learn how to stitch and dress wounds," she said. "I was always too impatient—my sister Sibbi is much neater than me—but at least I have some small knowledge." She looked across up at Mellette. "He has a fighting chance."

The old lady studied the wolf banner which Hawise had tied to one of the hanging poles at the head of the bed. "That is what the FitzWarin men have always had," she said. "A fighting chance."

# 35

$\mathscr{I}$N HIS PRISON CELL, JOSCELIN SAT UP ON HIS STRAW PALLET and stifled a groan. His skull felt as if someone had hacked open the top and poured molten lead inside. The night had been full of strange dreams and time had not been one smooth continuum but had passed in sudden flashes followed by long, motionless stretches.

He knew he was feverish. His heart was pounding too close to the surface of his skin and he could feel his own heat. Likely he would die here, which he supposed was appropriate since he had spent most of his prime fighting to hold it...and in the end he had failed. He wondered which Sybilla would rather have: his memory, or his return with his hands full of nothing. Last night he had dreamed of her and her hair had been the sea-coal black of their first years together, streaming down her back like a maiden's...or a mourner's. He had tried to tell her that he loved her but there had been no power in his voice. She must have heard him though, for her eyes had glowed from within like hard, blue jewels and she had held out her empty arms to him. "Then give me Ludlow," she had said and evaporated from his dream. More nightmares had followed, the same scene playing over and again in his head: Brunin struck by de Lysle's lance; FitzWarin choking on a faceful of powdered lime. Ludlow burning, as he was burning.

He was in one of the lower rooms of the Pendover tower,

one that never had a fire and smelled of damp stone. It was used to store barrels; fishing nets; ropes and other sundry equipment; wooden sleds for the winter; ladders for the apple season. The light came through a narrow aperture in the stone little wider than his wrist. A warped shutter stood on the floor beside it. It had to be lifted into place and thus far Joscelin had not bothered. The cool air felt good on his fevered body and the sight of daylight helped him to cope with the sensation of being pressed out of existence by the weight of stone above him and the knowledge of his own helplessness.

De Lacy had not been without compassion, if such it could be called. At least Joscelin had not been chained or manacled, and the wounds he had sustained in the last battle had been dressed in a perfunctory fashion, the bleeding stanched and linen bandages applied. He had several cracked ribs but had not been offered any binding for them. Yesterday evening a guard had given him a large chunk of reasonably fresh bread and a bowl of bacon pottage. A pitcher of ale had been provided too. Small mercies, but Joscelin did not believe that any higher grace would be offered. Why should it? In de Lacy's place he would have done the same.

He fell into a restless doze, punctuated by more bloody images of red sword edges and of fighting when he was too tired to carry on. He wanted to stop, to break free, but still his arm rose and fell, searing with the agony of pure exhaustion, and there was no way out. He jerked awake with a cry that almost tore apart his aching rib cage.

The trap door leading down to his prison had been thrown back and a guard was descending the steps in a square of light. Joscelin's gaze darted to one of the fishing nets as he considered grabbing and throwing it over the man, but he knew that he didn't have time or swift enough reactions. Besides, there would be more than one guard. The soldier reached the foot of the steps, turned, and faced him with sword drawn.

"Stay where you are," he warned.

Joscelin found a sour laugh. "You must think me a great threat indeed," he said. "Where am I likely to go?"

The guard said nothing, but clamped his jaw and looked toward the steps, which another man was descending. As his face came into view, Joscelin's heart kicked in his chest.

Gilbert de Lacy stepped off the last wooden rung and advanced to the bed. Joscelin's first impulse was to rise to his feet. He was taller than de Lacy by almost a full head and shoulders, but it would have been an act of bravado and he was not even sure that he was capable of standing. Instead he reclined on the bed and stared at his old adversary with what he hoped passed for disdain.

De Lacy raised one brow to show that he was neither fooled nor impressed. "One of the women will come to tend you," he said. "I do not forget the courtesies you extended to me when I was your 'guest.'"

"You expect me to thank you for such generosity?" Joscelin sneered.

"I expect nothing save your curses." De Lacy gave a grim smile and sent a glance around the room. "I could have walled you up in a darker, damper place than this and left you to rot, but that would be unchristian of me and a slight on my manhood. Some of my knights think that I should do away with you. It would be easy to claim that you had been killed in the heat of battle, but that would be a lie and it would prick my conscience." He rubbed his thumb along his jaw and added conversationally, "I'm going to have that old eyesore of a chapel pulled down and rebuilt in gratitude to God for answered prayers."

"What makes you think you are going to keep Ludlow?"

"The fact that you are my prisoner and that Fulke FitzWarin is dead and most likely his son too. Accept it, you are beaten." De Lacy folded his arms. "I have always respected your abilities, but you have nothing left."

Knowing how easy it was to be magnanimous from a position of victory, Joscelin gave a bitter laugh. "Do not be too sure of that."

He saw de Lacy's eyes flicker. He wasn't as certain of himself as he seemed. It was all bluff and counter-bluff.

"I hardly think that your son-in-law or your wife are going to arrive with a relieving army," de Lacy said. "You have no one else. The Plugenets are not strong enough, and I can call upon the Mortimers if I have need. Best to make an end of it here and now."

Joscelin pulled himself up on the bed, although it cost him much in pain to do so. "Take your sword then," he said through clenched teeth. "Thrust it through my ribs. Some of them are broken; it won't take much."

De Lacy bestowed him the kind of look that a priest or school-master might reserve for a recalcitrant child. "I thought you might be more sensible than this, but I thought in vain."

Joscelin gave a shallow gasp of humorless laughter. "Sensible!" he choked. "How much sense have you had for a score of years? Your grandfather was deprived of lands for treason. Ludlow is my wife's right."

"A matter of opinion. Enough." De Lacy made a casting motion as if throwing Joscelin's words away. "The point can be argued forever without gain. I am here to propose a bargain to you."

"A bargain," Joscelin repeated, thinking that an ultimatum was probably more likely. After all, de Lacy was right. He had nothing left to bargain with…except perhaps the King's favor once Henry came to deal with the dispute, and there was no guarantee of that.

De Lacy's eyes were bright and fierce in the gloom. "Relinquish all rights in Ludlow and I will release you. I will even be prepared to discuss my cousin Sybilla's interest in some of the manors beholden to the castle."

"And if I refuse?"

De Lacy's voice hardened. "Then stay here and rot."

Joscelin stared at him. "I have nothing to lose by doing just that," he retorted. "If I die here, the walls will cry out for vengeance."

"You have been listening to too many troubadour's conceits," de Lacy said curtly. "I will give you two days to think on the matter. And then I might begin considering what I should do about those other manors…" Turning on his heel, he went to the stairs. The guard stayed where he was and, after de Lacy had left, the trap door remained open, sending a slant of light down to the beaten-earth floor. Voices murmured at the top of the steps and, after a brief hesitation, there was a light tread on the rungs and two women descended to the prison. Joscelin's gaze sharpened at the sight of the second one.

"You!" he snarled and lunged upright. Pain lanced through his head and rib cage but he ignored it for the rage coursing through him was stronger by far. "You have the gall to come here now! You truly are a whore!"

The guard took two rapid strides and pointed his blade at Joscelin's throat, fear flickering in his eyes. "Stay where you are, or you'll be singing out of your windpipe!" Joscelin leaned back from the threatening tip of the sword. "Get her out of here," he said hoarsely. "I would rather you poured Greek fire over my wounds than allow her to tend them!"

"Might be arranged," the guard said with a nasty grin. "The lady asked personally to see you."

Joscelin glared at Marion. Her face was pinched and white, her eyes as huge as moons. "Whether it be to gloat or to confess, I want none of her! Let her carry her own burdens." He lay down, closed his eyes, and turned his back.

"Please," he heard her say softly. The words curled around his bleeding heart like lute wires and cut from him a response he did not want to feel. Amid the rage and revulsion came red pulses of tenderness and pity. "You are dead," he said in a husky voice. "It is your ghost that talks to me. I will not listen."

"I didn't want this to happen."

He clenched his fists and willed her to leave. She did indeed sound like a ghost, her voice thin and thready and lost. He remembered taking her up on his saddle, a tiny little girl with finger-thin braids, crying for her dead mother and clinging to her cloth doll as if it were life itself. And then he thought of everything that she had done and the image of the weeping child was swept away on a dark and bitter surge.

He heard the scuffle of her feet on the earthen floor and then her rapid ascent up the steps. His heartbeat pounded in his ears like a dull, fast drum.

"Looks like you frightened her off," the guard said. He gave a loud sniff. "Best for you that you did. Lord Gilbert don't trust her further than he can throw a spear."

Joscelin ignored the guard. The other woman came around the side of the pallet so that she was facing him.

"Lord Gilbert said we were to look at your wounds," she said in a brisk voice.

"They don't need looking at," Joscelin growled.

"Lord Gilbert gives the orders, and he wants you alive." Her tone was practical and brisk. She had a double chin and teeth like an old horse. Her eyes were small and deep-set, but they sparkled with good humor. "The sooner you let me tend you, my lord, the sooner you'll be left in peace."

Slowly Joscelin sat up and let her have her way. She was quick and efficient. Her hands were large and mannish, but they were deft too.

"She's trouble, that one," she said, jerking her head toward the stairs. "Only got three wheels on her wain, as my mother used to say. Keeps insisting she's going to have a grand wedding when all this hue and cry is over, but if that happens, I'll eat my wimple." She gossiped on as she worked, as if Joscelin were another woman. "Told her, I did. Ernalt de Lysle's duped more silly lasses than there are herrings in a barrel. Of course, she'll pay for it. I've seen her puking of a morn. Only way her child will have a father is if Lord Gilbert forces him to put a ring on her finger, and Lord Gilbert won't be keen to wed one of his best fighters to a lass with brains like a cracked pot."

Unable to command her silence, knowing that the guard would

not because he was listening in amusement, Joscelin detached himself. If he had taught Brunin everything he knew, then Brunin in his turn had taught him a little of the art of retreating inside one's own mind.

The woman anointed his wounds with some foul-smelling unguent and gave him a tisane to drink which she said would calm the raging of his blood. "Too much choler," she said. "Red hair's always a sign."

When she went, the silence was as blissful as a trickle of cold water on his hot brow. The guard went to follow her out. "Griselde'll be returning," he said with a grin. "Don't think you've escaped."

❖❖❖

Marion would have collapsed on the bed she shared with Ernalt and cried until she was a husk, but her stomach kept her at the garderobe, retching and retching until she ached from shoulder to groin. She had tried to tell Joscelin she was sorry, that she hadn't meant it to happen like this, but it had all come out wrong and the way he had called her a whore with revulsion in his eyes had been more than she could bear. She wasn't a whore…she wasn't! Whores lifted their skirts for any man who had the money to pay for their services. Whatever she had done had been for love and for not being loved enough.

Ernalt came into the chamber and walked into the garderobe. "Sick again?" he said, arching one golden eyebrow.

She stood up and wiped her mouth with an offcut of linen from her sewing. Her stomach was so sore that she stood half hunched like an old woman.

"I hear you went to tend Joscelin de Dinan," he remarked, leaning in the doorway and blocking her exit. "What did you want, his forgiveness?" His tone was dangerously soft.

Wordlessly she shook her head.

"Or perhaps you went to gloat." He reached out to wrap his forefinger around one of her braids

Marion gave him a reproachful look. "No, not that."

"Then what, sweetheart? To help him escape with a rope or a knife?" He twisted his hand, binding her braid across the width of it as if it were a bridle to tame an unruly horse, and pulled her toward him. "I know how open you are to persuasion."

She turned her head away, afraid that the smell of her breath would sicken him, and afraid of him too. "I...I just wanted to see him, that was all."

"Out of curiosity then." He snorted. "Jesu, you must think me a lack-wit." He fondled her breasts with his other hand. Her nipples budded but the underlying soreness made her flinch and immediately she realized her mistake.

"I love you," she whimpered.

"Show me then." He delved beneath his tunic to his braies. "Show me just how much you love me."

He took her from behind, standing up in the garderobe, with no more finesse than a soldier taking a whore in a stinking alley. Within moments he reached his release and, breathing harshly, leaned on her, forcing her body against the wall. "Whatever reason you went to Joscelin de Dinan, you will not see him again, is that understood?" he panted against her ear. "Wounded or not, he is a dangerous man and you obviously still harbor some regard for him. Who knows what you might hatch between you." Straightening, he adjusted his clothing and left. Marion tottered over to the bed, collapsed upon it, and folded herself into a ball. But unlike a hedgepig, she did not have the protection of spines. All of her was soft and open to attack.

❖ ❖ ❖

Brunin sat up and eased himself to the side of the bed. Pain shot through his body and he had to swallow the groan that swelled in his throat, knowing Hawise would latch on to it straightaway.

"You shouldn't be doing this," she said, watching him with anxiety.

"It's been twelve days now," he replied stubbornly, "and I'm mending well."

"Yes, you are, but that wound almost killed you and it's going to take longer to heal than a scratch." Her voice filled with exasperation. "It is one thing to rise from your bed, go down to the hall, and conduct business, another to mount a horse and ride to the King."

"I feel strong enough."

"You do now, but how will you feel in five miles' time?"

They locked stares and wills.

"Probably I will feel like admitting you were right," he said, "but that won't stop me." He beckoned for his shirt and tunic.

Hawise gave an impatient cluck of her tongue. "I am as mad as you are," she capitulated as she handed the garments to him. "I ought to tie you to this bed and lock you in here for a month at least."

Although in some pain, a gleam filled his eyes. "If that's a threat, I'll take you up on it," he said, "providing that I can have you beneath me."

"I wouldn't want to take advantage of an invalid," she retorted. "And stop trying to distract me with foolishness."

He widened his eyes in innocent affront. "It was you who suggested tying me to the bed."

"That wasn't foolishness," she replied with tightening lips. "The true folly is in what you are about to do…and before you say that it is for my father's sake, you know that he would not expect you to do this in your condition…whatever is happening to him." Her voice faltered a little and she raised his chin, her eyes fierce, daring him to take advantage.

He sobered. "I know what your father expects of me. That is not the question. It is what I expect of myself and of the King. It has to be settled—like a wound has to be cleaned out before it can heal." He reached out to stroke her face. "I will take care, I promise."

Hawise laughed mirthlessly. "I have heard you say that before." She brought him a clean pair of braies and chausses from the coffer and insisted on looking at the healing wound before he put them on. There was still a considerable hole, and the dressing had to be changed twice a day, but the flesh was healthy with no sign of taint, or even laudable pus. He had been lucky, very lucky, and she wanted that luck to hold.

"I mean it this time," he said. "I've seen what a single moment of carelessness can do."

By the time he was dressed in his gambeson and hauberk, cold sweat was dewing his brow. With tightly pursed lips, Hawise watched him latch his swordbelt. "Don't wear your dagger on your left," she said. "It'll chafe the wound."

He flashed her a look from beneath his brows. "Mother hen," he said, but with a smile, and swiveled the mounting to the back of his belt. "Does that suit you?"

His not going at all would suit her best, but there was no point in saying so. At least she was accompanying him, which meant that she might be able to prevent him from too much exertion.

As he turned on a short, cautious step to collect his helm, his grandmother entered the room. She was not using her stick and was walking as stiffly as he had been doing these last few days, but that was neither here nor there. What was a cause for eye-widening was her gown of moss-green silk decorated with wide bands of gold embroidery. She had pulled the side lacings in so tightly that even with a chemise beneath, the contours of her body were outlined: the remnants of what had been a slender, supple waist in young womanhood, a small mound of belly, and breasts like two flattened purses pressing against her lower rib cage. She had discarded her usual face-framing wimple for a gauzy veil edged with seed pearls and gold beads and her braids hung down beneath it in straggly silver ropes.

"Jesú," Brunin whispered. He had to suppress the urge to cross himself.

Unsteadily but without hesitation Mellette approached him.

"*Madame* grand-mère?" he said, his hair prickling at his nape.

A frown crossed Mellette's features. "Why do you call me that? Do I look like your grandmother?"

"You are my grandmother." Brunin darted a glance at Hawise who took a step toward the older woman, her hand extended.

Mellette ignored her. "You have no right to insult me," she said angrily. "You would be nothing without me and well you know it. Your position depends on my father's favor and that can soon be lost."

"I think perhaps you are a little confused, my lady," Hawise said gently. "This is your grandson, Brunin."

"I know full well who he is...and who you are." Mellette's voice filled with low venom. She turned to Brunin. "Husband, I have some news that will please you."

"You do?" Brunin said in a choked voice. He looked again at Hawise. She shook her head and moved away to summon the maids. Mellette gave a small, satisfied nod.

"I am with child. Isn't that what you wanted to hear? You need not share my bed any longer, and that will be a blessing for us both." Her eyes snapped with pride, challenge, and anger. "But I will not have your slut under the same roof. If you must couple with her, do it in the barn where you both belong."

Brunin stared, dumbfounded, filled with pity and a darker stirring of revulsion. "I know I resemble my grandsire, perhaps the more so in my armor, but I am not him, Grand-mère. He was Warin. I am Brunin."

A shadow of doubt crossed her face and, raising one hand, she pressed her knuckles to her forehead. "There is a veil across my eyes. I do not...I do not feel..."

Hawise returned with Sian and a maid. Speaking softly, the women guided Mellette to a window seat and gave her wine. The old lady's voice sounded querulous and lost for a moment, before it sank to a murmur and her head drooped. Looking worried, Hawise returned to Brunin.

"She thought I was my grandfather," he said with a grimace,

"but then all my life she has compared me to him. I suppose it is not so far a step to see us as one." He rubbed his chin. "Is this the first time that her wits have gone wandering?"

Hawise frowned. "She has been a trifle forgetful of late—calling people by different names...probably those from the past, I see now. Yesterday she called me Eve when she demanded a tisane for the ache in her joints, but the lapses have been small—compared to today's."

"Is she fit to travel?"

She considered, then reluctantly nodded, her sense of fair play not permitting her to do otherwise. "Yes, she is...and not so confused that she will not notice us leaving without her. She is quite capable of summoning an escort and riding to Gloucester on her own." She screwed up her face. "In truth, she is probably more fit to travel than you."

He didn't answer her remark because she was right, and he wasn't prepared to admit it.

❖❖❖

Henry's entire court and administration were crowded into the city of Gloucester and there was not a lodging room to be found anywhere. Barons and lesser knights, serjeants and common soldiers had pitched tents on various areas of sward, and Brunin found himself having to do the same. At least it wasn't raining and the weather was mild.

Ralf gazed at the vast array, the tents jammed together like teeth in a jaw that was a fraction too small. "How in God's name are we going to get near Henry, let alone petition him?" he asked as they left the women and the baggage attendants erecting their shelters.

"I don't know, but we must do it," Brunin said grimly. He was tired and in pain. The strain of sitting across a saddle was tugging on his wound and he wanted nothing more than to lie down and sleep for a week. But wanting and having were miles apart...unlike the press of tents. Brunin rubbed his forehead. He was aware of

Ralf waiting for him to lead them…Ralf who had always wanted to be the leader in their childhood, but now recoiled from it—and with good reason, Brunin thought grimly.

"First we go to the cathedral," he said, "and seek out Bishop Gilbert."

"Why should we do that?"

"Because he has the King's ear. Because he knows us and is sympathetic to our cause. We don't have to ride through a wall if we can find the postern."

Ralf still looked slightly nonplussed and Brunin almost smiled as he thought that Ralf's way of doing things was indeed to ride through walls.

The streets were crowded with townspeople and soldiers, jostling cheek by jowl. Ralf spurred to the front and, as if Brunin's thoughts had been transparent, began forcing a path through for their entourage. People were swift enough to leap out of his way, even if they did shake their fists and curse after him, but Ralf was impervious, except to remark that the citizens of Gloucester were a surly bunch.

Outside the cathedral door, the beggars of the town clustered with their wooden bowls, their sorry stories, their sores. Brunin doled out a handful of silver and wondered for how much longer he would have such largesse in his purse. The manors he owned were not big when compared to the size of the estates that he and Hawise had lost. There was also the matter of the death duty owing to King Henry in order that Brunin could inherit what remained.

"God bless you!" cried a milky-eyed bundle of rags with torn black fingernails and a mouth of yellow stumps. More largesse than this wretch here, he thought, and crossed himself. Dismounting was difficult and he was slow, pain pulsing with every movement he made, but Jester seemed to understand and stood still until Brunin had both feet on the ground. He expected to feel the sudden heat of fresh blood, but the wound appeared to have withstood the strain. He steadied himself against Jester's warm bay flank, then straightened as much as he could. He tied the horse to the hitching bar and, hand pressed to his side, walked slowly toward the ornate cathedral entrance. Ralf shooed away some small boys who were turning somersaults on the bar and, gesturing the other knights to stay with the horses, followed his brother.

The cathedral was as busy as a market place and reminded Brunin of the fair at Shrewsbury. Within the open nave, men were conducting business. Scribes were hiring their services to those who wanted letters either written for or read to them. Ink-grinders sat at small tables surrounded by their wares: oak gall and gum arabic; egg white; precious powdered lapis. A trader was selling little knives for trimming pens, and beside him a woman had laid out a cloth on which were quills fashioned from the feathers of different birds: goose and gull, swan, heron, and peacock. Old men sat on the benches at the side of the nave and gossiped. One pair were deeply engrossed in a game of merels. Nearby a mail-clad soldier was making an assignation with a gaudily clad woman. Brunin saw money change hands and watched them leave the cathedral with quickening pace.

"Bishop Gilbert probably isn't…" Ralf began to say, then stared as a colorful array emerged from one of the chapels and advanced down the nave. Surrounded by monks and courtiers came three of the most powerful men in the land, their progress marked by folk kneeling as they passed, the effect like a scythe through a wheat field. Flanked by his chancellor, Thomas Becket, and Gilbert Foliot, Bishop of Hereford, King Henry moved down the nave with a bouncing walk, as if each stride threw his energy into the ground and reflected it back up through the soles of his feet. His eyes were bright, his red-gold hair was sticking up where he had raked his fingers through it, and there was a dangling thread on his tunic where a cluster of seed pearls had torn off.

Ralf stared open-mouthed and then dropped to his knees and

bowed his head. Brunin was slower to kneel, easing down, cold sweat dewing his brow. But he was exulting too. There could not be a more fortuitous opportunity.

Thomas Becket looked down his patrician nose as if he were offended at the time it had taken Brunin to make his obeisance. Gilbert Foliot studied the two young men with shrewd and narrowing eyes. Henry stopped so precipitously that those following behind collided with each other.

"Brunin FitzWarin?" He stared. "You are newly arrived at our muster."

"Sire," Brunin said.

"Is your father here?"

"No, sire...he is dead, God rest his soul." He crossed himself.

Henry's gaze widened in surprise. He gestured Brunin and his brother to stand. Ralf set his arm beneath Brunin's elbow and helped him rise. "And you are sore wounded, by the looks of you," Henry said. "There is a tale here."

Brunin drew several shallow breaths and waited until the pain had abated sufficiently for him to speak. "I sent a messenger when my father died, but it is less than a month ago, and your scribes may not have counted the matter important." His tone was carefully even. What mattered to him did not necessarily matter to Henry. "He had been ailing with a bad chest for some time, but he breathed powdered lime at the fight for Ludlow."

"Ah, Ludlow." Henry compressed his lips and from his expression it was clear that he knew at least something about the matter. "Is that how you have come by your own wounds?"

"Yes, sire. I have come to plead for justice and petition you to intervene."

Becket made an impatient sound. "Then you will have to wait your turn. Think you that the King has the time for this just now?"

Henry held up his hand to stay his chancellor. "Peace," he said. "It was I who spoke of a tale, and I would hear it."

Becket's nostrils flared and he made no attempt to conceal his irritation. Bishop Gilbert gave the chancellor a glance filled with dislike and smug pleasure that Becket had been overruled.

Succinctly, Brunin gave Henry the meat of the matter and watched the King's cheekbones flush and his eyes brighten with anger. "This storm between de Lacy and de Dinan has gone on for too long," he said tersely. "You say that Joscelin is now de Lacy's prisoner."

"If he still lives, sire," Brunin replied. "When last I saw him he was wounded and receiving rough treatment from de Lacy's knights."

"De Lacy has ever served his own interests," muttered Gilbert Foliot. "During the war he changed sides more often than a nurse changes a baby's swaddling clouts."

"I recall that de Dinan changed sides too," Henry said with a sharp look at the Bishop.

Foliot shrugged. "Only the once, and in your lady mother's favor. You know his loyalty, sire."

"I know that while they are warring with each other, they are not serving me," Henry said tightly. "You were right to bring this to my attention. I will deal with the matter once and for all."

"Sire," Brunin said, knowing that for better or worse the brake was about to be applied to the runaway cart.

"And have one of the chirugeons look at your wound."

"My wife is here, sire, she will tend to it."

Henry nodded and made to move on, then he paused and looked at Brunin. "I will be fair," he said, "but I promise nothing."

Brunin bowed and the royal entourage continued its scything path down the nave toward the great cathedral doors.

"What did he mean by that?" Ralf asked, frowning.

Going to one of the benches at the side of the nave, Brunin eased himself down. "He meant," he said bleakly, "that we might not get Ludlow back."

# 36

A MIDWIFE FROM LUDLOW TOWN HAD BEEN CALLED TO attend the birth of one of the soldiers' women. The ordeal over and the mother safely delivered of a son, the midwife was now attending another summons in one of the private chambers. A few questions, a deft examination of Marion's belly, and she stood away from the bed.

"Well?" Marion questioned, anxiously wringing her hands.

"Mistress, you are indeed with child. You have all the signs."

Even though Marion had suspected the worst, the confirmation sent cold panic flooding through her limbs. "You are certain?"

The woman looked affronted. "I have followed my calling since the days of the first Henry. I am certain, my lady." She folded her hands loosely in front of her own stomach, rounded with a fondness for ale and the march of time. "I judge that the babe will be born next year, in the summer."

Marion sat up, icy sweat dewing her armpits. "What must I do?"

"In what way, mistress?"

Marion swallowed. "M-my mother died in childbed. I don't want...I don't want that to happen to me."

"You are not your mother, mistress," the woman said tactfully, keeping to herself the observation that Marion was as narrow as a weasel through hip and flank. Unless the child was small, she would not have an easy time. "You must rest all that you can and avoid heavy foods." She pursed her lips. "You should also pray to St. Margaret and make offerings in her name."

Marion nodded, absorbing the detail with greedy desperation.

"Of course, should you wish to bring on your flux, there are certain herbs that will…regulate your menses," the woman hinted. "But once you reach the stage where the infant quickens, then it becomes too dangerous and a mortal sin."

Marion chewed her lip. "What—what will happen if I take the herbs now?" she asked nervously.

The midwife shrugged. "You will suffer vomiting and severe cramps in the belly as your womb purges its contents."

"There will be blood?"

"Like a flux, but heavier. It is not as dangerous as childbirth, but it still remains a risk. On rare occasions the bleeding does not stop."

Marion turned white, as if the words had the power to drain all the blood from her body. For an instant she had thought there might be an escape, but it was a blind alley. Besides, this was Ernalt's child growing in her womb: his heir. He would have to hasten the marriage now. All she had to do was live through the ordeal of the birth. "Help me choose," she whispered.

The midwife withdrew slightly. "I cannot help you do that, mistress. The decision must be yours."

"But I cannot—" She broke off as Ernalt stormed into the room.

"Pack the baggage chests," he commanded, ignoring the midwife as just another servant. "The King's officials are in the hall and we've to ride to Gloucester." His features were flushed and agitated.

"Gloucester?" Her eyes widened. "Why?"

"Because that's where the King is," he snapped. "Make haste. We're leaving now. Make sure you pack my court tunic. I've got to go. Lord Gilbert's waiting for me." He banged out again.

Dismissing the midwife, Marion rose from the bed and went to Ernalt's traveling coffer. She had never been to court before, had only heard about it from the lips of troubadours and occasional guests who had attended there. Even Sybilla with her important connections had never been. Perhaps Ernalt would marry her at court before the King and all the high barons of the land. That would be an occasion indeed, a glittering moment and the fulfillment of her best dreams. Her hand descended to her belly. She was fecund with Ernalt's child. A son, it would be a son, the birth would be easy, and she would be a great lady. It was all going to come true.

She set to packing the coffer, her mood swinging between euphoric hope and terrified despair.

❖❖❖

The trap door squeaked open again. Joscelin eyed it with trepidation. He could tell from the quality of light in the window-slit that it wasn't time for one of Griselde's pungent visits to assess the state of his health. She had taken a fancy to him. He had tried being rude, but that only encouraged her. Refusing to respond meant that he had to listen to her verbal assault without the satisfaction of retort and it by no means deflected her. Her response to civility was a simpering familiarity that chilled his blood. Clenching his fists, he rose to his feet, putting distance between the bed and himself.

No one descended the ladder. Instead, he received a command, phrased as an invitation, to come up. Joscelin rubbed his grizzled chin. Either he had been ransomed and was about to be set free, in which case he was probably now a landless pauper, or de Lacy had tired of keeping him prisoner and had decided to execute him. Neither were reasons to set foot on the steps, but he had no doubt that if he refused they would come down and get him.

He applied himself to the rungs and was not pleased to discover that his legs were trembling. His ribs had begun to heal, but they still twinged sharply as he climbed, and he had to narrow his eyes against the increasing brightness of the light. He was like a mole, he thought, squinting out into the open, perhaps to meet the vicious blow of a club.

Two guards hauled him up the last few steps and into the

ground floor chamber. There was no sign of de Lacy, but the knight de Lysle was in the room, together with a pair of squires and a barber. To one side a bathtub steamed, and the smell of infused herbs wafted in Joscelin's nostrils. Mercifully the dreaded Griselde was absent. He absorbed the scene with relief and curiosity. Obviously he wasn't about to die, otherwise there would be no need to spruce him up and a priest would have been present.

"You are summoned to answer before the King," said de Lysle, looking as if his mouth were full of vinegar. He gestured to the bathtub. "In mercy my lord has chosen to give you your dignity."

Joscelin snorted. "In 'mercy,'" he scoffed. "What you mean is that if I am brought before the King looking as I do, it will reflect badly on my gaolers and generate dangerous sympathy."

"Read it as you will, my lord; it matters not."

Knowing that he would be forcibly stripped and scrubbed if he did not comply, Joscelin stood passively while the squires removed his sweat-stained, filthy garments. "So, the King has come to Ludlow?" he asked.

De Lysle hesitated for a moment. "The King has sent his summons from Gloucester."

"And am I summoned alone, or does Lord Gilbert ride to Gloucester to answer to the King as well?"

De Lysle gave him a cold look. "Lord Gilbert does indeed ride to Gloucester," he said, "but to do homage for his new castle."

Joscelin returned the knight's gaze in similar wise. Whatever Henry intended for Ludlow, he would not entrust such a declaration to a common messenger. It was too important.

He stepped into the tub and the hot water stung his flesh. Gazing down at himself, he saw the ravages of time and battle. There were thin white scars and newer ones, pink and red. His muscles might still be iron-hard, but the skin no longer clung to their contours: it was folded over them in narrow, crêpy pleats. One more battle, he told himself. One last battle to fight.

❖ ❖ ❖

Marion disliked riding and it was a long time since she had sat on a horse. Usually she had opted to travel in the women's baggage wain, but since there wasn't one of those and since Ernalt hadn't wanted to share his saddle, she was forced to ride on her own. Her mount was a hard-mouthed brown mare that kept wandering out of line and trying to crop grass at the roadside. Twice Marion had almost fallen off and she was mortified by the mingled amusement and irritation of the better riders.

She wanted to speak to Ernalt but he was traveling ahead with the men and she was at the back of the line, relegated to a place just ahead of the servants and baggage ponies. It was not until they stopped for the night in Hereford that she was able to talk to him, but he was distracted and bad-tempered.

"What is it?" he demanded impatiently, casting a glance over his shoulder toward his companions, who were talking around the fire. They were staying in Hereford Castle, which was currently held by a royal caretaker. Ludlow too was in royal hands for the moment. As Gilbert de Lacy had ridden out a royal garrison had ridden in and occupied the battle-scarred wall walks.

"I...I have some important news." She had envisaged telling him in the garden at Ludlow, or a sun-flooded chamber with bird-song cascading through the open shutters. Not here in haste and impatience with the other knights laughing in the background. But if she was to be wed before the court, he needed to know.

"Yes?" he prompted.

"I'm...I'm with child. The...the midwife says I am."

He looked her slowly up and down. "Are you indeed?" A slow, almost smug grin spread across his face as he took her by the waist and pulled her against him. She felt the heat of his hand through her dress and the hard pressure of palm and fingers. There was a gleam in his eye like that of a barnyard rooster about to tread a hen. He looked over his shoulder again, but now she knew that he was considering where he could find some privacy to couple with her.

"One of the knight's wives said that you have got women with child before."

He shrugged. "What of it? All men sow wild oats, but who knows if a furrow has been ploughed and sown by others."

"This child is yours," she said swiftly.

He gave a low chuckle. "Sweetheart, I know that. If I thought you'd been spreading your legs elsewhere, I'd kill you here and now and castrate your lover. You are mine." His forefinger probed the cleft of her buttocks. Mortified lest someone should see, she tried to pull away from him, but he held her fast and ground his loins against hers.

"I thought..." She swallowed. "I thought that when we reach Gloucester, we could be wed. You said it should be a grand occasion and what could be more grand than before the King and the court?" She hated the notes of anxiety and pleading in her own voice. "And now that I am with child..."

The urgency of his movements ceased.

"We both have our court gowns," she continued hastily, "and the matter of Ludlow is to be resolved. There could not be a better time."

"I am not so sure about that, sweetheart."

"I know it is sudden. I would have told you before but—"

"Hush." He set his hand over her mouth. "Be still." He removed his palm and stroked the side of her face and then down over her breast to her supple waist. He was torn by conflicting emotions, some of them bewildering because he did not understand them himself. The masculine pride and pleasure that his seed had taken root in her belly was simple enough to comprehend, as was the raw lust that her frightened vulnerability fired in him. If she hadn't mentioned marriage, he might have taken her to bed and been content, but, whatever her appeal, he had no intention of making her his wife. She was too needy, too demanding, and had no great dowry. He wanted her, he didn't want anyone else to have her, but he didn't want her enough to make her his wife.

"We'll have to see what can be done," he said, soothing her with his hands so that she would not make a scene in front of the other men in the hall. What he said was true, but its meaning was open to interpretation.

And being Marion, and needing desperately to believe, she chose the meaning that she most wanted to be true and smiled at him. When he took her from the hall and had his way with her in the chamber where the spare mattresses were stored, the smile remained on her face even though the force of his thrusts hurt her. A few more days and she would be Lady de Lysle.

# 37

*B*ISHOP GILBERT HAD FOUND BRUNIN AND HIS ENTOURAGE lodgings in a house owned by the Church. The former owner, an elderly man who had bequeathed it to the abbey, had but recently died and it was in a state of neglect, the floor rushes rank underfoot and the thatch much in need of repair. Still, it was better than a tent and Hawise, Sian, and the maids set out to make it habitable. Brunin said to Hawise with a tired smile that he had slept with her in more ramshackle surroundings and when she looked at him askance, murmured something about a certain charcoal burner's hut in Tockington Forest that made her blush.

The rushes were swept out into the midden pit and replaced with fresh ones; the corners were brightened with beeswax candles; the hearth cleared of its choked accumulation of ashes and a new fire laid. Mellette supervised the work and dealt out a constant stream of commands. Sometimes she recognized Hawise, but sometimes she addressed her as Eve, at others as Mald, who was the girl responsible for keeping the fire at Alberbury. When she saw her near Brunin, she would narrow her eyes and mutter imprecations against sluts and whores.

She had refused to remove her fine gown and silk veil, saying that she had to be ready for a summons to the court. "The King is my uncle," she kept repeating, as if she had shouted the words in a cavern and then swallowed the echo. But the King in the confused labyrinths of her mind was the first Henry, and she continually referred to people she had known in her youth who were long in their graves.

It was early evening and Sian was stirring a beef and barley stew in the cooking pot. In such cramped circumstances it was a necessity to feed the household out of one cauldron. Bread had been bought from a nearby bakery and Emmeline was eating a hunk smeared with honey. Ralf sat on the doorstep, whittling a tent peg out of a piece of wood, and Brunin slept on a pallet, one forearm bent across his eyes. Hawise knew that the ride to Gloucester and the subsequent meeting with the King had exhausted his strength. He needed to rest...although such opportunities had to be snatched at, and this hovel was not the ideal place to do it. She was worried for him but dared not show her worry lest she be accused of fussing.

Suddenly Ralf stood up, his body quivering like that of a dog spying a hare. Leaving her scrutiny of Brunin, Hawise hastened to his side.

"What is it?" Her heart lurched. "Papa!" she shrieked. Seizing her skirts in her fists, she ran toward Joscelin who was mounted on his old roan cob and accompanied by two men she did not know, one wearing rich but ordinary garments, the other a knight in full mail. Reaching his bridle, she gazed up at him, joy blazing in her eyes.

"Hawise..." His voice was as dry and light as a husk. With a weary effort, he set his hands to the saddle pommel and eased down off the horse. She had been going to run into his arms, but when she saw how gingerly he moved, she held back.

"I'm all right," he said. "Cracked ribs, healing wounds...battered pride." He opened his arms and she went into them and felt them close around her as they had done all of her life. Only now there was no certainty of safety and protection. Now there was simply the mutual clinging of two shipwrecked survivors washed up on foreign shores. She bit back a sob and after a moment drew away from him. The flesh had fallen from his bones, revealing the sharp angles of recent strain and illness. His rich copper hair had a greater dilution of white so that he was now the same roan as his elderly mount.

Swallowing hard, he searched her face. "I…Brunin…is he…" Then he raised his head and looked past her to the figure standing in the doorway. "Christ, boy!" The moisture from his eyes flooded his voice and swept it away. He strode toward Brunin and stopped. His breath sawed in his throat and his chest rose and fell in shallow, painful spasms. "I saw you pierced by a lance…" he managed to choke out. "I thought you were dead!"

"It would take more than that to kill me," Brunin replied, a smile lighting in his eyes.

"It nearly was the death of him," Hawise said, joining her husband. "He rode all the way to Alberbury with the stump in his body, and how he managed that, I will never know."

"Out of need," Brunin said simply. "I knew that if I could reach you, then I could close the door against the wolves."

They exchanged a look that made Joscelin feel happy for them and utterly bereft. He wanted Sybilla, but was not sure that she would want him. He was exhausted, still half-sick from his wounds, and not in good condition to face what was to come. Nor, from the looks of him, was Brunin. He did not need to count the days to know that the young man was on his feet perilously soon after receiving so bad an injury.

The two men clasped each other, but in a precarious, careful way that took account of each other's frailties.

"I did not know if you were alive either," Brunin said. "I wanted to ride with the royal contingent to Ludlow, but I was refused permission." He gave a bleak smile. "It was probably a good thing that I was. I'd have been too weak to finish any brawl I instigated…and I know I would have instigated one."

Joscelin found a smile in response, although mirth of any kind felt strange to him—like a garment that had once fitted well, but was now too ragged and threadbare to protect him from the world. "They put me in the Pendover tower store room and set a dragon called Griselde to watch over me," he said. "I'd be there now if it weren't for this summons—for which I gather you are responsible."

"There was nothing else I could have done."

They looked at each other, both knowing what was at stake. Joscelin clenched his right fist and turned his wrist so that he was looking down on the bunched muscle of his forearm. Beneath his creased and aging skin, the flesh was still rigid and the tendons thick. A swordsman's hand; a warrior's hand. There were few enough who lived to see the slow degeneration of the years. Even fewer who turned their backs on the dusty circle of the arena and walked away. "No," he said, "there wasn't." He looked around. His escort was waiting with polite patience for him to finish, but they had neither dismounted nor ridden away. He was not a captive, but he was in their custody.

"There is a bed for you here if you wish it," Hawise said with a glance at the men, "although little more than a mattress on the floor."

Joscelin smiled and shook his head. "No, I am expected to sleep in the King's hall tonight," he said. "Where I sleep on the morrow..." He gave a small shrug and turned to his horse.

"I have sent for my mother," Hawise said. "She will come."

Joscelin paused and she saw him clench his fists. "I do not know if that is a good or bad thing," he said heavily, "but you were right to do it. She ought to be here."

❖ ❖ ❖

The court was preparing to move on to Woodstock and would do so as soon as Henry had completed his business in Gloucester. Approaching the castle, Brunin and Hawise had to maneuver their way between baggage carts and pony trains, between squabbling merchants, toiling grooms, and irritable soldiers. A wine tun had been dropped between cellar and cart and a pungent, vinegary aroma blended with the stink of dung and sweat and burning bread from someone's too-hot oven. Two cart drivers began a brawl over who had right of way. One of them accidentally stepped back on a tiny long-haired dog that began to yelp, the ear-splitting noise out of all proportion to its diminutive size. The owner, a gaudily dressed woman, plucked her pet off the ground and waded into the men with a voice pitched at the same level as the dog's.

"It's always like this," Brunin murmured out of the side of his mouth as he negotiated a steaming pile of olive-green manure. "The Bishop of Winchester says that traveling with the court is death to the soul."

Hawise gave a smile of sorts. "I cannot imagine why he should say that," she replied as they narrowly avoided two porters carrying what looked like pieces of a dismantled bed. She supposed that it was the same as her own family moving between their manors, but on a much greater scale. Not only was the King's household on the move, but all the households of every magnate and baron summoned to attend him. She realized anew how fortunate they were to have found any sort of bed for the night.

The usher on duty at the door passed them through for a consideration of silver. Hawise frowned and Brunin gave a resigned shrug. "It is the way of the court," he said.

"So only those who can pay receive audience?"

"Not necessarily, but you have to be prepared to persevere. I could have offered to knock his teeth down his throat, but I'm hardly capable just now and there's always a price to pay of one sort or another. Nor is he defenseless." Brunin nodded toward two mailed guards lounging against the wall and watching all who passed over the threshold. "Observe the dog's teeth," he said.

They had scarcely advanced into the room when a commotion at the door caused them to turn. The lounging guards had come to life and were escorting a struggling, swearing Ernalt de Lysle out of the hall, whereupon they threw him into the mired street.

Beneath her hand, Hawise felt the rigidity of Brunin's arm and was assailed by a jolt of panic. "Don't do anything foolish," she warned. Outside Ernalt was picking himself up and brushing himself off. Marion was with him and, as she tried to help him, he shoved her aside with a snarl.

Hawise was horrified when Brunin removed her hand from his arm and walked back toward the door, but he merely paused before the steward and whispered something against the man's ear. More silver changed hands. When he returned, there was an expression of grim satisfaction on his face.

"What have you done?" she demanded.

"Since I'm in no condition to do 'anything foolish,' I've ensured that the hall stays out of bounds to undesirables," he said. "De Lysle won't be getting a second opportunity."

Joscelin joined them. His expression was strained and now that he was not wearing his cloak, Hawise was frightened to see how thin he was. His court tunic of blue wool hung on his body and his seal ring of thick gold was loose on his middle finger. It was as if without her mother, and without Ludlow, he was diminished.

A fanfare of trumpets announced the arrival of the King. Brunin struggled down on one knee and beside him heard Joscelin hiss with pain as he too was hampered by his wounds. Despite the gravity of the moment, Brunin found himself grinning with dark humor.

The King seated himself on a throne on the dais, magnates and bishops to either side of him. Henry was wearing a formal tunic in the same shade of purple as the cushion padding the seat of the throne and a pleated undergarment of wine-red silk. The colors clashed with his fox-red hair, and the brooch at his throat was lopsided, but even at the best of times Brunin knew that Henry cared little for the formality of appearance—unlike his chancellor. Thomas Becket was resplendent in a gown of red silk, stiff with gemstones and embroidery. His expression was stiff too, as if he had been curling his lip at a stink beneath his nose and his face had frozen.

There were other marcher barons among the gathering, some allies, some not, but mostly men who were neutral in the contention between de Lacy and de Dinan. It was not the only argument over which Henry had to make judgment, and since the court was waiting to move on, the King was disposed to be swift. He dealt with a couple of land disputes and the matter of awarding custody of the juvenile heir of a recently deceased baron to a guardian, and then he addressed himself to the business of Ludlow, commanding Joscelin and Gilbert de Lacy to approach the foot of the dais.

Henry leaned his elbow on his raised knee and propped his hand on his chin. "Ludlow," he said. The gray eyes flickered between Joscelin and Gilbert de Lacy. Both men had known Henry when he was a stripling youth with an army of rag-tag mercenaries at his back, striving to win a kingdom, striving for something he saw plainly as his yet held by another man. Now he was a king and, despite the clashing hues of his garments, despite the skewed brooch and the way he sat on the throne like an artisan, there was still no mistaking his charisma and authority.

"I have heard all the arguments, all the reasons why and why not. Time and again I have heard them and been reminded by your warring." He glanced briefly at the men gathered around him. "Some here have counseled me to punish you both and keep Ludlow in my own hands, and I admit I have given that notion more than passing consideration." He paused to add weight to his words and let their implication settle upon the men.

Beside him, Brunin felt Hawise's breathing quicken and saw her bite her lip. This was it. The moment when all was won or lost. Gold or dust. He took her hand in his and felt her fear, as icy as his own. In the heat of battle he could be as steady and indifferent as granite, but that was not how he felt now: for this was a different sort of battle...and there was nothing he could do for Joscelin.

"However"—Henry stroked his beard—"I suspect in so doing I would be cutting off my nose to spite my face."

There was another long pause. Brunin surmised that Henry was rather enjoying the drama of the moment and the exercising of his royal power.

"You both have a claim on Ludlow. Lord Gilbert through his father, who had the castle taken out of his hands for fomenting rebellion in the time of my great-uncle, King William Rufus, Lord Joscelin through his wife Sybilla Talbot, who is of de Lacy blood through her mother." Henry looked between the two men and raised his voice to encompass the barons standing around the throne. "I call upon all present to bear witness. It is my ruling that Gilbert de Lacy be given full seisin of the castle of Ludlow in perpetuity, to be held of him and his heirs by me and my heirs."

Joscelin stood as rigid as an effigy. For a moment de Lacy was frozen too, and then a beatific smile broke over his face—as well it might, for the King's words were a vindication of all the long years of struggle. Brunin bowed his head and stared at the floor. He could feel the rage and disappointment shimmering inside him like a heat haze on a summer day.

"No," he heard Hawise whisper. "Dear Jesu, no. He cannot do this to us."

He had done it at Whittington, Brunin thought, but that was nothing. A mere pinprick compared to an open sword wound.

"Nevertheless," Henry said into the silence of shock and joy created by his decision, "Joscelin de Dinan and Sybilla Talbot are due compensation for their loyalty to my mother and myself during the long years of the war. Therefore I give to them in perpetuity our manor of Lambourn and its appurtenances, worth in total seventy-six pounds a year."

It was in all senses of the word a kingly gift and, even if it was not Ludlow and had no castle, was almost a fitting exchange. But still, the initial humiliation and swallowing of pride came hard, as did the acknowledgment of defeat. Joscelin bowed his head. So did de Lacy, but raised it again, his gaze incandescent with triumph and joy.

There was little more to do after that but for the men to make their oaths to Henry for their lands, to put their hands between his and receive the kiss of peace. And then to give the kiss of peace to each other. All eyes were upon them and for an instant the tension was as tight as a drawn bowstring. Joscelin hesitated. So did de Lacy. Brunin's hand went to his sword hilt for reassurance and found no comfort. No man was permitted into the King's presence with a blade at his hip.

Gilbert de Lacy held out his hand to Joscelin. "It is over," he said. "If I cannot call you friend, then at least let us no longer be enemies."

There was grace in the words and Joscelin responded to them with a stiff nod and slowly raised his hand to clasp de Lacy's. The men leaned toward each other and performed the ritual of the kiss of peace. It was a brief salutation and they parted quickly, but a look passed between them, compounded of all the volatile emotions that had dogged their struggle down the years. Perhaps the best that could be salvaged was a grudging respect.

The audience broke up on the heels of the decision, for the King desired to be on his way to Woodstock and the outriders had already set out to secure grazing for the horses and lodging for those who were accompanying the royal household. Gilbert de Lacy left too, to secure his confirmed inheritance and retrieve it from royal custody. Joscelin remained where he was, staring numbly at the empty throne. An attendant had removed the purple cloth from the seat and carried the fabric out of the hall to one of the baggage carts. Men eyed him sidelong and avoided him with embarrassment and uncertainty in their faces. The world swirled and moved around him in a bright array of courtly color and left him both at its center and on its periphery.

Slowly he became aware of a presence beside him and looked up, expecting to see Brunin and Hawise. He both dreaded and desired their sympathy and comfort, knowing he was not ready to face them. But it wasn't them, it was Sybilla, which was infinitely more satisfying and infinitely worse.

Her garments were mud-spattered and she was gray with fatigue, but her eyes were burning as they had burned in his dream. He tried to meet them, yet, unable to sustain the contact, turned his head aside. "I am glad you were not here when Henry gave Ludlow to Gilbert de Lacy," he said. "I could not have borne it." His voice cracked. "Indeed I am not sure that I can bear it now."

He did not look at her because he feared what he would see. Anger, rejection, disappointment, anguish? In the early days of their marriage, when she was still mourning her first husband and hostile with grief, he had sworn to her that he would hold Ludlow. He had set out to prove that he was as good as the man she had lost—perhaps better—and he had failed.

"Henry did not wait for me," she said. "I thought he might have done me that courtesy at least."

"It would have changed nothing, and at least you were spared." Joscelin clenched his fists. *And at least I was spared your presence as he stripped my pride.*

"Perhaps I did not want to be spared."

"No," he said bleakly, "but how often do we get what we want? He has given us a rich manor out of his own estate in compensation."

"Yes, Lambourn. I saw Hawise outside with Brunin and they told me."

"But it isn't Ludlow."

"No, it isn't."

Her voice was pitched low and he wondered if he imagined the note of bitterness. Probably not. "I know it meant everything to you...I have failed..." The only way to leave was to face her and it took all of his courage. Two attendants brushed by them, their faces studiously blank, but Joscelin could almost see their ears stretched like trumpets. The men picked up and removed the throne, leaving indentations in the new green rushes.

Sybilla barred Joscelin's way. Her eyes were swimming with tears and new lines of care tracked her face. Although she stood erect and proud, Joscelin could see the price she was paying. His heart turned over as strongly as it had done the first time he laid eyes on her: standing in Ludlow's bailey, a small daughter under either wing, and her head high as he rode through the gates to take the castle, and her, in King Stephen's name.

"I do not deny that Ludlow means much to me," she said tremulously. "How could it not when I have loved and lived and laughed and mourned there since being a new bride. But you are wrong: it is not everything, and if you think that, then I too have failed."

He shook his head "No, beloved, no...you have never..." He could not continue.

"Oh, I have, and we both know it." She moved closer and raised her hand to touch his face. "There are times when we have ridden the storms of each other's differences and resentments. You have trodden paths on which you would never have set foot were it not for my urging—" She broke off and searched his face. "But you need to know that I would follow you barefoot in my shift and still be the proudest woman in England."

The declaration closed Joscelin's throat. He turned his head and kissed the palm of her hand, tasting salt and the grit of hard traveling.

"Let us go to Lambourn," she said. "Let us cease striving and sit in the sun for a while at least. Ludlow was my pride, but I still have my soul...and the greater part of my heart. In the end, it is not the stones that matter, but the people who dwell within them. I do not want to end my days like the lady Mellette—an embittered old woman locked up in a barren fortress of her own making."

Joscelin shook his head and managed a tentative smile.

She gave him a questioning look. "What?"

"A moment ago I was on my knees and looking into darkness," he said in a fractured voice. "And now, out of nothing, you give my pride and esteem back to me...but you are wrong."

She eyed him askance. "Why?"

"I would not have you follow me, but walk at my side."

They kissed like young lovers and it was a sweet and poignant moment that gave a brightening of hope to defeat.

❖❖❖

"Oh, in Christ's sweet name, there isn't going to be a wedding!" Ernalt snarled at Marion. "The court's going to Woodstock and we are bound for Ludlow." Temper flashed in his eyes. There were dung stains on his tunic where he had been thrown down by the usher's bodyguards and he was spoiling for a fight.

Marion bit her lip. "But you said—"

"Whatever I said was to keep you quiet, like a nurse giving a babe a honey sucket."

She stared at him with stricken eyes. "Then when are we to be married?"

"Haven't you understood yet?" he said, taking pleasure in the expression that his cruelty put on her face. "You're a tasty morsel when you're not whining, but men do not marry their morsels." He turned his back on her and strode off toward the sward where the de Lacy tents were pitched.

Marion stared after him, her world dissolving. The woman Griselde had warned her but she had preferred to pay no heed. She could appeal to Lord Gilbert, but she doubted she would reap much cooperation from that quarter. He had been prepared to use her to gain his ends, but the fact that she had been willing to betray her own people meant that he viewed her with suspicion and would rather not accept her as a legitimate part of his household.

She had nowhere to go, no one to take her part unless…Weeping, she turned toward the castle.

❖❖❖

Since the court was leaving the city, there was suddenly a glut of accommodation far better than the ramshackle hovel where Brunin and Hawise had spent the previous night. Unlike Henry, they had no plans to move on until the morrow at least and thus transferred themselves to the castle's great hall. Leaving Hawise talking to her parents and his grandmother seated at a bench on the dais, imagining herself a great lady at court, Brunin went with the knights to bring Jester and the other horses from the outbuildings at the rear of their former dwelling.

He was returning to the castle when Marion stepped out across his path and he had to clutch the bridle close to the headstall to prevent the horse from barging her with its shoulder. She had ever been foolish like that. About as much sense as a headless chicken when it came to being around horses...and men, he thought grimly. "Go on," he said to the knight following immediately behind him and handed over Jester's reins. "I'll join you in a moment."

With a ferocious scowl at Marion, the knight clicked his tongue to Jester and continued on his way. The grooms ignored her, omitting to bow, and the serjeant bringing up the rear spat in the dust at her feet and growled a curse under his breath. Marion's expression filled with distress.

"What did you expect?" Brunin said with curt hostility. "What you have done is unforgivable, except by God. You always wanted to bring men to their knees. Well, you have your wish. Are you pleased?"

She looked at him through shimmering eyes. "I never meant it to happen like this..."

"Well, it has, and it's too late to undo any of it," he said, his tone growing savage in order to negate the pity stirring inside him. "You have made your bed, so now go and lie in it."

She started to cry and, as the tears spilled over her lashes and ran down her face, she pressed her hands to her belly. "I can't," she sobbed. "He wants me for his whore, not his wife, and I am carrying his child."

"Why should any of us care about that, except to say that you deserve it?" He made to move on, but she shot out her hand and grabbed his sleeve with thin, bird-like fingers.

"Please...Lord Joscelin once offered me safe haven in a

nunnery. I thought that you might…that you might find it in you to speak for me."

Brunin shrugged her off in disgust. "He would not listen," he said. "And why should I speak for you?"

"I thought that at one time…that you cared…that you—"

A horse clopped around the corner of the building. Marion looked up at the sound of hooves and gasped as Ernalt de Lysle advanced on them on his stallion.

"Please…" Marion grabbed Brunin's arm again, her fingernails digging through fabric into flesh.

De Lysle dismounted. "Marion, come here." He extended his left hand in a peremptory gesture. His right was already reaching to his sword.

"Why?" she sniffled. "You don't want me."

"I didn't say that."

"No, you are very fond of 'not' saying things."

"I said come here." His nostrils flared with temper. Watching him, Brunin tried to read the flicker of his eyes, the motion of his body. He couldn't reach his own sword because Marion was trembling against him, barring his way.

"Leave her alone," he said.

De Lysle took two paces forward. "Still playing the preux che-valier, FitzWarin?" he sneered. "I remember you at Shrewsbury Fair, a puling coward with piss running down your leg."

"You seem to have strange notions of what is and is not yours for the taking," Brunin replied evenly, although his heart was pounding in swift, hard strokes. "And of the difference between courage and cowardice. It takes no courage to terrify a child into pissing himself or to beat a woman into submission. That is the coward's way."

Drawing his sword, de Lysle strode forward and wrenched Marion away from Brunin, flinging her aside so hard that she fell. And then he lunged. Brunin had watched the hand, not the eye, and ducked under the flash of the blade. The site of his healing wound burned with pain but the instinct to survive kept him moving. He came up, reached for de Lysle's wrist with his right hand, forced it back, and struck with his left.

De Lysle reeled, blood blossoming from his split lip and dribbling down his chin, and Brunin drew his own sword.

"No!" Marion screamed. "No!" She went unheeded. A crowd began to gather, drawn to the fight like hounds to the scent of meat. De Lysle recovered and aimed a slashing blow at Brunin's left arm. Without a shield, Brunin had to parry with his sword and the shriek of steel on steel was agonizing. Fine splinters of metal sparked from the blow and the impact ran up Brunin's arm, leaving tingling fire in its wake. He knew he had to end it quickly. He was weak from his wound and had been unable to train. De Lysle was strong and swift and it did not take vast intelligence to see how this fight was going to end.

He ducked beneath another blow and as he straightened and recovered, felt a trickling heat in his side. Again de Lysle came at him. Brunin parried and felt the blades sliding against each other. He pushed and twisted, flicked his wrist, cast de Lysle off with a heave that brought the wetness of blood through shirt and tunic, and then cut hard with the back edge of the blade.

De Lysle cried out and involuntarily heeled onto his back foot. Blood poured from the knuckle joint of his forefinger, which had been curved over the hilt guard. Now half the finger was gone. Brunin followed through, whipping off his cloak, casting it over de Lysle's head, and swiping the knight off his feet. De Lysle flurried his way out of the heavy cloth by which time Brunin had a sword edge at his throat. He allowed the blade to bite and watched the thin line fill and overflow with red.

"Stop it!" Marion shrieked. "Stop it!" She threw herself against Brunin, and her weight struck him on his damaged side. Agony whitened his vision and he grunted and gave ground. De Lysle raged to his feet and prepared to attack again, but his hilt was slippery with blood and, as Brunin parried, de Lysle lost his grip and his weapon sailed from his hand and landed in the street with a metallic clatter.

"God's sweet life, enough!" bellowed Gilbert de Lacy, forcing his stallion through the crowd to the drama at its center. "What goes forth here?" There was a dangerous light in his eyes. The knights of his entourage, mounted up and ready to leave, formed a phalanx, mail-clad and grim-faced.

Brunin knew that de Lacy was fully expecting to hear the word "Ludlow" on his lips and to act accordingly. "Honor," he gasped through bared teeth. "And cowardice."

"What?" Nonplussed, de Lacy glowered at him.

"They was fighting over the wench, sir," piped up one of the spectators, pointing a grimy forefinger at the weeping Marion.

De Lacy's scowl deepened. Uncoordinated with pain and exertion, Brunin staggered to Marion, hauled her to her feet, and thrust her toward de Lacy.

"In God's name," he said, "see her safely into a convent, my lord."

De Lacy's mouth twisted in distaste. "I doubt any house of nuns worth its reputation would harbor her."

"Give her to me," de Lysle said hoarsely. "She is mine." He held out his undamaged hand toward Marion and beckoned.

She stared at his outstretched fingers and slowly, with measured tread like a sleepwalker, went to him.

Nausea coiled in Brunin's belly. He wondered what he had just been fighting for. Behind him the sound of rapid hoofbeats announced the arrival of his own men and Joscelin's. Hawise rode at their head on Jester, her gray eyes aglitter like her father's when he went into battle. Brunin could see the potential for renewed bloodshed. Sword hilts rattled against scabbard mountings, spear hafts clacked upon mail as de Lacy's knights presented their weapons.

De Lacy spoke sharply to his men. Brunin held out his hand to stay his own and looked at Marion.

"Well?" he said. "What is it to be?"

She stared at him from within the pinion of de Lysle's arm, her eyes wide and blank like empty mirror cases. Then she lowered her lids and turned inward toward her lover, laying her palm on his mail-clad breast. He covered it with his mutilated, bleeding hand and gripped.

"You see how it is to be," de Lysle snarled with raw triumph. "She comes with me." He signaled a squire to bring up his stallion and, once mounted, pulled Marion up behind him. She clung to him, burying her face against his spine, hiding herself from the world.

De Lacy mounted his stallion. "Keep your distance from Ludlow," he said. "You and all of your kin."

"All claims are quit," Brunin answered stiffly. De Lysle was having difficulty controlling the sidling dun. Already the reins were slippery with blood. Still Marion would not look up.

Brunin watched de Lacy and his entourage clatter off down the road and as the tension left his body the pain struck with a crimson vengeance. He staggered and gasped, and Hawise was immediately at his side.

"You stupid, purblind fool!" Her voice was pitched low so as not to carry, but it was filled with vehemence, rage, and a tremble of tears. "What do you think you were you doing?"

"As you say, being a stupid, purblind fool," he answered and swayed. She unlatched his swordbelt, jerked his tunic and shirt out of the way, and looked at the damage wrought by his exertions. With tight lips, she beckoned two of the soldiers forward and somehow, between their brawn and Brunin's fading strength, they managed to get him across Jester's back.

"God help me," she said. "I want you alive for the rest of my days, not for the few that you seem to be making of yours!"

He tried to smile. "Are you sure about that?"

She gave him a look swimming with tears. "If you have to ask then you are indeed a fool."

❖ ❖ ❖

In a small side chamber off Gloucester's great hall, Brunin watched the candle burn on the pricket and wondered what hour of the night it was. He was wakeful now that the effects of the soporific wine had worn off. Hawise and Sybilla had cleaned his reopened wound with stinging salt water and astringent herbs, Sybilla informing him without sympathy that he should stop arching like a scalded cat and it was a good thing that men didn't have to undergo the ordeal of childbirth, or God's earth would be without a population. The women had packed the hole with soft linen bandages, given him wine infused with more herbs including white poppy, and left him to sleep. Now he was wide awake and thirsty. His side was pulsing and sore, but he was not in agony.

A flagon stood on a stool at the bedside, with a cup, but to reach it he would have to lean across his sleeping wife. He studied the candlelit shine of her hair: dark red as garnets, strong as wire, and soft as moss. He remembered its abundance in his hands on their wedding night: the clean, sweet aroma; the erotic sensation of it trailing over his skin. Thought transferred itself to flesh and, despite the distractions of thirst and pain, he was suddenly hard.

Stealthily he raised himself up on one elbow and reached toward the flagon. A drink would settle his thirst and the other matter would go away if he didn't think about it. He had just succeeded in hooking the flagon in his fingers when she turned over with a sleepy murmur. Gingerly he lifted his arm to avoid spilling wine on her.

"What are you doing?" she mumbled, opening her eyes.

"I needed a drink, and I didn't want to disturb you...but plainly I've failed."

She made an irritated sound. "You should have woken me. You don't want to open your wound again." She reached for the cup and turned to him, then eyed what the disturbed covers had revealed.

"I was thinking of your hair," he explained.

She bit back a smile. "Just my hair?"

"That was enough."

"Do you want me to put more poppy syrup in this?"

"No."

She removed the flagon from him and poured wine into the cup. His eyes never left her face as he drank it down. She watched the movement of his throat, and the soft glow and shadow of candle flame on his body.

"More?"

He shook his head and she replaced the flagon on the stool. When she turned back, he reached for her.

"Your wound!" she protested, her eyes flickering between his groin and the bandaging at his hip.

"…is in less need of succor than other parts for the moment," he said, his hands busy with the lace of her chemise.

"But we can't, you—"

"You don't want to?" He transferred his attention to the hem of her shift, bunching it upward, and she shivered as she felt the palm of his hand against her skin.

Hawise swallowed and felt her body grow liquid with lust. "I don't want to hurt you."

"You won't." He fastened his other hand in her hair and brought her mouth down to his; as they kissed, his fingers were very busy beneath her shift, banishing her misgivings. Brought to a pitch where modesty was forgotten, Hawise broke the kiss to remove the chemise. And then, because she was uppermost, and because it seemed to her the best way of preventing him from putting strain on his wound, she straddled his thighs and, after a moment's fumbling, succeeded in sheathing him. She did the latter slowly and watched his face. The expression in his eyes, the sharp hiss of breath through his teeth, told her everything she wanted to know and sent a ripple of pleasure arrowing through her loins. She knew that the Church would view such carnality as a sin and that penance would be due, but she was willing to be sorry on the morrow, not now.

"Am I hurting you?" She raised up and sank back down, the movement leisurely and calculated. The tips of her hair trailed lightly over his body.

A grimace crossed his face and he placed his hands on her hips, holding them still. "I would call what you are doing more like torture," he gasped. "And of an injured man too."

"Hah, shall I stop and let you be?" Although she had been hesitant at Brunin's first approach, Hawise was enjoying herself now. There had been little opportunity for such play in their marriage bed, but with each new encounter she was learning—and recent abstinence had sharpened her appetite...as it had obviously done her husband's. She could tell from his breathing and the fine dew of sweat on his body that he was riding a knife-edge.

"Do that and I will never, ever forgive you."

Hawise laughed and let herself rise and fall, rise and fall, while beneath her Brunin gasped and clung to control by a thread, every muscle in his body knotted with tension. The sight, the feel of him, the novelty of the position flooded through her and, added to that abstinence, brought her to a knife-edge of her own and, almost without warning, her climax struck like a stone hurled into a pool and the ripples cascaded through her body in flexing rings of sensation. She heard his breathing catch across his larynx, felt him let go and shudder with the pleasure of his own release, and then by slow degrees relax. His clenched fists fell open. He looked at her through heavy lids, his eyes glazed.

"And how is your need now?" she asked, gently leaning over to kiss him.

"Comfortably buried," he said against her lips and she felt him smile.

Later, the wine drunk down to the lees, she curled against him and ran her forefinger over his bicep, following the line of a vein running down the muscle. "What will happen to Marion?" she asked and felt his flesh tighten beneath her touch.

"I hope that de Lacy will put her in a convent."

"And if he doesn't?"

He turned awkwardly to face her and ran a strand of her hair through his fingers. "That is his concern," he said softly. "Whatever I might have done for her was finished today when she turned back to de Lysle." He made a face, as if he were lying on tree roots instead of a soft feather mattress.

"I don't hate her," Hawise said. "But she haunts me…"

"That is how I feel too."

Silence fell between them; Hawise was slowly drowsing back to sleep when he spoke again. "As soon as I can ride any distance, we'll go to Lambourn and to Alberbury and begin anew."

She nuzzled against his shoulder and murmured agreement.

"There is still Whittington to recover," he said. "There are writs to be sought and pleas to be made, but that is a way forward, not back." His hand closed on her hair and he pulled her against him. Soon his breathing was even and steady. Hawise watched the measured rise and fall of his chest, and if she was pensive about their future, she also knew that it held nothing they could not overcome together.

*38*

MARION STOOD BY THE WINDOW IN HER CHAMBER AT Ludlow. The attendants had just trooped out of the room after depositing her traveling chest against the wall. Ernalt's shield was propped against the chest; his naked sword lay across it, awaiting the attention of polish and grindstone.

There had been little point in taking the coffer in the first place; no need for the fine silk gown and gauzy veil. No wedding. Ernalt lay on the bed with his boots on, the muddy soles spoiling the coverlet she had embroidered with such painstaking care. That would not have happened in Lady Sybilla's household. Sybilla would have given a single look and the offending male would have immediately removed his boots. But then the male would not have offended in the first place—even though he had the right. Sybilla had always commanded the respect that kept such lack of consideration at bay. Marion knew the kind of respect that she herself commanded. Even if by some miracle Ernalt did raise her from concubine to wife, she would never have what Sybilla and her daughters had. When she thought of the future of the child growing in her womb, son or daughter, she felt an aching despair.

"Stop staring like a lack-wit and pour me wine," Ernalt commanded tersely.

She went to the pitcher and the cups set beside it. Lord

Gilbert's chirugeon had dealt with Ernalt's injuries. His mutilated finger was bandaged and wrapped in a leather archer's guard and the sword cut on his neck had been left to scab over in a crust of beaded blood.

"You should not have run to FitzWarin," he said as she handed him the wine.

Her throat tightened. "I…We were once children together. I thought he might help me."

"That was a stupid thing to think," he said softly.

"You said you wouldn't marry me; you said I was a whore. What else should I have thought?"

"And what did he say?"

She made to turn away, but he grasped her wrist with the hand not holding the wine and held her fast. "Tell me, what did he say? Did he call you a whore too? Would you have lain with him if he asked it?"

Marion tugged again and managed to wrench herself free. "He said…" She swallowed. "He said that my bed was of my own making." From somewhere within her lacerated mind, she found a last spark of defiance. "And yes, I would have lain with him had he asked it."

He came up off the bed, but tiredness and injury hampered his speed. Marion ducked under his arm and ran for the door, but tripped on her gown and sprawled her length. He strode after her, seized her by the arm, and flung her back into the room, slamming her against the coffer. Her thighs caught the lid and she sat down on it, the air punching from her lungs. His exertion had opened the wound on his neck and the drip of blood onto his hand made him stop and raise his arm to his throat to examine the extent of the damage. Marion's fingers encountered the hilt of his sword. She groped, wrapped her hand around the grip, and, panting for breath, brandished it at him.

He looked at her over his bloody hand with a mingling of astonishment, laughter, and growing rage.

"Put that down or I'll use the flat of it to beat you into next week," he said huskily.

"I'll use it, I swear I will." Her voice was thin, her hands shaking.

"You truly have lost your wits. Give me that." He took a step toward her and Marion made a token thrust with the weapon. His swordbelt was hanging over the edge of the coffer and as he reached her he caught his foot in the strap and tripped. Marion's gesture of feeble bravado would have done nothing on its own, but the force of his falling weight caused the blade to pierce his chest.

His eyes locked with hers. There was lingering fury in them and then an expression of wide bafflement. "What have you done?" he said.

In panic she snatched her hand from the hilt and tried to push him away, but his body leaned into her, forcing the sword in deeper. He tried to speak again, but all that emerged was a wordless croak. His chest shuddered but he could not draw breath and he fell upon her, pinning her under him on the coffer.

Weeping, gasping for breath, Marion forced herself out from beneath him. He fell to the floor with a dull thud, limbs flopping like those of the cloth doll she had owned in childhood. His gaze was fixed and blank.

"Ernalt…?" She crammed her fists against her mouth and stared at him, but he didn't move. A draught from the open shutters blew over him, lifting the fair hair off his brow, but his eyes did not blink.

"Ernalt, get up." She stooped, touched him, and then retreated with a small scream as a thin trickle of blood ran from his mouth corner. Her knees buckled and she collapsed against the coffer. Whimpering, she sat in the rushes, folded her arms around her midriff, and rocked slowly back and forth.

She did not know how much time passed. Someone knocked on the door, but it was barred and when she didn't open it, they went away. The breeze outside strengthened and a shower blew over. She heard rain hissing in the air and the light in the chamber darkened. When she roused herself, the light had returned and drenched birdsong was filtering through the window. There was a steady drip, drip of water onto the embrasure seat where the direction of the wind had gusted the rain into the room. Marion clambered unsteadily to her feet. Nerving herself to touch Ernalt, she took hold of his arm and dragged him toward the bed. Her eyes were drawn to the sword hilt and the protruding inches of steel beneath it and the way the weapon shook as she struggled with his dead weight. It was impossible for her to put him on the bed as she wanted—he was simply too heavy—and finally she arranged his body on the floor beside it, drawing his legs together, straightening his tunic. She fetched a ewer and cloth and wiped the blood from his neck wound and the corner of his mouth. She closed his eyes; she combed his hair until it shone like wheat-colored silk. Fetching his cloak from the coffer, she spread it over him from throat to knee, concealing the sword in his chest. Now he looked as if he were sleeping. She had always liked him best in repose, the harsh words and judgment silenced, the handsome features smooth and relaxed. No threat and nothing to contradict illusion.

For a long time, she stared at him. The room darkened as it rained again, then brightened. She stripped off her traveling gown and dressed herself in the brocade gown in which she had intended to be married. The gold brooch Ernalt had given her secured the deep neck opening, and his ring was on her heart finger. Marion unbraided her hair and combed it out with the same comb she had used on Ernalt, until it was a skein of golden silk. Over it she draped her best veil, the one edged with the little seed pearls that had been a gift from Joscelin one Christmastide. She secured it with golden pins and, as she pushed the last one into place, went to the window. There was another raincloud on the horizon, but as yet the sky sparkled and a rainbow stood out against the incoming gray. Her eyes on the sweeping arch of color, Marion slipped off her shoes and stepped up onto the ledge, her bare feet traced with shadowy blue veins. She had to squeeze herself sideways for the aperture was not large, but there was space enough. Perched on the ledge, one side of her body facing the open sky, the other the enclosing chamber, she looked down. It was a dizzyingly long way, but she had been falling for a long time and for much further than the distance between here and the base of the rock-cut ditch from which Ernalt had once climbed up to her. Her gaze turned inward one final time and embraced the enshrouded knight on the floor, and then she looked out, fixed her stare upon the rainbow's vivid hues, and flung herself toward them, arms outspread like wings.

# 39

IT HAD BEEN A HOT DAY AND THE DUSK WAS WOVEN WITH THE scent of dust and the green aroma of new-mown hay. Seated on a bench against the manor wall, a cup of sweet English ale in his hands, Joscelin watched the swallows dip and swoop over the manor house and outbuildings. His tunic was folded on the bench beside him and his shirt was pushed back to the elbows, revealing sinewy, freckled forearms. The hair sprouting on them was still red, unlike that on his head where only his nape now showed a tinge of the original strong auburn. He was entering his winter years, he thought ruefully, the time of brittle hoar frost. He had many regrets—things not accomplished in the swift summer season—but he preferred not to dwell on what could not be changed. Spring always followed winter; new shoots, green with sap, took the place of the old and sere, but born of the same roots.

"Deep thoughts?" Sybilla asked with a smile. She had brought her sewing into the evening warmth but the light was now not strong enough for her eyes to see her stitches.

"Melancholy," he replied with a self-deprecating smile that deepened the creases in his cheeks.

She gave him one of her questioning looks and he shook his head.

"It is no more than a pang at wondering how many summers of swallows we have left to watch."

Sybilla laid her hand over his, her skin mottled and veined like an autumn leaf. As many as God is merciful enough to give us," she murmured.

He chuckled softly. "Wise as ever."

They sat in silence again. When they had first come to Lambourn, Joscelin had been dubious about how content they were really going to be with such an alteration to their circumstances. But the manor was tranquil and prosperous and its atmosphere had drawn them in like a sunlit embrace. For Joscelin, it had been like the relief of shedding his hauberk. When he donned his mail, he always felt a sense of strength and power, perhaps even arrogance, but after a while the weight became oppressive and he was glad to remove it and relax. Coming to Lambourn had felt like that, but he had never been certain that Sybilla felt the same.

They had heard that Gilbert de Lacy had taken Templar vows and gone to fight in the Holy Land, leaving Ludlow to his son. A merchant who had recently visited Ludlow had told Joscelin and Sybilla that, before he left, Gilbert de Lacy had demolished the old wooden chapel and replaced it with a domed one built in stone, representative of the Temple in Jerusalem. New gates had been furnished and a program of rebuilding set in motion. In a way, Joscelin was glad. The more de Lacy altered Ludlow, the less Joscelin felt that it still belonged to him. Sybilla had absorbed the news with barely a flicker, but for a few days had immersed herself in the business of Lambourn with a quiet desperation. That had faded now and she seemed to have found a new equilibrium. He supposed it was one thing to remove a hauberk, quite another to go barefoot in one's shift. Such adjustment was bound to take longer.

The guard on duty on the wooden wall walk above the gatehouse suddenly straightened up and shouted a warning. For a moment, Joscelin's stomach wallowed, but no more than that. These days such shouts were few and presaged visitors, not attack. Momentarily hampered by the complaint of stiff sinews, he creaked to his feet and moved carefully toward the gates. Sybilla sent a maid to warn the kitchens of more mouths to feed.

Determined not to let the stairs defeat him, Joscelin clambered to the top of the gatehouse and stepped onto the timber walkway—by which time his heart was thundering in his ears and his knees were afire.

"It's your son-in-law, my lord," announced the guard, whose name was Ascelin. At Ludlow, he had been brawny and muscular. Now he was as plump and comfortable as a well-fed barnyard hen, his belly reclining on his sword-belt. He pointed a stubby forefinger toward the approaching troop. Summer dust was rising from the hooves of a troop of horses and the light was at that stage of day when every color was as sharp as glass. Joscelin fixed his eyes on the yellow, black, and red of Fulke's wolf banner, borne by the standard-bearer, and then on the familiar bay gelding and gray mare pacing behind it. Joscelin's heart continued to pound. He summoned all the breath he had left in his body and, cupping his hands, turned toward the bailey to bellow the news to Sybilla.

He had to negotiate the steps again, which, although not as exhausting, was just as difficult as climbing up them because one slip would have meant a bone-breaking fall. By the time he reached the foot of the stairs, two serjeants were swinging the gates open to admit the troop.

Just inside the archway, Brunin drew rein. Pointing toward Joscelin, he murmured in the ear of the small boy who had been sharing his saddle and carefully slipped the child to the ground.

Very gingerly, Joscelin crouched to his knees and watched his grandson run toward him. He could not believe that this confidently agile little boy was the same round-faced infant to whom he had bidden farewell last autumn.

"And who might you be?" Joscelin asked, through a sudden tightness in his throat as the child reached him and for the first time hesitated.

"I'm Fulke." The voice was confident too. Joscelin found

himself staring into the mirror of his own eyes: dark flint-gray and bright with curiosity. The boy's hair was crow-black like his father's, but the way he stood, sturdy and foursquare, reminded Joscelin very much of Hawise as a little girl.

"And do you know who I am?"

The child nodded. "You're my gandpa." The word came out slightly mangled, but considering Fulke was not yet three years old, it was a passable attempt.

"Have you ridden a long way?"

Fulke gave another vehement nod and suddenly turned shy.

"Well, only from Worcester today, but we've been on the road almost a week…haven't we?" Brunin arrived and ruffled his son's hair. "A good thing he likes riding." Joscelin eased from his crouch and Brunin embraced him hard.

Sybilla greeted their visitors, her face bright with pleasure, and Joscelin warmed to see her like that. She kissed Brunin, cuddled her grandson, and then hugged Hawise, who presented her with a swaddled bundle.

"And this is William," Hawise said.

"Although he has been called other names in the middle of the night," Brunin said drily.

They entered the manor house and, as the dusk gathered, the attendants closed the shutters and lit beeswax candles. The women retired to coo over the baby and catch up on almost a year's worth of gossip, and the men sat at the table, cups of wine to hand, legs comfortably stretched out. Little Fulke sat with them, snugly ensconced in his father's lap, and slowly chewed his way through a piece of bread.

"Well," said Joscelin, "you will never get to command Ludlow, but I do not suppose that matters now you're in charge of provisioning a great keep such as Dover."

Brunin smiled and gave a wry shrug. "I would rather it was Ludlow."

Joscelin grunted. "So would I, but be glad for what you have."

"I am." Brunin tousled his son's black hair and the child looked briefly up from his preoccupation with the piece of bread. "Daily…"

"I was sorry to hear about the death of your grandmother."

Brunin sighed and for a moment a vestige of the old shadows filled his eyes. "The end of her life was better than the rest of it put together," he said. "Since Dover is a royal castle, she thought she was at court. Thought her place had been recognized at last." He smiled bleakly. "She was convinced that I was her husband, which was awkward at times."

"You are indeed the image of your grandfather to look upon," Joscelin said. "I can see how her confused mind might make the comparison. The resemblance is a strong strain in the blood." He glanced toward the women and the dark-haired, dark-eyed baby that Sybilla was dandling on her knee. Emmeline sat with them; a young woman now, she had Eve's bones, but was all raven and sable like her brother.

Brunin looked thoughtful. "People say that, saving the hair, our eldest is like you…and I hope that is true in all senses of the word." His arm tightened around the sturdy child in his lap.

"Hah." Joscelin waved the sentiment away with an embarrassed hand. "He'll do well enough being himself, won't you, boy?"

Busy with his bread, but aware that a question had been asked, Fulke merely nodded vigorously and Joscelin laughed.

"I am fully aware that Henry gave Dover to me as a gift for family loyalty and a sop to keep me quiet," Brunin said.

"He would not have done so unless he thought you had the ability. Henry is no fool. He knows men, and he knows how to use them."

"Henry has hinted about giving Fulke a squire's place at court when he comes of age."

Joscelin's eyes brightened. A place at court was a sure way to royal patronage and greater things. A sign too of royal favor should any more signs be needed. "That is good news."

Brunin rose from the trestle and lifted Fulke onto his shoulders. "A hint is not a promise and a promise is nothing until it is fulfilled," he said.

"Ah." Joscelin rose too. "The matter of Whittington, you mean. I take it you are no further down that road than you were before?"

Brunin shook his head. "I have writs and pleas in the King's court but so has Roger de Powys. I am further down the road in that I can't see the start of it when I look over my shoulder, but I can't see the end either." His expression hardened with determination. "I won't give up, though," he said, clasping his hands around his son's legs. "This one will have his full rights when he comes to manhood. I can be patient. Hawise and I have a family to raise and a life to build out of what we have."

Together the men left the dais and joined the women's candlelight, while outside the summer night settled over the land in a star-scattered mantle.

# Author's Note

$\mathcal{M}$Y NOVEL LORDS OF THE WHITE CASTLE WAS PUBLISHED IN 2000. Not only was it shortlisted for the Parker Award for the best Romantic Novel of the Year, the response from readers was phenomenal and the emails just poured into my inbox. It tells the story of medieval outlaw Fulke FitzWarin and his endeavors to have his family lands restored. *Lords of the White Castle* was based upon the FitzWarin family history, which had been written down in the thirteenth century as a rhyming story and was the sort of tale that would have entertained a medieval household in the great hall of an evening.

*Lords of the White Castle*, however, is only the latter part of the FitzWarin tale. When I read the family's earlier history, I realized that it was every bit as fascinating as the later material and was crying out to be told, and thus *Shadows and Strongholds* was born.

The original rhyming romance has a core of solid truth, but in the interests of making a ripping good yarn, the chronicler played fast and loose with many facts, especially with regard to the timing and placing of some of the major players. For example, he thinks nothing of attributing part of the career of Brunin's father to Brunin himself or moving the Welsh attack on Whittington by thirty years after the likely occurrence. Mellette Peverel, Brunin's grandmother, has yet to turn up in any genealogy and it is doubtful that the FitzWarins were in any way related to the English royal house. Obviously if you have read this far, you will realize that for dramatic purposes I have colluded with much of the chronicler's deception, but since this is a work of fiction, I am not as constrained as a historian or academic. While keeping to a general truth, I have mostly followed in the footsteps of the aforementioned chronicler. Since his timing is so erratic in the early part of the romance and further research has turned up details of which I was unaware when writing *Lords of the White Castle*, readers of both books might find a few minor anomalies between the novels, but nothing, I hope, that horribly jars. As far as timing issues go, I have been fairly vague, although occasionally you may encounter a date. This has been a deliberate ploy on my behalf, caused by following the wonderful, but winding path of the original medieval writer of the FitzWarin romance.

Following on from the above, I thought I would write a couple of paragraphs on the known historical facts because I realize that readers often like to know what is truth and what is fiction and follow up details for themselves.

Brunin FitzWarin of *Shadows and Strongholds* was known in his adult life as Fulke le Brun, so described because of his swarthy complexion. Brunin is a diminutive of that description and might well have been a childhood name. Red-haired heroines often populate historical fiction, but in the case of Hawise de Dinan it is plausible because her father had ancestors in the male line with the appellation "The Red" and Hawise and Brunin's third son, Philip, was called "Philip the Red," suggesting that he had auburn coloring. I therefore felt it appropriate to give red hair to Hawise. Incidentally, there was some antipathy toward red-haired people in the Middle Ages. It was seen as a manifestation of undesirable traits, including bad temper and inconstancy!

The chronicle tells us that Fulke le Brun (Brunin) spent his squirehood at Ludlow and this aspect of the tale is highly probable. Both Joscelin de Dinan and his FitzWarin allies were self-made men who had risen from minor positions to more powerful baronial status by their own effort and ambition.

During the mid twelfth century, Joscelin de Dinan and Ludlow were under constant threat from Hugh Mortimer of Wigmore and Gilbert de Lacy. It seems likely that it was in fact Hugh Mortimer who was held for ransom at Ludlow, not de Lacy, but the writer of the FitzWarin poem states that it was de Lacy. Certainly the latter had a strong claim on Ludlow through the male line and Henry II ruled that he should have it and gave Joscelin de Dinan Lambourn in exchange. The tale of Ernalt de Lysle and Marion de la Bruere may seem to be part of the chronicler's imagination, but some historians believe that it has a core of truth and that the castle was indeed taken by help from inside during a fierce private war between Joscelin de Dinan and Gilbert de Lacy. Marion's presence is still said to haunt the foot of the tower from which she flung herself and visitors may sometimes feel a cold frisson as they pass the spot.

Whittington Castle too was a source of dispute. From what I have been able to glean, it was owned by the Peverel family but, before they had set their Norman stamp on the estate, it had been held by the ancestors of a Welshman called Rhys Sais. The FitzWarins were the Peverels' sitting tenants who took Whittington for their own when their overlord went on crusade, probably having entrusted it to them. When he didn't return, his estates were divided up between his four daughters. The FitzWarins, a family on the make, quietly appropriated Whittington and, in the chaos of the civil war between Stephen and Matilda, set about consolidating their hold and raising their profile. Dates are obscure but at some point in the mid-years of the twelfth century, Whittington was taken from them (probably lost in a Welsh raid) and given into the custody of the de Powys brothers, Roger and Jonas, descendants of Rhys Sais. The FitzWarins appeared to have thought of this bestowal as a temporary measure (unlike the exchange of Ludlow for Lambourn) and began suing through the courts for the restoration of what they plainly saw as their castle and their lands.

For readers wanting to investigate the subject for themselves, I would recommend Glyn Burgess's excellent work *Two Medieval Outlaws: Eustace the Monk and Fouke FitzWaryn*, published by Boydell & Brewer (ISBN 0 85991 438 0). For Joscelin and Sybilla's story I have found *Ludlow Castle: Its History and Buildings*, edited by Ron Shoesmith and Andy Johnson, published by Logaston Press (ISBN 1 873827 51 2), an invaluable guide.

I welcome responses from readers and can be contacted either from my website (which is updated when I have the time!) at www.elizabethchadwick.com or by direct email at elizabethchadwick @live.co.uk.

# Acknowledgments

$\mathcal{J}$'D LIKE TO EXTEND A BRIEF BUT HEARTFELT NOTE OF THANKS to the support team working in the background while *Shadows and Strongholds* has been in the writing stages.

Please take a bow before the audience: Carole Blake, my agent par excellence and fellow Meat Loaf fan.

Shana Drehs, my terrific editor at Sourcebooks, who is great to work with and is always able to see the bigger picture and blend together the best ideas from both sides of the table.

Dominique Raccah, founder of Sourcebooks, to whom I am eternally grateful for having such vision and boldness in the changing world of publishing. She is a huge inspiration to all her authors.

My husband and sons Roger, Ian, and Simon, who keep me grounded in reality and make sure that my tea drinking and chocolate eating habits are thoroughly indulged during the course of my writing.

Our dogs, who make me laugh and whose walks in all weathers gives me plenty of thinking time and enable me to really appreciate the changing seasons.

All the great friends I have made on the Internet, but particularly the members of the Penman Review list who have provided so much fun and genuine support, Historical Fiction Online, and also many members of the Historical Novel Society. The many members of Regia Anglorum Living History Society who have put up with my endless questions and charred offerings from the cooking pot, and especially the members of the Conroi de Vey. I promise that whatever superficial similarities there may be, I have not based the characters in my books on any of you.

A special thanks goes to Dr. Gillian Polack for Brunin's name—a possible childhood diminutive of Le Brun.

# *Outlaw Knight*

## The Palace of Westminster, December 1184

*A*LTHOUGH IT WAS NOT MUCH PAST MIDDAY, THE MURKY winter afternoon was already yielding to dusk. The sleety rain, which had put a stop to weapons practice outside, hurled against the shutters like glass needles. Every torch and sconce was ablaze, every brazier in use. Beyond their puddles of light and warmth, in the stairwells and dark walkways of Westminster's sprawl of buildings, a dank chill waited to envelop anyone foolish enough to step outside without a cloak.

Seated in a window embrasure of the White Hall, Fulke listened to the growl of the wind and buffed his new shield to smooth the scores and scratches sustained that morning. His father had given it to him at Martinmas when Fulke had turned fifteen, a man's accoutrement quartered in the FitzWarin colors of indented red and white.

"Hah, sixes, I win!" cried a triumphant voice.

Raising his head from the shield, Fulke glanced over at the dice game that was occupying Prince John and the other squires of Ranulf de Glanville's retinue. Money chinked as a curly-haired squire swept a pile of coins from the trestle into the palm of his hand. Prince John, who was almost eighteen, scowled and reached into the pouch at his belt to toss more silver onto the board.

Fulke might have joined them except he had no more than a silver half-penny to his name. Had the sport been arm wrestling he would have taken part. Unlike Madame Fortune, skill and brawn were dependable and he possessed an abundance of both.

The other lads had called him bumpkin and clod when he arrived from the Welsh Marches nine months ago. They had stolen his clothes, tripped him on the stairs, and emptied a piss-pot over him while he slept. It had taken them a week to learn the hard way that whatever Fulke received was returned twofold. They still called him bumpkin, but these days it was a nickname, a sign of acceptance into their company, if not their rank.

That he had a position in John's retinue was by way of a favor to his father from King Henry who valued the loyalty of the FitzWarin family. Fulke knew that John would never have chosen him for a companion, and the feeling was mutual.

Fulke looked again at the dice players. John caught his eye and glowered. "In Christ's name, stop making love to that accursed shield and bring some more wine." He waved his empty cup at Fulke. An amethyst ring flashed on his middle finger.

"Sir." Fulke laid his shield carefully aside, fetched the flagon from the sideboard, and approached the game.

"Fancy your chances, Bumpkin?" asked the curly-haired squire.

Fulke smiled, his flint-hazel eyes brightening. "I fancy yours more, Girard." He nodded at the new pile of coins on the trestle. "I'll arm wrestle you for them if you like." Having poured the wine into John's cup, he left the flagon for the others to help themselves.

Girard snorted. "I'm not falling for that one again!"

Fulke's smile broadened into a grin and he flexed his forearm where rapidly developing muscle tightened the sleeve. "That's a pity."

Girard made a rude gesture and scooped up the dice. Fulke stayed to watch him throw a total of three and lose his winnings, then sauntered back to the window embrasure and his shield. Two padded benches sat either side of the latched shutters, and between them was a gaming table on which John's tutor, Master Glanville, had placed a heavy wooden chessboard.

Leaning on his shield, Fulke contemplated the ivory pieces with a feeling of nostalgia bordering on homesickness. He imagined his family's manor at Lambourn, the faces of his brothers etched in firelight as they played knucklebones by the hearth. His mother sewing by the light of a sconce; he and his father playing chess in an embrasure just like this one, his father's brow puckering as he considered his next move. Fulke knew he was gilding the image for his present comfort, but there was still an underlying truth and solidity to the picture. While not wretchedly homesick, he missed the warmth and companionship of his family. He often thought it a pity that his father's next move had been to send him here to learn the skills of knighthood among the highest in the land.

"It is a great honor that King Henry has done our family," Fulke le Brun had said to him last spring having returned from attendance at court. "Not only will you be tutored by Ranulf Glanville the Justiciar, but he will mingle with men of influence who may be able to help us." Fulke could remember the flush to his father's sallow complexion, the spark of ambition in the deep brown eyes. "Whittington could be ours again."

"What's Whittington?" Fulke's youngest brother Alain had piped up. He was only four years old and unlike the older boys had yet to have the FitzWarin cause célèbre drummed into him blood and bone.

"It's a castle and lands belonging to us," said their mother, gathering Alain into her arms. "Your papa's family held it in the days of the first King Henry, but then it was taken away from them during a war and never restored. Your papa has been trying to get it back for a long time." It was a tale told in simple terms that a small child could understand and her voice was level, omitting the antagonism and bitterness that had built and festered over the years of striving.

"Too long," said Fulke le Brun. "Roger de Powys claims Whittington as his, but he has no right."

"If King Henry loves you enough to make me Prince John's attendant, why doesn't he give you Whittington?" Fulke had wanted to know.

"It is not as simple as the King's word," his father had said. "Our right has to be proven in a court of law and sometimes if a matter is awkward or seen as a mere quibble, it is pushed aside for more pressing concerns. God knows I have tried. The King has made promises, but it is not as important a matter to him as it is to me." He had looked intensely at Fulke and gripped his shoulder, man to man. "Ranulf de Glanville is well positioned to hear our plea, and he will be your tutor. Do your best for him, and he will do his best for you."

And Fulke had done his best because it was not within his nature to shirk and he had as much pride as his father. His ability to fathom accounts had increased beyond all measure beneath the Justiciar's instruction and he had picked up the broader points of Latin and law. What Master Glanville made of him, however, he did not know for his tutor was a solemn man in late middle age, not much given to open praise.

Fulke pushed his hair off his forehead and grimaced. He was not sure that being educated at court was a grand privilege at all. Being at Prince John's beck and call was a nightmare. At home, Fulke was the heir to his father's lands, cherished, sure of his status, lording it affectionately over his five brothers. Here he was of minor rank, a nobody to be used as John saw fit.

There was a sudden flurry at the dice table as Prince John shot to his feet sending the flagon that Fulke had so recently replenished crashing to the floor. "You thieving sons of whores, get out, all of you!" John gestured wildly at the door. "You're all leeches. There's not one of you worth a pot of piss!"

Fulke slid out of his corner and started to follow the other squires from the chamber.

"Not you, Bumpkin," John snarled. "Get me some more wine."

"Sir." Expression blank, Fulke stooped to the flagon in the rushes near John's feet. An ugly dent married its silver-gilt belly.

"You shouldn't have left it on the table," John said petulantly. "It's all your fault and you can pay for a new one."

It would have been wiser to keep quiet but Fulke refused to bow to tyranny.. "That is unjust, sir."

John eyed him through narrowed lids. "Are you arguing with me?"

Fulke stood up, the damaged flagon in his hand. "It is true that I left the flagon here when I should have replaced it on the sideboard, but I did not knock it off the table."

John jabbed a warning forefinger. "You'll pay and that's an end to it. Now fetch more wine and make haste."

Scarcely bothering to bow, Fulke strode from the room. Despite the winter chill, he was scalding with fury. "I won't pay him a single fourthing," he muttered as he flung into the hall beyond the chamber and marched down its length to the butler's table at the far end.

"For Prince John," he said woodenly to the attendant.

The butler eyed the damage with pursed disapproval. "How did this happen?"

"An accident." Even though Fulke wanted to throttle John, honor and discretion fettered his tongue in front of others.

"That's the third 'accident' this month then." The butler set the flagon beneath a wine tun and turned the spigot. "These flagons don't grow on trees, you know. Cost half a mark each, they do."

Close on seven shillings, Fulke thought grimly: a week's wages for a mounted sergeant and beyond his own reach unless he appealed to his father or spent an entire week arm wrestling for the funds.

Although John had bid him make haste, Fulke lingered over his return to the royal apartment, giving his anger time to cool. He was partially successful. By the time he banged on the door and entered with the flagon, his resentment had banked to a smolder.

John had unlatched the shutters by the chessboard and was leaning against the window splay, gazing into the stormy dusk. Darts of wind-driven sleet hurled past the embrasure. The court-yards and alleys were in darkness—no torch would remain lit in this weather—but there were glimmers and flickers of light from the occupied halls, and the watchmen had built a brazier in a sheltered corner of the ward. Further away, the windows of the great abbey glittered like dark jewels.

John turned, one fist curled around his belt, the other resting on the shutter. "You took your time."

"There were others waiting the butler's service, sir," Fulke lied and poured wine into John's cup. "Do you want me to leave now?" He tried to keep the hopeful note from his voice but knew he hadn't succeeded when he saw John's expression grow narrow and mean.

"No, you can stay and keep me company. You do little enough to earn your supper." The Prince gestured to the flagon. "Pour yourself a measure. I don't like to drink alone."

Fulke reluctantly tilted a couple of swallows into one of the squires' empty cups. The wind whipped the wall hangings and the candles guttered in the sconces, threatening to blow out and leave them in darkness.

"How many brothers do you have?"

Fulke blinked, unsure what to make of the Prince's mood except to know that it was ugly. "Five, sir."

"And what do they inherit?"

"I do not know. That is for my father to say."

"Oh come now. You are his heir. Everything will go to you."

Fulke shrugged. "That may be true, but none of my brothers will go wanting."

"And you think there will be no resentment that you receive the lion's share?"

"Not enough to cause a lasting rift between us," Fulke said. "Even if I quarrel with my brothers on occasion, blood is still thicker than water."

John snorted with sour amusement. "Is it indeed?"

"In my family it is." Fulke took a mouthful of wine and knew that he was standing on perilous ground. John was the youngest of Henry's children, born after the family inheritance had been apportioned among the other sons, none of whom was willing to give up one iota of what was theirs. John Lackland he was called, often to his face. Glancing at the wild, dark night, feeling the sting of wind-borne sleet against his skin, Fulke began to understand. And that he, in his favored position of eldest son, his inheritance secure, was being made a scapegoat. "My father says we are one body. The head cannot function without a torso or limbs. What you do to one, you do to all."

"My father says," John mimicked. "Christ, do you know how often you trot that out?"

Fulke flushed. "If I do it is because he speaks sense."

"Or perhaps because you are a child who has not learned to think for himself." John cast him a scornful look and closed the shutters on the wildness outside. The candles ceased to gutter and a sudden silence settled over the room, permeated with the smoky scent of burning wax. The Prince sat down moodily at the chessboard and fingered one of the bishops. "What do you say to a wager, Bumpkin?" John gestured to the chessboard.

"A wager?" Fulke's heart sank.

"Defeat me at chess and I'll let you off the price of the flagon."

Fulke did not miss the taunting note in John's voice. The Prince was an accomplished chess player and his skills had been honed by their tutor Master Glanville, whose incisive intelligence had led to him being appointed Justiciar. Fulke's own skills were erratic, developed not so much from logic and instruction as enjoyment of the game and the ability to think fast on his feet.

"If you wish it, sir," he said with resignation and sat down.

John smiled and swiveled the checkered board so that the white pieces were his. "My move first," he said.

Fulke knew that whatever he did he could not win. If he lost to John then he would have to find the price of the flagon. If he were victorious, John would find other, subtle, malicious ways of punishing him. The safest ploy was to lose as quickly as possible and then lather the Prince in flattery. It was what any of the other squires would do.

# The Greatest Knight

## The Unsung Story of the Queen's Champion

### Elizabeth Chadwick

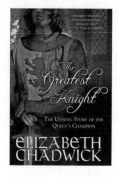

### *A Forgotten Hero in a Time of Turmoil*

A penniless young knight with few prospects, William Marshal blazes into history on the strength of his sword and the depth of his honor. Marshal's integrity sets him apart in the turbulent court of Henry II and Eleanor of Aquitane, bringing fame and the promise of a wealthy heiress, as well as enemies eager to plot his downfall.

Elizabeth Chadwick has crafted a spellbinding tale about a forgotten hero, an ancestor of George Washington, an architect of the Magna Carta, and a legend of chivalry—the greatest knight of the Middle Ages.

### *Praise for Elizabeth Chadwick:*

"Elizabeth Chadwick is to Medieval England what Philippa Gregory is to the Tudors and the Stuarts and Bernard Cornwell is to the Dark Ages." —*Books Monthly, UK*

"Elizabeth Chadwick, with her gift of storytelling, historical accuracy, and ability to recapture lives, has once again written an impressive and absorbing book." —*Historical Novels Review*

### *For more Elizabeth Chadwick books, visit:*

# The Scarlet Lion

## Elizabeth Chadwick

### *How a Hero Becomes a Legend*

Already known as a knight of uncommon skill and honor, William Marshal has earned the friendship of King Richard and the love of a wealthy heiress. But when the Lionheart dies, leaving his treacherous brother John on the throne, William and Isabelle need all of their strength and courage to face a shattered world. Their sons held hostage, their integrity at stake, the two must choose between obeying their king or honoring their hearts.

Breathing life into history, Elizabeth Chadwick provides a riveting novel of an uncommon marriage between a man of valor and the only woman who could match him.

### *Praise for Elizabeth Chadwick and* **The Scarlet Lion***:*

"One of the landmark historical novels of the last ten years." —Richard Lee, Historical Novel Society

"I rank Elizabeth Chadwick with such historical novelist stars as Dorothy Dunnett and Anya Seton. Read *The Scarlet Lion* and see why." —Sharon Kay Penman, *New York Times* bestselling author of *Devil's Brood*

"Everyone who has raved about Elizabeth Chadwick as an author of historical novels is right." —Devourer of Books Blog

### *For more Elizabeth Chadwick books, visit:*

www.sourcebooks.com

# For the King's Favor

## Elizabeth Chadwick

### *A bittersweet tale of love, loss, and the power of a king*

When Roger Bigod arrives at King Henry II's court to settle a bitter inheritance dispute, he becomes enchanted with Ida de Tosney, young mistress to the powerful king. A victim of Henry's seduction and the mother of his son, Ida sees in Roger a chance to begin a new life. But Ida pays an agonizing price when she leaves the king, and as Roger's importance grows and he gains an earldom, their marriage comes under increasing strain. Based on the true story of a royal mistress and the young lord she chose to marry, *For the King's Favor* is Elizabeth Chadwick at her best.

### *Praise for* **For the King's Favor:**

"The best writer of medieval fiction…"
—Richard Lee, Historical Novel Society

"Everyone who has raved about Elizabeth Chadwick as an author of historical novels is right."
—Devourer of Books Blog

### *For more Elizabeth Chadwick books, visit:*

www.sourcebooks.com

# To Defy a King

## Elizabeth Chadwick

### *Spirited daughter. Rebellious wife. Powerful woman.*

The adored and spirited daughter of England's greatest knight, Mahelt Marshal lives a privileged life. But when her beloved father falls foul of the volatile and dangerous King John, her world is shattered. The king takes her brothers hostage and Mahelt's planned marriage to Hugh Bigod, son of the Earl of Norfolk, takes place sooner than she expected. When more harsh demands from King John threaten to tear the couple's lives apart, Mahelt finds herself facing her worst fears alone, not knowing if she—or her marriage—will survive.

### *Praise for* **To Defy a King***:*

"Chadwick's great strength lies in her attention to detail—she brings to life all the daily humdrum of the medieval age but also seduces with the romance of her characters and the raw excitement of their times. *To Defy a King* is Chadwick on top form." —*Lancashire Evening Post*

"You don't just read a Chadwick book;
you experience it." —*Shelf and Stuff*

### *For more Elizabeth Chadwick books, visit:*

www.sourcebooks.com

# Lady of the English

## Elizabeth Chadwick

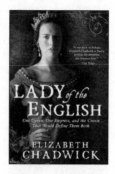

### *One queen, one empress, and the crown that would define them both*

Matilda, daughter of Henry I, knows that there are those who will not accept her as England's queen when her father dies. But the men who support her rival Stephen do not know the iron will that drives her.

Adeliza, Henry's widowed queen and Matilda's stepmother, is now married to a warrior who fights to keep Matilda off the throne. But Adeliza, born with a strength that can sustain her through heartrending pain, knows that the crown belongs to a woman this time.

### *Praise for* Lady of the English*:*

"The best writer of medieval fiction currently around."
—Richard Lee, founder and publisher, Historical Novel Society

"I rank Elizabeth Chadwick with such historical novelist stars as Dorothy Dunnett and Anya Seton." —Sharon Kay Penman, *New York Times* bestselling author of *Devil's Brood*

"Elizabeth Chadwick is to medieval England what Philippa Gregory is to the Tudors and the Stuarts, and Bernard Cornwell is to the Dark Ages." —*Books Monthly, UK*

### *For more Elizabeth Chadwick books, visit:*

# A Place Beyond Courage

## Elizabeth Chadwick

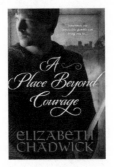

The early twelfth century is a time for ambitious men to prosper. John FitzGilbert is a man of honor and loyalty, sworn to royal service. When the old king dies, his successor rewards the handsome and ambitious John with castles and lands. But King Stephen has a tenuous hold on both his reign and his barons, and when jealous rivals at court seek to destroy John, he backs a woman's claim to the crown, sacrifices his marriage, and eventually is forced to make a gamble that is perhaps one step too far.

Rich with detail, masterful in its storytelling, *A Place Beyond Courage* is a tale of impossible gambles and the real meaning of honor.

### Praise for Elizabeth Chadwick:

"Picking up an Elizabeth Chadwick novel is like having a Bentley draw up at your door: you know you are in for a sumptuous ride." —*Daily Telegraph*

"The best writer of medieval fiction currently around."
—Richard Lee, founder and publisher, Historical Novel Society

"A star back in Britain, Elizabeth Chadwick is finally getting the attention she deserves here." —*USA Today*

### For more Elizabeth Chadwick books, visit:

www.sourcebooks.com